NULLARBOR CHASE

Christopher Coxhead

This is the first time I have ever written a book, it has been a thrill to write and I would like to thank Maureen my wife for her support and great proof reading.

I wish also wish to thank Richard our son, for his enthusiastic support, technical help and constructive criticism, Jennifer his wife for her helpful comments and my sister-in-law Pamela, who said without asking that she really enjoyed the novel and spent two hours one afternoon , in her busy life reading it too the end.

Finally without Gabrielle my teacher at Formby College, you made me believe it was possible.

NULLARBOR CHASE

TABLE OF CONTENTS

17th FEBRUARY - AM GLENDALOUGH PERTH

Isla came round slowly, she cautiously opened her eyes, they felt really gritty and stuck together with sleep; light from a nearby window silhouetted her body where she lay on her back on the light brown parquet flooring.

She grimaced as the sunlight in her eyes caused her head to start thumping with pain.

At first everything was a blurred haze, she blinked her eyelids to clear them of the glutinous sleep mess which was gumming her eyelids together, even though her brain seemed like it wanted to explode from her fragile skull everything seemed slightly better now she could see.

'Where am I?' she thought to herself.

'Christ what's that smell,' turning her head to the right towards the source of the smell, Isla observed a sickly mess close by on the floor, running her tongue round the inside of her mouth and tasting the nauseous contents of her throat, Isla identified the mess as her own vomit.

Alice screamed, and Isla's gradual return to the living world was hastened by the child's yell.

Quickly she raised her head and upper body from the kitchen floor where she lay to get to the screaming child. Isla immediately felt dizzy, nauseous and hung over, her body appeared to ache all over and the sudden movement made her feel extremely dizzy.

She forced herself to stand.

It all came back to her,

'I'm in the apartment in Glendalough.'

'That bastard Ryan has done it again,' she remembered, 'no wonder I feel awful, he's beaten the crap out of me after we've had a few beers

'That's right,' Isla recollected.

'We were at the pub, the Lake Tavern.'

'We ate there, the idea was to go home after eating, we got chatting then we both shifted some beer, sometime later we got chucked out because Alice was crying and other customers were complaining to the Manager.' She remembered.

Isla evoked the memories of Ryan screaming abuse at the pub's manager and patrons as she had dragged him outside whilst struggling to pull the crying Alice in the buggy along behind them.

Isla recalled some of the journey home, Ryan had got abusive when she wouldn't let him drive.

He had wanted to drive them back in the Ute. He had no sense at all when he was pissed. They had both been obviously too inebriated to drive and would certainly have been stopped or had an accident.

They had staggered home, Isla pushing the Alice he three year old in the buggy with Ryan 'mithering' her continuously, he had kept grabbing her tits and bum, she told him she couldn't it was the wrong time of the month but he wouldn't take no for an answer.'

It was less than a kilometre back to the apartment but seemed to take an age, with Ryan's interference, her inability to focus properly though her inebriation, it was difficult to take a direct route. She was also getting upset and angry with Ryan, who continued his attempts to fondle her body.

By the time he had managed to insert the key and unlock the front door of the apartment, both of them were shouting at each other, Alice in her buggy was crying and the whole thing was a disaster waiting to happen.

When they got through the front door of the rented first floor apartment just off Heard Way, Ryan had screamed at her.

'Prick teaser,' he had yelled.

Ryan had grabbed her long blond hair and smashed her head into the front door frame. Isla couldn't remember much more, she knew from the soreness between her thighs that he must have raped her but until now everything was a distant memory.

'Christ, I can certainly pick them,' thought Isla.

'The last so-called partner, Luca Mancuso, father of Alice had turned out to be a drug dealer on the quiet. It was only when WA Police had smashed in their door early one morning, when she was eight months pregnant, she realised something was wrong.'

Isla carefully walked round her own vomit to get to the upset three year old who had been securely strapped into the buggy all night

'I'm going to have to clear that bloody lot up,' she grimaced at the thought.

God she winced, 'I hurt all over, what the hell has he done to me?'

She could never remember feeling this bad before. Her head throbbed and it wasn't just the booze, her face must be a mess, both upper arms appeared to have black bruises coming through and her thighs were really sore.

The little girl, with tear stained face, dressed in her previous day's clothes; in her buggy by the front door, saw Isla across the living space and screamed:

'Mummy,'

'Coming darling, love you,' replied Isla as she staggered across the room.

Un-strapping, a very unhappy and scared looking Alice from the buggy, Isla realised what a mess she must look to the child.

Using the palms of both hands, Isla took a moment to push the strands of her blond hair back from where it was covering her face. It felt matted; she laced the fingers of her right hand through the hair trying to part the strands.

Looking at the hand as she pulled it away, Isla got a shock.

'Oh my God,' she trembled, 'it's dried blood,' she realised looking at the flakes of red and black, which were encrusting her fingers. Tentatively reaching up again she could feel a nasty cut just above her right ear.

Looking down she could only see, the remains of the wash faded, ripped, ochre 'T' Shirt, it appeared to be the only piece of clothing left on her body from the assault of the night before. Wiping her hands on the remains of her clothing Isla continued undoing the trapped Alice from the buggy.

At first Isla nearly collapsed with the weight of the three year old, when she lifted her from the child's buggy, the little girl gripped Isla tightly with both arms around her neck, her previous grizzling turning into a happier gurgling sound.

Even with all the other distractions Isla thought, 'what a mess we both are, Alice has wet herself, she is hungry and frightened and I've been beaten up, raped, been sick and got a bloody awful hangover and probable concussion.'

Through the remaining fog of the concussion and her alcohol fuddled brain, Isla made a decision, 'let's list the priorities,' she thought.

'First I have to survive this and get my act together for Alice's sake,' she decided.

'We have to get away, I have to sort my life out and make it better for both of us.'

'What a bloody mess!' Isla sobbed to herself taking care to turn her head away so Alice would hopefully be unaware of her mother's distress.

Alice, ever alert to her mother's moods started crying herself, Isla just about managed to carry the upset child to the kitchen counter; where she spotted a pack of digestives, giving Alice one, slowed the crying as the child now whimpering, gratefully grabbed the biscuit with both hands.

Alice sucked noisily on the nourishment unsure now about whether to continue crying or accept her situation had improved, trusting the gradually reviving Isla to hold her safe in Mummy's arms.

She uttered a sigh of contentment and smiled happily around the biscuit crumbs now coating her lips.

Holding on tightly to her little girl, Isla staggered slightly as she crossed the Living room. Her face exuded the pain she was feeling, her eyes were scrunched up and only partly open, there was a trace of lipstick, streaked across and marring her delicate chin, and the smell of her own puke pervaded the whole living area.

'Argh,' Isla shuddered as she made her unsteady journey across the living room from the kitchen area to the inner hallway and the bathroom. Dumping Alice and her part eaten digestive onto the bathroom floor, Isla checked the two bedrooms for any sign of Ryan. He not being present in the apartment Isla quickly put thoughts of him aside and felt a lot safer as she returned to the bathroom.

At least everything appeared right there, Alice appeared content Mummy was here and she had something to eat.

Isla acquired fresh towels for her and Alice, from the laundry cupboard and started filling the bath with hot water. She stripped Alice discarding the very smelly soiled clothing in the hallway outside the bathroom and the remains of her own ripped shirt followed.

17th FEBRUARY AM – ESCAPE FROM GLENDALOUGH

Half an hour later, a fresh smell of lemon bath salts and shampoo preceded two freshly bathed young ladies as they emerged from the bathroom.

The younger wrapped in a large pink fluffy towel toddled out first, one corner of the towel trailing behind, followed by a still very sore but partially refreshed, clean mother wrapped in an over large, sky blue, mans' dressing gown.

Looking towards the kitchen window high up on the rear wall, Isla could just make out the first rays of sunshine.

'It must only be about 6 in the morning,' she thought, 'we've hardly slept.'

Putting Alice down amongst her toys on the living room floor she double checked the bedrooms, again looking for Ryan; there was no sign so she threw some Cheerio's and milk into Alice's bowl and fixed coffee for herself.

Sipping at the caffeine laden brew Alice looked around her. 'What a load of crap,' she remarked to herself.

The kitchen although adequate contained a grubby old fashioned set of yellow units, the magnolia paintwork looked tired, there were black marks around the skirting board from vigorous use of the vacuum cleaner and the brown, closed, wooden venetian blinds helped to complete the picture of a just about viable rental for those who had nowhere else to go.

Isla thought to herself, 'At times I ought to question my sanity, how have we both ended up like this?'

Alice was busy with her breakfast, 'what did it matter if some of it ended up on the living room floor, at least she is happy for now,' supposed Isla.

For the first time she smiled to herself, and some of the lines left her face, 'Alice would survive on cereals if she had her way.'

Bracing herself, Isla grabbed a wad of white, paper kitchen towels from by the sink and a plastic bag from the cupboard underneath, hardly daring to look as she got to work, Isla cleared the vomit from the kitchen floor and dumped the dirty paper towels into the plastic bag, after this she wiped the now partially clean floor with more paper towels dipped in bleach before also dumping them into the plastic bag which she now tied up securely before dumping it ready for the trash outside the front door.

'That's better, that gruesome smell is gone, all I can smell now is bleach, fresh coffee and soap.'

Perching herself back onto a kitchen stool, Isla looked across the living room floor at Alice, the little girl appeared to be safely asleep, lying upon the pink fluffy towel, left thumb in mouth and surrounded by milk and cereal.

Sipping her coffee from a bright blue West Coast Eagles Barrel mug, Isla gripping the porcelain beaker tightly with both hands whilst both her elbows rested on the kitchen countertop, she tried to put her thoughts into order.

'What to do? Her mother Bethany was useless, besides which Mum was shacked up with her latest toy boy down in Bunbury, he was into Real Estate and was keeping mother in the style to which she wanted to stay accustomed,'

Isla thought about her mother and the initial cause of her problems.

Mum has only just passed 40, she always gets embarrassed if people realise she has a daughter of 25 and the final straw a granddaughter as well.

Mother had been, 'thrown out,' of her parents' home when Isla came along, a dalliance with one of the itinerant students on a working tourist visa the cause of the pregnancy.

After a catalogue of previous misadventures – pot smoking at school, including supplying other pupils, Doctors and Nurses in the barn with a number of older boys and thumping the Vicar for trying to remonstrate with her over smoking in the vestry. The pregnancy was the final straw and Mum had been kicked out of the family home.

The family were something to do with wine in the Margaret River area; Isla knew she had the same surname because there was no father listed on her birth certificate. All she knew was mum's elder brother, Uncle Brian, Isla's eldest and only known Uncle kept in touch with her mother whatever she did.

No matter what misadventure mother seemed to be involved in, her much older brother, Uncle Brian always seemed to be available to help his sister.

After Isla was born there had been a series of other 'Uncles,' whom her mother had taken up with in the intervening years, some were better than others although not all appreciated mum having a daughter in tow.

When Isla started to reach puberty, some of these 'Uncles,' showed the daughter more attention than the mother.

This often ended in rows between the two of them, with Isla often getting the blame for 'coming on,' to them, for wearing short skirts, low cut tops and obviously undercutting the boyfriends affection for her mother.

At 16 Isla had enough and walked out herself, since then until Luca four years ago she had been very much on her own.

Isla decided to assess their situation –

'I'm alright blonde, about 50kg, 1'7metres tall got a good body and can have any fella I want.

'I must be stupid, I'm living with a drunk and abusive partner,'

'The bastard has only ever done casual work, and hardly contributes financially,'

'We live in a rented 2-bedroomed 1st floor apartment which is a dump and needs renovation,'

'It's costing us more than we can really afford, without Luca's money we would be really knackered.'

,Luca, the father of Alice, is banged up for 5 years in Casuarina Prison out past the refinery at Kwinana, he was jealous as hell, fortunately he didn't know about Ryan otherwise there would be more than hell to pay.'

'He is also due for release in three months and I don't want to renew the relationship.'

'In conclusion we are booked in for a visit today and I better turn up with Alice otherwise Ryan might arrange for one of the 'family,' to visit to check up on us.'

Isla thought about her and Alice's financial situation, they had about $1500 in the bank, and $2500 on the credit card, Ryan didn't know about these savings otherwise he would have gambled and drunk it away by now.

They were overdue on the rent but Isla determined she wasn't going to pay it this time, 'that's Ryan's bloody job,' she decided angrily.

Isla owned a three year old, 2011 Ford Falcon GR XR6 outside, though in truth it wasn't hers, it really belonged to Luca, he had said 'you should use it to transport you and our beautiful daughter, can't have you walking or going on the bus.'

Isla didn't trust Ryan to drive the Falcon. He was never sober enough anyway and would be sure to get caught by a 'booze bus.' Besides Ryan had his own battered old white Ute which he used for transporting surf boards.

Isla reached for a brush, to further tidy the living room floor – in the process of clearing and sweeping the parquet floor Isla came to a decision, she and Alice would get out of here, they would contact Mum and find out where her Uncle lived and go there, surely she wouldn't be turned away, if she swore mother to secrecy, no one would know where they had gone.

First though, they would have to visit Luca at the prison today; otherwise the game would be up before she had even started.

Isla thought, 'If I get through the Visit,' without giving Luca cause for concern it will give us at least a weeks' start before he begins to realise we've disappeared.

After all Isla surmised, 'he doesn't know about Ryan, I don't need him to know now because Ryan is out of our life the filthy bastard.'

'I also don't want to stop the $1000 Luca makes sure hits our bank account the day after we visit. If we do it right today, Alice and me will be a grand better off tomorrow,' calculated Isla.

'The only problem at the moment,' thought Isla, 'was that sod Ryan, where is he?'

'If he comes in now everything will go to pot.'

Isla looked around for a weapon with which to defend herself, picking up a vicious looking 15 cm boning knife from the wooden, bamboo coloured knife block she placed it into her dressing gown pocket, picked up and tucked a sleeping Alice under her right arm and walked decisively towards the Master Bedroom.

'Now we have a plan, it might take a while to come to fruition but with a bit of luck everything will go in our favour,' she decided.

'If we are lucky Ryan has taken his Ute and gone surfing up at Yanchep, the big-headed bastard, has always fancied himself as becoming a pro-surfer which is why he could never held onto any job for too long.'

Isla, thought about why she had taken up with Ryan in the first place, 'His good blond looks and need for some sort of security after the police raid had been the problem.'

'I must have been sticking a sign out saying, available to first tosser with a smile,' Isla concluded.

Isla put the sleepy little girl into her bed and got packing, there seemed so much, at first it was overwhelming but gradually Isla made a dent in collecting their possessions together.

'Still at least I've made a decision and I'm in charge for once and making it happen,' Isla ruminated brightly.

Other than their clothing, nappies, toys and all the other young child's paraphernalia they didn't own much, most of her prize possessions being left at Luca's when they had been allowed to flee the scene after the Police Raid.

'Christ that had been a bad scene, they wanted to charge me with being an accessory, but with nothing being found in the house during the raid, they had no excuse to hold me.,

'Social Services would have been waiting to take Alice off me if I had been in prison,' she remembered shivering at the thought.

Since the raid 3 years ago, Isla's life had been crazy. A series of police interviews, Luca's lawyers and an unfortunate need to call mother for help as her waters broke, meant she had literally been left holding the baby, with nowhere to live.

Fortunately once Luca heard about the birth of Alice he had come through with two years in a swish 1-bedroom apartment in the QV1 tower, plus the Visits income.

'For probably only the second time in my life I took some control of my own destiny,' she recollected.

'When Luca said I should go and live with his parents I told him where to go, He didn't much like that, it hurt his Italian ego but being on remand he was in no position to argue.'

The apartment had been borrowed, almost certainly through Luca's drug connections, Isla hadn't known about previously. At the time she hadn't really cared as long as they had somewhere to stay after Alice was born.

Mother hadn't been too much help once she realised Isla and Alice had nowhere to live. She had been aghast and scared to death Isla would want to bring the baby and stay with her and the latest paramour.

Isla and Alice had visited Luca fortnightly, since the baby's arrival, throughout his remand in Hakia, just South of Perth then after conviction in Casuarina.

Luca had been pressing them to move in with his parents and in a fit of pique had stopped paying the rent on the QV1 tower apartment.

About that time Isla had met Ryan in a coffee shop up at Yanchep and in revenge for Luca's actions had jumped into bed with the itinerant surfer.

She had gone with Alice for a break from the city and had been served by Ryan who had been waiting on tables, to make some living money. Ryan seemed to love Alice, Isla fell for the good looks and smile, within 2 days they had moved into this near-hovel which Ryan had found through some surfing mate.

The sex had been good at first, the first time he had a few beers and smacked her around for refusing his advances, she was committed and it was too late to move out.

'We should have walked then,' thought Isla, 'I felt trapped though with the kid and everything.'

'Mind you now I'm taking control and we're getting out of here, and this time no-one is getting in the way,' she said to herself fiercely and with more conviction than she really felt.

Isla put everything they were taking in the centre of the Living Room so they wouldn't leave anything behind. She then made up her face, doing her best to conceal the marks left by Ryan's vicious assault.

Finally ready for the world Isla woke the sleeping Alice, lifting the baby out of the cot and tried to put her into the pushchair.

Alice screamed and decided she was going to scream and scream and scream, she also wriggled her body defiantly so it was almost impossible to put her safely into the child's buggy.

It was pretty certain Alice hadn't forgotten the events of the night before, they were obviously still fresh in her memory and had seared her mind, it became obvious very quickly that the little girl would not use the buggy as a means of transportation any time in the near future.

For Isla realisation took over 'the baby's pushchair was now defunct, Alice will probably never accept using it again, might as well discard it and leave it one less thing to carry out to the car,'

Decision made, Isla gave up with the buggy, cuddled and soothed Alice, Isla could smell the fresh baby smells of oil and talcum, she bribed Alice with another biscuit and placed her on the floor. The little girl soon settled as she chewed the biscuit in one hand and started to pull at the strap on a suitcase with the other.

Isla didn't want anyone to realise she had done a flit and inform on her to Ryan. She wanted to do that herself when she was a long, long way from Glendalough.

Isla decided she had better get dressed; earlier it had been difficult choosing something suitable to wear,

'I need to hide the bruises on my arms, they are too obvious and will cause awkward questions from Luca, hope the dress I've found is suitable.

During the packing she had found an old Summer Frock with sleeves down to the elbows. This appeared to cover the bruising on her upper arms; Isla hoped the bruises wouldn't show anyway because of the amount of concealer she had used on the lurid blue marks.

The cotton frock had a white background covered with some large pink flowers; it was quite high cut and showed off her legs really well, it had a pair of pockets at waist height.

'It should take Luca's mind off other things because it was so short and only just covered her bottom,' hoped Isla

A pair of white sandals and a necklace of white shells completed the look.

After dressing, Isla looked in the dressing mirror on the wardrobe door, 'don't look too bad, should pass muster, one bonus with the pockets, means I can keep the knife handy in the pocket on the dress,' she thought.

'Mustn't forget to leave it in the car when she got to the prison,' Isla remembered, 'otherwise I might be joining Luca, this time for trying to smuggle in a concealed weapon.'

Leaving Alice in the apartment, Isla went to fetch the Falcon from round the corner in Heard Way.

It was quiet as Isla went down the stairs from the first floor apartment, it appeared children had gone to school and working residents had left for their places of employment.

The day was starting to warm up, the sun shining brightly from the cloudless sky, there was little breeze and only the background noise of a lawnmower and the drone of the traffic from the nearby Mitchell Freeway.

'Just what I need, a bit of peace and quiet so nobody knows we're gone,' she thought hopefully as she parked the car by the outside stairway just below the front door.

Returning to the apartment unseen, Isla started the wearisome task of loading the car with all their possessions.

On the first trip to the car Isla tried to load herself up so things would go faster, but a combination of the aches and pains from the assault, the after-effects of the hangover and nearly falling down the stairs when she became dizzy on the first journey made her more cautious and careful on the following trips .

After about four excursions up and down the stairs. 'Time's going on, everything is taking too long,' she thought trying not to panic.

Isla bowed her head, gritted her teeth and concentrated on ignoring everything including Alice.

'Everything's conspiring against me, I daren't rush, otherwise I'll look a right mess afterwards and will have to do the make-up again, but I bloody well need to get this done. Isla muttered to herself trying not to get angry.

On her fifth trip Alice tried to follow, Isla stopped to give the little girl a drink and another biscuit and put her in front of the Television while she finished her journeys up and down the flight of stairs.

Throughout to what appeared to Isla the endless trips trudging up and down the stairs, they were fortunate not to see anyone, 'the apartment being at the end of a cul-de-sac must help,' surmised the exhausted Isla.

'Must make sure we take everything, I'm determined we're going to disappear from sight completely,' thought Isla as she ascended the stairs after packing what she hoped was the last of their belongings into the waiting Falcon.

Everything done and it only remained to dress Alice. Earlier Isla had left out ready a nice pink dress with frills around the neckline and the skirt. Isla dressed the little girl and hoped it would help to distract Luca.

Isla finished off Alice with some Baby Factor 50 on her exposed skin. They both departed the apartment, a happier Alice holding her Mummy's right hand as they descended the stairs.

Finally by 10:30am, everything was packed into the car; Alice was safely ensconced and secured in the rear of the vehicle.

Climbing into the Driver's seat, Isla reached across to check her handbag and purse, 'I bloody knew it Ryan's raided my purse again, bugger's taken all our cash and just left loose change.'

'What the hell, it doesn't matter the cards are secure and we only need an ATM to replace the missing money.'

A thought occurred, 'what about the smart phone?'

Isla dragged the phone from the recesses of her voluminous yellow handbag, as she retrieved the instrument, a few white crumpled tissues fell un-noticed from the bag's recesses onto the front passenger seat of the Falcon.

Concentrating on the phone Isla switched on the Nokia Lumia whilst cradling it in her right hand, glancing at the screen she realised, 'good it has about half a charge so it's good for a few hours yet,' Isla powered it off, 'I can ring Mum later, 'she decided.

Just as she was starting up the car, Mrs Crawley from No. 9 the apartment below hers came round the far corner of the building.....

17th FEBRUARY AM - CRUISE TO THE FORUM

'Hallo, Isla love,' Zelda shouted from alongside the opposite end of the buff coloured, shingle stone wall of the apartment block.

'Damn,' Isla thought to herself, 'nearly made it,' realising it would look suspicious if she just ignored Zelda, Isla switched off the engine of the Falcon, left the driver's door open and sidled along the ground floor wall towards her neighbour.

'I hope Zelda can't see all our possessions packed inside the vehicle, thought Isla glancing back over her outside left shoulder towards the now silent Falcon.

'Hallo Zelda, how are you?'

'Great love, how's it going, what's happening? Going to be another scorcher isn't it?'

Stopping so she was between Zelda and the car, Isla replied, 'it is isn't it, can't really stop, Alice is in the car and it'll be getting hot without the Air Conditioning.'

On cue came the perfect reminder, the sound of the little girl shouting, Mummy.'

'You better go now love, Alice has given us the perfect reminder, catch you soon?, Laughed Zelda as she headed off towards her own apartment whilst rooting in her own handbag for her front door keys.

Isla returned to the Falcon thinking about Alice and travelling in the car. 'She's never happy in the vehicle unless we are moving, only then when she can look all around her through the windows does it stop her from getting upset,

Isla eased into the driver's seat, the change in position of her body touching the warm fabric of the seat gave her a painful reminder of the bruising from Ryan's assault of the night before.

Still much relieved at their escaping the apartment unscathed, Isla turned on the Falcon's engine, pushed up the AC blowers to full, eased open the two front windows with the buttons on the driver's door and gradually eased off the entrance way onto Heard Way. All through this Alice had been complaining bitterly in her child seat in the rear of the Falcon.

Isla knowing her daughter well made no effort to comfort the child as she suspected as soon as they started moving Alice stopped her petulance, Isla could see the little girl rubbing both her brown eyes, her little hands curled into fists, whilst trying to look out of the window.

'Brilliant,' thought Isla, 'thank goodness, for modern baby seats, they're set up really high so Alice can see what is going on.'

With Alice safely ensconced in her seat, her natural curiosity at the passing and changing scenery could often keep her entertained for hours. The little girl liked pointing at things she considered exciting and yelling out loudly with her obvious pleasure at spotting different sights which often piqued her interest.

They eased their way carefully down and past the bungalows of Heard Way, outside each of which was an Acacia Tree, these hardy bushy trees appeared unaffected by the drought or sun and continued to thrive in their present environment.

Until the Air Conditioning cooled the local environment inside the Falcon, Isla didn't want to close the car windows, so the pleasant smell of the Acacias and local Tea Trees pervaded their senses, as they progressed gently through the avenue of mainly yellow brick houses.

It being quiet at this time of day, with hardly a pause, they eased left onto Ellerby Street, which was completely clear.

A moment or two and a block later the Green of the traffic light allowed them to turn left, straight onto the inside lane of the dual carriageway which is Jon Sanders Drive. At this point the Air Conditioning having kicked in properly and now sufficiently regulating the temperature inside the body of the car Isla closed the car windows and felt the relief at cool freshness keeping them pleasantly chilled.

Isla looked ahead getting ready to turn into Glendalough village with her mind only half concentrating on her driving and the other part of what she needed to do at the village centre; acquiring money, child necessities and other supplies plus Petrol from the Caltex.

Ahead of her on the centre division, partially obscured and waiting to turn right across the dual carriage Isla realised she could see a battered, rusty, filthy, white Ute.

There being nothing alongside or ahead of her as she started indicating, Isla flashed her lights to allow the Ute to turn into the Village ahead of her, the Ute tooted in acknowledgement and flashed across the two lanes ahead of the Falcon.

'Oh crap,' she swore.

Alice giggled loudly at hearing her mummy shout out loud

'Bugger, bet he's seen us,' realising too late, it was Ryan's Ute.

'We definitely don't want to meet up with him now, better get out of here smartly,' judged Isla near to panic.

Rapidly she bashed the indicator stalk so it indicated her turning right instead of left. Accelerating hard, and gripping the Falcon's steering wheel tightly, she forced the vehicle sharply into the outside lane aiming to turn right, so they could flee south down Harborne Street.

A large flashy red Holden saloon honked loudly as she cut it up rather badly.

'Crap I forgot to look, talk about bringing attention to ourselves,' Isla reflected, her heart beating rapidly with the alarm she felt.

Isla winced as the thoughts of what could have happened if the other driver hadn't been so aware, having visions of the pair of them being trapped in the mangled wreck of the car.

Sighing to herself and relieved that they had escaped safely, Isla lifted her right arm, and waved it vigorously in apology to the driver she had offended in the hope it would mollify their feelings.

Glancing quickly in her rear-view mirror, Isla could see the other driver, he was shaking his head at her but smiling as if accepting of her apology. Isla returned the smile.

'That's nice,' she thought pleasantly.

Even so Isla guiltily thought everyone must be staring at their vehicle, just like a small child she tried to scrunch down in the driver's seat as if to make herself invisible to everyone outside the car.

The Highway now being clear, Isla acted with more caution and was able to ease into the right turn lane without any more crises.

Isla knew that even if at worst Ryan was suspicious at them not following him and the Ute into the village.

'It will take him ages to get turned round and back out of the village, exiting the shopping centre is murder,' she remembered,

'Even if he knows which turning we have taken, before he can follow we'll be long gone,' she believed.

Isla's mind was still racing with lots of thoughts and it was becoming increasingly difficult to concentrate on her driving.

'Mind you, until he gets back to the apartment, he'll probably think we've gone shopping.'

'Ryan probably won't try and find us until he realises we've left, by which time we will be well out of here,' Isla suggested to herself to ease her own fears

Isla steered the Falcon left off the main drag onto Dodd Street towards the schools and the Lake Monger reserve.

'Better to avoid the highway, just in case,' she decided.

'Anyway we've plenty of time to waste and it's more scenic along here.'

Her breathing eased and her heart slowed down, it no longer felt as if it was going to burst out of her chest. Isla felt they were safe for now and the release of the nervous pressures of the last few hours helped to calm her nerves.

Glancing around, the reality of the passing normality and calm scenes began to impinge on Isla's senses, she relaxed into her driving.

'Christ that's painful,' she thought as her hands relaxed on the steering wheel, ' I must have been gripping the wheel so hard my wrists hurt.

They could see children playing in the grounds of the Lake Monger primary school on their left side, a mother pushing a toddler in a bright green tri wheeled push chair, with its large rear wheels and smaller front wheel' added to the normality. A pair of grey pigeons alighted from the road way ahead of them and flapped their way onto the verge

Leaving the school in their wake, Isla eased the Falcon, gently right into Gregory Street. Alice gurgled happily from the rear of the car.

Glancing in the rear view mirror, Isla observed the little girl smiling, waving her right arm in the direction of all the new things she could see, with left thumb in mouth and dribbling slightly from the right side of her lips.

Once they had completed the turn, there were expensive looking, comfortable, homes to their right and to the left stretching away past the occasional eucalyptus and over the summer browned grass of the reserve, was Lake Monger. The occasional, bushy, globular shaped Acacia with its pink flowers brightened the otherwise water starved, burnt, brown parkland.

There was a white van parked in the front of the third house, a low slung bungalow, in grubby condition, with white paint peeling from its wooden structured porch at odds with all the other more respectable structures along the rest of the road.

The vans rear was fully open and Isla could see it was full of tools and other implements neatly racked inside the vehicle.

A man in blue overalls peered out from under the bonnet of the green Honda parked alongside the van and waved away another in white shorts and tanned, bare torso who was trying to peer around the mechanic into the engine of the Honda.

All this passed in a blur but told its own story to Isla, 'must be a broken down car, with visiting mechanic and concerned vehicle owner,' she thought.

Isla remembered the school they had just passed, and fondly thought back to school and nature trips, 'when I was just a child, how brilliant it was at times; if I remember right it's and an urban wetland round here Lake Monger and with Lake Herdsman, they're the last two wetlands left in and around the City of Perth.' Isla smiled to herself pleased at being able to remember these facts.

Isla drove the Falcon carefully down Gregory, being careful to negotiate the occasional speed bump safely, with the occasional glance in the rear view mirror at Alice to make sure she was content and to check for signs of a possible pursuing white Ute.

'Alice looks happy for now, reasoned Isla gratefully, 'she's trying to watch everything still looking from side to side and gurgling happily, 'and long may it continue.' Isla.

Isla whilst still concentrating on manoeuvring the Falcon safely, deliberated about her next move, 'visiting at Casuarina isn't until 4.15pm, it being a weekday; we need somewhere to eat and hide out for the next few hours,' she reflected.

What else? 'I need to phone mother, we still need fuel for the Falcon, also got to get cash, and we require somewhere to stay for the night before running down to Margaret River to try and find Uncle Brian.'

Isla reflected on where they could go until visiting time at the Prison, 'we need somewhere to be safe, ideally we need to be able to do everything at once and we need lots of people so it's easy to hide,' she thought.

At that moment Isla had a brainwave, 'how can I be so daft it's obvious, we need a big shopping centre, they've got everything, and the Floreat Forum is just round the corner, after all it is one of the biggest of the Shopping centres in Perth?'

'It's only about 4k from here now, in that large car park we should be able to hide the Falcon amongst all the other cars and trucks and no-one will ever think to look for us so close to home,' assumed Isla brightening at the idea.

'It's always possible we might meet someone we know but it's most unlikely it will be someone who's likely to contact Ryan,' she concluded.

'We aren't going to tell anyone about our plans, are we darling?' said Isla out loud to Alice, pleased with the thought.

Isla smiled to herself at the thought of getting out of the heat, acquiring refreshment, and the chance to relax, clean up and make themselves thoroughly presentable for Luca.

'Don't want his suspicions aroused at all, got to look our best,' she reasoned.

Chatting away to Alice in the rear of the vehicle Isla said, 'a bit of shopping therapy is always a good way to brighten a girl's day, isn't it darling?'

Alice nodded her head and answered, 'yes mummy,' in agreement.

Isla watchfully approached the end of Gregory Street; now they had made a decision, she was going to have to turn the Falcon right across two lanes of traffic onto the centre median strip before she could even worry about turning West onto the dual carriage towards the Shopping Centre.

'God,' she thought, 'my head is pounding.'

Isla didn't know whether it was the hangover, the thumping from Ryan or a combination of the two. On top of the severe headache, she felt sore all over, driving the car hurt, turning the steering wheel at times felt like a huge weight on her upper arms although the necessity of having to use the muscles appeared to be loosening the stiffness.

The turn onto Grantham Street, leaving Lake Monger in her rear mirror wasn't as difficult as expected and in less than five minutes, they were soon arriving at the 'Forum,'

Isla thought to herself, 'let's refuel the car first and get that out of the way.'

Isla turned the car left off the Boulevard into the Petrol Station on the North side of the Floreat Forum, even though under the awnings, Isla gasped as the heat hit her when she alighted from the Falcon, the air was very still, there was little relief from the sultry temperature outside and the stink of gasoline made her nauseous.

Stumbling along the car to the pump, level with the hose, using her credit card Isla fought her way through the questions on the pump screen so she would be able to fill up and avoid the necessity for going to the kiosk.

Isla mopped her brow with a tissue taken from the passenger seat of the Falcon as she leaned against the vehicle while the fuel gurgled noisily into the car's fuel tank.

Watching the cost rise inexorably on the pump's screen, Isla mused to herself, 'why it is some pumps are slower than others? This one seems to be taking forever, or perhaps it's the weight on my sore arms.'

The reek of the gasoline and its fumes rising from the filler made her slightly queasy, the vapours from the re-fuelling appeared to surround her. Glancing into the car she could see Alice in her seat in the rear of the Falcon watching her through the side window of the car.

Finally after what seemed an age, the sensor on the pump caused the fuel to stop its progress into the now full fuel tank of the Falcon. Isla withdrew the nozzle from the car and put it back onto the pump, put the filler cap back into place and collected her receipt from the pump.

Exiting the petrol station, Isla manoeuvred the vehicle into the North Car Park, leaving the 'Cambridge Library,' on her right and now knowing how hot it was she pulled over, in a child parking space, as close as possible to the library building, completely forgetting all about hiding the Falcon in the middle of the car park amongst the other automobiles.

'That's it safely parked up, we're on the South side of the library, and as the day wears on the car will gradually become shaded from the harsh rays of the sun. By the time we return the car should be fully shaded,' remembered Isla from their previous visits to the Forum.

Isla decided against using the Windshield sun shade, 'it's Luca's, it's really garish and unique, with its Italian stallion motif in luminous, green, white and red. It will easily identify the car to others who know him,' she concluded.

'Without it, our cars just another blue Falcon,' isn't it? Isla said to Alice as she unstrapped the little girl from her seat in the rear of the vehicle.

Alice hugged Isla tightly as she lifted her out of the car, she groaned and winced as the pain from her injuries hit her, viciously slammed the rear car door shut as if to obviate the pain, locked the Falcon with the transponder and headed slowly and gingerly, towards the Shopping Centre air conditioning.

Isla knew where she was taking them and advanced through the shopping centre to the far end, she knew they both required sustenance and the best place to acquire it was 'Happy Cafe.'

'There's everything the pair of us need in there, high chair for you Alice, a friendly welcome and good home-made food for both of us and the best coffee in Perth for me,' said Isla over her shoulder to the little girl.

Alice was diverted by the sights, sounds and colours of the shopping centre and Isla was adjusting to the little girl's slow pace as they made their way through the shopping centre.

Isla thought about the fresh coffee and almost drooled about idea of the caffeine kick. 'At the cafe they'll fuss all over Alice and look after us both without any awkward questions,' she thought.

Glancing through the Happy Café's glass surround, Isla spotted a seat in the middle of the cafe, there were at least another dozen mother and baby units throughout the café, there was plenty of friendly noise of chatter, babies and young children.

Isla walked in with Alice and smiled as she entered the Unit, 'wow it is busy, at least there's people we know it will help us to pass the time,' she thought gratefully.

In the middle of the café was a set of three tables for four joined together, to make a long bench type table, the tables were black and set low, like coffee-tables? These were surrounded by the café's black tub like chairs, mothers, push chairs, baby paraphernalia, of course the children and some grandparents plus of course food and coffee interspersed with baggage, it

all littered the enlarged table. This made the centre of the café appear enclosed by its own private cocoon.

'Hi Isla, how's it going,' greeted Bryony the first to see them, this was followed by a number of halloes and other greetings from all those around the table, themselves frequent visitors to the same ante-natal clinics, mother and baby groups and now nursery as Isla and Alice.

Happy Café though not large was a friendly raucous place, the young men behind the counter were cheerful, lively and prepared to give as good as they got from their generally young clients.

The wall behind the counter was covered in a psychedelic portrait in blues reds and greens, there was a line-up of many multi-coloured plastic ducks greeting the customers at the counter and a collage of Polaroid photographs of agreeable customers by the door.

It was located at the East end of the Forum and was of its own particular concave design. The windows were on the completely curved edge and travelled from floor to ceiling; overlooking the sunlit East end of the Upper Car park.

Isla was much relieved when Bryony grabbed Alice and the harness from Isla's shoulders.

'Take some weight off, coffee is it? Said Bryony as she placed Alice onto the lengthened table.

With much relief Isla slumped into one of the tub, black chairs and grimaced as she realised how sore she was now she had been relieved of the baby carrier.

Other girls sitting round the table greeted Isla with ribald comments and continued their chatter about children, boyfriends and husbands.

'Not going to get much sympathy, but plenty of assistance and help if I ask; I'll also able to phone mother in peace, while the others keep an eye on Alice, decided Isla.

'At least I'll have some idea about what we're going to do after we visit Luca at the prison.'

After coffee and muffin and lots of chat, Isla said to the rest of the group, 'can you girls keep an eye on Alice I've got to telephone mother?'

'Of course girl,' came back from a number of voices in their conclave, 'with one ironic quip, 'hard luck Isla,' they all knew of her mother's 'caring reputation it had been remarked upon previously.

Amazingly, her mother answered after one ring of the mobile, normally Isla would have to leave a message and hope her mother called back.

'This must be some sort of record,' thought Isla

'Hallo Mum,'

'Good morning Isla, how are we today,' mother must be somewhere she considered posh, she was giving out in her posh Mrs Bouquet voice today, decided Isla.

'Mum,' Isla said, 'I just want to ask you...'

'Isla I must tell you where I am and who I'm with,' Mother rudely interrupted in a very excited voice.

Isla thought to herself, if I don't blast back at the stupid woman I'll never get a word in edgeways for the next twenty minutes.

'Mum,' Isla shouted down the mobile, 'just bloody listen for once.'

A passing elderly couple looked aghast at the aggressive way Isla was shouting down her Mobile Telephone. Other passers-by stopped their window shopping and looked on in interest.

It appeared there was shocked silence from her Mum so Isla thought she had got the floor, in a more normal voice and trying to turn away from those in the shopping centre who were now taking an notice of what was happening Isla said;

'Mum I need to know where.......'

'Isla don't you dare to speak to your own mother like that, I am sure everyone round my table heard what you said. Have you no pride, of course you haven't.'

Then in a whisper; 'I am so embarrassed by the way you spoke to me. I'll never be able to live it down if anyone here heard the way you spoke.'

 'Mum,'

'No, you can have your say in a minute when I've finished.'

Admonished by her mother, who continued to rant, 'the way you speak to me after all I've given and done for you over the years.'

Mother continued to conveniently put aside her own many indiscretions and continued to criticise Isla further.

Mother must have removed herself from her public gathering because her voice rose and she continued to pontificate further.

'I suppose I should expect no less, the company your keeping, an eyetie drug dealer as father of your baby, the bugger's incarcerated in prison, and now an idle bloody surf bum who beats...'

'Bloody hell that's enough,' decided Isla and cut her mother off in full flow by switching her mobile telephone off.

'They say truth hurts, we all make mistakes but we don't need to be reminded of it by our own kith and kin. Especially mother whose reputation isn't exactly spotless is it?' concluded Isla.

When Isla returned disconsolately to the 'Happy Cafe,' the party was starting to break up and most of her friends were ready to go. Although feeling disillusioned by her mother's antics but refreshed by coffee, food and paracetamol; Isla thought, 'mustn't arouse suspicions about our plans to depart from Western Australia, so better put a brave face on everything.'

With a smile from ear to ear Isla said goodbye as everyone departed the Café, with many air kisses, they all said goodbye to each other and went off in different directions, most towards the car park and a few like Isla and Alice back into the Forum.

17th FEBRUARY LUNCH – KNIFE AT THE FORUM

Isla didn't want to catch the others because she could do without being questioned too closely, so she stood Alice on her two feet slowly allowing the rest of the party time to leave.

With the little girl in tow they toddled their way out of the Café and into the Forum. Alice grasped Isla's right hand tightly with her own small left hand, Alice excitedly kept gesticulating at the colourful sights and sounds of the shopping centre, trying to pull her mother from one exciting shopping window to another.

Occasionally they wandered into a shop if something took Isla's eye or if Alice was insistent.

Isla decided, 'a bit of shopping therapy is a great way to use up time before the visit and hopefully all this walking will tire Alice somewhat.'

Alice was starting to get a bit fractious when they arrived at Woolworths and wanted to be carried so Isla made a decision.

'Need to go in here anyway darling, we must stock up on fruit, food and drinks.'

Without giving the little girl chance to complain, Isla picked her up and plonked her smartly into the child seat of one of the stores many large wire trollies.

Alice was too shocked at first at the sudden change in circumstances and began to whimper. Isla countered the little girls' dissatisfaction by propelling the store trolley at different speeds and constantly changing course as they moved throughout the supermarket. This changed the little girl's perspective on things and she kept laughing throughout their visit, enjoying the new game.

'Thank goodness Alice likes our game,' thought Isla looking down at the little girls excited, flushed cheeks as they whizzed round the corner of one aisle, nearly colliding with a young man stacking tinned fruit onto a shelf.

By the time they reached a cashier Isla had achieved her shopping aims, Alice was content with placing Isla's purchases into the trolley and trying to acquire some of her own when they passed close enough to a shelf for her to reach an item.

By the time they left the store Isla was fully laden once again, with two shopping bags in her left hand, Alice dragging at the other arm and voluminous white handbag hanging from the same shoulder.

Isla said to Alice, 'mummy must look like a cart horse, still we aren't going far, only to the family room, to get us both looking presentable, what do you, think?'

Alice replied in a serious voice, 'yes mummy,' and letting go of Isla's hand decided to try an launch into a march, while getting her arms all crossed up.

The family room was tucked away at the rear of a Dollar store, Isla, Alice and all their baggage managed to shove open the entrance door.

She literally fell into the room, 'good and quiet darling, no one else to bother us,' said Isla dumping the shopping onto a large table at the centre of the room

Glancing round the room Isla was reminded of how friendly and pleasant the room was, the walls were covered in murals in congenial pastel colours, Alice wandered over to a set of wooden multi coloured building blocks piled into a play corner at the far side of the room and started to pile them one on top of the other.

Isla glanced at her yellow Swatch watch, 'crap its only 1pm we still need to waste a lot of time,'

Alice giggled at her mother's swearing and returned to her bricks which were now reaching mini tower block proportions and teetering on the brink of collapse.

'Visiting isn't until 4.30pm and the prison is only about 45 minutes driving time.'

'I know it's always best to be early as there is all that security to pass through, if we allow an hour we've still got three and a half hours to waste,' Isla said aloud.

'Once we are sorted in here, we can use the ATM, for cash; drop into Australia Post to look up motels around Margaret River, take the shopping to the car and then take a leisurely route via the coast to Casuarina.'

Isla reflected, 'Funny though if we have to go down to Margaret River we will literally have to go right past Mother in Bunbury. I'm not going to ask her again, Alice and me will find Uncle Brian on our own.'

'Won't we Alice?'

Perhaps it's all for the best, Mother could quite easily grass us up to Luca, Ryan or both if she's pressured.'

At that moment the entry door banged open and a little boy dressed all in blue came scurrying into the room.

There was a crash the ensuing draught being the finally straw, Alice's creation collapsed noisily to the floor.

'Hallo,' he shouted loudly at Isla , 'I'm Max,' and promptly raced off to join Alice in the toy corner, from where after a brief pause he erupted with a model aeroplane in his left hand he started careering round the room making what he imagined were aeroplane noises.

'Hi Isla,' said a voice from behind Isla, whose gaze had followed the little boy as he rushed into the room.

'Oh Hallo Kylie,' replied Isla to Max's mother.

'Christ,' she said to Isla, 'some bastard has given you a right thumping haven't they? Couldn't be your Italian Stallion could it, he's banged up isn't he?'

'No I mean yes,' exclaimed Isla in surprise 'I thought I had covered it all up.'

'Girl,' laughed Kylie, 'you might convince a half blind man at forty paces but you'll never convince anyone else. Will she Max?' she said to her youngster, who was blindly oblivious to what was being said or going on around him.

'Let's get Alice sorted then we'll sort you out Isla, won't we Max?'

Max turned round this time his mother's voice this time having broken through his present thought train.

'My mum beaut..., beauty,' Max stuttered, then dropping the aeroplane toy, turned back to the other toys and concentrated on his new task of trying to make his own tower of wooden bricks.

Kylie laughed, 'you always get it not quite right, don't you handsome, Mummy loves you anyway.'

'He really means Beautician,' she explained to Isla.

Kylie a tall, vivacious, woman; with a ready smile about 1.80 metres tall, fit, healthy and about 25, loved by everyone and the best friend anyone could have. She lives in an apartment somewhere near the centre of Perth, her husband Mike, besides being an up and coming financial expert, does some sort of Martial Arts for fun. Isla had met them when circulating with the young and high flying, whilst accompanying Luca to the latest party. The men started discussing the latest investment idea and the women hit it off immediately, since then they had been the best of pals.

Together the women cleaned up a protesting Alice, whilst Max looked on with interest, his own tower of wooden bricks having collapsed once too often.

Out a large cavernous brown handbag, Kylie produced a toy car for Max; who immediately grabbed it and stated pushing it round the room while making Brrrm, Brrrm noises. Alice by now sitting on the floor, with left thumb in mouth, made happy noises watching Max with what appeared to be a look of amazement.

Kylie now produced from the depths of her capacious bag, all she needed to turn anyone from 'Ugly Betty' to a fairy tale Princess. She then proceeded to improve on Isla's amateurish efforts of the morning, by the time she had finished 30 minutes later, Isla couldn't believe the transformation, and she gasped with approval and surprise, when Kylie opened a large make up mirror for Isla's benefit.

'That's terrific Kylie, how can I ever repay you.'

Isla's petite, 1.6m, blonde haired frame looked ravishing in the half-length mirror of the family room and she felt so much better.

'Just let Mike know, where the bastard who did this is likely to be, that would be enough thanks to see him get his come-uppance. The tosser,' answered Kylie with vehemence.

Isla now felt a whole lot better; she still ached, her headache was more in the memory rather than its earlier debilitating form and she still felt sore all over, paracetamol were controlling the headache and some of the other pains.

Looking and feeling more confident helped with the injuries.

Effusively, Isla thanked Kylie once again, giving her friend a big hug and kiss on the right cheek. To which Kylie said. 'Hey watch it you dumbo, I've just cured all the damage you don't want to mess it up immediately, do you?'

Isla laughed at the thought, 'no, but thanks again what would I do without a pal like you.'

They and the children, left the Family room together.

Kylie disappeared off towards the car park with Max rushing ahead

Isla and Alice entered the relative quiet of Australia Post, there was a small queue at the two opened counters where two young Post ladies in their smart uniforms were serving the dwindling line of patient customers.

Once in Australia Post, Isla found a WA travel guide, and was able to quickly pay for the book before they returned to the concourse and made their way slowly towards the car.

Here on the car park they were met by the baking lunch time heat; unfortunately the Fremantle Doctor, the cooling south-easterly which blows just after lunch most summer afternoons hadn't started to give relief to this part of Perth.

A trickle of sweat ran down Isla's brow and into her left eye, she dabbed at the eye tentatively with her right fist, not wanting to spoil Kylies incredible make up. This stinging salty liquid was now really beginning to irritate the eye and rubbing it wasn't helping her vision making both the eyes blink almost continuously. Wanting to attend to the offending eye and needing to get something softer to dap away the perspiration, Isla jogged the short distance to the Falcon and dumped her shopping at the rear.

'Bloody hell I can hardly see a thing,' Isla thought raging to herself as she reached inside her handbag for a tissue to treat the irritated eye.

Alice who had been roused by the short rush across the car park started to complain loudly because of the blinding heat.

'Enough Alice,' said Isla sharply to her daughter, whilst dabbing the offending eye with a tissue now salvaged from the handbag.

Alice started to sob because of the reproof from her mother, Isla just wanting to get on, retrieved the keys and remote from her bag and unlocked the Falcon, which was now well shaded by the library.

Before sorting Alice, Isla grabbed her two shopping bags and hurled them across Alice's seat in the Falcon onto the other rear passenger seat.

Now taking an annoyed, wriggling and fractious Alice from the tarmac, Isla started to put the little girl into her child seat, Alice was determined it wasn't going to happen and was contorting her body into the most awkward of positions whilst shouting, 'no mummy no car, no car.

Suddenly Alice stopped wriggling, fell back easily into her car seat, and excitedly pointed her chubby right fist over Isla's right shoulder.

'Ryan, Ryan,' repeated the little girl

Before Isla could react, a large hand groped her right breast and another grabbed her round the waist pulling her away from the car.

'Leaving me, were you,' shouted Ryan in her left ear, 'You can't leave, and bugger off just like that!

Letting go of a partially secured but now screaming Alice, Isla screaming inside herself at the unfairness of life, reached into her dress pocket with her right hand, pulled out the boning knife and sliced open the outside of Ryan's left wrist.

17th FEBRUARY LUNCH - CASUARINA PRISON

Its 1230, and in Casuarina Prison, just inland from the oil jetties of Kwinana, things are simmering in the cauldron that can only be a modern maximum security prison anywhere in the world.

The whole Establishment is locked down, there's a big search going on, these only happen in the most severe of circumstances, there has to be information about some possible serious breach of security, no Superintendent of a prison is likely to take the decision to lock down lightly. Explanations will be needed right up to State Government level.

Word amongst the prisoners is the 'screws,' think there is a gun in the prison somewhere. How that got in nobody knows but although the disruption may be a break in the monotony of prison life it's scary because it impinges on normality and everyone's safe secure environment.

Everyone thinks Visits should still happen but except for meals and an hour on the yard no one thinks much else is going to occur today. Prison routine is gone for the day, if a prisoner has hidden anything; they hope they have done a good job. Lock Downs seem to energise Officers, searches are often better targeted and more thorough. There is also the chance for staff to settle some scores by being right on top of the troublemakers, little faults are likely to picked on more than normal.

Down in Cell Block B, cell 7, a grey concrete walled cell meant for a single prisoner, are two in bunk beds it being the only comfortable place for them both to live in the cell as there isn't much room to move around.

It has already been searched earlier in the morning. Luca Mancuso lies on the top bunk, his head propped up on two pillows, he is lying on his back with his knees bent dressed only in boxer shorts and white grubby singlet with a mobile telephone gripped in his right hand and held to the same ear.

The top bunk is Luca's choice, if he preferred he would tell Spike his cell mate to move and because of Luca's status amongst the other prisoners there wouldn't be a problem. After all what's the point of being top dog if you are going to literally lie under someone else, better to be in control at all times is Luca's way of thinking.

He could also have a cell to his own but he prefers the security of having his fellow cell mate close by.

'Spike,' his prison moniker, a very large, morose, Aborigine, 2m and nearly 300lbs of very fit beef, with dark wiry curly hair, seated on the edge of the lower bunk similarly dressed in shorts and singlet, now works for Luca as one of his heavies. Spike would do anything for Luca on account of Spikes extended aborigine family up in Port Hedland being 'well looked after,' by Luca's extensive contacts.

Luca, is a third generation Australian/Italian, his grandfather, Luigi a conscripted cook, an ex-resident of Naples, had been captured in his Field Kitchen in the Egyptian Desert by Australian Troops on the Egyptian/Libyan Border in December 1940, when the Commonwealth Forces battered the Italian 10th Army in 'Operation Compass.'

After a number of travails, including being incarcerated in the hold of a Liberty ship attacked by the German commerce raider, Adjutant in the Indian Ocean Luigi had ended up in a POW camp at Jarrahdale, a small town about 45 miles south east of Perth.

Whilst in camp, Luigi had been sent on 'Parole,' to work on country farms where he met a local girl and two years after the war married her before moving to Perth.

Luca's father, Walter, a child of that union, married an Italian girl, fresh off the boat, herself an émigré from Naples in the early 70's, it was an arranged marriage, with the girl Francesca, a distant niece being personally nominated by Luigi. Like all good catholic families there were a number of children, Fabio being the last and Luca the next youngest.

The 'Family,' had been involved in illegal activities around the Fremantle Docks since the 60's, this had passed from grandfather down through the family.

Luca had improve on these connections to branch out into the illegal distribution of drugs.

Luca, the brains of his outfit had been as he called it, 'stitched up,' by the police when he had been arrested and a serious amount of amphetamine, found in his car.

In reality Fabio had put the drugs in place and anonymously called Crime Stoppers. The result had been Luca's incarceration but not the control Fabio so desperately wanted.

Luca is lying on his bunk, speaking into the mobile telephone. He isn't meant to be in possession of such an item but when the search happened, it was in a plastic bag stuck up Spike's backside. It would take more than a few brave Prison Officers to ask Spike to drop his kegs and bend over.

Luca is running his drug empire from Casuarina and he is in a conference call with his acolytes spread over Perth and the rest of Western Australia. Luca has also found a new outlet for his talents since his incarceration.

Smuggling drugs into the prison; there is no risk to Luca:-

1. It's a lucrative business, the drugs are paid for by friends and family outside the prison.
2. The mules who come on the visits take all the risks as do the prisoner receivers.

3. The drugs cost three times as much if they make it through the Prison Security.
4. People also only get paid if a smuggling run is successful; often the mule is paid with drugs on conclusion of the run so no money changes hands.

Luca thought about the previous inefficient team which used to run the rewarding business of selling drugs in Casuarina, they couldn't guarantee delivery as they didn't have a great deal of success trying to evade the prison security.

On Luca's arrival and with his contacts both inside and out, it had been explained to the previous suppliers that they would have to stop their activities or suffer the consequences.

This hadn't gone down well but a bit of persuasion, by Spike and his assistants had closed down the opposition very quickly, after all nobody fancied spending more time in hospital, even if the one in Casuarina was comfortable, it wasn't worth losing a finger for.

Having checked around the rest of his lieutenants, Luca spoke to his right-hand man and younger brother Fabio.

'Well Fabio, business appears to be thriving out there as well as in here.'

'Yeah' said Fabio, 'the supplier is doing alright; he's got three meth labs in operation now we are getting as much as we can use.'

'Alright,' replied Luca, 'I'm expecting Isla and Alice this afternoon make sure she receives her money tomorrow. Have you done anything about renting a new place for them yet?'

Fabio, who had been discreetly keeping a careful watch on Isla and Alice, was well aware of her relationship with Ryan. Something he was hoping to use to his own advantage at a later date, answered Luca reassuringly.

'Of course the money will go into her account in the morning, we will find her something nice down the coast, I think, perhaps something near Mama and Papa in Rockingham on the beach. They could see more of their grandchild then; they are always complaining Isla never visits. '

'That would be brilliant Fabio, use my personal account to finance it, no renting we might as well legitimately invest in property. Until she is moved in, I want a careful eye kept on Isla, I don't want any other character mucking about with my daughters mother.'

'Alright Luca, I'll put the Twins onto it, they aren't very busy at the moment,' he answered, 'must go now ciao.'

The Twins, were used by the brothers for enforcement when necessary; mind you if word got out that they were on your trail, you soon conformed or suffered at least brutal and sometimes fatal injuries, they were very good at breaking bones.

Fabio had already decided, Ryan had outlived his usefulness and needed teaching a lesson besides Fabio was jealous and had a fancy for Isla himself, he would need his brother well out of the way though, Casuarina Prison wouldn't be enough to avoid Luca's ire if Fabio got too close to what Luca regarded as his personal territory.

Fabio hadn't previously kept an eye on the two girls as previously requested, thinking it a waste of time, a sarcastic comment about 'while the mice were away,' from a contact up in Yanchep, and a complaint about never seeing 'the girls' from his mother, had alerted him to the situation and he had investigated himself the previous week and realised Isla had been playing away.

'It will be a nice persuader to hold over when I'm ready,' decided Fabio to himself.'

'Better do as Luca wants and put the Twins to work,' he decided.

Meanwhile, Luca switched off the mobile, 'hear Spike grab this will you,' said Luca, as he leaned over the edge of the top bunk and handed the phone down to his cell companion.

Spike grunted an acknowledgement, his whole attention was concentrated on their shared Television; it was 1pm and time for Doctors, on Channel 10. Spike was nuts over soap operas and tended to get really upset if something interfered with any screening; 'Lock Down' was a bonus he would normally miss the last ten minutes as he would usually have to go the shoe workshop. He concealed the phone temporarily under his mattress and got back to his viewing.

Luca decided to get his head down, 'Spike give us a shout at three so I've time to get ready for my visit, I'm going to get my head down for a couple of hours.

'Right Boss,' came the muffled reply

17th FEBRUARY PM - ESCAPE FROM RYAN ALONG THE BOULEVARD

At the time Spike was switching on the television in Casuarina Prison, the Falcon was screaming, rapidly west along the Boulevard.

Grim faced, Isla was desperately trying to drive hastily through the traffic, her eyes blurred due to the tears streaming down her cheeks, blood all over her carefully chosen dress and Alice only partially secured and screaming fit to burst in the rear of the vehicle.

With her hazy, tear-stained vision, Isla drove almost blindly straight through the Empire Avenue roundabout, it was on her before she realised and she just managed to flick the wheel left and right to avoid careering across its prettily decorated bush covered centre.

They were fortunate not to collide with a yellow mini cooper, which had entered and was making its way across the roundabout from their right.

They roared across its front and continued onto the Boulevard, they could hear a squeal of brakes and honking of the Mini's horn astern of the Falcon as Isla left the outraged motorists in their wake, she didn't have time to notice the palm trees on the nearside verge as she just about kept control of the car as they flashed by.

Fortunately a Natural gas powered, Grey and Green, 'Trans Perth,' No. 82 Bus for City Beach was pulling out of the stop before Thurles Road, and a brown UPS truck coming the other way east bound along the Boulevard made Isla come to her senses.

'Christ what am I doing,' she suddenly realised, they had nowhere to go, the Falcon with them inside was headed for disaster.

'Bloody hell,' Isla screamed out in terror as she practically stood on the brakes, and brought the Falcon to a shuddering halt, just before it collided with the rear of the slow moving bus.

They were so close to the rear of the vehicle in front, Isla realised she couldn't see its rear window through her windscreen.

'The front bumper of the car must be practically touching the rear of the bus,' she realised.

The pain of being slammed with force into the harness of the seatbelt made her remember the little girl only partially secured in the rear; Isla looked over her left shoulder as the Trans Perth bus pulled away from the now almost stationary Ford.

Fortunately Alice had enough of the harness around her to keep her in the back of the car without being injured, the little girl's screams had turned into a whimper at the shock of the car's deceleration and her mother's yells of frightened anguish.

Shaking violently with the tension of it all, Isla gripped the steering wheel tightly and got herself under control and started to accelerate slowly away from the scene of the near collision.

The recent violent scenario and everything that had occurred since, flashed through her mind:

'I just reacted when Ryan grabbed me, I must have hit something bad there was blood everywhere, it must have been bloody painful, he let go of me immediately, and screamed loudly,' were the onrushing thoughts which crowded her mind.

Isla wiped her eyes, with the sleeve of her dress, to clear away the tears as the Falcon followed the bus sedately westwards and trembled as she continued to remember what had happened.

'The knife went into his wrist so easily, I pulled it clear immediately, actually straight away because he screamed in my ear so loudly, mind you it made the bugger let go of my tits pretty quickly,' she took some pleasure at the thought.

Feeling the pocket of her dress Isla could feel the blood stained knife back in her pocket, 'I don't remember putting it there.'

'I just remember wanting to get away from the scene as fast and as quickly as possible.'

Nearby shop goers, had stopped and looked interestedly at the scene, they couldn't have seen much, that side of the car being hidden by the library and the Forum.

Ryan's yell and he leaping round, cursing and trying to staunch the flow of blood from his left wrist had attracted the attention of everyone who could see some of what was happening.

Worried, confused and panicking Isla recalled, slamming the near side doors shut; Alice had started to cry, the poor girl hadn't understood what was happening.

She remembered trying not to panic too much, her racing round to the other side of the Falcon and jumping into the driver's seat, then it had been like a bloody farce, 'I sat in the driver's seat and realised I had no car keys.'

'I couldn't think for a moment, mind went blank then realised I had left the bloody things on top of the car.'

Isla now driving more sedately and following the Trans Perth bus, had to think for a moment, 'how then did I end up here driving us along behind this green monster?'

She thought back, 'I slammed open the driver's door, leapt up on the door sill and grabbed the keys from the Falcon's roof and got out of there as fast as we could go.'

'We left Ryan sitting on the kerb sobbing and calling me a bitch, he must have dragged his bright yellow 'T' shirt off, leaving his upper torso naked. The yellow cloth was fast turning crimson as we departed the scene,' Isla recollected.

Isla also remembered, noticing out of the corner of her left eye, two, what, appeared to be, female security staff, cautiously approaching the scene.

'It took me two attempts,' Isla recalled, 'to insert the key into the ignition, I was shaking so bloody much.'

'Once I got the engine started, I must have been panicking I revved it too hard, its scream made all the pigeons scatter, the tyres squealed as we reversed out of the parking space and the two approaching Security staff had leapt to one side, thinking they were in danger.'

'Even though I was freaking out, I must have had some modicum of common sense,' recollected Isla.

'I remember driving cautiously down the rows of parked cars until we reached the exit, poor Alice didn't know what was going on and was sobbing her poor little heart out,'

'In front of us as we had turned into the exit there had been that bloody battered Hi-Lux with two brown country dogs racing around its open rear compartment, barking excitedly at everything that moved.'

Alice seeing them, had stopped her crying and pointed, 'dogs' she had yelled.'

At that point Isla remembered, 'I hadn't been interested in the bloody dogs, except as a way of keeping Alice happy, the Hi Lux had been trying to turn right but had stopped across both lanes blocking our exit left onto the Boulevard.'

She had kept banging the horn of the Falcon in frustration, only to be greeted by the driver sticking a hairy, brown, tattooed arm out of the Hi-Lux window with the index finger raised skywards.

Being stuck Isla had remembered having the presence of mind to look in the Falcon's rear view mirror, 'I could see the two female security personnel trotting across the car park towards us, it made me bang the steering wheel in frustration.

'It had seemed an age but in reality had only been a few seconds, the Hi-Lux cleared off to the right, departing with a cheeky honk on his horn.' Isla hadn't cared she had been just glad to get out of there.

Not caring at that moment, trusting nothing was coming she had roared out of the junction at speed, nearly T Boning another car in the process, fortunately those moments of panic have been interrupted by the No. 82, Trans Perth bus.

'That brought me to my senses.'

Now she had to slow down to the speed of the bus it gave Isla time to think, 'I must stop panicking. Ryan might want to kill me but he daren't go to the police, after all I was protecting myself whatever he said and I've got the bruises to prove it. I've just got to avoid him, I need to be less predictable, and best stick to the plan,' were the many jumbled thoughts that flashed through her mind.

'I know we are banking everything we have on an Uncle I can't really ever remember meeting but from what mother's always said I'm sure he'll come through,' Isla concluded hopefully.

'We need somewhere to stop as soon as possible Alice, we've got to secure you darling and somehow I've got to get out of this dress without anyone seeing us, commented Isla to Alice who had stopped crying and was trying to extricate herself from the partly secured seat belt.

As if to remind her about the blood, Isla looked in the mirror and tried to wipe some of the blood off her chin, only to transfer it straight onto the steering wheel when she returned her hand to the task of manoeuvring the car.

'I've got it,' shouted Isla excitedly.'

'The Acacia Aquatic Centre is up here on the left, it has got a huge car park, with loads of shady hidden spaces under the eucalyptus trees, this time on a weekday it will be dead quiet and there is a good chance we might even be able to use the rest rooms without being seen.'

Alice who was still struggling with the seat harness didn't look up and just said, 'yes mummy.'

Almost as soon as Isla had her idea the entrance to the Aquatic Centre was upon them, a hand-painted white sheet with Swimwear sale, in green letters, marked the entry and Isla swung the Falcon left off the Boulevard and eased the vehicle into the tree and bush lined driveway.

Isla approached the Car Park with a certain amount of trepidation; after all she was covered in blood, she was only guessing about how busy the Centre would be and really couldn't be sure the place would be as empty as she first thought.

Depressing thoughts rushed through her mind, 'everything else keeps going wrong, it's like a roller coaster, every time something goes right, like meeting Kylie something else immediately falls apart.'

'There will probably be buses of school kids or something else,' thought Isla pessimistically as she eased the Falcon slowly towards the colourful, low slung buildings which are the entry to the pools.

She felt tired, exhausted even, it might only just be afternoon but it had already been a long, adrenaline fuelled, eventful day.

'Some things do go right, the car park is nearly empty, it looks like there can only be a few customers, there's a few cars here and there all over close to the buildings, brilliant,' enthused Isla to Alice.

'Some of those half dozen cars in sight have to belong to staff,' Isla suspected, the place must be nearly empty.'

She took an immediate hard right as they entered the car park and parked in the north-western corner under a convenient shady eucalyptus tree, and as far away from the Centre's buildings as it was possible to be, slumped back in her driving seat and switched the engine off.

17th FEBRUARY PM - FLOREAT FORUM, RYANS TRAVAILS

'Bitch, bitch, bitch,' inwardly screamed Ryan, the pain in his wrist was excruciating; he wasn't sure whether it was worse when she stuck him with the knife, or pulled the bloody thing out.

'Can't care about that now, it's obvious I've bloody well got to stop the blood,' he realised.

He barely noticed the Falcon exiting the scene; he managed to staunch the wound by ripping his yellow T shirt from his upper body and using it as a makeshift and not very clean pressure pad, although some blood still dripped onto the pavement in front of him.

Looking round him Ryan thought, 'bugger me, being stabbed is bad enough and now I've got other bloody problems.'

The departing Falcon left him in clear sight of everyone close by, he was sitting in the corner of the car park, two uniformed women from Forum security, who had at first tried to stop the departing car were cautiously approaching him and now only 30 metres away.

None of those forming a circle of curiosity round him were offering help but just gawping at him and the blood soaked scene.

'One chance,' decided Ryan, 'got to get hold of myself and get out of here.'

Clutching the T shirt tightly around the wound with his right hand, Ryan got up and walked rapidly away from the scene and hastened into the Forum.

One of the security women realise what was happening and shouted at him to stop.

Uncertain what to do she conferred with her colleague and by the time they had made up their minds as to the priority Ryan was into the Forum and long gone.

Ryan's speedy exit from the scene gave him the element of surprise; he was well ahead of any possible pursuers when he careered into the Forums shopping area and proceeded to the one place he knew well, the nearest pub.

The Hotel was situated at the west end of the Forum and set over a number of levels, including the lower car park where Ryan's battered Ute lay safe, cool and waiting for him.

Moving rapidly through the curious shoppers, Ryan diverted through the Best and Less shop, nicking a sports shirt in the process, he was in enough trouble anyway, he thought, 'a bit of shop lifting wasn't isn't going to cause me many more problems.'

Ryan pulled the new shirt over his head only then realising it was an AFL 'T,' and his least favourite team the Magpie colours of bloody Collingwood, 'as a Carlton fan, 'this is the final sodding insult,' he thought moodily as he walked hurriedly into The Hotel.

Ryan, now in the hotel reception took a moment to look around; the two receptionists were busy with customers, when he looked back through the smoked glass doors of the Hotel entrance back into the Forum, he could see one of the security guards, stopped, looking all around, and speaking urgently into her personal radio.

Presumably they had lost him and were asking their control to find him on the CCTV cameras. He should be alright where he was for the moment; he wouldn't expect them to have connected cameras in the Hotel.

Ryan assumed Security would have called the cops, if he tried to leave in his UTE from the basement car park; he reckoned CCTV would soon pick him up and pass him onto the cops. He could do without the cops but if they were going to get close to him he would be better off hiding out in the open and the best thing for curing all ills was a beer.

Ryan headed for the bar, on arriving at the basement level hostelry; he selected a barstool at the left end of the bar to be able to keep his throbbing left wrist hidden between his body, the wall and below the level of the bar.

It smelt like any bar anywhere in the world, the scent of beer and polish, although the glass bar top and the mirrors behind the optics and the shelves below appeared spotless, there was the aromas of vinegar and food from those dining in the main body of the room. It was cool due to the Air conditioning and dimmed lighting gave the whole place a relaxed feel.

On the opposite side of the bar from Ryan, were floor to ceiling windows with blinds to shade the room from the searing sun, through the partially opened blinds could be seen an inviting patio with metal chairs and tables for sun-worshipping drinkers and diners.

'Christ, how has it come to this,' Ryan said to himself.

Perhaps he had been a bit over the top last night, but he was sure she had been gagging for it, he hadn't meant to hit her so hard but she had asked for it trying to turn him down like that. After all she had a lot to thank him for:

He had found their apartment, who looked after Alice when Isla didn't feel up to it?

'Mind you he had to admit she was gorgeous and he wished Alice were theirs.'

'Who else would put up with a girlfriend visiting a jailbird, drug dealer every fortnight?'

'She might be paying the bloody rent but he had his surfing competitions, she couldn't be expecting him to work all the time otherwise he would never make it to the worlds and the luxury life for them all. Business class and 5-star hotels all the way,' he dreamed.

Earlier he had spotted the Falcon when she flashed her lights allowing him to cross into the village, he had only been going to top up the gas tank on the Ute, he had tooted her back and assumed she would follow him into Glendalough village. After filling the tank he couldn't see her and the kid anywhere so he went back to the apartment.

It was only when he dumped his stuff in the kitchen he realised something was wrong, the lack of Alice's toys and clothing was the first thing he noticed; at first he thought Isla had been tidying up then he realised something was really wrong; he ran to their bedroom and on seeing open doors of the wardrobes with the emptiness beyond he realised she and the kid had done a runner.

Grabbing a beer from the fridge he had slumped onto the red, faux leather sofa and thought about what he could do, 'he couldn't stay in the apartment, they were already late with the rent, the next month's was due tomorrow and the landlord would be knocking at the door.'

Isla didn't know, Ryan had appropriated last month's rent and told the landlord they would pay it up next month i.e. tomorrow.

'Crap,' he had thought, he had meant to get some extra hours in at the Yanchep Coffee House, that's where he had been this morning, doing the Breakfast shift.

He had needed the rental cash as a down payment on a new board which the 'Yanchep Surf Shop,' owner had told him was the bees knees, direct from Hawaii, he didn't know he fell for that crap, but he always did, the board, when he tried it, was no better than any other he owned. The Bastard at the Surf Shop wouldn't take it back and was getting snotty about Ryan's tab as well.

He wasn't going to let Isla go that easily he would have to find her quick; he knew she would be at Casuarina this afternoon; he needed to find her before she stitched him up with Luca. Ryan suspected Luca might have some nasty friends around Perth and he didn't want to meet any of them too soon.

He thought about where Isla might go and decided she would need to top Alice's food and belongings. That meant shopping; she hadn't gone into the village, obviously because she had seen him, so she would go somewhere close. He knew Isla liked the Floreat Forum so he had thought he would try there first, once he had finished his beer and worked out an exit strategy from the apartment.

Isla and Alice had been easy to find, he had watched them in the Happy Cafe, followed their progress back towards the car, through the shopping centre. He had been going to follow them into the Family Room, when Kylie pushed past him with her kid in tow, so he waited.

They were absolutely ages; he got so concerned he had walked rapidly down the corridors each side to check there were no other exits.

He didn't want there to be a scene with all the other shoppers looking on, so he had followed them back to the Falcon. He had only been going to give her a little fright and she had stabbed him. So here he was hiding in the bar waiting for some service.

An uninterested barman, eventually left his mobile phone texting, and approached Ryan, before reaching him Ryan shouted for a Swan on draught, the young barman obliged, leaving the schooner on a paper bar mat, in front of Ryan.

'Open tab,' gestured the barman waving his right hand towards the till.

'No thanks,' replied Ryan, aiming to be pleasant and avoid suspicion, 'just the one, cool me down after that heat out there, warming up and no Doctor yet,' he commented

He reached for his wallet, crap it was in his left pocket. With much difficulty and much to the barman's surprise, Ryan struggled to extricate his wallet with his right hand, with much difficulty and cursing under his breath he eased from the pocket and dropped it; Ryan swore under his breath, looked up at the young barman.

'Let me get that for you sir,' suggested the barman as he went towards the exit from his domain.

'That's all right, I've got it,' exclaimed Ryan as he slid off his bar stool, clipping it with his left hand.

He did swear then, quite vociferously, halting the barman's progress in his tracks.

The barman turned back towards Ryan and politely, giving Ryan a chance to withdraw his bad language, queried it by saying;

'I'm sorry sir did you say something?'

Ryan who was by now awkwardly trying to regain his seat, with his dropped wallet now firmly ensconced in his right hand, grimaced and apologised to the barman.

'Sorry mate just banged my foot,' hope I didn't offend you.

No that's fine sir, anything else I can get you,' replied the barman.

'Nothing thanks,' answered Ryan, who had by now resumed his position and retrieved a $5 bill from the offending wallet.

'Keep the change,'

'Thanks,' said the barman, collecting the $5 bill before making change, placing it in the till and the remainder into a tip jar.

There being no-one else at the bar, Ryan felt safe for the moment, and although there were other customers they all looked to be lunching at tables throughout the bar.

The barman was avoiding him, probably due to his previous actions; Ryan didn't care he needed peace and quiet as well as time to think. He nibbled nuts from the complimentary bowl. The pain in his wrist had become a dull throb; he appeared to have staunched the flow of blood, there was none dripping onto the floor below, although if anyone got to look at the drench soaked T shirt surrounding his left wrist, he might have some explaining to do.

He decided he would nurse his beer and think about what he was going to do to take revenge on Isla; after all he had his pride, no self-effacing bitch like her was going to stab him. Sure he had hit her but she had been asking for it refusing him his conjugal rights, where did she think she was coming from, supercilious tart.

Ryan had never in his life let anyone get one over him, sure he might appear a laid back surf bum and he did want life to be a blast, but no-one ever was going to take him for a ride so Isla had it coming to her full style.

At this point, there was a commotion behind him, he glanced up at the bar mirror, to see two WA cops surveying the room from the far entry door.

He didn't dare look up and tried to contract his body into the corner of the bar so he would be less noticeable, without appearing to look up he was able to follow their movements out of the corner of his right eye, as they sidled across the rear of the room. His heartbeat rose and a line of perspiration furrowed down his brow, inside he wished he could curl up into a tiny ball and disappear.

Perhaps fortunately they didn't appear very interested or couldn't see him in the far corner of the room and exited through a patio door, he hadn't realised until he gasped for breath, he must have been holding his breath throughout. Ryan took a huge gulp of beer, draining the glass.

Abruptly before the barman could come across to him again; he departed the bar through the far door. On his way across the sparsely populated room, he made sure to keep his injured left arm close to his side whilst avoiding eye contact with everyone he passed.

Arriving at the far exit of the room he acquired a Cricket Australia cap from the hat stand just inside the doorway, departed the Hotel and entered the Lower Ground Car Park, whilst placing the cap so the peak was clearly covering his forehead.

Nothing seemed awry there was the odd shopper moving between their cars and the shopping Forum. There appeared to be no cops and no Security, keeping his head down, pressing his chin tightly into his chest and his tightly wrapped left arm down by his side he made his way into the car park.

Fortunately it appeared dark in the car park, due to the bright contrast of the outside daylight, the area smelt of burnt rubber and petrol fumes and there was the occasional squeal from cars making the tight turns around the parking bays, there was little chance of him being really noticed on the CCTV as long as he made no moves which would bring him to the attention of the watchers.

Ryan made a beeline for the Ute cutting between the parked cars; where possible avoiding the walkways and other people, as he passed around a battered old, green, Holden Commodore he nearly jumped out of his skin when some bloody little yappy dog, started barking fit to burst. It took a moment before he realised the dog that was racing round the inside of the Commodore, was barking at him. He moved away quickly putting distance between himself and the wretched pooch.

'Sod it, I'm having all the luck today,' thought Ryan, trying to avoid other's gazes by keeping his head down as he moved towards the Ute.

'Lucky CCTV doesn't have an Audio listener otherwise I'd be right messed up.'

Arriving at the Ute, he positioned himself in the driver's seat and realised he would be unable to use his left hand to drive, reaching across himself with his right hand he selected reverse and eased back into the drive way as he reached across to select drive he was positioned directly under a camera which he hoped was pointed elsewhere.

Leaving the car park onto Floreat Road, Ryan set off to return back to the Glendalough apartment. He would get himself fixed up there, look at and clean the wound with TPC, bandage it up, hope like hell the knife had been clean so there wouldn't be an infection, take some paracetamol and then get down to the prison where he would be waiting to greet her when she finished with Luca.

Up in the control room a local Police Officer who was liaising with the Shopping Centre Security, was trying to gain the registration of the Falcon from the CCTV. This was proving difficult, Isla obviously hadn't bothered with a car wash recently and the plates were obscured with dust.

Giving up the Officer said to the Head of Security, 'I think there's not much more we can do, the guy obviously isn't going to make a complaint and we would only give him a bollocking for nicking the T Shirt.

'If he turns up at A and E we might find him otherwise I think we should call it a day.'

The Head of Security wanting to keep in with the local constabulary agreed and the situation was left as it was.

17th FEBRUARY PM - THE POOL

Recovering a whimpering tear-stained Alice from the rear of the Falcon, Isla placed the little girl on the ground with Teddy, the toddler was now shaded by the body of the car and the Eucalyptus tree. The concrete car park was covered, in a light layer of sand and in the corner where they were parked, were plenty of strips of loose eucalypt bark. Alice immediately grabbed a strip and started to wave it around like a sword as if to show her prowess off to Teddy.

With the heat of the day, lack of wind and continuing dry period, the indigenous, menthol cough drop smell, of the Eucalyptus trees was pleasant but almost overwhelming. For Isla it helped her think and react positively to the present situation, keeping a careful eye on her daughter, who was trying to stand up with Teddy in her left hand and the strip of bark the other, she opened the trunk of the Falcon, fortunately lying on top of the suitcases and other packages were half a dozen summer dresses she had laid on top to try and prevent creasing.

Isla looked at her hands, she didn't dare pick up the clothing like she was but she also couldn't approach the cafe and toilets of the Aquatic Centre covered in blood.

Isla grabbed a large bottle of drinking water from the back seat, a purchase from Woolworths in the Forum, splashed it over her hands and face. Not caring who was watching, it was a swimming pool park anyway, Isla ripped off the bloody dress and bra, sluiced the bloodstains off the rest of her body and used the clean part of the discarded dress to dry herself.

'Hopefully that makes me look more presentable,' she thought grabbing a bright red short sleeved summer frock and black bra from the trunk she quickly got dressed.

'That's better,' she thought admiring herself in the offside wing mirror of the car.

Suddenly Isla realised it was very quiet, too quiet, she looked anxiously round her for Alice, only to find the little girl toddling off towards the brush, Teddy grasped in the right chubby hand and long piece of bark in the other in happy pursuit of a wallaby. Until their arrival it had been quietly sleeping in the shade of a bush of kangaroo paw.

'Alice,' screamed Isla in panic whilst rushing from the tarmac in pursuit of the little girl.

The wallaby which hadn't been bothered by the approach of Alice, was immediately disturbed by Isla's scream hopped furiously away.

Isla rushed up to rescue the child from her expedition, the little girl had plonked herself onto her bottom, dropped her piece of bark and was looking and pointing, with a look of amazement on her face into the undergrowth where the Wallaby had disappeared

Isla wasn't too worried by the wallaby but more the probability of them disturbing sleeping snakes in the undergrowth.

Hauling Alice up, Isla walked the little girl back to the car.

Isla grabbed her bag with her right hand, shut up the car, by pushing the doors shut with her right knee, shouldering the trunk closed, locked the doors and rapidly headed for the cafe and adjoining rest rooms.

It was really hot and sultry now and as Isla approached the centre, she didn't really have any idea how she was going to make herself look right for Luca again.

'We have time but I'm still stiff and sore and now I feel filthy because of Ryan's blood, hope the washroom's good in here? Speculated Isla.

Isla chatted to Alice about the nice Wallaby as they walked across the concrete of the car park, out of the corner of her eye she spotted the word crèche in front of the entry door, looking closer she realised the centre had a crèche.

Isla thought quickly, 'I could leave Alice while I get myself sorted out. It's only $5.40 for 90 minutes, we have time, I could even have a swim, get showered and get ready in time to make our way to the prison.'

Ten minutes later, Alice and Teddy were contentedly ensconced in the crèche and Isla dressed in a new cheap black one-piece from the swimwear sale, was happily doing lengths in a practically empty swimming pool.

Isla could feel the refreshing kick of adrenaline you get from hard exercise, the warm water appearing to ease the muscle pains and kinks in her tendons. She wished it could go on forever; the trouble was she had responsibilities and battles to fight so after about 15 minutes she headed for the changing facilities.

An hour later having put herself back together, drinking a fresh latte from the cafe, Isla felt ready for the world again. Thanks to Kylie's ideas she had done a lot better job of covering the bruises with makeup. She needed to, her red dress was sleeveless, low-cut and only just covered her bottom.

'Mind you with this dress Luca was hardly likely to notice anything else but me,' she determined.

Picking Alice up from the crèche was only a problem for the little girl, Isla suspected Alice had enough excitement for the day, and there were tears as they left the complex.

Isla didn't really need the tears but understood and hoped Alice would sleep in the car.

Isla wanted to concentrate on the next stage of their adventure the visit to Casuarina.

Carefully exiting the buildings with a cheery goodbye to the receptionist, Isla carefully checked the car park for interlopers, before approaching the car, once bitten, twice shy and she wasn't intending to make the same mistake as at the Floreat Forum.

Isla felt safer when she saw a couple of Mud larks (magpies,) on the grassland alongside the Falcon; 'they wouldn't be there if someone was hanging around the car or close by in the bush,' she thought.

Properly securing Alice in her rear seat and after making sure she had washed clean and dried her own seat and the steering wheel, Isla sat back and re-thought her options.

It's now just after three; I reckon it will take about an hour to reach the prison. Normally I like to be early so we are at the front of the queue but today doesn't really matter, it's was going to be our last visit; we can always blame the traffic, after all it's happened before.'

Isla decided as they were close they would take National Route 1 down the coast, she didn't fancy going through the city. It was a much more pleasant run close to the seaside and kept Alice more interested with the passing scenery.

Decision made, Isla eased the Falcon out of the Bold Park Aquatic Centre and left onto The Boulevard, traffic was starting to increase; she could see schoolchildren in their distinctive uniforms cycling along on the tracks either side of the highway, they ended pulling out onto the highway behind a very shiny, purple metallic, Ford Falcon Ute with three colourful surfboards laying in the rear.

Isla looked into the rear mirror, Alice was fast asleep, her left thumb was in her mouth and occasionally her lips would move as she sucked onto the digit.

Isla could see a golf course on her left, part of the Wembley complex; she had been there with Luca for a wedding in happier days. It had been a full Italian do,' and gone on almost all day, she remembered the couple being given cash presents by everyone.

In those days Isla dreamed of happiness with Luca, having no knowledge of his nefarious activities and thinking him something in Investments, the only bonus in the last three years had been the arrival of her gorgeous little girl Alice.

'God, they had made a handsome couple then,' she mused, whilst gently directing the car westwards, 'him with his dark good looks and suit from Saville Row, London of all places and her in a black Kirrily Johnston Babylonia dress, with her blond hair and simple jewellery.'

'God we wowed them all back in those days,' Isla remembered with a secret thrill, 'now it's all a bloody disaster.'

On their left were some newly built roads ready for their future new housing developments, gradually as the road crested a small hill, they reached more mature housing, set well back from the highway with aged eucalyptus trees on either verge. The trees were all leaning towards the north east, as a result of the punishing Fremantle Doctor. The road turned to the left and she could see the sea in the distance, the sight of it always pleased and refreshed her, it had always been like a cleansing spirit. The Doctor, must have just started, Isla could see whitecaps on the distant but closing watery expanse of the Indian Ocean.

Within moments the road started its downhill descent towards the dark blue, white flecked sea, the twin carriageways were separated by a grass covered central median which was also used for the thin, tall, T shaped, twin, road light structures. The Falcon appeared to leap towards the sea between the bush covered dunes. It only seemed like moments and they were turning left and south, onto the West Coast Highway towards North Fremantle.

The road flattened out now they were close to sea-level and it's all part of Tourist Drive 204 as the regular brown signs reminded Isla.

The drive was pleasant, the road all dual carriageway and divided again by a grassed central median. Some Horticulturist must have had fun planting different types of trees at frequent intervals along the central median, there were small and large palms; tall thin conifers, with long thin branches sticking out horizontally, looking just like two dimensional Christmas trees; acacias, and eucalyptus of various sizes.

Every time she had to stop at a junction, Isla became extremely nervous; the sight of a white Ute would cause her heart rate to jump, just in case it was Ryan. It didn't matter that there was no way he could have found them, the thought of the possibility was still very frightening.

Isla was religious about keeping to the speed limit, it was bad enough every cop in the city knew this car belonged to a drug dealer but she couldn't afford to get pulled over now with everything that had already happened that day.

The road started to run into the western suburbs, there was more traffic about and on her left was the Trans Perth Fremantle rail line, a silver, with green stripe commuter train bustled north in the opposite direction.

Not feeling up to the traffic on the Stirling highway and wanting to stay at a leisurely relaxing place, Isla left most of the traffic behind as they followed Curtin Avenue into North Fremantle, keeping the railway to their left and now passing suburban residential housing to their right.

Shortly after passing Mossman station the traffic began to build up and at the Marine Drive roundabout the traffic came to a standstill briefly as the two southbound single lanes of traffic came together.

It was relaxing to drive slowly along the beach side road, the first of the surfers were taking advantage of the rising waves caused by the Indian Ocean swell and the start of the Doctor. The sun beat down on the blue sea its rays making the ocean gleam in the sunlight.

Ahead were the cranes of the nearly completed shopping and residential complex which was part of the expanding North Fremantle. Isla felt refreshed by the sights and opened her window to get a breath of the fresh sea air.

They crossed the Swan River on the older Queen Victoria Bridge.

On her right Isla glanced towards the busy port of Fremantle, her view partially obscured by the railway bridge, there appeared to be a slab sided, green car carrier manoeuvring in the port, she could see the flocks of seagulls, hungrily circling the area over the fish docks.

'There must be newly arrived fishing boats, and it must be a cacophony of noise around the fish dock with all those birds trying to get a late lunch,' laughed Isla to herself.

Checking the rear view mirror for the umpteenth time Isla could see a newly woken Alice looking around her with interest at all the different sights her blond hair was tousled by the breeze through the open window.

For the first time that day Isla smiled inwardly, 'after some setbacks my initial plan is starting to come together.

'I don't know where we are going to bed down tonight but we look free and clear for the moment.'

17th FEBRUARY PM - VILLA NAPOLI FREMANTLE

About the time the Falcon with Isla and Alice was crossing the river a meeting which would affect everyone was taking place close by in Fremantle.

In the Italian themed restaurant, the Villa Napoli, on the High Street in the old historical part of Fremantle, there was a meeting entirely about Isla and Alice of which they knew nothing.

'Hi boss,' said Aleksander as he approached Fabio, following closely behind was Andriy who acknowledged Fabio's wave of hand in greeting as they took their seats opposite Fabio, at their reserved table in Villa Napoli. The dining chairs groaned and seemed to sag under the weight of each of the twins.

The Twins were originally from Kiev, they had been caught out enforcing for the wrong boss. Safety being preferable to valour, they had left town very quickly and ended up in Australia five years before.

Somehow they had persuaded Australian Immigration in Perth to grant them a Tourist Visa and never left.

They were both about 40, similarly, around 2metres in height and weighed in at around 130 kg. None of this body size was fat, regular daily workouts saw to that – neither had a hair on their head and they exuded violence.

One of them alone was enough to scare any self-respecting citizen – people had been known to walk the other way when the two were strolling the pavements of Fremantle together.

Rare, for such characters and perhaps even more frightening, neither of them had the modern habit of exhibiting tattoos. They didn't feel they needed them, their vicious personalities being enough to exude their influence.

The pair were both well dressed in matching light grey summer weight suits with white short sleeved shirts and matching grey woollen ties.

Fabio being third generation Aussie was more down market in tailored light blue shorts and collared matching plain short sleeved shirt.

Luca had acquired the pair from a previously defunct business about three years ago, the twins had preferred the more lucrative offers of the Italian brother so they had persuaded their previous boss to retire rather than get into a dispute over territory with Luca and Fabio.

Things had been quiet recently, after Luca's arrest and incarceration there had been a period of consolidation, areas of influence had been agreed with other main dealers.

Disagreements about territory affect business, even in the trade of illegal drugs; Luca and Fabio had decided to let the dust settle.

With the twins onside there had been little prospect of the competition taking advantage of the initial disarray caused by Luca's arrest.

Luca had decided and informed Fabio that like all good businesses there are times when you need to sit back and take stock.

After ordering beer and large portions of pasta, Fabio got down to business.

'Luca, wants you to keep an eye on his girlfriend and their kid, he doesn't know about the boyfriend but it's about time the reprobate was warned off.'

Andriy, the younger brother by ten minutes but the spokesman for the two said, 'how far would you like us to go,' in guttural English.

'A friendly warning, I think.'

'He needs to be leaned upon. We don't want it bad enough so the cops are involved, her being known, might make them look further than we would really want.'

'You will need to give us some details about where they are living and any movements,' answered Andriy.

'She will be at the prison visiting today from 4.30, I've written down the address where you might find him, he's a beach bum who mainly surfs at Yanchep so you shouldn't have any problems finding him,' replied Fabio whilst handing over a slip of paper with the Heard Way address and Ryan's description.

'OK,' grunted Aleksander.

'One other thing she's driving my brothers' dark blue Falcon, she and the kid are to be treated with kid gloves and not know what's happening,' said Fabio.

'You should be able to identify her and follow them, when she goes to the Falcon in the Prison visitors Car Park after visits, about 5.30pm today.'

'That's alright, after we've eaten, we have time to get up to Glendalough, have a chat with this Ryan character, explain the facts of life and be at Casuarina before she completes her visit, ' decided Andriy for the two brothers.

At that moment, two waiters appeared with large steaming plates of pasta and glasses of beer, the smell of the sauces was enough to make their mouths water, and the three of them settled down to some serious eating and drinking.

'We're all agreed then;' said Fabio, delicately wiping some tomato sauce from his moustachioed top lip, with his bright red linen napkin.

'The girl and kid should be heading down to Bunbury in the next day or two to my parents, I'll be renting a house for them down there in the next few days and I'll keep you informed.'

Andriy, wiping beer froth from his lower chin with his right wrist replied, 'alright boss we'll hit the road shortly, and contact you on the mobile later, to let you know what's happening.'

'That's fine,' replied Fabio, 'remember though to be careful what you say over the mobile, we don't know who could be listening in.'

'Fair enough,' replied the brothers in unison.

About 30 minutes later the two brothers saluted Fabio as they departed, they headed for their Holden Commodore Ute, the latest SV6 Z-Series in 'Perfect Blue.' The Twins loved these big Australian vehicles it was like they were made for big hunks of manhood like themselves.

Aleksander was their main driver, although Andriy got behind the wheel when necessary, as to be expected from illegal immigrants neither had Australian licences.

It didn't really matter to Aleksander about a licence, he was an extremely proficient driver shortly after the split from the Soviet Union, when all sorts of private enterprise became possible, he had driven souped-up Volga's as getaway vehicles.

About 30 minutes after Isla, Alice and the Falcon had crossed the Swan River southbound, the Twins and their Perfect Blue Ute went in the opposite direction northbound, to the Stirling Highway and Glendalough beyond.

17th FEBRUARY PM - CASUARINA PRISON

Isla, Alice and the Falcon, had just passed the turning for the Royal Australian Navy base, southbound on Rockingham Road when she made the decision which was to partially alter everything that was to happen the next ten days.

'Best to change our routine,' she decided, 'we don't want to drive up and park in the visitor's car park at Casuarina, best we park at Kwinana Railway Station, on the Park and Ride and get the Visits Bus in at 3.45. That way if Ryan is outside watching the car park he'll probably think we have given visiting a miss.'

With the BP Refinery on their right, Isla eased the Falcon into the left filter onto Thomas Road which would take her directly to Kwinana Station, as she waited a white Ute, raced across her front.

'Bloody hell,' she swore aloud in fright attracting Alice's attention in the rear of the vehicle.

'Sorry darling.'

'That nearly gave me a heart attack,' before I realised it belonged to someone else, for Christ's sake, it wasn't even the right make, there was no way he could be here now after the mess I made of his wrist.' decided Isla reprimanding herself under her breath.

Thomas Road was very busy with trucks and tankers and it wasn't easy joining the filter to turn right across the highway, there were no traffic lights and because of the queue, Isla was worried they might find a large fuel tanker up the backside of the Falcon. Eventually they were able to make the turn, it was 3.35 and they had 10 minutes to meet the bus.

Fortunately the car park was next to the highway and very close and they were able to park just across the road from the bus stop.

Alighting from the car Isla checked herself over, smoothed down her dress with both hands and used the drivers' side wing mirror to check her face. She took enough money out of her purse, for the parking and bus ride, retrieved her passport and Alice's ID, to prove their identities at the prison and locked her bag in the trunk.

Leaning over to unfasten a sleeping Alice, Isla felt a hard lump pressing on her right hip and suddenly remembered,

'Christ the Boning knife.'

'I would be in a heap of crap trying to get that through prison security.'

Quickly slipping the knife under the driver's seat, she grabbed a bottle of water, a drink for Alice, picked the now unstrapped dozing little girl from the rear of the car and strode out rapidly towards the waiting bus.

They had used the bus before; it had been easier when they were living in the city to take the train.

Boarding the bus, she was greeted by some friendly acknowledgements from regulars like herself.

One of the girls joked about Isla coming down in the world and returning to real society if she had to catch the bus again.

There was the usual mixture of concerned parents, wives or partners like her and children; plus the mules.

Everyone on the bus knew who the mules were. Skinny girls with pinched faces who looked like they hadn't eaten for a week, vacant glassy looks confirmed their own drug use making them obvious targets for the visits searchers when they arrived at the prison. They were usually too scared to acknowledge the greetings from the other visitors.

At exactly 3.45, the driver closed the doors and the bus left the Station car park on its short drive to Casuarina.

Everything appeared to be going right now; the traffic lights were on green as they crossed the Kwinana Freeway on Thomas Road, soon they were turning off Orton Road and into the prison car park. The visits bus pulled up in the front of the gaol and Isla, with a somnolent Alice stretched out in her arms looked out past the staff car park towards the visitors car park in the far distance.

She breathed out with relief; no battered white Ute but she knew Ryan could still turn up before visits were complete.

Joining the crowd leaving the bus, Isla felt she could almost touch and smell feel the fear of those who were going to try and smuggle something into the prison for their partners.

There was the resignation of those who were going to visit untrusting prisoners, who for whatever reason always believed their other half was in bed with someone else, they knew they had to visit but they were going to end up having an argument, and were steeling themselves for the impending storm.

'Like myself,' thought Isla, 'if I don't get this exactly right.

Isla grimaced at the thought then prepared herself for the inevitable search and impending visit.

To counter the gloom of most of the, primarily women visitors, there was the predominantly happiness and joy of the young children who didn't properly understand why, but who gleefully understood they would see Daddy today.

When they entered the Gate, there was already a queue for the search teams of dogs and prison staff.

Isla put her few coins into one of the re-useable lockers, locked it and carried the key in her right hand so it was obvious when she came up to be searched.

Alice who felt like a dead weight in Isla's arms, slowly opened her eyes and looked around curiously; she appeared quite content lying across her mother's shoulder, although the pain from her beating had Isla wishing she could get her daughter to walk.

The queue of visitors progressed slowly in fits and starts towards the entrance of the search tank.

Visitors were being taken into the search room six at a time. Up to now there had obviously been few problems, they had moved forward quite regularly.

It was obvious no one was getting caught yet, trying to smuggle contraband; the queue kept stopping and starting but moved on at a reasonable pace.

Just when they thought they were getting close the queue stopped.

'Damn,' said the blousy, middle-aged blond woman just behind Isla and Alice.

This made Alice wake up properly and to Isla's relief the little girl wriggled and Isla was able to put her down and let her walk, while the woman continued.

'Looks like someone's got nicked, still be less time fighting off the Old Man's groping hands, won't it girls?, she said loudly and light-heartedly to the rest of the queue.

Some of the, queuing visitors nodded their heads and smiled nervously an odd one laughed in unison.

Eventually after what seemed to take forever but was in reality only about ten minutes, Isla and Alice arrived at the Search room.

At the entrance a lady Officer in white blouse with dark blue epaulettes checked their ID's carefully and informed them of the search procedures.

They were third into the search room, each of the six of them were expected to stand on one of the six taped X's on the pale, beige, linoleum flooring.

'Each of you please stand on a cross. Lady,' she said indicating Isla, 'can the little girl, stand alongside you?'

'Yeas she usually does,' replied Isla.

Alice held onto Isla's right leg with both her arms, looking expectedly towards the other door, she giggled happily.

Isla looked ahead, 'yes there is a search dog,' she noted, eyeing up a friendly black Labrador sitting alongside its handler at the other end of the room.

Alice loved this, she loved the big black Labradors sniffing her, while stood alongside her mother.

The Officer looking after dog said to them all, 'please stand still the dog will walk around you and return, it will only take a moment.'

The young girl next to Isla looked unhappily at the Officer, she didn't look old enough, you had to be 18 to visit a prisoner on your own, and she was shaking with fear.

'Oh, Oh,' thought Isla, 'this could take a while,' expecting something to happen, and for the girl, to almost certainly be questioned about her age.

The Black Labrador and its Male Officer handler, bustled down the room.

'Good dog Max, find, find,' encouraged the handler as the dog ran down the line of visitors.

Max with sleek, back, tail wagging furiously ran in an S shaped pattern, and in the same way back to his handler.

When the hound passed Alice she tried to reach out to him but he was too fast for her, she was a great fan even though she was never able to catch any of the dogs.

Max barked and ran back to the young female visitor, sat down and pointed his nose in the air. Immediately two other male Officers standing to one side approached the young girl and asked her to follow them to another room. She burst into tears and half collapsed, the Officer on her left, quickly and gently grabbed her near elbow to steady the poor girl and helped her from the room.

The handler raced to his dog and gave him a battered looking yellow tennis ball, Max chuffed with his reward, barked happily and bounced his way happily back to the end of the Search room with his Handler.

The Lady Officer apologised, 'Sorry, please stay where you are, we'll have to do this again.'

Max set off again, returned to his handler and they went and sat at the end of the room, the dog panting with pink tongue hanging out of its mouth and tail wagging furiously.

Everyone sighed with relief and through previous experience they headed off towards the metal scanners and the Search Team on the other side of the room.

Isla and Alice followed along slowly, the latter gripping Isla's right with her own left hand. They walked together through the metal detector arch, Isla leading Alice through, trying to avoid the sides as they cleared the structure.

It beeped, Isla wanted to fall through the floor, for a moment she thought she still had the boning knife in her pocket.

Grinning at her the Officer overseeing the search, said to Isla, 'it won't be you love, that dress couldn't hide anything,' laughing he continued, it will be the little girls shoes, betcha!' and he pointed at Alice's pretty little red shoes with their metal buckles.

Isla sighed with relief, all the stress of the day, must have really affected her, how could she forget about Alice's shoes, they did this every two weeks and it always happened.

'Excuse me?' said one of the other lady Officers, 'please just stand over here,' she said to Isla indicating a space away from the walk through metal detector. Grabbing a hand held metal detector, she ran it down either side of Isla and then around Alice, sure enough the little girl's shoes, caused a beep, beep, beep, from the machine.

'Thanks,' said the Officer, 'please go over there,' indicating the gate to the Visits room.

17th FEBRUARY PM - THE PRISON VISIT

Standing by the indicated gate was an uninterested tall rugged, male Officer, who looked like he would be more at home playing Aussie Rules stood holding a large set of keys, attached to a long metal chain, which was itself held onto his belt by a large round metal ring.

As they approached he unlocked a metal barred gate and then a wooden door before allowing them through into the Visits Room

Picking Alice up, Isla braced herself, fixed on a smile and looked at her watch, '4.30, visits ended in 55 minutes.'

'Just have to survive that long,' she thought to herself.

'Mustn't argue about anything, must agree with anything he wants. After all, once this is over we don't intend ever seeing Luca again,' she promised herself.

'Which prisoner,' questioned the Officer?

'Mancuso,' answered Isla.

'Table 14, over to the right' said the Officer, 'don't forget to check in at the top table first,' he continued as he unlocked the gate to the Visits room and ushered them through.

There was the almost overpowering reek of cleaning fluid affecting their senses as they passed through the gate, this soon passed and as they made their way into the brightly coloured expanse of the Visit's space.

Isla could see Luca sitting at their visits table, he waved and Isla picking Alice up showed her off and encouraged, 'wave to daddy darling,'

Alice needed no second bidding and waved vigorously at Luca halfway down the large room.

Isla showed their ID's to the two Officers on the top table and went over to Luca. He rose and greeted her with a big bear hug, nearly squashing Alice between them. Before she could protest his tongue was right down her throat as he kissed her passionately, his hands gripped her bottom tightly and she could feel his manhood pushing at the front of her dress.

In severe pain due to the bruising from Ryan's assault and the tightness of Luca's grip, she held on and tried not to gasp with the agony of the tight embrace.

Isla knew the Officers' wouldn't allow their passionate clinch to last too long and it would all be over pretty quickly. Brief hugs and kissing was allowed only briefly at the beginning and ending of each visit.

Alice started to protest and wriggle, when from just beside them a tall smartly turned out Officer, in a firm, gruff voice whispered into Luca's vacant left ear.

'Enough Mancuso, sit down otherwise your visit will be curtailed.'

Luca knowing how far he could push the envelope, let her go, while still taking the opportunity to stroke her left breast with his right hand as they sat down.

Isla sat Alice onto the table between them; it was about 70cms square and the similar in height, had four thin metal legs, one on each corner of a heavy plastic coated red top.

The visits room was painted in a variety of bright pastel covers, on a dais at the front of the room were the two Officers Isla had reported too, when she entered the Visits room. There were four long rows of tables like the one they were sitting at, evenly spread throughout the Visits room. In one corner was a crèche overseen by two women in nurse's uniform, opposite this and in the corner to the right of the seated Officers was a canteen from which Prisoners could buy refreshments for their visitors.

Glancing around as they sat down Isla thought.

'Considering its purpose the space is well maintained, bright, airy and fit for purpose.'

Luca, held out his long, perfectly manicured hands to his little girl as she tried to reach him from the top of the Visits table. Picking her up, he held her in his arms and told Isla he was going to take Alice and get them all a drink and some chocolate from the canteen.

'Thanks,' said Isla.

A contented Alice and her smiling father, left the table, to obtain everyone's refreshment. The little girl gripping his neck tightly, with both arms, while her head lay across his shoulder as they made their way across the Visits room to the canteen.

'Sod it,' Isla thought.

'Alice is getting as bad as her mother, must be in our genes, every one of our men wants to control us.'

'Bloody Ryan battering me and now Luca, thinks he owns me.'

'OK I did want a sodding coffee, he could have asked me not just assumed he was right, she grumbled to herself.

This made Isla more determined, Alice and her were definitely going to disappear.

'Just got to be all sweetness and light for the next 40 minutes and then we'll be out of here and away from this bastard and his bloody family forever.'

Father and daughter returned from the canteen with coffee for the adults and a beaker of orange for the child,

Isla assumed a look of happiness, and fixed a 'happy smile,' to her face and said,

'Thanks for the coffee darling.'

Luca said, 'we haven't got long and we need a chat, so I'm taking Alice over to the crèche so we aren't interrupted.'

Alice happily left for the crèche, this time holding her Daddy's hand as they manoeuvred their way across the visits room.

'Crap here he goes again, doesn't ask me if it's alright for Alice to go to the crèche, just bloody assumes,' seethed Isla, trying to smile but scratching her nose with her right hand in case anyone noted her frown of disapproval.

'This is the one place I'm are sure to be watched, especially visiting Luca.' Isla assumed to herself.

'Right,' said Luca on his return from the crèche.

'I've decided you need help, you're to dump that place in Glendalough. It's not right my girlfriend and daughter are stuck there.'

'Tomorrow I want you both packed up and down to my parents in Rockingham, Fabio will have a decent place, somewhere close by, for the pair of you next week.'

Isla took a moment to consider this to give her chance to decide on her answer.

'I had better agree, but only after I've had argued a bit, otherwise he might get a bit suspicious. He isn't used to me always agreeing.'

'But we are happy there,' Isla started to say.

Luca interrupted, 'no argument love, it's a done deal; I should never have let you be stuck in Glendalough anyway.'

'Besides what have you been doing?'

'My parents are complaining because they haven't seen either of you for months, except that brief visit at Christmas.'

'That's all I bloody need,' believed Isla, 'they would smother the pair of us and disapprove of everything I do.'

Isla thought, 'I wouldn't be able to go anywhere, Luca's mother, Francesca would be querying every move and Walter, the old man would watch me like a hawk.

'He's a dirty old man anyway I'm sure he wants to get into my knickers, he makes my skin crawl every time he looks at me,' she reflected.

'The pair of them only accepted me because of their grandchild Alice, but totally disapprove of me because I don't have any Italian connections, sod them.'

'Well,' said Luca impatiently.

'Alright we'll go down there but we need a couple of days to pack and give notice, Alice has her jabs tomorrow,' lied Isla

She reached across the table and grasped both hands in hers tenderly to show she was acquiescing gracefully.

Inside Isla was fuming.

'I don't like Fabio being responsible for housing us, I would trust him as far as I could throw him. He is a snivelling, crawling, little pipsqueak.'

'I'll castrate him if he tries anything on,' she mused smiling at thought of him losing his balls.'

After a lot of talk from Luca about how much he loved them and the promise he would soon be up for parole, Luca went back to the crèche to collect Alice.

For the remainder of the visit they gave their attention to Alice, although Luca was constantly reaching across and grabbing her hand. For Isla it appeared to go on forever, for Luca the time flew.

Luca had time to tell Isla about the lone prisoner two tables along, 'he's in trouble, no visit, she's supposed to be bringing stuff in today.'

'He's already in debt to me; they better have a good reason for not coming through today, I've got customers waiting.'

'Bloody Hell, do you have to be involved in drug dealing especially in here?' responded Isla whispering vehemently, her cheeks going red with the anger she felt.

Isla reprimanded herself, thinking, 'behave, be all sweetness and light, remember you have only to get both of us through this visit.'

Luca laughed at Isla's response and grinning while putting both her hands between his said, 'Don't you realise where all the money comes from, they'll never catch me, I have too many people between me and the deals, everything is up here,' he said pointing with his right hand to the side of his head, 'nothing is on paper.'

The waiting prisoner looked desperate and kept anxiously watching the Visits entrance, even with the coolness of the Visiting Room air conditioning, the man was sweating profusely, his face was a pasty green colour and he kept wiping it with a grubby white handkerchief.

Isla thought of the young girl taken away from the Search Room when the dog sat, on her. She didn't say anything to Luca but almost felt sorry for the guy, She felt especially upset for the young girl, she would be in serious trouble even though she was so young and probably too naive to realise what she was getting herself into.

Soon enough, one of the Officers at the top table rose and said loudly. 'Time everyone finish your Visits please.'

Immediately all the prisoners with partners stood up and grabbed their other half's, putting Alice on the floor for safety, Luca grabbed Isla and started to grope her everywhere while kissing her passionately.

God he thought, 'she feels good, it's going to be another two weeks before she comes again, its bloody murder.'

Luca didn't feel Isla wince under his strong grip; fortunately for her he hadn't noticed any bruising, but Isla was hurting badly from this final embrace.

After what appeared moments to Luca and was an absolute age to Isla, an Officer appeared alongside, cleared his throat loudly as if hinting and Luca had to let Isla go.

Cursing under his breath, Luca picked Alice up and gave her one last hug before handing her to Isla.

'Bye Love,' he said 'see you in a fortnight, love to Mum and Dad.

'Bye darling,' said Isla.

Smiling with relief because the visit had ended, she put Alice over her left shoulder and marched off purposefully towards the exit, this was jammed by visitors trying to wave their last goodbye and Isla had to gently push her way through the throng.

Arriving in the Search Room on the way to the exit, Isla felt exhilarated, she had done it, they had survived the visit there was no way Luca could have any suspicions they were home free.

'Well nearly,' reasoned Isla

'There's only Ryan, the parents and Fabio to avoid but stage one of the plan, has been achieved.'

Isla emptied their locker and retrieved the small change, with Alice walking alongside, looking curiously at everyone in the crowd around them, they made their way out of the prison and onto the Kwinana Station bus.

17th FEBRUARY PM - ZELDAS APARTMENT GLENDALOUGH, RYAN

Ryan pulled into Heard Way with some relief, although it was just under 5K, it had been a struggle at times having only one hand to drive his Ute.

'Still just about there,' he thought.

He pulled into a parking space across from the apartment, bumping the kerb as he did so.

Ryan could see a bunch of his female neighbours on the lawns in the front of the apartments. They looked up from their conversation, to look disapprovingly at Ryan and his noisy Ute.

'Christ,' Ryan reflected, 'don't want that bunch of nosy buggers checking up on me, they're probably only nattering about the latest soaps.'

Switching off the engine Ryan looked down at the blood stained, yellow 'T' Shirt, covering his left hand.

'I can't go past that lot looking like this, they'll give me some real stick and ask some real awkward questions.'

Just at that moment, Zelda walked across and looked in the driver's window.

'Hi Ryan,'

'You beauty, what the bloody hell have you done to your hand, get your backside out of this bloody machine so I can have a look at it, it's a right bugger by the looks of it.'

Ryan thinking quickly and succinctly for a change, realised here was a heaven sent opportunity.

'Thanks Zelda, could you? I don't think Isla is in, I've cut it gutting a sea bream me and the boys pulled out of the sea up at Yanchep.'

'Of course, come in, bye girls,' she said to the other women, 'work to do, man's got a little cut that needs seeing to.'

The other women laughed as they sidled away, a dark haired, middle aged housewife from further down the block said.

'When you've finished with him send him along to me, I'll finish him off for you.'

Everyone laughed uproariously. Ryan's tanned cheeks flushed red with embarrassment.

With some difficulty, Ryan alighted from the Ute, grabbed his blue duffle bag, which went everywhere with him and followed Zelda through to her apartment and into her kitchen.

On their way into her apartment Zelda muttered, 'you've got to be daft trying to drive with that mess of a hand, why didn't you get the lifeguards to sort it out.'

Ryan just shrugged and followed her into the Living Room, it was the same layout as upstairs, but nicely decorated and the place looked spotless. The parquet floor was shining; with the blinds being open the outside light lit up the room with its light pastel colours and made it look totally different.

'Wow Zelda it looks totally different compared to our rented dump upstairs.'

Zelda didn't comment as Ryan followed her into the kitchen area.

'Grab a stool and bung your arm up on the worktop.'

Zelda said indicating one of the tall tubular metal brown seated bar stools on the Living room side of the Kitchen counter.

Zelda opened her larder and pulled out an old, battered, mainly red, tartan covered, Scottish, Shortbread tin.

'Got everything to fix that mess on your wrist in here,' she said pointing to the injured limb.

'Can you manage to remove that thing you've got wrapped around your wrist?

She asked, as she laid a large, fluffy, salmon pink, bath sheet on the kitchen work top.

'Don't worry about messing it up,' said Zelda indicating the towel.

'It will soon wash out.'

Ryan placed his left elbow onto the towel and gingerly started to un-ravel the bloodied yellow T Shirt. At first it didn't want to come apart, the dried blood having stuck the folds of the cloth together. With some gently tugging, Ryan managed to ease the shirt away from his wrist; the difficult part was when he pulled the final section of shirt away from the wound.

'Bugger,'

Ryan yelled and winced as the pain struck.

The wound started to weep blood without the benefit of his temporary bandage.

Ryan looked anxiously at the 30cm diagonal slash across his left wrist'

'Stand back,' let the horse see the saddle,' said Zelda, all business, as she slapped a large dressing onto the wound.

'You've made a right mess of that my lad,'

'Do you want me to sew it up?' She asked, smiling to herself.

'It's only like a bit of embroidery after all and I'll do a better, neater job than some fly by night nurse, besides it'll save you 4 hours and awkward questions in casualty.'

'Can you really do it?' asked Ryan surprised, filled with trepidation and worried about painful it would be.

'What about when they are supposed to come out?' he said grimacing, 'how will I know? And w-w-what sort of thread will you use?' he stuttered anxiously.

Zelda laughed, 'only kidding Ryan, I've got these butterfly grips, once we've stopped the bleeding, they'll bind the wound together and you'll have a bit of a scar to boast about.'

'Thanks.'

'Hold that dressing tight onto the cut, if you keep pressure on it, the bleeding should stop, we'll give it 5 minutes. While we're waiting I'll put the kettle on,'

Zelda filled the kettle with cold water before switching it on, and said,

'I'm off to the bathroom, I should be back before the kettle boils, it'll switch itself off if I'm not back in time, you just keep the pressure on with that dressing and wait there.'

Ryan nodded his thanks

With Zelda disappearing, even if only temporarily, Ryan had some time to think and calm down:

'Isla's attack on me with the knife was a real bummer, I hadn't thought she could be so pissed off at me.'

'If I'm honest with myself, I had it coming to, it's alright being laid back and enjoying life, I've really not been thinking about her and the kid, I just thought everything was alright and it was all going great.'

'Getting pissed last night has buggered it all up I'm a right tosser.'

'Suppose I've got away with sponging of everyone else, living on the edge all the time, I should have done better, after all she told me that she came with the kid, can't say I wasn't warned.'

Ryan looked at himself in the reflection of the cooker door.

'Look at me, nearly 30 and middle-age is round the corner.'

'Living with Isla and Alice for this last year has been great, I love looking after the kid and Isla's bloody gorgeous a right catch, I've been so bloody lucky to be alongside the pair of them.'

'I'm a bloody idiot,' he concluded

'I need to get a life.'

'I need to admit I'm never going to make it as professional surfer, and to show I mean it, the first step towards this is to flog all the flash boards, clogging up the truck.'

'I need to stop bloody drinking, I'm a right bastard when it's in me.'

'I need counselling then I don't know where the violence comes from but I've got to stop.'

'Finally I need to get a permanent job.'

Ryan felt a little better and calmer, having he felt resolved some issues, and setting these list of objectives left him smiling to himself.

 Ryan's mood then blackened as he realised it was alright resolving issues in his head but there wouldn't be much point if he couldn't make everything right for Isla and Alice.

'I love the pair of them,'

'How the bloody hell am I going to get the pair of them back after that?'

Ryan remembered the anger, the vehemence and violence of Isla's attack.

'It was a real shock to the system, it made him realise how much he owed them for trying to bring some reality and growing up to his life.'

'I need to bloody grow up.' Ryan shouted angrily aloud to the room.

Just as Ryan was coming to this final angry conclusion, Zelda returned,

'You alright, thought I heard you shouting?'

'Fine thanks just shouting at myself for being so daft.'

'I'll just brew up and then we'll have a look at your wound,'

'You don't look like your putting much pressure on it.'

Ryan shook his head and realised he had forgotten about the pressure he was supposed to be exerting through the dressing onto the damaged wrist.

'Sorry.'

'Don't worry about it; it's your blood,' said Zelda smiling at him as she was pouring hot water into a couple of large white mugs.

'Sugar.'

'No thanks just as it comes.'

'Right let's have a look and see what we've got' she said, as she carefully lifted the dressing from the wound.

'Phew.' Winced Ryan, gritting his teeth and not trying to show the pain as the dressing was ripped from the long cut across the top of his left wrist.

'You big softy, it's not bleeding now,' said Zelda as she dabbed the wound with cotton wool soaked in strongly smelling antiseptic.

Ryan didn't say anything, just grimaced, held his breath and concentrated on watching the second hand ticking round, on the wall mounted, large, white kitchen clock.

He gasped as Zelda, dumped the dirty plug of cotton wool in the kitchen bin and let go of the arm.

'Hold on while I put these steri–strips across the wound, I reckon five should do.'

As Zelda attached each strip, she pulled the sides of the wound together so the body could more easily take on the task of repairing the injury.

'I'll put a dressing over the top and bandage your wrist, you'll need to change it in a couple of days and the important thing is to keep it clean, so no surfing for a while, right!' She emphasised as she took a sip of her tea.

'Tell Isla, I've got plenty of First Aid stuff if she needs it, she'll be able to re-dress it for you.'

Ryan realised he would have to own up to the present situation, and facing up to his recent resolve, gulped so it looked like he was swallowing his Adam's apple said.

'Well it's like this you see, Isla's cleared off with the kid and it's all my own fault.'

Zelda barked at him angrily.

'You're a bloody idiot, how could you mess up so bad, those two are absolutely brilliant.'

'I know, I know, I'm a stupid idiot and I regret it all, here's what happened.'

With only slight embellishment, so as to not make himself to appear totally unscrupulous, Ryan explained to Zelda about Isla leaving and the real reason for his wound. He didn't try to justify himself, just laid it all out there for his neighbour.

Angrily Zelda laid into Ryan.

'I think you're bloody lucky, after what you've done I'd have slit your stupid throat.'

'I know, I'm so very sorry about everything but I've made a resolution to make everything right for them,' whimpered Ryan.

'I'm totally off the grog, I need them, I've really messed up everything.'

He apologised very quickly and tried to explain his new resolution, this calmed Zelda somewhat, she still though gave him a right rollicking.

'You must be really thick; you've got a ready-made family there, they really cared about you, all you've done is used and abused them, and they've done the right thing and buggered off.'

'You've deserved everything that's happened to you.'

'If I was Isla I wouldn't have you back anyway, either way you owe her big style.'

'You should get on bended knee and pray for her forgiveness;' Zelda, continued really laying into the now repentant Ryan.

In the face of this maelstrom from his neighbour, Ryan was blushing with embarrassment, feeling really contrite and ashamed of his actions.

'I know, I know, I'm really sorry,' he said meekly.

'It's not me you should be apologising to, it's them.'

Ryan now feeling like a total worm, rose from the kitchen stool, and stepped away from the work top,

'I had better go now.'

'I'll remember what you said and try and contact Isla later, I hope she'll have me back, don't know what I'll do without them.'

He admitted as he left Zelda's apartment.

Ryan, picked up his duffle bag and made his way home to the upstairs apartment, he had tears in his eyes. 'Hell.'

'I haven't cried since my pet hamster died and I must have been about ten.'

17th FEBRUARY PM - GLENDALOUGH ASSAULT

Ryan felt tired as he entered the apartment, he realised how empty it looked, and there were no toys or other girl's paraphernalia littering the main living room. There was only the dirty buggy which they had acquired from a generous neighbour.

Knowing there was no point trying to ring Isla as she would be at the prison visiting, 'that jerk Luca,' Ryan decided to get his head down and try and catch up on some missing sleep. His body was sleep deprived from, 'too many late nights, and too many early mornings recently,' he thought to himself.

Meanwhile a couple of streets away, a 'Perfect Blue' Commodore Ute was just turning into Glendalough Village, Andriy had decided the Ute needed fuel and being unsure of the exact location of Ryan and Isla's apartment they decided to confirm its location, when they refuelled in the shopping complexes, Caltex Garage.

Aleksander refuelled the Ute, whilst Andriy went into the Garage shop to pay and ask for directions.

There being only one cashier, Andriy calmly waited in the queue to shell out for the fuel, he was third in line and in no hurry as he could still see Aleksander refuelling the Ute.

Reaching the counter he asked the cashier for the directions to the apartment, meanwhile behind him a rather large, burly, tanned, middle-aged trucker started to complain to everyone, about being held up by people who didn't know where they were going.

Andriy having the common sense and confidence of someone who has the ability to handle anything physically, calmly listened to the Cashiers explanation. Once he was certain he fully understood, he told her the number of the pump where Aleksander was just completing his refuelling.

The trucker objected strongly, grabbing Andriy by the shoulder to pull him aside he said.

'Move out the way you bloody Pom, let a real Aussie get served.'

'Excuse me.'

Andriy said apologetically to the cashier.

Turning to the trucker, Andriy placed his right hand on the left shoulder and squeezed into the pressure point, pinching the nerve.

The trucker collapsed like a sack of spuds; there were gasps from the cashier and the rest of the queue.

Turning back to the cashier, Andriy reached into his right side back pocket, pulled out a large wad of dollars and said to the cashier.

'How much, please?'

'He'll recover in a moment but should be more polite in the future,' he added.

After paying for the fuel, Andriy calmly left the shop, leaving a shocked bunch of customers, cashier and very contrite, quiet, recovering trucker.

He returned to the Commodore Ute and relayed the directions to Aleksander as they left the village.

Approaching the apartments, Aleksander and Andriy agreed they should turn the vehicle around so it was facing back towards the exit, in case of trouble and a need to leave the scene rapidly.

From their directions and the address gained from Fabio, they quickly identified the Apartment of interest, noting it was a first floor apartment they looked around for people who might take an interest.

Although they were always prepared, it didn't do to advertise their profession unless really necessary.

Other than some children on the grass in Heard Way and a mangy looking grey haired mongrel sniffing at a nearby lamp post things seemed to be very quiet, it was after school closed but before most people would be returning from work, a momentary quiet period and ideal for the twins.

Leaving and locking the vehicle, they passed Ryan's battered white ancient Ute, as they approached the stairs to the apartment, the mongrel sensitive perhaps to the tension emanating from the men, ran over and started barking while closely following on the heels of the brothers.

Aleksander muttered under his breath as they took the wide stairs together two at a time.

The mongrel realising there was nothing to be gained by following, sat yapping at the bottom of the stairs.

The noise annoyed Zelda and she opened her front door to reprimand the hound just in time to see two large pairs of feet disappearing towards her upstairs neighbours.

The cause of all the noise, stopped barking and rushed over to Zelda, in the hope of human company or more likely some sort of food. She wanting an excuse to listen to what went on above her, spoke quietly to the dog and passed the grateful hound a digestive biscuit which she had been going to eat herself but for the interruption.

Meanwhile above her Andriy knocked politely on the door of Ryan and Isla's apartment.

Nothing happened.

Andriy knocked again this time with more authority, the door and its screen rattled under his fist and the echoes of the banging on the outside of the door reverberated around the apartment.

Ryan, who hadn't heard the first knock, still partially clothed in a clean, red, Oahu surfers, T shirt and light blue underpants was lying on the top of the double bed in the master bedroom; awoke with a start when Andriy interrupted his beauty sleep, with the louder banging of the second knock.

'What the hell's that,' thought Ryan, as he rose unsteadily from the bed, rubbing his eyes with his clenched hands?

Grabbing a pair of knee length, navy blue, cargo shorts from the floor; Ryan nearly fell over trying to put them on, his left leg catching as he was standing only on his right, he headed for the front door of the apartment.

Aleksander said 'he y?' (not in,) in Ukrainian.

Andriy looking at him angrily replied, 'in English you fool, you don't know whose listening.'

'Anyway doesn't matter, some ones in,' he said noticing a shadow move behind the blinds, 'I can see movement.'

Zelda below now patting the itinerant hound heard the exchange above and began to worry about Ryan's safety.

Ryan totally unaware of the threat outside the door, pulled it open, saying loudly to the brothers, 'who the hell are,'

His question was interrupted when Aleksander drove his large right fist into Ryan's midriff. Ryan promptly collapsed back into the apartment, he didn't hit the floor completely because as he was about to strike the parquet, the twins like a well-oiled machine grabbed him, each to an elbow, with Aleksander on Ryan's right side and frog marched him backwards before throwing him into the nearest lounge chair. Andriy slammed the front door shut after them, and with Aleksander stood on either side of a gasping Ryan curled up like a ball in the chair.

Andriy said to Ryan in a polite but chilling voice with slight Eastern European accent.

'Listen carefully Ryan, I will explain the situation to you only once, if you talk, my brother here,' indicating Aleksander on his right; 'will take it that you are being argumentative and not cooperating, if that is the case he will take appropriate action, which will be very painful to you, do you understand?'

Ryan having been awoken so painfully and still not fully comprehending his situation, in between gasping for breath went to reply as he opened his mouth to speak, Aleksander grabbed Ryan's left wrist with his right hand and with his left promptly broke Ryan's left forefinger.

Ryan screamed loudly and hugged his left hand to his body sobbing from the instantaneous pain.

_-***-_

Down below, Zelda already very suspicious, left the happy mongrel to his wanderings and rushed back inside her apartment. Picking up her telephone she dialled 000, it seemed to take forever but the receiver at the other end of the line only rang twice before her call was answered.

"Police Fire or Ambulance" answered the Telstra operator.

Zelda now in an absolute panic interrupted, 'Police there's someone being killed here.'

Fortunately, Zelda had used her own telephone, the Telstra operator could see where she was calling from, so she immediately transferred the call to the Police Emergency Response Team.

The Police emergency operator, whilst signalling for a police response asked Zelda her address to confirm the situation.

Zelda in a panic shouted down the telephone, 'Apartment 1.'

Ryan screamed again.

'Bloody hell they're killing him up there, send the cops quick.'

The operator after finally calming Zelda explained a police response was on its way, and to tell her the address of the emergency and what might be happening. While Zelda was explaining the crisis, another operator listening in, was translating the situation to a two-man patrol car which was responding from the area of the Floreat Forum.

-***-

Upstairs, Andriy said to a very scared, cowering Ryan, 'nod your head if you understand me now, you will not speak unless I tell you.'

Ryan nodded his head vigorously, worried there might be another painful misunderstanding.

Andriy happy the lesson had got through, nodded to Aleksander.

Aleksander dragged Ryan's left arm away from his body, Ryan whimpered with the pain of his broken finger. Aleksander twisted the arm, while pulling it straight out so the forearm was bent against the elbow joint, he held the forearm with his left hand gripping Ryan's wrist and the right the elbow.

Ryan winced and whimpered, 'this really hurt, Christ I wish I could scream,' he thought, biting his lip so much, blood ran down his chin, on top of this the very painful broken forefinger was hanging off the hand at a strange angle.

Through this pain filled fog Ryan heard Andriy say,

'My associate has decided you will never see Isla and the child again, do you understand?'

Ryan still held fast by the other twin nodded.

'If you attempt any contact, my brother,' said Andriy, indicating Aleksander, 'will break your other arm, do you understand?' he said again.

Ryan nodded; he had never felt such pain, 'What did he mean other arm?'

'That's because this one is about to be fractured' said Andriy nodding to his brother.

Aleksander fully prepared with Ryan's arm already twisted against the joint, broke the forearm and let it drop.

17th FEBRUARY PM – GLENDALOUGH TO ROYAL PERTH HOSPITAL

'Aaah,' screamed Ryan, nearly jumping out of the chair with the shock of the increased pain.

Andriy just shoved him back down with the palm of his right hand, leaning down and over Ryan he said quietly into Ryan's right ear,

'We will be watching, when anyone asks, you slipped, there are always more bones to break, no police.'

Andriy didn't ask Ryan if he understood, with his brother, he turned and walked out of the apartment, leaving a sobbing Ryan, slumped in the chair with a useless left arm dangling over the arm of the chair.

As they walked back out onto the trellis, shaded first floor balcony, they could hear sirens in the near distance.

Without rushing but increasing their pace, they made rapid progress to their transport and drove carefully down Heard Way, as they reached the corner, Aleksander, slowed and politely pulled the Ute to the gutter to allow a WA Police cruiser, with blue lights flashing and siren blaring to rush around the corner in the opposite direction.

'Some nosy neighbour, I suspect,' commented Andriy to his brother as they continued on their way, 'the prison next, I think.'

-***-

Zelda, cautiously peering out through the blinds over her front window, heard Ryan's final scream, to her it sounded like one of real excruciating agony and worried her intently.

'Where are those bloody coppers,' she wondered in near panic.

Just at that moment she heard the bang as the front door above was slammed shut. Moments later she heard the steps of the Twins as they descended rapidly down the stairway, before glimpsing them briefly as they passed in front of her apartment.

She heard the rumble of a big engine starting and the noise of the vehicle disappearing as it moved down Heard Way.

Thinking it safe, Zelda recovered her First Aid Tin from its position on the kitchen worktop, she hadn't chance to put it away since Ryan's recent departure.

Leaving her own Apartment she scurried up the stairs to the scene of the crisis, she could hear the police siren as the cruiser rushed up the Avenue.

Stopped, panting at the top of the stairs, she realised she couldn't do anything for Ryan, the door must be locked. She banged on the door hopefully, concerned about Ryan's safety and hoping he was fit enough to answer. Zelda put her left ear to the door shouting into the apartment.

'Ryan it's me Zelda, they've gone now, the Cops are here,'

Zelda heard their police vehicle scream to a halt below in a cacophony of noise and lights.

Inside the apartment, Ryan was in agony and in a quandary, he didn't know what to do, he had been told he couldn't talk to the cops. They were here though and anyway Zelda must know most of what happened, you could hear almost everything through the thin walls and floors of these Apartments.

He didn't know where to put his arm or how he was going to get to the front door, he realised if he didn't get there soon the Cops would just bust it down. Calling out weakly but loud enough to hear, he said.

'Zelda I'm coming.'

Zelda who was busily leaning over the balcony was screaming in fearful anger at the two male Cops, who were just alighting from Car, 'shut that bloody noise off,' referring to the police siren,' and get your useless, bloody, backsides up here.'

Ryan with his left arm and hand hanging loosely and uselessly, by his side, stumbled across the Living Room to the front door of the apartment; he could hear Zelda outside screaming at the Cops, through all the pain, the noise of the siren was the final straw, he just wanted to collapse onto the floor, curl up in a heap and let the world end.

In front of the apartments, one of the Cops silenced the siren and both came bounding up the stairs.

Zelda couldn't believe her eyes the first one in his bright blue uniform shirt peaked cap and navy blue trousers didn't look like he should be out of school.

'I must be getting old,' thought Zelda, 'the Cops look younger every time I see them.

Following behind his colleague, was an older Officer who reached the scene a little breathless after mounting the stairs at a run. He immediately took charge and asked Zelda for a full explanation.

Zelda wasn't prepared to waste time telling her story she wanted action now.

'There could be a dead body behind that door,' she screamed at the unfortunate Officers, 'you need to get in there immediately, there were two thugs in there beating up my neighbour, he could be dead while you're asking stupid questions,' she added.

On hearing this, the younger Officer started banging on the outer door to Ryan's apartment.

'Are you alright in there sir? We need you to open this door.'

He stopped as a haggard looking Ryan opened the screen door, struggling to hold this back whilst opening the front door with his only available right hand. The young Officer took control of the door as soon as it was unlocked.

Zelda rushed towards Ryan and ushered him back into the Living Room, leading him by his good arm she made him sit down on the sofa whilst saying.

'It'll be alright Ryan,' in a sympathetic voice.

In a louder voice she yelled at the older Officer,

'Call a bloody ambulance, quick, you can ask him questions later.'

The Officer standing just inside the front door was already onto dispatch ordering the said vehicle.

He had quickly realised, from Zelda's original call, what little she had indicated when they arrived, the state of the victim that they almost certainly had a serious incident on their hands.

Speaking again to Dispatch he said.

'We will almost certainly need a Serious Incident Team, can you warn the Incident Room please.'

Ryan was by now safely ensconced upon the sofa, Zelda on his left side, telling him to hold his broken arm as tight to his body as possible.

'The body will act as its own splint temporarily.'

'If you can manage it I will strap the arm to your body and that will ease the pain.'

Ryan who still didn't know what to with the broken limb, tried to follow her instructions which only made the pain from his injuries worse.

'Where was the bloody ambulance?'

He thought exhaustedly as Zelda lashed his left shoulder to his body with a bandage from her voluminous, 1st Aid Box.

The younger Officer knelt with his right knee on the floor on Ryan's right side and tried to reassure him.

'If you can tell us something as soon as possible sir, we can get after these thugs for you. The Paramedics are on their way, my partner has asked our Dispatch to send them ASAP.'

Zelda tried to interrupt, 'can't you leave him alone,' she tried to say.

She was interrupted by the older Officer by the door.

'Come on darling if no one tells us anything how the hell are we supposed to catch the vicious buggers.'

Zelda realising the futility of arguing because the Cop was right, finished strapping Ryan to himself said to both of the Officers.

'Shouldn't one of you be taking notes, to save me repeating everything?'

The younger Officer cleared his throat and showed Zelda the open notebook and pen he was holding.

Zelda slightly embarrassed said, 'Sorry,' before launching into her story.

Ryan who was only too pleased for Zelda to tell her story so the Cop's would for the moment ignore him, already felt a little more comfortable thanks to Zelda's ministrations, concentrated on managing the pain in his mind, he could hear another siren in the distance, which he presumed to be the St John's Ambulance rushing to his aid.

Everyone ignored Ryan as Zelda told the Cops of, ministering to Ryan's cut earlier, him leaving, the two large men who had gone up to Ryan's apartment, the banging on the door, Ryan's screams and the rapid departure of the thugs, whom she guessed had given Ryan these very visible injuries.

'What were they driving,' asked the younger of the two policemen.

'I'm sorry I don't know I couldn't see, I think it was big, blue and a Ute. I couldn't see it properly.'

The older policeman sighed with exasperation and passed this information on to dispatch to go out to all duty vehicles.

'All units to watch out for a large, blue Ute with two large bald headed men leaving the vicinity of Glendalough, to be approached with caution as wanted for questioning over a serious assault.'

He concluded to the Dispatcher, who repeated the message back to him. He then confirmed he would need someone from the Serious Incident Team when available.

Moments later there was an all units message heard over the police radio repeating his request.

Hearing the ambulance closing the scene the younger Officer who had completed his note taking of Zelda's statement, went out to meet the paramedics and direct them to the apartment.

The older policeman asked Ryan if anyone else was in the apartment, he shook his head. The Policeman said.

'You won't mind if I check will you?'

Ryan, who was beyond caring, just nodded in agreement. The Officer taking this as his cue and taking out his notebook and pen began a serious tour of the apartment. He decided not to ask any further questions of Ryan yet, it was important to get a feel for who else might be living in the apartment and now he had free rein what he mind find there, legal or not.

Making a careful note of the discarded, damp towels in the bathroom, dirty child's clothes, the child's buggy on the living room floor, the Officer soon realised at least one other occupant of the Apartment was a small child.

This concerned him an opened up a number of unasked questions,

'Was this, an abduction?'

'Was there a mother?'

'If so where were they?'

Feeling there were too many unanswered questions the older Officer felt Ryan would have to provide some answers quickly. There were lots of other intangibles.

'Where were the remaining inhabitants of the Apartment and were they in danger?'

On returning to the Living Room, the older Officer found paramedics attending to Ryan, one was administering gas and air to relieve Ryan's pain and the other was fixing a vacuum splint around the his fractured limb.

Realising there was no way he could ask any questions of Ryan the older Copper, decided to question Zelda once again, indicating to his partner that he should keep an eye on Ryan, he pulled Zelda to one side.

'I know a child and a woman have, or are living here, what's happened to them?' asked the Cop.

'They're alright, they've split from him, I saw them leaving this morning,' said Zelda, indicating Ryan with a nod of her head towards the invalid.

'Don't know where they've gone but they left about 1030.'

'I waved them off, and before you ask they were fine.'

'Right,' said the Officer, 'I'll need their names, just in case we need to make sure they're safe, and the car type and registration please.'

'I'm not very good with vehicles, it's a huge blue thing, I always thought it was too big for her but Isla said it was dead easy to drive, mind you being that size she always had room for all Alice's gear,' answered Zelda launching off at a tangent.

The Officer tried to get her back on track, 'did it have a badge?'

'Oh yes an oval one front and back with blue writing,'

'That's a Ford,' said the Officer kindly.

'Oh yes, like those on the Tele at the V8 racing,' Zelda added.

'Will Davidson, he's a hunky bugger, he drives one,' added Zelda digressing again.

'Well done,' complimented the cop, 'we've obviously got a Blue Ford Falcon.'

Don't suppose you got the reg. or know anything else the vehicle luv.'

'Oh,' said Zelda now more confident and getting into her stride.

'Isla said it was only a couple of years old and had all sorts of gadgets, she tried to show me some when she took me to the village the other day. '

'I don't get all that new-fangled stuff, waste of time,' she added.

Just as the Cop was about to ask about the number plate again, Zelda in full flow now gave him the answer.

'Don't you be asking me for the number plate again either, I can't remember my own never mind someone else's.'

'I do know it was a personal one; don't know what it was though,' she said scratching her nose with her right forefinger.

At that moment, the paramedics helped Ryan into a portable wheel chair; one of them covered him with a blanket and put the portable oxygen unit onto Ryan's lap. Ryan himself was holding the oxygen mask onto his face, with his good right hand and appeared much better for the ministrations of the medics.

Ryan momentarily dragged the mask from his face, 'my bag,' he gasped, 'I need my duffle,' he pointed indicating the blue bag lying on the kitchen unit where he had dumped it earlier.

'Okay,' said the paramedic, retrieving the duffle and putting it onto Ryan's lap,

'Got all your important stuff inside, has it?'

Ryan oxygen mask back in place, nodded furiously and relaxed back onto the stretcher.

The younger Cop told his colleague and Zelda that Ryan was being taken to the Casualty Emergency Room at the Royal Perth.

Zelda inquired of the Officers, 'what happens now?

'We are going to have to secure the Apartment until Ryan is questioned because we don't yet know why he was attacked.'

'We're unsure what's happened to the woman and particularly the child, my colleague,' he said indicating the younger Officer, 'will stay here and I'll follow the lad, to the Royal Perth. I'll trust you will give my mate all the information you have about the apartment's residents.'

He left following the ambulance in his cruiser.

Zelda, explained to the other Cop that she really didn't have any more to tell him and she needed to get her Husbands and her own dinner ready as he would soon be returning from work. She left leaving the young man in charge of the empty apartment.

17th FEBRUARY EVENING - MISSED BY THE TWINS

The twins watched with interest the Police Cruiser as it passed them on the corner of Heard Way.

'Someone must have heard the screams,' laughed Andriy.

Aleksander just grunted a smiling reply in agreement.

Andriy reached into his right hand back pocket and pulled out his mobile.

'I'll just keep Fabio informed,' he said.

Aleksander concentrating on negotiating the right turn off Powis Street onto the Mitchell Freeway, south bound slip road, just nodded in answer to the observation.

'Fabio Ciao,' said Andriy, as the former answered the telephone call.

'First job done, a little pain caused, message passed and we think, properly understood.'

'Someone called the Cops but we were well gone,' said Andriy his black 'I Phone,' held open, on speaker so Aleksander could take part in the conversation if he wanted.

'Fine,' said Fabio, what's happening now?

Andriy replied, 'we're off to the prison and should be there well before 5.30 when Visits finish. It's only 4 now and we are 30 minutes away. We're going to park up in the Visitors Car Park and keep an eye on the Falcon for when they leave the Prison.'

'OK, I'll leave it in your capable hands, speak to you when you've delivered them,' instructed Fabio as he ended the call.

They had just continued from the Mitchell onto the Kwinana Freeway when they could suddenly see a rash of red lights ahead and the traffic started to back up, they had only just reached the North side of the Narrows Bridge, and almost from nowhere all five lanes of traffic were jammed up.

Aleksander realising he was going too fast hit the anchors, correcting the Ute's tendency to screw to the left, they came to a shuddering halt just astern of a large, silver, Caltex road tanker.

Finally remembering the position of the Hazard Lights, switch, he turned it on to warn the speeding car behind.

The pair of them looked around; they had just reached the North side of the Narrows Bridge, even though it was the beginning of the evening rush hour, and they were on the main south bound artery out of Perth, they had never seen a jam like this. All five lanes were stopped except for a little forward movement on the inside lane.

Andriy cursed and looked across the Ute's cab to his brother, 'Bloody traffic, better switch onto 720ABC and check what's happening ahead.'

'Christ after all of this, what if we miss them? The brothers aren't going to be pleased.'

Aleksander who had a much more sanguine outlook on life, laughed, 'you're always worrying Andriy, if we miss her, we'll ask for other contacts and take it from there.'

'She can't go far with a little child to look after, children need things and need to be regular otherwise they cause problems.'

'Stop worrying.'

At that Aleksander, glancing in the rear view mirror to check traffic behind was safely parked and nothing was likely to rear end the Ute, switched off the Hazards and turned on the radio.

Immediately he could hear Perth's Magic FM, DJ, announcing, 'Perth traffic is at a standstill south bound, there's a tanker overturned at the Canning Bridge Station slip road and only the outside lane is open, avoid the Kwinana Freeway and the Narrows Bridge if you can. For those who are in the jam, you're listening to Perth's home of easy listening and over to Frank Sinatra to help you while away the waiting time.' The radio then switched over to Sinatra crooning 'New York, New York.'

Andriy stared morosely through the windscreen, trying to wish the traffic into moving, whilst almost constantly glancing at his watch as the time inexorably passed.

Aleksander was beating his hands on the steering wheel in time to the music, whilst singing the tune rather badly in a deep, excruciating, base mumble. He was happy enough.

'What would happen, was always going to happen, in the end they would work it out and things would come together as they always had,' he meditated.

On their outside, a white vehicle with green decals, St John's ambulance, siren shrieking, blue lights flashing, raced past in the emergency lane.

The inside lane was still moving slowly presumably traffic was exiting at Mill Point Road, into South Perth just south of the bridge. They were only moving a couple of car lengths occasionally, so Andriy began to encourage Aleksander to move the Ute across the traffic at every opportunity in the hope they could make the exit.

''Quick grab that space.'

'Shove him out of the way.'

Were some of the shouts coming from his passenger as Aleksander used the size of the Ute, flashing lights and his horn to bully their way across to the nearside lane, where they gradually moved towards the first Exit south of the Narrows Bridge.

Andriy, though still watching the time felt relieved that they were at least making progress.

On his side of the vehicle he could see the mainly white sails of small yachts scudding before the Northerly Breeze in the Swan River. Over his left shoulder, as he looked back towards the city, he could see a blue hulled, white accommodation, Fremantle Ferry Boat leaving the Barrack Street Jetty.

'Everything would be good,' he thought, 'if only this bloody traffic would start moving.'

They were now moving in batches of 10 to 12 cars as the traffic lights at the bottom of the ramp started to have an effect. Andriy pulled out the 'Melway,' map book showing all the streets in Perth, he would map a route through the back streets to clear this mess of traffic.

'Bloody hell it's nearly 5,' he ranted as they crossed the Mill Point lights.

'There is no point turning right yet it will just be clogged with traffic.'

'Keep heading east until we are well clear of the jam, at that point I'll direct you back south, it will be longer but in the end I'm sure it'll be faster.'

Thirty minutes later, after some fancy driving by Aleksander, and judicial use of the 'Melway,' by Andriy they were headed West, on Thomas Road towards Casuarina Prison.

Aleksander signalled left onto Bombay Drive, it was 5.40, as he turned the Ute into the turning, he could see a Trans Perth Bus approaching the turning in the opposite direction, with its left turn blinker flashing.

Neither of them thought anything of this as they continued their progress towards the prison.

Andriy said fiercely, 'Watch out for the Blue Falcon with a woman driving and a kid in the back, they surely can't have left by now?'

Aleksander smiled to himself and thought, 'there he goes worrying again, she'll either be there or she won't, we'll still find her eventually.'

'Okay,' he agreed.

They pulled into the visitor's car park and drove round the Parking Bays. There were a variety of cars, Ute's and vans loading up with visitors but no sign of the designated Falcon.

'Damn,' screamed Andriy loudly.

17th FEBRUARY EVENING – CASUARINA TO ROCKINGHAM

Isla now safely on the bus was busy chatting with some of the other female visitors, a fully awake Alice sitting alongside her peering out of the window at the passing traffic.

Isla didn't notice the Ute headed in the opposite direction with the two large, bald headed, east European, thugs but a little boy, about eleven years old, with fair hair, green shirt and shorts did.

'Wow it's a Perfect Blue Ute' he shouted, 'look Mum, Dad wants one of them when he gets out.'

His mother, a frequent visitor smirked at the idea, 'he'll be lucky, the only way we'll afford one of them is if he nicks one.'

To humour her eager son she said, 'why's it called Perfect Blue son?'

Her son, quite chuffed, thinking he knew something his Mum didn't said, 'Wow don't you know Mum, Holden made them in the colour Peter Brock used to rally in the 70's, to celebrate his life as the greatest Australian racer ever.'

His mother, who had vague recollections of Peter Brock answered, 'that's really interesting, well done you're full of facts aren't you?'

At that the bus pulled into Kwinana station, the sun was getting low in the west, Isla, who in her mind had been ignoring the situation, realised she was going to have to decide about where they were going to go from the car park.

They needed somewhere to stay quickly; Alice was all messed up and out of routine, it had been a hell of a day. The pair of them needed somewhere decent with a bed for herself, and hopefully a separate one for Alice plus a proper meal.

Isla mad up her mind, 'we'll head for the coast; there is always something decent out there, it now being the end of the summer there should be some vacancies.'

They said goodbye to those other regular Visitors they knew, as they disembarked the bus at Kwinana. There were plenty of hugs and kisses from the regulars for Isla and Alice. There were also plenty of smiles and relaxed faces, Visits were over for at least two weeks and everyone could get on with managing their own lives no matter how difficult.

The pair, made their way across to the Falcon, Alice dragging on her mother's right arm, thumb in mouth, Isla kept a careful watch for a battered white Ute, there appeared to be no sign.

The car park was busy with commuters departing the station, having just left a southbound train from the city.

Alice, tired after such a long day wasn't too happy now, and started crying as Isla secured her into the rear of the car.

'There, there, darling we'll soon be safe and sound,' she said fastening the seat belt and trying to calm Alice at the same time.

Sticking to the plan Isla quickly turned the car west out of the Station Car Park following a rash of commuters through the slip road onto Thomas Road towards the dying sun, its rays dazzled her momentarily and she quickly pulled the visor down to shade her eyes.

Alice's fractious mood had declined to occasional whimpers, the changing scenery appearing to have the necessary soothing effect on the little girl.

They were soon turning south onto the Rockingham road. On their left as they made the turn there was a large red and brick wall with Kwinana etched into the centre. The Highway had dual carriageways with a grass central reservation; the traffic was heavy with the remains of the rush hour south from Perth and Fremantle.

Isla settled the Falcon into the inside lane, following a working, green Commodore Ute, full of gardening tools, hoses and lawnmower. The browned grass covered but sandy verges, suggested dunes and their closeness to the sea, the view to the Kwinana refinery was obscured by large windswept Eucalyptus and smaller bushy Tea trees.

After about 5K, and seeing the sign for the Kwinana Beach Road, Isla took the opportunity to turn right off the main carriageway towards the ocean, hoping the sign meant houses and possible accommodation.

Alice's interest in the surrounding countryside and traffic was waning, and at times there was a certain amount of tears and louder crying from the rear of the Falcon.

Isla was getting desperate now and tending to push the speed limit, whilst still looking out for somewhere for them to stay.

'It's a beach road Alice there's got to be something with vacancies along here.'

The Falcon bumped as it crossed a rail track, the refinery entrance marked with a large CSBP sign could be seen on the right. Isla hoped she hadn't made an error, the area looked industrial, although a brown road sign said Tourist Drive 202, it directed them to the left where a few 100 meters later they bumped across another railway track, there were three big white round oil tanks on their left just beyond another railway track, while on their right trees, bushes and some large white buildings obscuring any opportunity of a view of the beach.

The road took a hairpin to the right before turning even more sharply to the left at the entrance to National Farmers Unit, the Kwinana Beach cafe was passed on the Falcons left whilst through the trees on the parkland to the right could be seen the azure blue of the Indian Ocean. There was still no sign of housing or hotels.

In fact to Isla's frustration the road ahead yawned empty, except for sandy scrub on either side.

The hope of accommodation had failed to materialise, this was a country road with some Industry and gradually they closed with the sea until the beach was almost alongside the road, the water looked blue, cool and refreshing. They passed a jetty servicing the refinery; a large, blue tanker alongside.

Finally they reached a roundabout and housing, there was a trailer park to the left and housing all along the shore side of the road.

'Must be on the north side of Rockingham,' thought Isla, 'if we continue along here there has got to be Hotels and other accommodation.'

Speeding up with impatience and hope, Isla fairly made the Falcon shift until within what seemed moments she slowed to enter the town itself.

She reduced their speed to a crawl looking around hopefully for some sign of accommodation, getting desperate she pulled into the side alongside a Realty Office where half a dozen young people, dressed for the beach were about to cross in front of her.

'Can you help?' she shouted through a now open driver's side window, a young man of about 16 with yellow swimming trunks, matching flip flops and a colourful Body Board detached himself from the group.

'Ma'am can I help,'

'We need somewhere to stay,' Isla replied exhaustedly indicating herself and Alice.

'That's easy, turn left at the next turning go down three blocks turn left again at Emma Street keep going to the next Main Road, Wanliss Street and you'll see it on your left when you cross over. It's my aunt's Guest House she'll look after you.'

'Thanks,' said Isla, 'appreciate the help, will she have vacancies'?'

'I know she has, it's autumn and midweek, you'll be alright she loves little ones,' he waved at Alice.

'Thanks again I really appreciate your help,' shouted Isla after the young man who was now, with Body Board hooked under his left arm, chasing his friends towards the beach, no doubt hoping to catch the last of the sun's rays before it departed in the west.

'Say hello for me,' he shouted back, while waving with his right arm as he disappeared onto the beach.

Her car window open, Isla could smell the freshness from the sea and the cool sea breeze whisked up by the Doctor. Quickly putting the Falcon into drive, she eased it round the corner and followed the directions to the Guest House.

Thanks to the young man's directions, the guest house was easy to find, at the open gated entrance was a friendly sign inviting guests to drive in and park. Isla manoeuvred the car into a parking space close to the entrance door, released a grizzling Alice from the back seat and rang the doorbell for attention.

The house was two stories with a balcony running right around the property; the main building was constructed of red brick and the balconies of highly polished yellowing wood. With the lights shining from all the windows in the gathering dusk, the place looked wonderfully welcoming to an exhausted Isla.

Isla was just about to ring the doorbell again when the door opened; in the doorway was a woman of about 50, straight auburn hair to the shoulders, well-tanned complexion, wearing a yellow short sleeved, calf length dress, fluffy white slippers and topped with a white apron covered in red, just because I love you, figures.

'Good evening, how can I help you?' she said in a booming voice, beaming bonhomie as she spoke.

'Hallo, your nephew said you might have a room,' Isla enquired.

'Of course my dear, come in, let me take her,' she said relieving Isla of the dozing child, 'the pair of you look exhausted come through to the Living Room.'

Isla followed dutifully, it seemed like somebody else was in charge, suddenly she felt safe and anyway she was just about beyond caring.

As they entered the Living room with its two big brown leather sofas, four matching chairs, old fashioned country house fire place containing a vase of yellow flowers, a man of similar age to the landlady, in brown slippers, long khaki empire shorts and matching collared, short sleeved, shirt rose from the far sofa.

Still trying to watch the cricket on the LCD TV above the fireplace he crossed the room towards them. 'Hi I'm,' he was interrupted.

'Arthur' boomed the landlady, this is, sorry haven't asked your names, she enquired.

'I'm Isla and the little one you're holding is my daughter Alice.'

'Lovely,' said Arthur looking wistfully back at the Television.

'Help Isla get her luggage and put it in the Country Garden Room, then move the cot out from storage and wipe it down so its fresh,' instructed the lady of the house.

'I don't think it will be long before little Alice will be needing it.'

Tickling Alice, who was now giggling, under the chin and saying to her, 'will you my dear?'

'I'll be in the kitchen giving the little one something to eat,'

'Isla you get organised then you can have dinner with us its nearly ready.'

'I'll look after little Alice here, won't we dear,' she said speaking directly to the child putting her down on the tiled floor.

Alice, who normally was upset around people she didn't know, appeared, like Isla overwhelmed by the proprietors kindness and authority and calmly accepted all this extra attention. She didn't even appear concerned when she was taken off to the Kitchen and her mother disappeared towards the front door.

Isla was concerned what Arthur would think of her fully laden car, he didn't bat an eyelid and helped her find their overnight things, even going out of his way to suggest some toys for Alice. Isla embarrassedly asked Arthur for his wife's name, explaining she had no chance to ask.

Arthur grinned, 'Well you can tell who's in charge here, I just follow along, Moira is great, she's a heart full of gold and as you can see loves children.'

Now he was free of his other half, it appeared to give him the opportunity to digress more.

'You've been dead lucky, we're empty, there was a whole wedding party due for three days, they were staying all over town, including us but they say,' he said tapping his nose with his right forefinger, 'that the Bride has run off to Hong Kong with the Best Man. It takes all sorts doesn't it,' he grinned pleasantly as he hauled Isla and Alice's belongings into the Guest House.

'Follow me and I'll show you the room then fix Alice's bed, I'm sure you'll like it,' he said as he opened a first floor green door into the most exquisite, large bedroom.

The bedroom wallpaper was chosen to make the room look like an English Country Garden; it was decorated with wonderful flowers and grasses with fully leafed deciduous trees in the background, the curtains, quilt cover and pillows matched the decor with tasteful green and brown stripes on a white background.

The room contained a kettle with a full set of brewing materials, a small LCD TV, fitted wardrobes and a large, glass, double balcony doors onto the wooden balcony where there was an inviting sun lounger.

'Where's the bathroom? Enquired Isla.

 Arthur laughed, and pulled on a handle which appeared to be a section of wall, he grabbed the handle and sliding the hidden door to the right, revealed a small but tastefully decorated white bathroom.

'It was my idea, her indoors wasn't sure but this time I got my way.'

 Isla giggled almost uncontrollably at this statement, it was a mixture of the way Arthur had talked about the bathroom, his wife and the release of tension.

'If you're sure we've got everything we had better go down and see how the other ladies are doing, shouldn't we?' Arthur queried. 'Also I've to sort out the cot yet.'

Isla stifling her giggles, with one last lingering look at the comfortable double bed followed Arthur down the stairs to the kitchen….

17th FEBRUARY EVENING - ROYAL PERTH HOSPITAL

Once the paramedics pushed Ryan off the lift into the Ambulance they made him comfortable, strapping him onto the stretcher. The two checked all Ryan's vital signs before getting ready to leave the area outside the apartment.

Now he was being looked after properly and despite his injuries, Ryan was recovering well, the liberal use of gas and air to ease the pain and his natural physical fitness meant some colour was returning to his face.

Ryan felt safer and somewhat healthier in the more secure environment, of the St. John's Mercedes Ambulance. Realising he had at least three broken bones, Ryan plucked up courage to speak to his saviours, the paramedics.

'I know I'm a mess but what happens now please?' he asked, partially moving the mask from its position covering his nose and mouth.

The smaller of the two, a bespectacled paramedic in his forties, dressed in short sleeved pale green uniform shirt and dark green uniform trousers smiled kindly as he re-packed the blood pressure unit, said, 'My mate Barry here,' pointing to his younger colleague, similarly clothed, 'will in a moment whip us off to A & E at the Royal Perth, and we'll hand you over.'

'What happens then?' Said a concerned Ryan, who was worried about police questions.

'We'll pass on the information about your injuries, a nurse will triage you, a clerk will take your details, depending how busy they are, is how long you'll have to wait. You won't be a priority because we've got you nicely splinted up.'

'Oh and by the way one of those Coppers is following because he wants another chat with you.'

'That's all I need, more questions.'

'Thanks,' he said to both of the paramedics and reached for the mask to hide his distress and ease the pain from his injuries.

'Right we'll be off shortly,' said the younger paramedic as he closed the rear doors of the vehicle, 'no lights or sirens,' came his muffled voice from outside the Ambulance as he made his way to the driver's door.

Ryan could here as they pulled away the crackle of the Ambulance communications radio. Shortly after they pulled away, he could hear it crackle to life, there was a lot of communications traffic but indistinguishable to Ryan. He heard their driver speak to his controller and suddenly they started to speed up and he could hear the siren screaming its raucous tone- also the reflection of the flashing lights could be seen the windows of the passing buildings.

Barry shouted through, 'big smash on the Kwinana, all available needed, got to get rid of this body fast. '

'Royal Perth is ready for us, they're gearing up for the big crash.

'Best give the Mitchell a miss then.'

'I know, get out of the bloody way, silly sod,' he shouted at some obstruction outside the ambulance.

The paramedic sitting next to Ryan, pulled his seat belt tighter and said to Ryan,' don't worry lad, you're going to get there a bit quicker we're needed elsewhere, sounds like there's a problem south of the river, just keep taking big breaths of the gas and air, you'll not feel anything,' he said smiling, pointing at the mask.

'How do you feel?'

Ryan, securely harnessed onto the narrow stretcher, could feel the movement of the vehicle through his body as the paramedic manoeuvred it in an out of the traffic, replied.

'Fine thanks, I never realised how much difference the gas and air makes, he's really shifting isn't he?' Ryan said pointing towards the front of the ambulance with the mask in his right hand.

'Must be something even more serious after you, an RTA southbound on the Kwinana this time of day will cause absolute havoc with the traffic.'

The ambulance leaned as the driver turned hard right, 'coming off Wellington Street,' said the paramedic, 'be there in just a second.'

The ambulance lurched to the right again, the siren died and the vehicle came to a smooth halt. Within seconds the rear door opened and the paramedics were hauling the stretcher out of the ambulance and pushing Ryan rapidly but cautiously into A & E.

'Right Ryan,' said the older paramedic, 'we'll find an empty cubicle and someone to take over.'

A pretty, petite, brunette, experienced, triage nurse, dressed in her white uniform dress with red epaulettes bustled up the entrance corridor towards them.

'Hi guys, in here,' she said pointing to a spare cubicle.

Ryan's stretcher was pushed alongside the bed in the cubicle; the portable oxygen cylinder and mask were retrieved by the driver of the ambulance, the other paramedic, carefully but quickly released Ryan from the protective securing straps.

'Ok love,' said the nurse, 'can you switch beds yourself, or will you need a hand.'

'No that's fine I'll do it myself,' said Ryan as he wriggled his way across to the cubicle bed with the help of his fit right hand.

'I feel exhausted,' he thought, realising the movement had caused him to start sweating profusely.

Ryan slumped on his back onto the bed relishing and savouring the comfort of the fresh, clean, sweet smelling, bed-linen. He carefully positioned his splinted left arm alongside his body in the most comfortable position.

'What have we got then?'

The bespectacled paramedic looked up from his notes secured to a black clipboard, 'Suspected fracture, about middle of lower, left, arm to both Radius and Ulna, also definite fracture, same side forefinger.'

Adjusting his glasses between his right thumb and forefinger, he looked down at his notes again he carried on.

'Caucasian male, Ryan, 30 no awkward signs, blood pressure up slightly, probably due to the trauma.'

'All injuries down to suspected assault, policeman who attended scene is on his way over. Alright, we are apparently needed urgently elsewhere.'

'That's OK boys you get off,' the nurse said taking the proffered notes from the paramedic.

'Be careful out there,' she added to the departing ambulance men.

'Right young man,' she said sternly to Ryan, 'you may be quite a while, there's a big pile up on the Kwinana Freeway and we are on standby to receive casualties.'

'We'll get you down to X-Ray first, then the Doctor can see what's what.'

'Are you comfortable?' She asked as she parted the curtains to leave the cubicle.

Ryan, who felt extremely comfortable and only slightly bothered by the pain of his injuries, replied meekly to the Nurse, 'I'm fine for now thanks.'

The curtains swished shut behind the Nurse as she answered 'OK,' from the corridor, on her way to her next patient.

Ryan, lying on his back, lulled by the gentle chatter from cubicles around him and the safe antiseptic hospital smells, dozed off almost immediately; it had been a long, difficult and tiring day.

Noises from the busy casualty area occasionally broke through his torpor, even the pain from his broken arm and finger was overridden by his exhaustion.

About 2 hours later he partially woke, when a large elderly man in light grey overalls whispered in his right ear, 'you just stay there mate, we're off to X-Ray.'

Ryan dozed easily as he safely ensconced in his hospital bed, was wheeled into the radiology department, where they waited briefly before being moved into an X-Ray room.

Ryan's escort left and said, 'they'll call someone when you're due to return,' indicating the female radiologist as he left.

After a number of X-Rays of his injuries, Ryan was taken back to a cubicle in A&E, safely ensconced in the bed Ryan had almost forgotten about the police, he was more concerned about the increasing pain from his broken forearm and finger.

'Hallo Ryan, feeling any better,' said his nemesis the older copper as he stepped inside the cubicle facing Ryan from the far end of the bed.

'I've just a few questions.'

Ryan sighed, 'it was obviously put up or shut up time,' he thought.

Remembering his earlier resolution about turning his life around, Ryan decided to tell the truth.

'It's a long story he began...............

After about ten minutes he had explained about Isla, Alice, Luca, and the two east European thugs, his connection, his estrangement and his resolution.

'Right,' said the policeman, 'I'm not so concerned about the mother and little girl now, they're obviously organised and not missing, C.I.D. will be interested in the Mancuso connection.'

'Do you want to press charges against the two large gentlemen who did this,' he said indicating Ryan's injuries with a nod of his head.

Ryan not sure what to do cautiously asked, 'what would happen if you catch them?'

'On your evidence we'll charge them, we'll check for some forensics and take a statement off the woman in the apartment below. Otherwise they'll probably be bailed with a warning to stay away from you.'

Ryan remembering the calm, cool, way the twins had inflicted their violence on his body, thought the officer had no idea but to humour him said, 'fine whatever you want.'

'Oh by the way is this blue duffle yours, only there appears to be stuff falling out of it.'

'Yes it is,' replied Ryan fearfully, realising there was something he didn't want the Copper to see.

'Oh dear Ryan what's this?' said the Officer smiling as he picked up a plastic bag from the detritus that had fallen out of the duffle bag.

'I suspect you've been using something you shouldn't haven't you?' he declared, indicating the brown herbal like substance in the plastic bag.

'Alright, yes its cannabis, but it's for my own personal use,' admitted Ryan, flushing even through his pained features.

At that moment the curtains to the cubicle were whisked back and their conversation was interrupted by the arrival of a young male Doctor, stethoscope wrapped around the back of his neck and a middle aged female nurse.

'I'll be seeing you,' said the policeman as he backed out of the cubicle.

'I know you might be tempted but don't leave town, I've a feeling you've been involved in more than you're been telling me.'

'Let me know where you are staying when you get out of hospital,' the constable added handing over his card to Ryan.

I'll be wanting to see you again in the next couple of days about this,' stated the Officer waving Ryan's plastic bag of cannabis in its now sealed evidence bag.

'Don't forget to call me, I would hate to have to come looking for you,' was his final parting note as he disappeared through the screen round the cubicle.

'Alright what have we got here nurse,' said the Doctor.................

17th FEBRUARY EVENING - END OF THE DAY

The Twins, now in a bar back in Fremantle were discussing the events of the day over a couple of imported Obolon beers, even though they were twice the cost Andriy and Aleksander still preferred the beers of the old country.

Aleksander wanted to speak in Ukrainian but knew it would annoy Andriy, who was forever reminding him about fitting in and not bringing themselves to the attention of others. Putting the half empty bottle to his mouth he took a good slug of the cold, refreshing alcohol, before signalling to the bar for two more.

'The boyfriend should be no problem now, how are we going to find the girl and baby?' He asked Andriy.

'It might be easy; we know they've scarpered from the apartment in Glendalough, if Fabio is right they can only go to his parents, there's nowhere else,' he answered.

'Maybe we don't need to do anything, we'll find out from Fabio tonight or tomorrow.'

'Anyway here's to a few more of these,' Andriy said raising his bottle of beer in salute.

-***-

Isla sat back, 'that was delicious she said tiredly,' to her hostess.

Isla put her right hand politely in front of her mouth as she tried to stifle a yawn.

Her hostess smiled back sympathetically, 'I think you better join Alice, bed for you I should think, don't you?

'What about paying you?'

'We'll worry about that in the morning, won't we Arthur?' she said to her erstwhile husband sitting at the other end of the dining room table.

'I can't actually see you two doing a runner on us can you?'

'Anyway we've already been paid for the next three nights thanks to the eloping bride.'

Isla pushed her chair back from the table, 'I don't know how we'll ever thank you,' she started to say.

'Not to worry it's our pleasure my dear.'

'It's great to know we are able to help you two young ladies, off you go to bed, Goodnight, God Bless, sleep tight.'

'Goodnight,' said Arthur as Isla made her way out of the room.

Isla launched into a huge yawn as she made her way up the stairs, she couldn't believe their good fortune.

Moira the landlady had just taken over.

Alice had been bathed, fed, changed and given to her ready for bed as soon as Isla had emerged refreshed from the shower.

No sooner had she tucked the fully contented Alice into the cot, than the little girl was asleep, lying on her back, left thumb tucked safely in her mouth and innocent look upon her face.

She had gone back downstairs to be greeted with Supper with her hosts, when Isla protested that they were doing too much for her. The couple had, or rather Moira insisted she always made too much for the two of them so it would be unfair if Isla didn't sit down and join them.

Arthur just grinned nicely and nodded his head in agreement.

After getting herself quickly ready for bed, Isla sunk gratefully in between the sheets and was asleep as soon as her head hit the pillow.

-***-

Ryan woke, it was difficult opening his eyes, it was like a heavy weight was keeping them closed, his mouth felt dry and he felt nauseous. The lights above him on the ceiling, he could feel rather than see through his partially closed eyes

The he remembered the Doctor, having seen the X-Rays had wanted him operated on immediately. There had been loads of questions, he had been fortunate the important things were in place so they could operate.

'He hadn't eaten for hours.'

'His Medicare Card was in his wallet along with his Professional Surfer's Insurance Card.'

Next thing he had been on a different bed, lying on his back, a nice young lady in blue scrubs had injected him and told him he would soon feel sleepy.

Ryan remembered the metal side rails of the bed being pulled up and the corridor lights flashing past above his head as he was pushed rapidly down a hospital corridor.

He vaguely remembered a cluttered room through swing doors, other doors ahead of him; he could see a big round operating theatre light through the far swing doors, they were closed but had windows in the top half. The room he had been had appeared cluttered with the bed, the people, and shelves full of, couldn't really remember but it was just lots of medical stuff.

At that point the lady in blue scrubs had asked him, 'are you sleepy?'

For some reason he had said, 'no,' that was the last he could remember.

Now more fully awake, Ryan turned his head, whilst still keeping it jammed to the pillow, slowly to the left and looked at his injured arm. What he could feel, felt heavy, like a big lump.

The arm was by his side, covered in white, 'oh that's right,' he remembered, 'a cast.'

The Doctor guy had said about him having one of them, the cast brought back memories.

When he was a kid he could remember a school mate having a cast on a broken leg, the rest of the boys in the class, had all been jealous because everyone could write or draw on the cast. The lad had got it autographed by some Dockers and other AFL players.

'We had all been jealous,' he recollected.

'Hallo Ryan, see you're awake, are you feeling alright?

'Would you like something to eat?' said a female voice.

Ryan turned his head while unsure of what to do kept it firmly ensconced in his pillow, he could see the smiling and concerned face of a nurse in her white uniform.

'A bit fuzzy, not sure of how much I'm allowed to move, yes please to food although could really do with a drink.'

'We'll just sit you up,' said the nurse, helping Ryan to raise his upper body to a sitting position while plumping up the pillows behind him.

'Now lean back, there's water on the table here,' she said indicating a freshly filled jug of water and glass on the bed side locker to Ryan's left.

'Oh, that's difficult,' realising the locker was on his injured side she quickly wheeled it round to the other side of the bed.

Ryan now sitting sunk back into the pillows, they had their own smell of freshness and he could smell antiseptic and the aroma of a light perfume.

'Must be the nurse's scent,' he concluded.

'It's nearly midnight, I'm going to get you a sandwich, check your obs, temperature, blood pressure and stuff.'

'The surgeon says your operation was fully successful so I'll tell you more in a second,' she said as she exited the room.

With his right hand, Ryan gripped the cast and lifted it from his side and rested it across his body, just above his knees. The cast went from just below his elbow to his hand- the plaster was only just dry; he looked at the splint on his forefinger.

'That might be a bit awkward, sticking out from the cast like that; I'm going to catch it against things unless I'm careful,' he thought.

Moments later the door opened and the nurse returned bearing gifts, a pre-packed BLT sandwich on brown, some medication and a hot drink of coffee in a ceramic white mug.

Putting her items down on the bedside locker, the nurse went back through the door, only to return a few moments later pulling a medical trolley.

'Ryan, I'm going to do your obs,' she said as she pulled a file from holder attached to the bottom of the bed.

As she took Ryan's Blood Pressure, temperature and checked him over she explained to Ryan what the surgeon had done during his operation.

'You've a clean break in each of the Ulna, and Radius, the two bones in your forearm. The surgeon has attached a plate to each of them to help stabilise the bones. The cast is to support and protect the forearm. The forefinger is also a clean break, the surgeon had to straighten it out but it will now heal inside the splint.'

'Have you any questions?'

Ryan felt stupid because he couldn't think of anything to ask, 'no not at the moment.'

'First I want you to take these,' she said handing him the medication with a glass of water, 'eat your supper and get some rest, if you need us there's a buzzer here,' she said indicating a red plastic button attached to a white cable resting on the bed alongside his pillow.

'Press it any time you need us.'

'Keep drinking when you're awake.'

'If you need the toilet, press the buzzer, you've just had a major operation and we don't want you breaking something else by falling over, do we?

'Thanks very much,' said Ryan reaching for the sandwich.

Ryan tore off the wrapping and gulped the sandwich down, only stopping briefly to quench his thirst with a large slurp of water.

It seemed like only moments after the sandwich demolition that he suddenly felt tired again; he yawned and awkwardly moved his pillows so he could lie down.

'This is going to be awkward,' Ryan thought, 'I can't lie on my left side, that's the side I normally sleep on.'

Lying on his back Ryan felt uncomfortable; he didn't think he would be able to sleep like this. Within moments the medication did its work and Ryan was snoring gently......................

18th FEBRUARY AM – SAFE IN ROCKINGHAM

Isla woke slowly from her uninterrupted reverie, she felt really comfortable and relaxed, it was difficult opening her eyes, rolling over from her right side onto her back, Isla using her fists gently rubbed the sleep from of her eyes and looked up at the white painted, mottled ceiling.

Waking up properly and realising where she was, Isla wondered why it was so quiet. Lifting her head from the pillows brought a sharp pain to the right side of her head, a painful reminder of the last 36hours. Isla looked across the sunlit room to the cot.

Alice wasn't there, Isla had a moment of panic and her heart skipped a beat, until she heard Alice laughing elsewhere in the house. There was a lukewarm cup of tea on the bedside table; it was obvious she had overslept and someone had already been in their room.

Unsure what to make of this, Isla rose quickly from the bed, borrowing a white, cotton dressing gown off the a peg, on the inside of the bedroom door, she didn't dare glance in the mirror, Isla left the bedroom and gingerly descended the stairs, besides the sore head she still very sore around the inside of her thighs and was tender elsewhere.

'I suspect the bruising is really showing today,' she grimaced at the thought.

Once downstairs, she followed the noise of the laughter, emanating from Alice and their hostess all the way to the sun dressed kitchen.

'Good morning Isla, did you sleep well? I brought you a brew, you were sleeping like a baby, so I left it by the bed.'

'This little one,' she said indicating Alice, was wide awake, so we decided to leave you to your slumbers.'

'Didn't we Alice?' she said patting the little girls head.

Alice giggled happily and stretched out her arms, 'Mummy,' she said.

Alice was sitting safely secured in an old wooden high chair, which was decorated with colourful transfers of Disney characters. On the table in front of her were the remains of something that looked like porridge, some of which was spread around her lips.

Isla went across and kissed the top of Alice's head.

'I'll just clean Alice up,' she said.

'Don't worry about the mess, I'll sort that out, we've just had breakfast, what would you like, you can have anything, cereal, fruit, a fry up, the lot or part of- whatever you want.

Isla who couldn't remember the last time she had been looked after like this asked meekly, 'would it be possible to have some scrambled eggs on toast?'

'Of course,' replied Moira her hostess rubbing her hands together, 'sounds good to me.'

'Can I make a suggestion? Grab a drink, take Alice to the bathroom and sort her out, do whatever you need to and in thirty minutes I'll have your breakfast already.

Moira smiled at Isla but didn't say anything about the nasty bruise on the side of her head.

'Somebody has given the poor girl a right belting,' she realised, 'at least the kid looks OK.'

Isla poured herself a glass of fresh Orange Juice and drank it straight down, grabbing a paper kitchen towel from the work surface she cleaned Alice of her breakfast and carried her upstairs to their bedroom.

Putting Alice on the bathroom floor, Isla quickly showered, talking to Alice all the while.

The little girl was quite happy playing with a plastic, yellow duck which Isla had found on the side of the bath.

'Come here darling,' said Isla, now dried after the shower and wrapped in a big brown, cotton bath sheet.

'Let's get you cleaned up,' she said using a freshly rinsed matching brown flannel.

Alice screamed in annoyance and wasn't best pleased when Isla washed her face and tried to wriggle away from Isla's grasp.

Standing up Isla went to clean her teeth, wiping the steam from the mirror above the wash basin; she also saw the bruises on the right side of her face and wanted to cry.

There was a blue bruise on the right side of her forehead, a healing cut just above the same ear, the lower half of which had its own bruise extending just below the sore lower lobe.

'What must Moira think?' Isla thought.'

'Still what's to worry she's said nothing and she can't have missed seeing it.'

'They're really nice our hosts, pity we have to leave,' Isla surmised.

Quickly brushing her hair into some semblance of order, Isla picked up Alice and they returned to the kitchen. They were greeted by a sparkling clean kitchen; there was no evidence of Alice's breakfast or the High Chair. Instead there was a single place setting at the kitchen breakfast bar, in front of it was a single pink rose in a single stem glass vase, a Tower of London placemat and two accompanying drinks mats. Moira was just placing a large steaming plate of scrambled eggs, topped with a fresh sliced tomato onto the table.

'Put Alice down, she won't come to any harm, grab yourself some more juice from the fridge,' she said indicating a rack of glasses alongside a very large refrigerator.

'Do you want brown or white toast with your eggs, we have some nice breakfast marmalade and what would you like to drink, tea, cold tea, coffee, herbal tea, hot chocolate, said Moira ticking them off on the fingers of her left hand.

Isla who was trying to watch Alice, the little girl was happily exploring her new surroundings, walking around and peering up at everything, had to think for a moment.

'Brown toast and Black coffee please.'

'Good, don't worry about Alice there is nothing to hurt her in here, we get lots of little children through this kitchen, besides which I have six grandchildren, so far, they're always wandering about in here and none of them have hurt themselves yet,' explained Moira.

At that moment there was an anguished cry, both women looked round anxiously and laughed. Alice had managed to get herself twisted around the legs of a bar stool at the other end of the counter and had fallen a short distance straight onto her face.

After the first yell, Alice managed to extricate herself, shook her head, ignored the concerned women, pulled herself up and continued her exploration.

Grinning at each other Isla returned to her breakfast and Moira to the kettle and toaster.

-***-

Half an hour later both women were sitting in colourful striped canvas beach chairs on the guest house patio with a now sun creamed Alice, complete with sun hat, sitting on a straw mat playing with some rag dolls. There was the smell of Acacia and Tea trees all around them and they could hear the squabbling of cockatoos in the surrounding trees

'I'm not going to interfere, and if you think I'm a busybody please tell me so,' said Moira turning and looking directly at Isla.

'Obviously something's not right, if you want to tell us some of it and we can help we will.'

'You are obviously a nice person who's had some bad luck, otherwise we wouldn't offer,' she added.

Isla was nearly overwhelmed by the kindness; she rubbed her eyes with a tissue in her right hand to stop the forming tears. Alice alive to her mother's distress rose unsteadily to her feet with the help of her mother's beach chair and said,

'Mummy,' with a querying look.

Isla glad of the excuse to have time to think, picked her up and sat the little girl on her lap. Alice took the opportunity to cuddle up to her mother's chest, stuck her left thumb in her mouth and promptly went to sleep.

'You promise you won't judge,' said Isla.

'No of course not, I wouldn't offer if I didn't think you looked in need of a helping hand.'

There will be no judgement or criticism here,' she added with a charming smile.

'Besides, except for you two, what else am I going to do for the next couple of days; we're all paid up due the wedding elopement and Arthur is going to use the excuse to belt some little white balls around the golf course, with a couple of his mates.'

Isla mind made up told Moira everything, Uncle Brian, her mother's estrangement, Luca, the prison and finally Ryan.

Moira was a good listener and didn't say a thing until Isla finished her epic, 'appears you've never properly been looked after,' she commented, 'amazed you've survived, looks like the only people who care about you are your little girl and probably this Uncle Brian.'

Moira got up and walked across reached down and gave both the girls a big hug, Isla started crying this woke Alice who also copied her Mummy by crying herself.

Once everyone had stopped crying and settled down, Moira made fresh cold drinks for all, Alice recovered now because Isla was alright, was back on the floor with the dolls, supping juice from an orange Goofy beaker.

Moira said, 'What do you want to do?'

Isla replied, 'I want to go down to Margaret River and find my Uncle, I'm sure he'll help us, I know he works at a big vineyard, he's the winemaker somewhere there. I think he's married with grown-up children,' she added.

'Best place to look is the White Pages, we'll go inside and I'll get the computer warmed up, then you can find him on there.'

18th FEBRUARY AM – RYAN GETS OUT OF THE ROYAL PERTH

Ryan's hospital room was illuminated by a nurse switching on the lights, this woke him from his medically induced stupor.

'Morning,' said the person responsible for this unexpected interruption of his very necessary slumbers.

It was the nurse who had said goodnight the previous evening, 'sorry to wake you, it's just after 7 o'clock in the morning, have to check your vital signs and record for posterity before I go off duty at eight.'

'Did you sleep well?'

A groggy Ryan who was still blinking his eyes against the unexpected light, trying to get his brain working through the final effect of the previous night's sleeping pills, answered while rubbing his eyes with both fists.

'Thanks, it is true then they do wake you up early in hospital, you would think they would let you a man lie in and get better.'

The nurse who was just binding his left arm before taking Ryan's blood pressure laughed.

'I know what you mean but there's a reason for all this, we have to prove all of you are as well as can be expected when we go off duty.'

'The surgeons and specialists have to see you all before they start their clinics and surgery, so you all have to fit in with our routines.'

Blood Pressure now checked the nurse was making notes on Ryan's charts, 'you need to drink lots of fluid, got to keep that intake up, don't want you dehydrated do we?' She commented.

Ryan who had a really dry throat realised how thirsty he was, grabbed the jug and poured water into the glass on his bedside table. He gulped down the first glass before pouring himself a second.

As if to remind him the nurse coming to the end of her checks asked, 'have you been?'

'No I've been asleep all night, but it's a good reminder,' Ryan said easing himself and his cast off the hospital bed and scurrying to bathroom.

When he returned to his hospital bed the nurse said, 'all your vital signs are fine, I suspect they'll discharge you and send you home by lunchtime.'

'Thanks very much' he said to her departing back as she left the room.

'Oh crap,' he thought, 'what am I going to do?'

'I need to get me and my stuff out of the apartment before the landlord sends someone around to evict us.'

'Isla won't have paid the rent and the bastard will be on to us quick if I don't move rapidly.'

'Even then I've nowhere to go really, I'm not going crawling back to Mum and Dad again, the Old Man will laugh his bloody head of if I do, there'll be the 'told you so,' crap all over again.'

'I'll worry about where I'm going to go later, I'll get a couple of mates to pick up my stuff and the Ute, they can park it up at the cafe in Yanchep and I'll sort it from there somehow. At least there's people up there who'll help if asked,' Ryan surmised.

Ryan got on his mobile telephone and arranged with a surfing buddy to pick up the apartment and Ute keys from the hospital, he said he would bring another person to drive the Ute and suggested parking the Ute at his place near the boardwalk up in Yanchep. He also offered Ryan a place to sleep on his settee for a couple of nights if things got difficult.

Breakfast arrived with the Surgeon from the day before, two young looking Junior Doctors and a nurse carrying a black clipboard with paper attached and pen at the ready in her right hand.

'Hallo Ryan,' said the surgeon with a smile as he picked up Ryan's left arm in its cast and held it out horizontally, can you lower your arm yourself, if I let it go?'

'Sure,' said Ryan confidently, bracing himself.

The surgeon let his arm go; even though he was ready Ryan only just managed to control its descent back to the counterpane on top of the hospital bed.

'Phew,' he thought, 'that was close.'

'We'll get you X-Rayed again this morning just to see you're alright, if the pins look good, we'll get rid of you just after lunch.'

'You need to come back to my clinic in about a month, medication for the pain and don't go getting thumped again will you?'

'Please arrange that,' the surgeon said to the nurse.

'One of you check the X-Rays, I think, if they're okay let the ward know so this gentleman can be discharged,' he said nodding his bald pate towards Ryan.

'Right who's next? Goodbye,' said the Surgeon as him and his entourage rapidly departed the room.

Ryan now he had the chance greedily reached for his cooling breakfast, except for last night's sandwich he couldn't properly remember his last meal.

-***-

Shortly after two in the afternoon, Ryan cast held in a sling, wearing a now grubby T Shirt and jeans from the day before, was standing outside and under the shade of the A & E canopy waiting for his buddy from Yanchep.

Earlier Ryan had tried telephoning Isla's mobile and was surprised when after the first ring it went to a voice message. 'This is now a discontinued telephone number; please check you are dialling the right number and try again.'

'What's happened to her?' he thought, 'I'm definitely dialling the right number, it's been in my mobile telephone address book for ages and I've called her hundreds of times.'

'I'll try her mother later and see if she knows what's happening,' he surmised.

A large shiny metallic black Ute came barrelling around the corner and screeched to a halt in front of Ryan. The window wound down and his surfing mate from Yanchep stuck his head out of the open window, 'Christ you look a bloody mess mate, hop in before we get nicked or an ambulance comes wailing in.'

Ryan walked round the back of the Ute and carefully eased himself into the front passenger seat. He had no sooner sat down, than Mick reached across him pulled the door to with a loud satisfying clunk. Pulling himself upright Mick said, 'hold on,' and they were off with a screeching of tyres across the empty ambulance stands and out onto the one way system around Victoria Square.

The flash of oscillating blue lights and noise of sirens followed them briefly as a fresh emergency arrived at the Royal Perth, in the rear of a local St John's ambulance.

'Phew, that was close,' shouted Mick above the noise of Meat Loaf belting, Bat out of Hell from the twin speakers located in the rear of the cab. With both front cabin windows open Mick, right arm resting on the outer sill was making sure the rest of Perth was able to enjoy his taste in music.

Mick shouted to Ryan above the dulcet tones of the American pop star, 'got a bed for you back at my place, missus isn't best pleased but as I told her if the boot was on the other foot you would come through for us.'

'Anyway what's your plans?'

'By the way you look a right bloody mess, can't see you doing sodding much with that busted arm and the rest of the crap which looks sodding painful, you daft sod,' shouted Mick unsympathetically.

'You must have really upset the Gods, losing your bird who stabbed your bloody arm and then getting smacked around like that all on the same day.'

Ryan winced at the comments.

'Thank Christ my names not Ryan,' Mick roared with laughter as he swerved between two, for him, dawdling cars northbound on the Mitchell Freeway

Ryan who was uncomfortably hanging onto the passenger side seat, grimaced with pain having collided with the doorway during Mick's latest manoeuvre complained bitterly.

'It's all right for you, I deserved what I got from Isla, pissed out of my head again, but,' Ryan shivered at the thought, 'you wouldn't have wanted to meet those two bastards, built like brick shithouses and as cold a pair of fish as your likely to meet, not a caring bone in either of their bodies.'

'What you going to do about it then you soft sod.'

'I've got to warn Isla and the kid, they're really up the creek if those two crooks come calling.'

'How the hell you going to protect them the mess you're in.'

'I tried calling them before from my phone but it says is discontinued, don't know how that can be.'

'Least I can do is call her again to let her know, give us your cell, and we'll see if it's any different from yours.'

'Bloody hell why not use yours again, sodding hell mate you're always bumming stuff.'

'Oh what the hell, you're a mate and what are friends for,' said Mick grinning as he threw his mobile across the cab.

Ryan caught the cell with his good right hand and punched in Isla's number.

It rang and rang before transferring to the previous discontinued message.

'Oh shit thought Ryan I'm going to have to get hold of her Mum when I get my own cell re-charged cause if I try it now on this low charge it'll never last the time she'll be on the phone,' Ryan realised.

'The lads beat us, said Mick pointing to Ryan and another dirty white Ute outside the flat as they roared up to the flat.

'Better give us the keys and show us what you want from the apartment then we can bugger off before the landlord comes calling.'.........................

18th FEBRUARY AM – THE TWINS GET A BOLLOCKING

'Oh sod it what's that,' cursed Andriy as his sleep was interrupted by the persistent, noisy tones of his cell phone.

Andriy rose cautiously from his bed and stumbled across the bedroom to the chair holding his discarded clothing from the night before. The constant ringing of the mobile phone was beginning to really annoy him as it became entangled when he tried to drag it from his trouser pocket.

'Damn,' he swore as he tore part of the outside of the pocket from the trousers.

Finally having retrieved the phone, now really irritated, he managed to answer the call.

On answering Andriy was greeted by a tirade of abuse from an irate Fabio.

'What the bloody hell happened?'

'Where's the girl and the kid?'

'You've buggered it right up, the bloody cops are involved, and your thug of a brother caused too much damage to the ruddy boyfriend.'

Andriy whose pulse was by now really racing, angry at having been unexpectedly roused from his hard won sleep was by now was really annoyed, flushed red and approaching his boiling point started to count to ten in Ukrainian, 'один (one), два (two), три (three),'

'What the bloody hell are you mumbling about,' screamed an irate Fabio down the phone.

'I am counting to ten in Ukrainian, you will either treat us both with proper respect, or we will pay you a visit and things will not go easy with you, the boy was lucky.'

'But, but, you work for me I pay you both,' stammered Fabio.

'Incorrect, we work for your brother who we respect and in his present unfortunate position has to depend on a piece of shit like you,' answered the angry but calm Ukrainian.

'Now Fabio, were you going to ask us to sort out a little problem that may have occurred due to some incorrect information supplied by you,' said Andriy taking control of the conversation.

'I don't think your brother would like to hear about your mistake of the girl and baby not being at the prison in the Falcon do you?'

Andriy, now in control didn't want any awkward questions about their being late arriving at Casuarina. In their business traffic jams were not normally an allowable reason for incomplete commercial transactions.

Fabio realising his mistake and not wanting to be on the wrong side of the East Europeans, cursed to himself, lowered his voice and tried to inveigle his way back into the good books of the twins.

'Andriy, she and the kid definitely visited, Luca told me this morning, it was a great visit and they were certainly there until the visits time finished, she can only have got to Casuarina some other way.'

Thinking hard Fabio remembered about the Kwinana station visits bus, 'that's it,' he said.

'What,' interrupted Andriy loudly, still irritated by Fabio and still wanting to keep control of the situation?

Fabio now properly subdued at the thought of the twins ire, explained about the probable use of the bus by the girls.

Fabio, adopting a more reasonable tone of voice and wanting to ingratiate himself with the brothers stated the obvious.

'We have to find them as soon as possible, if Luca realises they are missing we'll all be in the crap won't we?'

Andriy realising he was now in charge of the situation replied reasonably.

'They're missing, who is likely to know where they might be?'

'The only person I can think of, is her mother, she's called Bethany Steele and last I heard is she's shacked up with some toy boy, an Estate Agent down in Bunbury.'

'What's his name and how do I find him,' queried Andriy straight to the point.

'I bloody well don't know do I, you get on the road and I'll have to get on the blower and see what I can find out.'

'Is that alright with you,' just in time Fabio remembered it would not do to annoy Andriy and his brother further.

'Fine, we'll get some breakfast, do the gym and get down there early afternoon, keep in touch,' he added.

Fabio shaking with relief, that the conversation which had become so dangerous had ended, slammed the telephone into its holder and slumped into the nearest armchair in his neat apartment on the Old Fremantle waterfront and thought.

'This things a right bloody mess, Bunbury might not be huge but I bet it has got to have a dozen estate agents at least, how the hell am I going to find the toy boy by lunch time?'

'I'm also going to have to tell Luca when he contacts me from the prison later today, if he finds out from someone else first he'll blame me and probably set those bloody east European goons onto me.'

Fabio forced himself out of the armchair and although early poured himself a Bundaberg rum, from the nearby oak stained drinks cabinet and a cold ginger beer with ice in a tall glass whilst adding a slice of lemon from the fridge. This to steady his nerves and give him time to ponder his next move.

Calm now, Fabio considered what little he knew about Isla's mother, 'she was a gold digger, so the toy boy must be loaded.'

'The toy boy either had inherited money or owned a lucrative Realty Agents, if the latter was the case it was likely to be something local, dealing in high end properties, it therefore couldn't be one of the State or National Agents.'

'I'm great aren't I, thought Fabio in self-congratulation, picking up his I Pad from the nearby glass coffee table and logging into Google, Fabio asked for Estate Agents in Bunbury, The results came through quickly and showed him a total of ten. He was able to discard six immediately because they weren't a local enterprise, two more didn't look feasible because they were just letting agents, which didn't fit with the toy boy character Fabio pictured.

Fabio logged into each of his two selected sites to look at the personnel involved at each realtor, the first was a family business which had been going years, was owned by a female matriarch and employed mostly young women, the son of the aged owner was in his fifties and didn't fit Fabio's expected profile of a toy boy in their thirties or younger.

With the second Fabio thought he had come up trumps, a picture over half the screen of a man in his thirties announced that Ray Lacy and his exclusive team were the people you needed to move your exclusive home in Bunbury and the surrounding country. The advert was a little bit garish but out to impress and make a well-off home owner feel, the company was exclusive to the area.

'That's got to be it,' shouted Fabio excitedly to the empty room, pumping the air with his free left fist.

'I'm brilliant,' he said to himself in self-congratulation as he reached for his I phone and dialled in the number of Ray Lacy exclusive Real Estate Agents of Bunbury.

After two rings a sweet young female voice answered.

'Ray Lacy and associates.'

Fabio thinking quickly, trying the personal touch and using the ultimate bluff said, 'Can I speak to Ray please, met him and his other half at a party recently, when he advised me about moving property.'

'Certainly sir who can I say is calling?'

There was a pregnant pause while Fabio suddenly realising he wasn't wanting to use his own name came up with an answer.

'Uh, uh, Tom Smith,' he finally came out with, thinking he had blown it.

'That's fine Mr Smith just putting you on hold for a moment.'

Spanish Eyes came drifting over the telephone, this though wasn't really helping to soothe Fabio's battered nerves.

'Bloody hell what am I going to say?' He thought.

'Good morning Mr Smith, Ray Lacy here believe you met Bethany and me at a party recently.'

'Got to be them,' realised Fabio, 'can't be that many Bethany's with young Realtors in Bunbury.'

Bluffing Fabio said confidently, 'I know you only normally move property in Bunbury, but I was so impressed I thought I might ask if you would be prepared to sell something in Fremantle for me.'

'Sorry Mr Smith, much though I appreciate your compliments we are staying here with our exclusivity for the next couple of years, after that mind....'

Fabio interrupted, 'alright then thanks for your help, some other time perhaps.'

Disconnecting the call, Fabio returned to the I Pad and the White Pages to ascertain the realtors home address, jotting this down he leaned back onto the couch retrieved his drink sighed contentedly and congratulated himself.

'That was so easy, it only took fifteen minutes,' he concluded smiling inwardly.

'I'll finish my drink then contact those two Ukrainian nutcases, with that Estate Agent in his office, they might just be in time to introduce themselves to her ladyship before lunch,' Fabio imagined...........

18th FEBRUARY – UNCLE BRIAN'S SURPRISE

By the way, I hadn't noticed, do you have a mobile? Moira asked.

'Yes,' said Isla, 'I didn't want to switch it on, I've taken the Sim card out 'I don't want anyone to know it's working, or where I am.'

Isla picked up Alice and all three of them went back into the house, Moira switched on the computer in the Guest House's small Office just off the kitchen. Moira sat on the swivelling, black, leather, office chair while Isla leaning on the clean white-painted door frame, stood holding Alice.

Moira said turning in the chair to face Isla, 'I think you should lose the mobile, even better trade it in at the Telstra shop.'

'You don't know where you're going so it would be best to get a cheap pay as you go or contract on this address so no one can make the connection, they say Telstra have got the best coverage throughout the state.'

Swivelling back so she was facing the desk Moira complained, 'this computer takes forever to load up, this broadband G stuff was supposed to make things faster.

'Not much bloody use though if the computer takes all day to warm up,' she added.

Isla nodded in agreement.

Moira, with the computer finally on line, went into the Australian White Pages through her local server.

'What did you say the name was?'

'Brian Steele.'

'There's only one Steele in Margaret River and it's a C. according to the map, it doesn't look very hopeful the address looks like a small apartment, do you want to try the number?' suggested Moira, reaching for the house phone.

'Might as well, have to start somewhere,' answered Isla.

Moira passed the telephone over, she had dialled the telephone number and Isla could hear the burring sound of the phone ringing at the other end of the line.

On the fourth ring the telephone was answered and a young lady said, 'Charlotte Steele, how may I help you.'

Isla's heart raced, she didn't know what to say she hadn't really thought it through. 'Ahem, hello,' she stuttered.

'My name is Isla Steele, and I am looking for a Brian, my Uncle, I'm really sorry to bother you, I hope you don't mind, I am really desperate to find him,' Isla suddenly couldn't stop it was like she had verbal diarrhoea.

'Sorry I'm going on,' she said in excuse.

'It's alright,' said the female voice at the other end of the telephone, 'I'm sorry though, I can't help, I know I'm the only Steele in the local phone book, I've only moved down here from Dubbo about a year ago.'

A disappointed Isla said, 'thanks,' and frowning, dejectedly returned the telephone to its receiver.

Moira walked across, put both arms around Isla's shoulders and gave her a quick hug.

Looking at the upset Isla she said, 'Come on love, it's only the start, just because he doesn't have a land line doesn't mean he's not there, he may be a mobile only user.'

You're going to have to go down there and ask at places like the Library, Cop shop and visitor centre.'

'Come on lets google up a map and work out a plan. If you want you can always come back here tonight.'

Once they had worked out a route to the Margaret River Visitor Centre both of them realised it was really too far to do a return trip in one day. It would take Isla about 3 hours in the Falcon.

'That's alright, I know someone else in the business down there.'

'Hand me the telephone please,'

After a couple of minutes and a brief conversation Moira turned to Isla while returning the telephone to its holder.

'All fixed, it's a B and B just outside Margaret River, met the lady at a conference in Perth last year, she'll be brilliant for you two.'

That's settled, what do you want to do? It's halfway through the morning now, by the time we get you and Alice sorted, you aren't going to make it down there much before tea time, we could always get you properly organised, new telephone and anything else you need before getting you both off nice and rested first thing in the morning.'

Isla considered this idea, after all she felt safe here at the Guest House in Rockingham, they needed to be properly prepared and perhaps she could try and negotiate with her mother again. She would surely know where Uncle Brian was.

'Just one other thing,' she said, 'when we go into Rockingham I want to try ringing my mother again, it may save us a lot of effort. If I switch on and use my mobile just before I part exchange it, no-one will have a chance to work out where I'm calling from.'

Isla was convinced that with all their contacts Luca and Fabio could trace her whereabouts if she used her own mobile.

Alright said Moira, 'let's put Alice down, get her organised and we'll stroll into town.'

An hour later, all three of them walked into the town, Moira looked rather fetching with a butterfly decorated parasol she had acquired in Japan, the previous year.

Isla had a white sun hat to protect her from the sun and a fully refreshed Alice was safely holding her mother's hand as they leisurely made their way into town.

Isla had worried about covering her bruised face with make-up, Moira had said she'd be better off without it, after all who in Rockingham knew her and was likely to take notice. Accepting her wisdom Isla had acquiesced, she felt a lot better out in the fresh air, walking into the newly blown up sea breeze during their short walk into the local shops.

Isla took her mobile out of her white pinafore dress pocket and dialled her mother's mobile. This time she was determined to break through her mother's selfish demeanour and was ready for her diatribe.

'Hallo,' said her mother without pause she added.

'I know it's you Isla, it says so on my phone, and what do you want now?

'Yesterday you cut me off in mid-sentence; you just don't seem to care how I feel.'

'I'm sure everyone I was with, guessed what was going on, cut off by my own daughter, how could you?'

Isla let the tirade wash over her, this time she wanted to get through to her mother no matter what it took.

'I'll just have to be patient,' she thought.

Moira who could hear parts of the tirade, walking alongside, Isla and Alice, pulled a face and began to understand part of Isla's problem.

'God, no wonder Isla and Alice have got problems,' she concluded to herself.

The one sided conversation continued for what seemed like forever to Isla, so much that at times as they continued their walk towards the shops, Isla put her arm out straight and held the mobile telephone as far away from herself as possible.

Moira found that quite funny, she had to laugh, it looked so delicious, there was this stupid selfish woman ranting and raving at the end of the telephone and no-one was listening except perhaps the squawking gulls making hopeful low passes, looking for discarded scraps of food.

Mother, hearing laughter over her telephone must have realised something wasn't right.

'Isla,' she shouted, 'are you listening to me?'

Isla, who now was trying not to laugh with Moira, said, 'no mother, are you going to listen to me?' She giggled, because Moira, totally unladylike was pulling faces for a bemused Alice.

Mother started to go off on one again, said loudly 'Isla...'

Isla interrupted, 'Yes Mum, my friend, Alice and I want to know if you are going to let me speak.'

Mother the ultimate snob, became embarrassed, realising that some other woman was listening in said meekly, 'Yes Isla, who's your friend?'

Isla didn't respond to that, after all the stupid woman hadn't even bothered asking about her Granddaughter. Instead Isla asked, 'I am trying to find your brother, Uncle Brian, he's not registered as having a telephone in Margaret River.'

Mother now intrigued said curiously, 'Why do you want to know where he is?'

Isla was ready for this.

'Actually mother, we're taking a trip down the Margaret River in the next few days and I thought I might take Alice, who is after all his niece, to make his acquaintance.'

That must have caused a real panic, a normally in control mother, must have had thoughts of her daughter and grandchild visiting her as well.

'Bunbury is after all right en-route for Margaret River, any visit by Isla and Alice would let everyone know I'm a grandmother.'

'I can't let that happen, nobody here knows my real age others are getting face lifts and using Botox and I haven't had to resort to that yet,' she reflected.

Isla, laughing to herself and grinning at the others as they walked along, waited for mothers panic to subside and the silence on the other end of her mobile telephone. She was fully aware of how scared Mother was of admitting to a Grandchild, she suspected mother's toy boy had no idea of her real age.

Finally Bethany roused herself to answer Isla's query, 'Isla dear, you know how much I would love you all to visit; it's just not possible at the moment.'

'That's alright Mum, what about Uncle Brian?'

'I've got his mobile telephone on this phone memory.'

'I'll text it to you when we've finished.'

I don't know how he is, I haven't spoken to him since Melissa died.'

'I really don't know why he hasn't rung me?' She continued whining.

'That's a laugh mother only ever telephones Uncle Brian when she has her own personal crisis, she's too selfish to think of anyone else,' reasoned Isla to herself.

'OK Mum, don't forget the text please, bye,' said Isla hopefully.

Isla knew that if something else happened in the next ten minutes in her mother's life, the promised text would be totally forgotten and Isla would have to ring back for the mobile number for Uncle Brian.

They walked onto the shopping parade at this point, Isla realised she couldn't change her mobile telephone number until Mother texted. Fortunately just at that point it beeped, pleasantly surprised Isla found the vitally important text from her mother with Uncle Brian's telephone number.

'Wow,' she thought excitedly, 'Mother has actually come through for once.'

Moira who had been listening to the one sided conversation with interest said, 'done it has she?'

'Yes, can't believe it would be that easy, do I ring him now or when I've got the new telephone?'

'New telephone I think, get the shop person to transfer all your numbers, it's supposed to be easy to do on these new-fangled phones my ancient brain hasn't caught up with this modern technology yet.'

'Try ringing your Uncle Brian when we get back, in the peace and quiet where you can concentrate.'

Moira pointed out the Telstra shop, they made their way past the other shops under the shade of their awnings, even with the fresh sea breeze, it was still very warm and they were glad of the chance to get out of the direct sunlight.

Meanwhile, Moira who said she had a few bits to fetch, relieved Isla of Alice and took her off round to the other shops while Isla completed her business.

It wasn't busy in the Telstra shop, a young man in his Telstra, blue-checked shirt was able to help Isla very quickly, within what seemed minutes but was in reality more like 30, Isla had been relieved of her old mobile telephone and was now fully equipped with a new Smart Phone and contract registered to Moira's address.

She had been assured it would do everything she wanted and had the widest coverage in Australia. Importantly all her old telephone numbers had been transferred especially Uncle Brian's newly gained number.

-***-

When the three ladies returned from the shops, they found Arthur ensconced in front of the Television watching cricket, a cold bottle of Swan bitter clasped in his right hand.

'Hallo everyone,' he said rising from the sofa to greet them, 'had a good visit to our local emporiums?'

'Fine thanks,' said Isla, 'how was your golf?'

'Great fun but I need to practise more.'

Moira laughed, 'he always says that but he really only goes for the man chat, anyway Isla you go up and make your telephone call, I'll put this shopping away and Arthur can play with Alice,' she said as she dragged the shopping bags towards the kitchen.

'Don't worry I'll look after her, you get on, 'said Arthur.

Isla relieved of her responsibility, excitedly raced up the stairs to their bedroom, putting the new Smart Phone on her bed.

Although excited about finally being able to speak to Uncle Brian, she was scared he wouldn't be able to, or want to help her. She felt really nervous and her hands were shaking as she tried to use the Smart Phone. Three times she made mistakes and had to start again; she could feel her heart racing, her hands were sweaty.

'Finally,' thought Isla as she could hear the Smart Phone dialling the number. It rang 5 times, instead of someone answering, it went to the answering machine, for a moment Isla was crestfallen.

Instead of the normal message Uncle Brian had left his own personal message, 'Hi, this is Brian Steele, winemaker to the stars, either leave a message or telephone me at Mulloneys Vineyard on the Maroondah Highway near Healesville speak to you soon,' at this point he laughed contentedly and the message ended.

Isla was distraught and racing down to the kitchen flung herself in to Moira's arms.

'Whatever's wrong child,' said Moira.

Isla tearfully, held out the new Smart Phone, 'please dial the number and listen.'

Moira did so and always wishing to reassure and be positive said, 'that's alright, we'll find the telephone number of this vineyard you can contact him there, there's always a way round any situation.'

'But,' said Isla, 'he's in Healesville, where the zoo is, that's miles away, he's near Melbourne, that's in Victoria isn't it?'

Victoria seemed like the end of the world to Isla she had never been further than a school trip to Albany on the southern coast of Western Australia.

'Let's go and look on the computer?' said Moira.

The two women went off to the little office again and switched the computer on, while they were waiting for it to warm up, Moira said, 'if we get hold of him, how are we going to get you both there, it's too far to drive.'

'I don't care, how far it is, I'm not giving up on the Falcon it's the only big asset we still own, I don't care how far it is, I'll get us and the car there somehow.........'

18th FEBRUARY LUNCH - LUNCHTIME BUNBURY

'That was a bit of a walkover wasn't it,' said Andriy as they turned off the end of the Australind Bypass onto a massive roundabout centred with tall eucalyptus trees and surrounded by well-trimmed sun-browned grass.

Aleksander grunted in reply, after all he was fully satisfied with their run down from Fremantle to Bunbury, the 170 kilometre trip had passed uneventfully in about 100 minutes, there had been few delays and the trip had been straightforward.

Aleksander eased the Ute onto Sandridge Road, in a westerly direction towards the town of Sunbury. The dual carriage way its central median as per its verges mainly lined with tall thin eucalyptus their green leaves glinting in the midday sun.

The traffic was light until they reached the commercial section at the Donnybrook turn off.

'Better find somewhere to pull off Aleksander and we'll ring that idiot back in the city and see if he has a location for us,' suggested Andriy.

'We don't want to go past the place do we?'

'Okay,' replied the other twin as he negotiated his way off the road alongside the Farmers Market, where Sandridge Road became Blair Street

Andriy dialled up Fabio's mobile and taking the piss said, 'Ciao Fabio, how are you now, our Italian stallion got all the details we need have you?'

Fabio now very concerned about the turn of events in his relationship with the twins cautiously replied, 'I think we know who the boyfriend is and the location of his Office.'

'I've got a home address for him as well,' he added.

'The bint you're looking for is in her early forties, is called Bethany Steele and fancies herself as something special.'

'She apparently doesn't acknowledge the kid and is too snobby to admit to having a grandchild.'

'How do you think she'll react to our visit,' asked Andriy.

'She'll no doubt get on her high horse and over react, it will almost certainly be all bluster, so you shouldn't need to use any physical force, the pair of you together should frighten her to death,' replied Fabio.

'High horse, what is this,' queried Andriy, not understanding the expression.

'Means if she can she'll treat you like some lackey, servant sort of thing if she thinks she can get away with it.'

'Ha, ha, that's funny,' roared Andriy now clear in his own mind what sort of woman Bethany was.

'Now what's the address?'

'9 Upper Esplanade I've looked it up on the computer, it's some sort of large bungalow facing the sea across Ocean road, it's white painted with a two door double garage, you shouldn't be able to miss it.'

'If there's no one there you can easily watch the building from Ocean Drive there appears to be lots of parking giving you a clear sight of the bitch's place.'

Andriy glancing at the blue sky above through the tinted windscreen of their Ute said, 'looks a nice day to be down by the beach so it will be easy waiting.'

'Anyway if she's in and won't open up, Aleksander can always take the door of its hinges.'

Andriy laughed maliciously at this thought.

Fabio despaired of the violence and the possible local reaction, he knew in small towns of Australia, people were more likely to react and report anything out of the ordinary. He was also worried about the twins reaction if he advised them to take a softly, softly approach.

Thinking quickly and preferring ingratiation Fabio said to Andriy, 'try and do this quietly please mate, if we go in to hard she's likely to faint or have a heart attack on us and we won't get the right answer for Luca will we?'

'Alright then we will try and take it easy but if she won't tell us we may have to get out hands a bit dirty alright?'

Andriy not remembering Fabio's comment about waiting asked 'What happens if she's not there, shall we pay the boyfriend a visit?'

'No, no my betting is the boyfriend won't even know she has a girl that age never mind being a grandmother, I bet she has nightmares in bed at night thinking about her toy boy finding out about her granddaughter.'

'I'm afraid you'll just have to wait, remember what I said it might be better to park on Ocean Drive and keep an eye on the house from there if she isn't in.'

'I think you'll find it to be a good spot, anyway it's up to you, I just need a result urgently.'

'Okay we'll do that, we'll let you know if we have any success,' replied Andriy.

'Ciao Fabio,' he said to Fabio as he cut off the signal fully aware of how much the Italian ancestry got up his employer's nose.

'Right Aleksander, let us find Ocean Drive and this Upper Esplanade, whatever that is, and then see if we can sort this bitch of a mother out so that we are able to find our missing duo,'

'Any idea how you spell it'? Said the other brother reaching towards the sat nav.

'Better you don't ask anybody if we have need of making an example of the woman while we are here, we don't want anyone remembering who we are.'

'Good thinking Andriy, try Upper, it's only a small town and there can't be many streets that begin with those letters,' answered Andriy not having thought to ask Fabio for the spelling of the street name, and never having heard of an Esplanade before.

'Got it,' said Aleksander, it's only 3k we'll go straight on from here.'

'Apparently Upper Esplanade is one back from the coast and Ocean Drive, the place we're looking for overlooks the ocean and the lower road so Fabio says.'

'Got that,' said the other twin after twiddling with the sat nav, 'I can see Ocean Drive on the map, Upper Esplanade runs off it and alongside, if we come in from the north,' he speculated.

'Right then let's go,' replied Andriy impatiently.

'Let's get this thing sorted and get out of here.'

'I hate small towns there's too many busybodies watching what is going on, much prefer the anonymity of the big city, the sooner we're back in Fremantle the happier I'll be,' added Andriy.

-***-

Meanwhile back in Rockingham, Alice was sitting in a high chair alongside the kitchen table, consuming her lunch.

The three adults were discussing Isla's next move.

Moira, who thought it was time, Isla's mother took some responsibility in the girl's lives said in between mouthfuls of her home made Cesar salad.

'I think it's about time you and your mother made peace, it's surely time she acknowledges Alice, don't you think?'

'Stupid bloody woman obviously doesn't know what she's missing being a grandparent is the best thing ever,' gruffly added Arthur.

'I can't though, she's only ever cared about herself and she's so selfish it's unbelievable.'

'Well someone has to do something,' continued Moira, your mother should at long last give you something back and I've an idea about how to do it.'

'First do your boyfriend's know where your mother hangs out nowadays?'

'No but....' Replied Isla.

Moira interrupted, 'this is what we'll do, if everything goes wrong you can come straight back here, but first had better cancel your B and B down at Margaret River.

'Second we'll pack you and Alice into the car with all your belongings after lunch and make it look like you left Perth in a bit of a rush with all the screaming banshees behind you.'

'Third, the pair of you'll drive down to Sunbury and throw yourselves on your mother's mercy.'

Isla was very unhappy with this and started to complain, 'Moira, she won't let us stay I know she won't she's so bloody awful she sobbed.'

Moira reached across and hugged the young woman.

'It's really all you've got left dear, you and the little girl can't drive all the way to Victoria.'

'If the worst comes to the worst and she turns you away, please come back here and we'll work something else out.'

'Won't we?' she commanded Arthur.

'Of course we will,' he replied with an aura of confidence.

'Alright we'll try and do as you say, if nothing else I can't wait to see her face when we turn up at her front door,' agreed Isla grinning through her tears at the thought of her mother's reaction.

Arthur got up from the kitchen table and said, 'right ladies how can I help?'

This persuaded everyone that the decision had been made and the three adults re-packed the Ford Falcon ready for the ninety minute trip down the road to Bunbury.

By 1.30pm Isla and Alice were on the road south, decision made, vehicle neatly packed by Arthur, with all their belongings, clearly visible and piled up high so Bethany would only be too well aware of the girl's exodus from the big metropolis to the north.

Isla half-hoped they would have to return to Rockingham and the other half dreaming of a proper family with her mother welcoming them both with open arms.

18th FEBRUARY PM – ROCKINGHAM TO BUNBURY

Meanwhile down in Bunbury the twins were closing on their destination, now on Symmons Street they could see a large cricket ground to their right, a number of what appeared new white two-storey condominiums to their left, and just past a roundabout the azure blue Indian Ocean.

The firmament above the ocean was only enhanced by a few white cirrus striating the light blue sky.

Following the sat nav's instructions Aleksander made their Ute veer left onto the unmarked road which they assumed to be the Upper Esplanade, sure enough within 250metres the dulcet tones of the lady in their sat nav were announcing their arrival at No. 9.

As previously agreed they drove gently past, easing along at a steady 30kph, Aleksander silenced the sat nav and made the Ute follow the road round until they reached the next roundabout, he turned right around a small roundabout towards the sea.

'Wow did you see that sculpture, weird wasn't it,' commented Andriy.

'Couldn't see it properly I was concentrating on getting round the turn, what was it?' asked Aleksander.

'Well as you could see it was a white stone sculpture it looked like a boy holding a sinking boat,' answered Andriy.

'Something different, must be loaded round here, if they can afford to leave pieces of art sitting on roundabouts for any thief to acquire,' said Aleksander who was negotiating the right turn onto Ocean Drive.

'Bit quiet around here,' commented Andriy as he looked back up the hill towards the Upper Esplanade.

The Ocean Road was split by a narrow burnt grassed median which looked in need of maintenance, they could look to their right and observe the similarly straw grass covered hill interspersed with the occasional bush.

On their left was a tarmacadam covered cycle and pedestrian track, low dunes before a yellow sanded beach lapped by a low Indian Ocean swell.

First there was a yellow bricked hexagonal building which was followed by a similarly bricked long, narrow, single-story building covered by a light grey, sloping corrugated roof. There were few windows and under the similarly covered porch on the wall Andriy could just make out a sign, with the words, 'Surfers Club,'

A second similar building followed before a car park on both sides of the Ocean Drive and a brown road sign advertising Back Beach on the seaward side car park.

'Pull in to the right here,' said Andriy sharply to Aleksander, concerned they would miss the turning.

'We have a brilliant view of the house from there,' he said pointing his right arm fiercely across the chest of his brother in the direction of the land side car park.

Aleksander pushed his brother's arm away, realised they were too late to turn across into the proposed car park, the slim central median now having intervened said, ' I've got it but we'll have to turn around before we can get in there.'

'Give us a bloody chance,' he added irritably.

Consequently the twins and their car returned to the initial roundabout where they first turned into the Upper Esplanade. Andriy indicated right, completed the turn right round the roundabout and returned to the car park Andriy had got so excited about.

'Face the car up the hill,' instructed Andriy, 'and don't park too close to any other cars.'

'Of course, of course, you think I'm daft, just relax Andriy this is going to be easy you'll see.'

Looking round him he had a change of mind, '

'You know I don't like this it's too open and to quiet, there's hardly any cars and too few people we are to easily noticeable and we are definitely rememberable.'

'Then we have to act like we belong, we'll park up facing these basketball courts, we've a terrific view up to the house, we'll have a close look now then go for a walk, there must be a toilet down there,' Andriy pointed indicating the buildings alongside the beach, 'and I for one am desperate.'

'Yeah you're right, the building isn't going to move, the garage doors are open to the elements, we've only going to watch for one of them closing or a car being parked up and we'll know we are in business.'

'I'll come with you, I have a need as well.'

-***-

Isla and Alice were meanwhile just leaving the inland route down the Forrest Highway where it became the Old Coast Road south of Lake Clifton.

There was very little traffic everyone was keeping to the 110kph speed limit, Alice, was fast asleep after her satisfactory lunch, there was a green car on Isla's forward horizon of which she would catch glimpses on straightaways, they would occasionally flash past a slower heavily overloaded truck and except for the traffic headed north there was little to break the monotony of white sand verges and row upon row of the inevitable tall bark stripped, reliable eucalyptus.

Well south at Myalup the trees became coniferous as they skated the State Forest, there was little else of interest and it gave time for Isla to consider how she was going to get over mother's prejudices about her and Alice.

'This time we are both desperate, surely she has to consider her family instead of putting herself first,' thought Isla hopefully.

Isla knew however it had rarely happened before in her life and the chances weren't good today but at least in Rockingham they had somewhere to fall back to if necessary.

She was however concerned that they were imposing on a fantastic couple of people and wanted where possible to manage their own situation.

Ninety minutes after leaving Rockingham and less than two hours after the twins had passed through, Isla steered the blue Falcon off the Australind into the same large roundabout, knowing where she was headed however she took a different route to them heading towards the city centre and the more northerly and easier route to the Upper Esplanade.

-***-

The twins whilst keeping an eye on the bungalow at 9 Upper Esplanade were perambulating along the nearby beach tanned, muscular, upper torsos exposed to the sun's rays, carrying their shoes and socks as they walked barefoot along the sands and relaxing whilst awaiting Bethany's arrival.

Just as they were at about the furthest from their blue Commodore Ute, Aleksander realised there was movement at the property they were meant to be observing.

A dark blue car turned into the driveway and a young woman exited from the driver's door and headed for the front door of the white bungalow.

Aleksander nudged his brother hard with his elbow and pointed to where they were meant to be watching.

'Andriy, Andriy, look, look, it must be her, isn't it a big blue car we're meant to be looking for.'

The next few moments were like a comedy of errors, Andriy sat down on the sand and went to put his shoes on.

Everything went wrong he had to undo his laces

'Christ I wish I hadn't just kicked them off now if I hadn't been too lazy to undo the bloody things even when I took the sodding shoes off,' he seethed to himself.

Andriy swore aloud, 'damn it's bloody, sod's law the bloody left lace has knotted.'

Heart racing and face going red with embarrassment, he fumbled the lace undone and slipped both shoes on while pushing the socks into his trouser pockets.

Meanwhile Aleksander still in bare feet, socks tucked into shoes tucked under his left arm ran ahead shouting, 'come on, come on, Andriy, stop buggering about it must be her.'

Some of the few spectators at the edge of the Indian Ocean, looked round curiously at the commotion and took further interest when Alexander's bare feet left warm sand and landed on the hot concrete of the pathway between the two beach side buildings.

Aleksander jumped high, attempting without succeeding to get the burnt soles off the incredibly sun boiled surface on which he had landed.

In his panic and reaction to his incredibly painful seared feet he dropped his shoes. Turning rapidly and grunting in pain every time a foot touched the ground, Aleksander retreated to the relative safety of the beach before slumping down into the sand.

Looking back down the beach, Aleksander realised Andriy was still attempting to retrieve his own situation and would have to manage his awkward position himself. He looked anxiously at his shoes about three large paces onto the sun-baked concrete and began to crawl on trousered knee and with sock covered hands to retrieve the much needed shoes.

Moments later and sitting on his behind putting his recovered shoes onto his feet the shadow of Andriy loomed over his large body.

'More haste less speed is the English saying I believe, meanwhile the girl is getting back into the blue car and I'm waiting for you.'

'Alright, alright, I'm nearly ready,' said Aleksander staggering to his feet relieved to get away from the now blistering heat of the concrete walkway.

'Let's go then, now you've finally decided to join me,'

The two lumbered across the tarmac towards Ocean Drive and their waiting vehicle on the far side.

-***-

Isla parked on the drive of her mother's residence on the Upper Esplanade, quickly realised there was unlikely to be anyone home when she had arrived and seen the two open and empty garages.

Half in hope, rather than expectation she pressed the gold ornate bell on the right side of the gold leaf, oriental motif decorated, otherwise white double size front door.

Isla could hear the notes of the first part of the 1812 overture ring out somewhere inside the bungalow.

'Mother must live here then it's all over the top,' she thought, looking at the ornate front door and hearing the closing tones of the music caused by her pressing the button of the front door bell.

Hearing and expecting nothing else from the house at that moment and hearing the fretful tones of an unhappy Alice through the open driver's door of the Falcon, Isla turned about and set out to return to her little girl in the Ford Falcon.

18th FEBRUARY PM - BUNBURY CHASE

As she returned to the vehicle, at the front of the bungalow, Isla could see out over the cobalt sea of the Indian Ocean with its white flecked waves pushed over by the south westerly breeze of the Doctor.

'Terrific view,' she thought jealously as she stroked her blond hair back into place, 'have to give mother her due she can't half pick her boyfriends they always appear to be loaded nowadays.'

Getting closer to where she had parked the car at the front of the drive, Isla could see more clearly, over the brow of the hill down to the beach and the two car parks either side of Ocean Drive.

There was little movement a couple of kite surfers were taking advantage of the Doctor and doing their best to catapult off the top of individual waves, some adults and children appeared to be paddling at the edge of the Ocean and two large men were running across the Ocean Drive towards her and a large deep blue Ute parked on the car park below. This vehicle was directly below the Falcon and the bungalow and it was facing directly up the grassy slope towards her.

'Crap, I know them,' she realised.

It felt like her gut hit the floor as she trembled with the realisation of who they were.

'It's them bloody Ukrainian thugs of Luca's.'

Heart racing, Isla ran quickly back to the car, slamming the vehicle's door, although shaking in fright she managed to insert the car key in the ignition and start the car.

She circled the vehicle round the large tarmacadam frontage of the residence on Upper Esplanade until she found herself facing down towards the coast and the palpable threat from Luca's two acolytes.

Isla had only met Andriy and Aleksander a couple of times when they had acted as bodyguards when Isla and Luca had attended a couple of public bashes in town. They had been used for show really, rather than protection but it had made the couple look special to the crowds, Isla remembered fondly basking in the adulation from those held back behind the barriers.

She had heard Luca refer to them as his muscle and had heard telephone calls when Luca had instructed the pair of them in something her partner had always referred to as protection. In those days not knowing Luca's history it had also been amusing to have two large dark-suited men make passage for the couple through the crowds when they attended fashionable parties of the West Australian glitterati.

Knowing they were now in serious trouble and having only her wits and doubtful driving skills as the only way out of this hole, Isla stopped the car so it was facing out of the drive and waited to see which way the twins would go.

With the dark tinted windscreen of the Falcon, Isla was aware the twins would be unable to see inside her car.

With the car stopped, Isla said to herself, 'don't panic, don't panic, just watch to see what they do first.'

'Whichever way they turn we'll go the opposite so at least we have a start on them,' she decided, don't panic,' she repeated to herself.

Alice perched up in her chair in the back of the Falcon had stopped her whimpering when all the action took place and Mummy turned the car round, she looked round her to see what would happen next, feeling the tension of her mother she started to cry.

'Alice, darling it's alright, we're going somewhere else because Grandma isn't in,' the shake in her voice betraying her concern.

Down in the land side car park the twins had returned to their Ute and Aleksander had started up the car.

-***-

'Which way,' said Aleksander gloatingly, thrilled with the thought that their objective was almost within touching distance.

'She can't have seen us, mind you she must have realised nobody is in and is going off somewhere else, her car is turned round now and facing outwards,' commented Andriy trying to assess the situation.

'What ever go right out of the car park then you won't have to cross any traffic.'

'Okay,' replied Aleksander, 'we'll take it easy at first and see if she reacts.'

'Whatever happens we've got them, there's nowhere for them to run, even in that machine we've got the beating of her driving I'm sure.

He reversed the Ute gently back not wanting to alert the two girls above them and moving forward turned north onto Ocean Drive, behind an old green Commodore with a blue 'p plate' on the rear window and a young man wearing thick black spectacles, making his way cautiously ahead of them.

'Damn, wrong choice,' observed Aleksander to his brother, 'can't get past because of the raised central median.'

'I know, I know,' said Andriy frantically flashing their vehicles lights at the dim sod ahead of them.

'Have they gone yet?'

-***-

Isla seeing the brother's make the decision for her said to the unhappy Alice, 'hang on darling,' and launched the Falcon southwards down the Upper Esplanade.

The accelerated past the single story, mainly blue painted concrete art shelter on the left, Alice stopped crying, pointed at the intriguing graffiti paintings and gurgled excitedly.

Isla didn't have time to notice she was fully concentrated on controlling the heavy Falcon whose front wheels screeched as they first spun at the fierce acceleration caused by her heavy right foot, which was pressing the accelerator pedal as far as it would go.

Within moments the northern end of the Upper Esplanade disappeared in the rear view mirror as the road bent left and the first junction was upon them,

Isla released the accelerator pedal and braked hard, she flicked the responsive car left into Haig Crescent, then realisation dawned on her as she accelerated up the hill, she was braking all sorts of laws as the school zone restriction signs on either side of the road reminded her.

Desperately not caring about their speed she looked for the next turning to disappear into. Even in her near terror, Isla realised it was especially important they get away from the school, the last thing they needed was a curious policeman or school crossing person preventing their escape from Luca's thugs.

At the next fork in the road Isla flicked the Falcon right narrowly missing a gentleman on a red bike freewheeling downhill with his right of way from her left.

Glancing in her rear mirror she realised she was now out of sight of the Upper Esplanade and not wanting to kill themselves or some poor innocent member of the public through her reckless driving she slowed the vehicle to a crawl and tried to work out what to do next.

Further down the hill now on Upper Esplanade, Aleksander and Andriy in their Commodore Ute were making rapid progress past where Isla and Alice had turned inland up Haig Crescent.

'Blast that P Plater,' cursed Andriy, 'it's almost like it was in the employ of those girls the way it stuttered onto that roundabout.'

'Where the hell have they gone?' shouted Aleksander looking down the almost deserted road ahead, his previous smugness now having deserted him.

'They must have turned off, they aren't on the coast road either,' he continued his rant

'Go left, left,' Andriy yelled at his brother, they must have gone back towards the town.'

'Alright, alright let me drive,' replied the other brother angrily as he swept left onto Scott Street leaving the roundabout with the white 'Russell Sheridan', 'Young Smithy' sculpture in their wake.

Within moments they were roaring over the crest of the hill up from the coast and could see no sign of the Blue Falcon ahead of them.

Aleksander slowed the Ute to a crawl, 'lost them for now, no point in getting done for speeding or someone ringing the cops because I'm driving like a lunatic.'

'You're right,' agreed Andriy starting to calm down himself.

Best make a sweep around, just in case she's hiding in some cul-de-sac and then we'll return to the coast and keep an eye on the house.

-***-

Isla realised as she coasted around the quiet residential street which is Withers Crescent that although the view from the road towards the city was very pleasant from atop this, that in the blue Ford Falcon they must stick out like a sore thumb.

Alice wasn't happy either, she frequently let out yells of unhappiness and even the sound of Isla trying to console her couldn't get away from the need to stop and attend to the little girl. Seeing a piece of brown grass next to an electricity sub-station on their left side, Isla pulled the Falcon over to the left of a weathered, wooden, telegraph pole and stopped alongside the sub-station out of sight of those below.

Alice was now continuously crying but before she could attend to the little girl Isla needed to double check around to see if they were visible from any other parts of the surrounding countryside.

Across the road from where she had parked the car was a concrete view point with a bush and two small trees shading the area, a steep downward path ran alongside into a hilly park covered in trees.

Isla could see to the harbour to the north end of Bunbury, looking down she could frighteningly see a recognisable Shiny blue Ute similar to the one the Twins were driving on the road below her sanctuary, if it was the same vehicle it was at least going away from them at the moment.

Although she couldn't possibly be visible from the Ute it was still enough to make her step cautiously back and peer through the convenient branches of the nearest tree. Her heart which had briefly calmed down started pounding against her chest cavity once again.

Screams from Alice in the rear of the Falcon reminded Isla of her priorities, returning to the vehicle, Isla released a very upset toddler from her seat in the rear of the car.

Retrieving Alice's rug from the trunk while holding the released, sobbing child tightly in her arms. Isla laid the rug carefully on the brown, mown grass in the relative shade of the car and placed the partially consoled child carefully onto the rug.

-***-

Down below Isla and Alice's lofty perch the Twins were following a narrow one-way Wittenoon street past the fairly newly constructed Church of Australia, with Andriy looking into all the side streets in the hope of spotting the Ford.

'I'm not sure that she saw us,' commented Andriy hopefully.

'Of course she did, how come they disappeared so quickly if they weren't running away?' Stated Aleksander.

'No she can't have known it's us, we've only met her a couple of times and that was long before Luca was incarcerated.'

'Doesn't matter does it, we now know she has come to her mother's and whatever she's going to return there, if not her mother is going to know where she's gone, isn't she?'

'Alright then whatever happens we win, if the girls return we've got them if they don't, we know Isla has got to keep in touch with her mother whatever.'

'We'll just go back and wait then,' added Andriy.

18th FEBRUARY PM – NEAR MISS

Isla now having given the little girl food and drink and also having refreshed herself from Moira's thoughtful emergency food parcel, was able to sit contented on the brown grassed verge, in the shade of the Falcon, at the top of Withers Crescent.

A much more contented Alice snuggled up into Isla's arms, relaxing into the relative peace and quiet.

Isla knew in her heart of hearts she would have to warn her mother about the impending disaster that was about to impact on her parent's life in the shape of the Ukrainian thugs.

She didn't however want to let her mother know her own new mobile number, Isla was still psychotic about being tracked by Luca's followers.

In her mind Isla made a decision, 'even though we filled up earlier we better find somewhere to top up, at least then we can out last the thugs if they follow us.'

'With a bit of luck we'll find a phone booth Alice, then we can ring your Grandma and warn her about what might be on her doorstep,' said Isla to the little girl.

Gently removing Alice from her grasp and laying her back onto the mat, Isla re-started the Falcon, put the AC on full blast, and partially opened the front windows to cool the vehicle.

Having set this in motion she retrieved their possessions, re-packed the car and secured Alice back into the vehicle.

Just at that moment the first children in their mainly blue with white and red striped sweat shirts came walking round the corner from the High School below, most of the children took the path down the hill through the park while some of the others gathered at the top of the path chattering amongst themselves.

Isla decided she would have to follow the crescent down towards the school and hope that if she headed back down Haig Crescent towards the coast, she should be hidden amongst all the traffic from parents on the school run.

'With a bit of luck we can head south away from your Grandma's and make our escape Alice, what do you think?'

Alice giggled in reply and looked contentedly around her. There was a lot to see a gradual build-up of cars, on the school run, had parked on the verges either side of Withers Crescent where it dropped down to the main road. Lots of children were milling about and there was lots of noise from the starting cars and passing children emanating through the partially open windows of the Falcon.

At this point Isla could see Haig Crescent as they passed between the school buildings, there were no cars parked here it being a restricted area but there were a number of school buses and a school crossing patrol.

Isla carefully manoeuvred her vehicle to the left, back onto Haig Crescent and doing her best to avoid the mess of people, children and traffic appearing at the end of a school day, she joined the queue of vehicles making its way downhill towards the coast.

The road bore round to the right leaving the entrance to their recent sanctuary, Withers Crescent on their left.

'It is such a short time since we scurried up there,' remembered Isla.

She had to concentrate fully here, there were cars parked on the brown sun-burned grass verges to her left and others half parked onto the pathway to her right. Children were everywhere, making their daily escape from the school environs of Bunbury High. Isla and Alice in the Falcon continued their crawl in the traffic, down the hill, with the Indian Ocean now visible in the distance ahead of them.

-***-

Andriy and Aleksander were parked up in the car park off Ocean Drive, this time as far south as they could get, looking through the netting of the basketball courts, the windows of the Ute were fully open to get the best value from the Doctor's south westerly sea breeze.

They too had become aware of the mass exodus from Bunbury High and now from their new position had the added advantage of being able to observe the upper bodies of the cars exiting Haig Crescent as well as reasonably clear sightlines down Coast Drive and partial views on the Upper Esplanade traffic.

'Can't see why she should be amongst this lot,' commented Andriy.

'Even so we had better keep a sharp lookout they've already managed to avoid us once this afternoon don't want it to happen again do we? Replied the other Twin

-***-

At the bottom of the hill, cars were attempting with some difficulty, to exit a jam packed car park to Isla's right, she let a white Toyota full of young uniformed, school children and harassed woman driver, slot their vehicle in front of her.

There were now three cars ahead of them in the queue as another vehicle cleared the junction onto the Upper Esplanade.

While checking Alice in her rear view mirror, Isla left a small gap in front of the car and was just about to move forward when their twin, another blue Falcon took the opportunity to bully his way in front of their own vehicle.

For Isla who was stressed enough as it was the arrogance of the driver in front was like scratching a festering sore, she lost it and swore at the bastard in front of them whilst hammering the horn of her own Falcon.

Alice giggled and went, 'Mummy,' severely, this made Isla realise the comedy in the situation.

'They were in no hurry so why the anger,' she thought to herself and smiled in the rear view mirror at her little girl.

The guy in the blue Falcon ahead, waved laconically back at her, his right fist out of the window with two fingers parted in an unpleasant gesture, while the uniformed boy turned in his passenger seat stuck his head out of the window and poked his tongue out at them.

This made Isla laugh out loud.

-***-

Down in the Coast Drive car park, Andriy and Aleksander heard the sound of the car horn and Andriy from the left side of the Ute could just see, the top of what looked like a deep blue coloured car, behind a white car exiting Haig Crescent.

'Start her up Aleksander, this could be it, I'll just get a better look.'

At that Andriy leapt out of their vehicle, clambered up and stood on the passenger side sill to get a better view.

Clambering back inside their Ute he exclaimed excitedly, 'if it isn't, it's the spitting image, let's get over there.'

'Go south, we can always come back north if it turns that way.'

Aleksander concentrating on getting their Commodore Ute down the road as fast as possible, crossed the Coast Drive and set its nose to the south with the sea on their right before seconds later turning uphill away from the Ocean towards the young smithy roundabout.

-***-

Presumably other school run cars were parked on the Upper Esplanade and this made it difficult to get space to turn out of Haig Crescent, eventually the annoying vehicle ahead of them managed to turn left onto the crossing road and departed with a derisory beep of his horn.

Shortly after with four cars in between them and the transgressor, Isla and Alice in the Falcon were able to follow the other's lead and proceed south down the Upper Esplanade.

Following the other cars down to the roundabout with the young smithy sculpture, Isla could see the other Falcon proceed straight on across the roundabout, the next car a red Echo, turned left into Scott Street.

The following car stopped at the junction because with right of way from below on the Ocean Drive appeared the Perfect Blue Commodore Ute with the twins safely ensconced inside.

Isla gasped fearfully, 'how the hell did they find us so quick?'

To her astonishment and great relief the Ute turned right and went racing southwards away from the girls in their Falcon, following the rude interloper of a few minutes before.

Gratefully Isla turned left up Scott Street and towards what she hoped were the reasonably safer environs of the City of Bunbury.

-***-

The blue Falcon, the twins were following had a head start and was fairly shifting, though Aleksander with his driving skills was easily able to whittle away the other cars lead, and they were soon in visual sight of the number plate but couldn't see inside because of the heavy dark tinting of the rear window.

'Can you read the number plate Andriy?'

'Yes but it isn't the one we've been given.'

'Do you think she could have got it changed?' Queried Aleksander.

'You wouldn't think so, but we don't really know her that well and she could have all sorts of contacts we don't know about who are quite capable of swapping plates.'

'Remember it's been quite a while she's been out there with that car, could have made all sorts of changes to the Falcon.'

Whoever it is going quickly, it's either her having spotted us or someone in a hurry,' commented Aleksander as he tried once again to pass the flying Falcon ahead of them.

'Careful,' cautioned Andriy, 'back off, just follow for now and let's see where we end up.'

The blue Falcon raced down the Upper Esplanade, followed closely by Aleksander and Andriy in their Commodore Ute.

The Falcon ahead of the Twins braked hard as the road turned ninety degrees right before heading back down and towards Ocean Drive.

The Falcon only paused briefly at the main road before flicking left and immediately speeded up on the near empty scenic road.

Aleksander followed behind, any chance of overtaking being prevented by the small, low central median.

On their right the Ocean still presented an enthralling scenic vista, at the turning off to Hayward Street, another sculpture was centred on the roundabout.

They didn't have much chance to see the hanging trousers, dress and wind gauge pointing to the East, which made up a mainly silver grey sculpture, called The Whalers, as they followed the Falcon on its seemingly urgent passage through the junction.

At this point Ocean Drive lost its central median but with traffic denser and the Falcon driver in an apparent rush there was little opportunity to overtake.

Ocean Drive started to diverge inland from its namesake the coast and moved inland, with green grass covered dunes between the car and the sea and Bunbury suburbia to their left.

Within a kilometre and without indicating the Falcon dived left between two sculptures of ladies with upper naked torsos' set on to orange brick dais. The sculptures another of Russell Sheridan's work, this time called The Maidens, was barely noticed by the Twins in their anxiety to retrieve the situation.

The blue sign on their right said Westwood Drive, Aleksander braked sharply at the unexpected manoeuvre of the Falcon, braked hard and swung the Ute sharply into its wake.

The front vehicle now had a good start and raced uphill through the suburban street of well found, set back, single structure homes, by the time Aleksander had chance to catch the speeding vehicle ahead of them, it had pulled up at a junction and turned left onto a dual carriageway.

'We've got them now,' said Andriy exultantly banging his right fist on the dashboard in front of him as Aleksander accelerated and quickly reduced the distance to their quarry.

'Hang on they're pulling over to the outside lane and indicating,' he indicated and followed onto the outside lane.

The Falcon seeing a space in the oncoming traffic whipped right across the oncoming dual carriageway, into what appeared to be a dead end into a sports complex.

'Get after them,' cried Andriy enthusiastically we've got them.

'Alright, alright, I'm trying we would be on them if it wasn't for this bloody traffic,' responded Aleksander as he waited impatiently for a rush of what appeared to be never ending, oncoming vehicles.

Finally after what seemed to be an age, the twins were able to cross the dual carriageway and into the sports area.

'The sign said Hockey Stadium, wonder what they are playing at?' questioned Andriy.

Aleksander followed the short road under the trees and into a large car park, ahead was and obvious sports stadium and a large car park in front and either side of the building.

Much to their surprise and disgust was the blue Falcon they had spent the last fifteen minutes chasing.

Its boot which was open and facing them was being used by a boy, about eleven years old, who was collecting a sports bag and two hockey sticks, while a man, probably the boy's father was holding the lid of the trunk ready to close it.

'Bugger, bugger, bugger,' swore Andriy, 'let's get of here and back to that bloody house before we miss those bloody girls again.'

-***-

Isla was glad when they had breasted the hill halfway up Scott Street and were halfway down the other side and no longer visible from the coast road, reaching the junction at the bottom of the slope and given no obvious sign of the way back into the city, Isla decided to turn left down Picton Crescent, and without realising took the previous route of Andriy and Aleksander earlier that afternoon.

Isla thought, 'at least going this way it's away from the relative threat of those two thugs.'

18th FEBRUARY EVENING - THE GIRLS BOOK IN

By the time the wearied Twins had returned to their previous location in the car park inland of Ocean Drive, facing the targeted bungalow on Upper Esplanade, neither were in the mood to be trifled with and were blaming each other and the world, for charging off after the smokescreen which was the other blue Falcon and its hockey playing child.

'Bloody hell Andriy, surely you should have realised with the wrong number plate it couldn't have been the right car.'

'Instead of us charging off to a ruddy hockey stadium, we should have been here watching out for the real sodding car with those poxy girls.'

Andriy replied angrily, 'I thought you were supposed to be the expert bloody driver, you couldn't even keep up half the time never mind get past that sodding car.'

'But, but,' expostulated a furious Aleksander, who was seriously thinking about thumping his annoying brother.

A realisation that something had changed prevented a possible over reaction.

'Look,' he shouted pointing up towards the bungalow.

'One of the garages is now closed, someone must be home, let's get over there and find out where those girls are.'

Calming himself and assessing the situation Andriy cautioned his brother.

'Patience, patience, let's think this through first, we've done too much wasteful chasing around without any success already today.'

Aleksander nodded his head in agreement and stopped the engine, he had just restarted in anticipation of heading towards the property above.

'What do you suggest we do?'

'I think we leave things for now, go and get some refreshment, top up the car and come back in about ninety minutes at sunset about seven. We're less likely to be noticed when we approach the house and with what may happen when one of them opens the door either way we'll be in a better position to take control of whatever occurs,' declared Andriy confidently.

'Seems sensible,' Andriy grunted and nodded his head in agreement.

He re-started the Commodore and set its head towards the city and some refreshment for the pair of them, Isla's Mother and partner could wait for a while.

-***-

Isla and Alice in the Falcon, having fortunately avoided the clutches had turned onto Turner Street and followed the Twins previous progress, over the road hump onto the 20kph restricted, narrow one way street which is Wittenoom.

At the end of the restricted one-way section a large white complex with overhanging, brown, timber roof appeared on their left hand side.

Set high to the right on the end of the building and in blue lettering were the words SOUTH WEST DISTRICT POLICE COMPLEX.

Isla stopped the car at the junction and thought, 'dare we?'

She shook her head and contemplated what might happen, 'Ryan could have made a complaint and I could be arrested,' she thought glumly.

'What would happen to Alice then?'

'Once they realise who we are and our connection to Luca they're not going to be very sympathetic or helpful,' she surmised.

Isla's mind was made up by a hooting from an impatient white panel truck astern of the Falcon trying to exit the one way street, its exit blocked by her indecision.

Isla's reverie interrupted, and with the embarrassment of realising she was blocking the road, had made her inattentive and she nearly shot forward into the side of a white Commodore police car which was exiting Stephen Street from her right.

With the near miss, Isla checked herself, double-checked their route was clear before pointing the Falcon north and setting it in motion along the continuation of Wittenoom street.

Proceeding easily along the tree lined street where there was a mixture of housing and light industry, they cleared three junctions before returning to somewhere Isla recognised.

Across from the car on the opposite corner of a roundabout was the Lord Forrest Hotel, somewhere Isla remembered passing when they were trying to find the Upper Esplanade.

Having a bit of a brainwave, wanting a bit of comfort and fed up with being chased around Isla drove the car up to the front entrance and parked outside, it was fortunate a white, with lower brown facing, topped with a yellow stripe, Roberts Luxury Tour Bus parked on the roadway was obscuring most of the Falcon from view.

Grabbing a sleepy Alice from the rear of the Falcon she marched inside the plushly decorated reception area and approached the efficient looking green and yellow uniformed receptionist with a shining Melanie name tag.

'Please can I help you madam?

'What a lovely little girl you have there,' she added.

Isla who had decided it was time to use mother's name, bluff a bit and cause her parent some awkwardness replied brusquely.

'Room that's booked please, with cot.'

'Name please madam.'

'My mother has booked it I believe, Bethany Steele.'

'Hold on a moment please,' said the receptionist typing into the reception computer.

'We know Ms Steele well she and her partner are regulars at functions in the conference room and often use Alexander's our restaurant,' commented Melanie the Receptionist.

She paused and looked intently at the screen before lifting her head and saying apologetically to Isla and a somnolent Alice.

'I'm sorry Madam there is no booking for you, something must have gone wrong, I do apologise most sincerely, I'm sure we can sort something out.'

'Damn,' said Isla making an effort to appear really irritated.

'I would ring mother but my mobile needs charging, I'll just have to put us back in the car and nip down to the house and see if she has returned yet.'

'Oh no madam there is no need to do that we'll phone her for you.'

Melanie entered mother's name into the computer and was soon dialling her mobile.

'Excuse me Ms Steele it's Melanie at the Lord Forrest here, I do apologise for bothering you but your daughter and granddaughter are here at Reception and tell me we have a room for them booked by you.'

Bethany, was momentarily taken aback by the telephone call but with years of avoiding embarrassment and quick on the uptake answered quickly.

'Oh is it today, haven't I booked them in?'

'Melanie I am so sorry, I'm sure you can manage something for me can't you?'

Melanie the receptionist surprised by Bethany's failure to remember her daughter and granddaughter visiting answered helpfully.

'Of course, of course, I'm doing it now, would you like this to go on the Company or the personal account?

'Oh personal please,' replied Bethany already trying to work out ways she would explain this to her partner Ray.

'Could I speak to Isla, my daughter please?'

'Of course Ms Steele, I'll pass you over now and by the time you two have finished talking, I'm sure we'll have everything organised.

'Here you are Madam, everything is arranged, your mother asked if she could have a word,' said Melanie handing the telephone to the waiting Isla.

Isla took the telephone from the Receptionist and said laughingly, 'hallo mother how are we today?'

'Alice is really looking forward to seeing you.'

'Isla, what are you playing at?'

Isla in a firm voice really needing to warn her mother about the probability of a visit from the Twins, replied, 'mummy I think you need to nip round immediately and see Alice before I put her to bed, otherwise you'll miss her.'

Isla who had never called Bethany mummy since her own early years, hoped the use of this terminology would make mother realise something was wrong and the urgency of the situation.

Isla couldn't say what was on her mind and warn Bethany because the receptionist Melanie, who was pretending or trying not to listen, couldn't help hear what was being said and would notice any change in the tone of the conversation.

Isla desperately didn't want to give the receptionist any idea something was wrong, 'I don't know what Bethany said to Melanie but it has certainly done the trick.' She concluded.

'I can't just leave home like this just because you say I have to, I'll have to sort myself out my hair is a mess and I'm all dressed wrong,' protested mother.

'That's brilliant mother, we'll see you shortly, and Melanie will tell you which room.'

Melanie was mouthing 302 at Isla as she cut her mother off and returned the reception telephone to the young lady.

'Melanie, please do you have someone who can park our car, and I'll get what we need for the overnight.'

'Of course,' answered Melanie reaching for the telephone to find help to move the Falcon to the secure car park.

-***-

Bethany cursed under her breath as Isla disconnected the Lord Forrest telephone.

'Blast, bugger, bugger, buggeration, how the hell am I going to tell Ray I have a granddaughter, he only knows about Isla?

Then remembering back to the telephone conversation, her curiosity aroused she reflected to herself.

'Why did she call me mummy?'

'I've always discouraged that, ever since Isla was tiny.'

'It must be something crucial for her to use that term,' Bethany decided.

'I had better get my backside round to the Lord Forrest right now,' she concluded to herself.

Just taking time to primp her hair in front of the hall mirror, apply a touch of pink lipstick, Bethany made her way to the garage and her silver mini cooper convertible.

'At least I don't scrub up too bad,' she praised herself as she swung the little car onto the Upper Esplanade, leaving both garage doors open as they had been earlier that day.

'Lucky Ray isn't due home till late, he's got a property to show up by the Inner Harbour, then he's got a Lion's meeting,' recalled Bethany as she pulled the Mini to a stop in the secure car park of the Hotel.

A few minutes later Bethany was knocking on the door of the girl's room after enquiring their location from Melanie and having had her credit card swiped on the machine in reception.

There was a noise the other side of the door and Bethany felt like Isla was checking on her through the room's spyhole.

Moments later Isla opened the door a half-naked little girl in her arms.

Isla beamed at her parent and said, 'come in mother, quickly.'

As soon as the door was securely shut, Isla passed over Alice, who and told Bethany.

'Here mother hang onto your granddaughter a moment, I desperately need the loo.'

Before Bethany could reply, Alice was hanging onto her neck with both arms and Isla who was making her way to the bathroom retorted.

'Alice say hallo to your grandma.'

At that Bethany was left with the little girl and staring at an already dis-ordered hotel room.

Suddenly feeling exhausted by the last thirty minutes and everything Isla had suddenly brought into her normally well-ordered life, Bethany slumped down into one of the room's two armless beige armchairs, still holding carefully onto Alice, who was snuggled up into Bethany's right shoulder, sucking her left thumb contentedly.

Isla in the bathroom sitting on the closed toilet seat, breathed a huge sigh of relief and thought.

'So far I've acted on impulse and got away with it.'

'Mother is here and for the moment we're away from the Twins, how much am I going to tell her though?'

'I've got to warn her about those Ukrainian thugs and what they can do.'

'Oh sod it I'll have to tell her about trying to find Uncle Brian and all the shit we're both in she decided, I'll have to make it look as if at least we're getting out of her hair.' Isla decided.

Decision made, Isla washed her hands, checked her hair and went back into the bedroom; she was pleased to see her mother and Alice getting on so well.

Alice was poking her fingers through Bethany's hair and Mother wasn't complaining but laughing with the little girl.

They both looked up as Isla returned to the hotel room from the bathroom.

Before Bethany had a chance to speak, Isla said.

'Let's go and have something to eat, I'm ravenous if we all eat and put Alice down for the night afterwards we can talk when she's asleep, we have to make some big decisions and you need to know what's happening.'

Bethany, who would previously have been unhappy in the present situation was quite surprised about how happy she was holding her granddaughter and to see her own daughter again astonished Isla.

That's fine darling, we eat here regularly the buffet is excellent, you can have as much or as little as you want.

'It also works really well, I had no plans this evening anyway, Ray is out until late, I'll give him a ring shortly to let him know what is going on.'

_***_

It now being close to 7pm and the light fading the twins were returning to Ocean Drive fully refreshed, Aleksander had insisted they refuel their stomach at his favourite fast food restaurant.

It had taken some time to find a Macdonald's, it was only when they saw the sign for the Bunbury Forum in the east of the city that they were able to satisfy Aleksander's hunger pangs and refuel the Ute as well.

Parking on the darkening car park the twins could see a few keen surfers returning to their cars and others trudging up the slope towards their homes in the nearby suburbs.

'Look,' said Andriy, 'the place is in darkness and both garages are open again, hope they aren't both out all night.'

'Doesn't matter if they're out until late, I'm content for a few hours yet,' replied Aleksander rubbing his replete belly.

'Won't be the first time we have had to wait for a while, we'll give it until about 1030 and then find a motel, better tell Fabio what's happening though, although the wop bastard doesn't really need to know yet,' answered Andriy.

After a brief telephone call, Andriy left a message for Fabio who wasn't answering his mobile the twins sat back to wait, a local country station playing popular music from the car stereo and the sky darkening over the orange, streaked, Indian Ocean behind them.

18th FEBRUARY EVENING – EVENING IN BUNBURY

Having made a decision about eating the two women and little girl made their way down to the Hotel restaurant.

Bethany was greeted like an old friend as befits someone who is a regular and valued customer.

Both settled for the buffet and Alice in a high chair alongside their table was doted on by the two waitresses every chance they got between serving the rest of the restaurant diners.

Settling back in their restaurant chairs with coffee in front of them and both satisfied by their excellent meal, Alice still playing with the remains of her pudding, Bethany was first to speak.

'I must admit Isla this is all very nice, even if it is going onto my credit card, and I'm more pleased to see both of you than I ever realised.'

'What on earth is going on and why all the secrecy?'

'It's all about Luca and the crime scene he is involved in, I've done a runner and Luca has sent two of his east European thugs after me. They were in Bunbury today, I've managed to avoid them, they were watching your house, I don't know how they managed to find you and it's so awful,' cried Isla bursting into tears with relief at being able to tell someone else part of her problems.

'There, there,' said Bethany patting Isla's nearest hand, 'come on it can't be all that bad we'll just call the police if they threaten you.'

'It's not so much me it's you I'm worried about mother.'

'They're going to try and use you to find Alice and me, and they won't do it gently if they get the chance believe me.'

'The things I've found out about Luca and his family this past few months, Alice and me need to disappear, which is why I rang you about Uncle Brian.'

'What about that surf bum Brian, you've been living with.'

'It's not Brian, its Ryan mother, and I've left him, he likes to hit on women when he has had few cans and a couple of nights ago was the final straw.'

'I can see the bruises, that was him was it?

I've been lucky I've only ever run into one like him and I made a right mess of him with a pick axe handle I can tell you,' said Bethany digressing.

'Yes it was Ryan, the bastard.'

'We left our pad yesterday morning without him knowing but I could be in real trouble which is why we need to get out of here,' she said including Alice with the sweep of her left arm.

Isla went onto explain about the happenings at the Floreat Forum and her use of the kitchen knife on Ryan's wrist.

'Don't worry about that darling, don't think he's going to the police after the damage he's done to you, think they might call it self-defence'

'I must have hit an artery, there was blood everywhere, he may be dead,' said Isla shaking with the thought, only just realising what she might have done.

Bethany answered calmly wanting to re-assure her daughter, 'if he was dead you would know it by now, it would be all over the news and they would certainly have stopped you in that car of yours.

'You think so.'

'Certainly, there's been no dead bodies in shopping centre car parks on the news yesterday or today.'

Partially re-assured Isla changed subjects.

'Everything we own is in that car, which is also ours because Luca transferred the ownership on it to me when he got put into that foul prison.'

'When you rang me last time I tried my brother, his mobile keeps reverting to message and I tried ringing that vineyard but no-one ever answers and it doesn't even appear to have an answer machine.'

'I know, I know,' agreed Isla the same thing happened to me, some very nice people in a bed and breakfast back in Rockingham were terrific and really helped us out last night.'

'I need to ring them when we get back to the room and tell them we're safe.'

'I think we had better go back to the room now,' said Bethany smiling at Alice who had just fallen asleep with her forehead resting on the table of the high chair.

Returning to the room Bethany helped Isla to undress, and put Alice to bed in the cot supplied by the hotel. Alice herself didn't complain and dozed in out of sleep throughout these ministrations.

Isla rang Moira on her mobile, assured her and Arthur of their safety and improved relationship with Bethany but didn't upset them by telling them about their near miss with the twins.

Bethany also telephoned Ray who was just arriving at his Lions meeting to tell him she would be late home as well and if he wasn't drinking as she suspected, would he mind picking her up at the Royal Forrest about 10:30 as she had a drink or two.

Ray agreed and jokingly asked who the other boyfriend was, Bethany said she would explain when they got home and told him she loved him.

'The way you were speaking to him mother he sounds a bit more special than usual,' commented Isla at the end of the conversations.

'I know,' coyly answered Bethany, 'he is a bit, I know he's a touch younger but he always makes me feel special.'

'Oh dear mother it has finally happened I think you're finally in love with a fella, amazing,' laughed Isla.

Bethany blushed with embarrassment and tried to change the subject.

'What are we going to do about the situation about these thugs, if they approach me?'

Isla took a moment before replying, 'call the police.'

'Won't that get you into trouble?' Answered Bethany.

'How can it, they can't admit to chasing me and if they make the connection to Luca the police are going to ask them a lot of questions.'

'Alice and I aren't going to be here anyway for the police or anyone else to worry about.'

Thinking further Isla added, 'I'm sure they can't afford to meet up with the police, I reckon they aren't in Australia legally anyway.'

'So what are you going to do, you and Alice?' Asked Bethany, 'much though I would like you both to stay here, I don't think it can ever be safe for you in Western Australia.'

'I think Uncle Brian is such a terrific idea,' she added.

'He would never let you down, he's always been there for me, he's a terrific brother, no matter what scrape I've ever got myself into,' said Bethany wistfully

'I'll book you both on flights to Melbourne tomorrow and you can go up to the Yarra valley and find him I'm sure,' declared Bethany decisively.

'No, no, you can't do that, all we own is the car and everything in it, I'm not prepared to give up the car especially, it's only just over three years old and anyway the airline will charge a fortune to carry all our baggage,' replied Isla.

'You must have a plan, you said yourself and we know you can't stay here can you?' Said Bethany reinforcing the point of the dangers of staying too close to home.

'I've already thought about that I'll drive Alice and me to Victoria it can't be that bad, after all people do it all the time don't they?'

'Isla don't be stupid it must be over three and a half thousand kilometres, that's crazy,' said Bethany, horror struck.

'I have to mother, we don't have a choice, sorry and all that but it's the only way we are going to escape undetected and keep everything we possess intact.'

'I understand darling but it's hugely worrying to think of you going all the way across the Nullarbor with only you driving and having to look after Alice as well.'

'Sorry Mother I've decided, this near thing with those thugs has made my mind up.'

'We are going in the morning and there's no changing my mind,' declared Isla decisively.

'Fair enough but before I go tonight, let's plan how you are both going to do it safely,' answered Bethany.

-***-

Back at the car park on Ocean Drive it was now well past 10pm and the Twins were getting bored and concerned. For a while their interest had been aroused by listening to the country music station and a walk down to the beach and along the moonlit sands.

Earlier in the evening they had been alone in the darkness of the car park, the interior of the Ute back-lit by the street lights of Ocean Drive but now the area around them was getting busy with mainly small cars of couples obviously interested in romantic liaisons starting to make the car park more hectic than it had been in the earlier daylight.

Peering through the windscreen of the Ute at their unlit target, Andriy yawned and uttered the first words between them for quite a while.

'There's nothing happening, is there?'

'I also don't like all these other cars around us, think we had better find somewhere to get our head down for the night.'

Aleksander answered, 'Yeah I think you're right, it's obvious the Falcon and its occupants must be hunkered down somewhere for the night themselves, she wouldn't keep the little girl up this long.'

'That's if they're still in Bunbury, if she realise it was us earlier, I reckon she'll be long gone which is why we've seen neither hide nor hair of them since.'

'You're probably right agreed Andriy, let's get out of here, I'm tired and need to find a mattress to lie on.'

'We'll need a late night pharmacy for toothbrush and stuff before we find a motel though,' added Andriy as Aleksander turned the Ute in the direction of the city.

Right Isla think you have a plan, it's not going to be cheap but if I transfer $2000 to your account tomorrow it should give you enough to pay for fuel and motels all the way across and shouldn't have you driving too far in any one day.'

'Thanks mother that's brilliant and saves me using everything I've got left,' said Isla looking up from the screen where they had been planning her route and booking motel rooms for the journey across the south of Australia.'

'I had better get out of here, you need to get on the road smartish in the morning, Kalgoorlie might be on the easiest roads, and it's still a very long trip on your first day.'

'I know but I need to get us as far away as possible before we stop on that first day and everything after that is only four hours or so a day.'

'Now I'm tied into the roadhouses and everything.'

'Alright then you get to bed, I'll arrange with Melanie to get you called at six, and have breakfast to your room thirty minutes later how does that sound?'

'That's great,' responded Isla hugging her mother.

'I forgot, what about your mobile it's not working.'

'I've got a new one, here I'll ring you so you've got my new number,' declared Isla reaching for her mobile.

'One thing mother,' reflected Isla, 'don't put us into your own mobile memory until I'm due to reach Eucla.'

'Why's that?'

'Then if you do get threatened or anything, or your phone gets checked you can honestly say you don't have my new number.'

'Are you serious,' said Bethany, a little annoyed, 'there's no way I'm going to let anyone have that number.'

'Yes very serious, it's important for all of us that if asked you really have no idea of the number, if you don't list it as mine it will only show up as unknown,' said Isla forcefully.

'Fair enough darling, whatever you say,' answered Bethany, deciding it wasn't worth arguing over, Isla being so determined.

At this point as if in agreement with her parent, Alice woke up in the cot on the other side of the room and both the women ceased their conversation to allow her to return to her slumbers

'I'm sure hope everything will be alright though, please be careful and stock up with lots of water and supplies before you leave Kalgoorlie.'

'What happens if Ryan rings,' remembered Bethany.

'Yeah even though he smacked me around a bit when we were pissed, I do feel guilty about the stabbing, it was a bit over the top.'

'Please find out if he's alright and you can let me know when I call you.'

'That's alright but what do I tell him, if he wants to know?'

'Just tell him we're fine and safe and it was good while it lasted.'

'Okay darling drive safely and keep in touch, looks like I'll be visiting Victoria if everything goes alright,' said Bethany tearfully as she hugged Isla tightly before leaving the girls to their fate.

19th FEBRUARY AM – BUNBURY ASSAULT

After Bethany had left the previous evening, Isla even though tired from her long day had prepared all their gear, ready for a prompt departure before crashing out on the large comfortable bed. She had little time to luxuriate in its comfort before falling into a deep sleep.

Fortunately the night passed without interruption, it seemed like no time before her heavy sleep was rudely interrupted by the loud rasp of the bedside telephone.

Isla unable to work out where she was in the pitch black of the hotel room was only brought to her senses by a yelp from Alice in her cot on the other side of the room. It took some moments to work out and find the telephone and she wasn't helped in her fumbling search by knocking over a half empty glass she had left on the bedside table alongside the telephone.

Finally having located the implement causing the horrendous noise she answered it while finding the bedside light switch, the telephone's automated voice told her it was 6 o'clock and that this was her requested call.

Grasping the nettle, and not taking the chance to turn over in the King size bed, Isla said, 'hallo darling,' as she passed her newly awakened little girl on her way to the bathroom.

Having completed her toilet, Isla picked up Alice from her cot, stripped herself and Alice, before taking them both into the shower. Alice thought this was great fun and both were fully refreshed dressed and wide awake when room service knocked on the door with breakfast at six thirty.

By seven with assistance from hotel staff, Isla and Alice in the Falcon were wending their way out of Bunbury bound for Perth, onwards to Kalgoorlie and hopefully South Eastern Australia.

-***-

Bethany and Ray, her partner lying next to her in their bedroom in the bungalow on the Upper Esplanade were still fast asleep as Isla, Alice and the Falcon made their way out of the city.

Bethany had arrived in reception of the Royal Forrest the previous evening just as Ray pulled up at the front in his latest silver BMW 6 series, just pausing briefly to wave goodbye to Melanie, Bethany had jumped into the passenger side of the car and said unsure of his reaction.

'Lots to tell you about Ray darling.'

'Let's get home, sit down and pour a drink and I'll explain everything.'

'Alright sweetness, sounds good to me,' replied Ray as he drove the vehicle the short distance to their residence on the Upper Esplanade.

Once they had settled down with their drinks, Bethany had owned up to Isla, Alice, Luca and his Ukrainian thugs.

Ray, who was settled, happy in his relationship with Bethany and laid back as they come, took it all in his stride. He even went so far as to make a joke of their situation when he realised Bethany's real age.

'Well I'm really pleased, you've got yourself a toy boy, and a step-grandfather, I never realised,' he chided the embarrassed Bethany whose complexion was turning a bright shade of red.

Then he had reached across the sofa hugged her, told her much he loved her and asked if there was any way he could help.

Bethany who probably for the first time in her life actually felt safe in a relationship, had gone to bed a happier more contented, secure woman.

_*** _

On the South Eastern outskirts of the city, Aleksander was awake in the Comfort Inn which was the only one they had been able to find with vacancies the previous evening.

The uninterested night porter had been only too willing to sell them a room even though it was after ten thirty.

By the time they had seen the brightly illuminated vacancy sign at the Comfort Inn, after being turned away at the three previous establishments which had all exhibited No Vacancy signs, they had been getting annoyed and concerned about where they were going to sleep that night.

'Andriy,' he shouted at his snoring brother.

'Get your arse up, you lazy sod, day's awake and we've things to do and people to find.'

Andriy not best pleased to have his beauty sleep interrupted, raised his head from the pillows and grunted.

'What's the time?'

'Nearly eight, I've been awake hours listening to your bloody snoring, you noisy bastard,' said Aleksander criticising his brother.

'Let's get out of here, buy some fresh shirts, get some breakfast and find them bloody girls and get back home to Fremantle, I'm getting really pissed off with this wild-goose chase,' complained a grumpy Aleksander as he headed for the bathroom of their motel room.

'Alright, alright, agreed,' answered Andriy in a conciliatory tone.

'Agree with you about fresh shirts, these are a bit ripe,' he said sniffing at the armpit of the red, checked, short-sleeved shirt he had worn the previous day.

After the briefest of showers, and necessary ablutions, the brothers had soon found a hardware with working men's shirts and replaced their smelly apparel of the previous day.

These were handed to the surprised retail assistant for disposal, before they departed and set out travelling up Blair Street in the Ute in search of breakfast.

Finding a café with a full breakfast had been easy and by nine fifteen the Twins were returning to the Upper Esplanade.

'No mucking about this time,' declared Andriy.

'Let's drive straight in and see who is at home, like you, I'm fed up with this whole business.'

Aleksander driving the Ute grunted in agreement.

-***-

At that precise moment, Bethany dressed in a white jump suit, long blond hair held back with a white scrunchie, was tightly hugging and kissing a smartly dressed Ray, in a grey lightweight suit with shorts, white shirt and red tie.

Ray was just about to make his way to the Realty Office and begin his working day, when Bethany had grabbed hold of him.

'Thanks for your support, you are really terrific you know, I don't know what I've done to deserve you,' she enthused.

'I love you, you daft sod,' laughed Ray.

'I've always known there was something else you had to tell me,' he confided, 'and I knew you would tell me at the right time, so that's all that's happened.'

'Better let me go,' he said kissing the top of her forehead and pushing her gently away.

'I'm meeting a client at the Office shortly in ten minutes,' he explained.

Laughing with happiness Bethany giggled, 'you'll look good then you've got lipstick all round your mouth.'

Ray smiled, looked in the mirror by the front door and wiped the lipstick from the corner of his mouth with a tissue from his trouser pocket.

'What are you going to do today?' he asked over his shoulder as he opened the front door.

'Firstly, I'm following you and fetching my Mini from the Lord Forrest,' she replied as picking up her white handbag.

'Drop you off if you like,' he suggested.

'No it's alright it's only a short walk and it will be nice to have the exercise, besides I can admire the view over the ocean, I never tire of it,' she enthused

'Bethany waited until Ray had left so she could wave him off, then she locked the front door, before starting to make her way onto the Upper Esplanade.

She stopped briefly at the front of the driveway, in the warm sunshine to look out over the Indian Ocean, there was little breeze, and the waves appeared hardly ruffled, she felt warm, thanks to the morning sun and so happy.

Even if Isla and Alice were escaping Western Australia, they were no longer estranged, she knew that had always been her own stupid fault but at least now they were together in spirit, her relationship with Ray had now taken a whole new and happy route and everything was so much more right with her world.

Like a little happy girl she skipped on the spot.

-***-

Coming slowly down the Upper Esplanade from the northern roundabout in the blue Commodore Ute, the twins were able to observe Bethany waving goodbye to her partner,

Andriy looked around, there was no other traffic on the road, the surrounding property appeared quiet and they weren't really observable from Ocean Drive or its car parks.

'It has got to be her, the description is right, doesn't she look like the girl?' observed Andriy.

Well grab her then, don't let's piss around,' whispered Alexander fiercely as he pulled the vehicle alongside the unsuspecting Bethany.

A fraction of a second later, just as the startled Bethany became aware of the Ute creeping up alongside her, Andriy leapt from the front passenger door and grabbed her from behind with his left arm round her neck pulling her off her feet and his large right hard covering her mouth squeezing her lips together, so she would be unable to scream.

Bethany tried to scream even so, the hand over her mouth prevented all but a stifled whistle penetrating Andriy's covering hand.

'None of that bitch, I'll wring your bloody neck if you so much as make a noise,' said Andriy into Bethany's right ear before dragging her into the Ute and dumping her between the seats.

Bethany uncomfortably perched between the two brothers, in a state of shock over her sudden change of circumstances whimpered at the sight of Aleksander picking his nails with a fierce, vicious, 15cm long, black handled, steel bladed knife.

Grabbing and squeezing Bethany's right breast with his left hand, Aleksander said, 'nice and friendly, I do like women with decent tits, these modern anorexic bitches have got nothing up top.'

'Yours are just what I really like to play with, something to get hold off.'

Bethany quietly sobbed, 'what do you want?'

Then more fiercely as if to reinforce Bethany's dire situation Aleksander continued.

'I am going to continue to enjoy your body, while my brother asks you some questions, every time you lie, will mean I will enjoy more of you,' said Aleksander rubbing his nether regions with his right hand, which was still holding the black handled knife.

'Do you understand me?' he said nastily as he placed the point of the knife under her chin.

Bethany nodded in agreement too shocked to speak while Aleksander continued to fondle her left breast through her top and bra.

From behind her in the passenger seat Andriy asked, 'are you Bethany Steele?'

Bethany hesitated just a moment trying to think of how she should answer the question, her last vestige of courage committed to do everything she could to allow Isla and Alice time to get away.

'You obviously didn't believe me bitch, did you?' Said Aleksander laughing, 'I'm going to really enjoy this.'

'You really do need to take us seriously,' continued Aleksander releasing her breast, and with his now free hand he grabbed the left shoulder straps of Bethany's jump suit and white bra, pulled them viciously off her shoulder before cutting them apart with one slash of the knife.

Roughly he exposed her left breast and started to fondle it roughly.'

'I can lie as well, don't forget.'

'You'll notice I went two stages in one that time.'

'You are completely in our control, we don't really care how much we hurt you.'

'Next time you lie or don't answer immediately we might take you into your pretty little house and give you a really good time,' said Aleksander smiling and licking his lips as he continued to knead Bethany's exposed breast.

'Yes, yes I'm Bethany Steele,' she whimpered her resolve to protect her girls completely gone.

'Where is your daughter Isla and her child?

'On their way to Healesville in Victoria, they left this morning.'

'Where were they last night?

'At the Lord Forrest,' whimpered Bethany totally confused by the constant sexual assault, the exposure and the calm questioning from behind her.

'What's that?' said the voice behind her.

'The hotel round the corner.'

'Why are they going all that way?'

'To get away from you.'

'They can't be just going to Healesville for no reason, there must be someone there they know.'

'Yes my elder brother Brian.'

'Where does he live?'

'I don't know,' gasped Bethany and panicking said, 'but he's head winemaker at Mulroney's wines in Healesville.'

'You don't know your brothers address,' said Aleksander, 'I'm not sure I believe you.'

At that he pulled down the top of her jump suit and grabbed her other breast, so now her naked upper body was exposed to all and sundry and the continuous fondling of her upper parts was starting to arouse her responsive body.

'It's true, it's true, please believe me, he's only just left Margaret River for a new job there,' she said trying to pull the top of her jump suit to cover her naked breasts.

Aleksander slapped Bethany's offending hands away, and said, 'no you don't bitch I'm enjoying this.'

'I think she's telling us the truth, do you want one, he said lifting and offering Bethany's right breast to Andriy.'

'Thanks don't mind if I do,' said Andriy reaching over and pulling Bethany's right shoulder so she was now partially lying down across the central console, he now grabbed the offered source of pleasure.

'Now where were we?'

'Where were they the night before last?'

'In a B & B in Rockingham.'

'What's her mobile number?'

'I don't know,' but quickly before either twin could react she continued, 'it's on my phone in my bag.'

'Okay,' said Andriy delving into Bethany's white handbag, extracting her mobile and thumbing through her address book.

'That's good, that's the one we have.'

'Anything else?' He asked Aleksander.

'No I don't think so,' he laughed 'look at that her nipples are all aroused, shall we take her inside.'

''No unfortunately we haven't the time,' laughed Andriy releasing Bethany's breast and stepping from the Ute.

Right out you come,' he said grabbing Bethany by her ponytail and dragging her across the passenger seat.

'If you go to the Police we will know.'

'If you warn your daughter we will find out when we catch her.'

'If you tell anyone else we will know.'

If anything like this happens and we find out we will be back take our pleasure of you, for as long as we want and then if you are lucky when we've finished with you, my brother will take away all your woes by slitting your throat.

'Do you understand,' he said reinforcing the threat by tugging hard at Bethany's pony tail as he dragged her out of the Ute.

'Yes,' she sobbed.

Andriy had dumped her kneeling in the gravel at the front of her drive, and left Bethany sobbing, her slashed jump suit clutched to her bruised bosom.

Andriy threw the white handbag onto the drive after her, as soon as he re-entered the Ute, it moved away rapidly, wheels screeching, peppering the part recumbent Bethany with gravel.

'That was fun,' laughed Aleksander as he manoeuvred the Ute through the City of Bunbury.

'I still say we should have taken her inside.'

'Don't be daft, your dick is talking, don't forget the threat is all we need, this way she'll be unlikely to call the police.

'Your way, it becomes rape and the Ute would have been really noticeable, a strange car parked outside makes neighbours suspicious.'

'More seriously, we have to tell Fabio and he had better speak to Luca to find out what he wants to do.

'Also get a shift on brother, if we're lucky we might catch the Falcon on its way back north on the South Western Highway.'

Dragging his mobile from his shirt pocket, Andriy, thumbed up Fabio's number and set it to ring.

This time Fabio answered immediately,

'Andriy what's happening?'

'Have you found them?'

'Where are you?' continued Fabio in a deluge of questions.

'Hang on, hang on Fabio,' if you stop asking questions I'll tell you what's going on.

Andriy grimaced at Aleksander shaking his head with frustration.

His brother replied by putting his right forefinger to his temple and twisting it while mouthing idiot back to Andriy.

Andriy glossed over how they had lost the girls the previous afternoon and concentrated on informing Fabio about the intention of, Isla and her daughter's plan to travel to Victoria in search of their relation.

Fabio thinking hard replied, 'I'm going to have to tell Luca, he's due to call at lunchtime, he'll do his bloody nut I'm sure, especially if he thinks he's losing his daughter.'

'Damn, I'm glad he's locked up in Casuarina our lives would be hell otherwise.'

'O.K., leave it to me and thanks for your efforts, will be in touch.'

The Twins in the Ute, speeding up the freeway towards Fremantle, relaxed, believing their part in the pursuit of Isla and Alice must be over unless they were lucky enough to spot the Falcon before they reached the city.

19th FEBRUARY AM - BETHANY INVOLVES RYAN

By the time the Twins had concluded their assault of her mother a determined Isla was taking the diversion off the Kwinana Highway onto the Roe Highway, or State Route 3 as it was referred to on her Sat Nav.

She had pushed north as hard as she dared wanting to clear the environs of Perth before attempting to make any stop.

Alice had at times not been best pleased, and in the parts of the journey such as in between the many kilometres of trees on the Forrest Highway she had grizzled quite incessantly.

Isla had countered this by judicious use of music from Curtin FM, a West Australian favourite of hers

Isla realised she was going have to upset Alice frequently by doing long stages on this epic journey, hardened her heart and hoped Alice would get used the idea.

-***-

Bethany had been left sitting at the front of her own driveway in the dust of the twins Ute, half naked, bruised and scared beyond belief.

She had somehow, while trying to cover her half naked body with the remains of her jump suit stumbled back to her own front door. Somehow with trembling hands, Bethany had managed, after three quivering attempts to insert the key into the lock of the front door and on opening it, collapsed sobbing onto the beige rug in the entrance way.

After some time, she dragged herself to the en-suite bath room and turned on the shower until it was scalding hot.

After tearing the clothes from her assaulted and bruised body, Bethany had discarded the offending attire into the corner of the bathroom. Only then had she stepped into the shower cubicle before losing control and starting to cry again at which point she collapsed sobbing in a heap into the shower tray.

After a few minutes the scalding water started to bring her round, Bethany rose and scrubbed herself hard all over as if this at least could take away the effect of the sexual assault on her body.

After towelling herself down and clothing herself in her comforting, white, fluffy, cotton dressing gown, Bethany went to the kitchen and put on her kitchen gloves before returning to the en-suite, where she retrieved the discarded clothing and threw the offensive reminder of the morning in the waste disposal.

Having got to this point unscathed, Bethany deciding she couldn't let her tribulations, no matter how awful get in the way of protecting her daughter and granddaughter resolved to beat those two horrible men by warning Isla.

To stiffen her resolve, Bethany opened up a white laminated cupboard in their living room picked herself out a cut crystal whisky glass and poured herself a generous slug of Ray's favourite 10 year old Tobermory malt whisky.

Carefully she picked up the glass full of the golden liquid in her right hand and in her left she plucked the telephone from its plastic holder on the kitchen wall and carefully positioned herself on a white couch in the living area.

Bethany sipping the smooth, velvety, malt whisky from the Isla of Mull, tried desperately to forget about the threats and sexual assault of earlier and concentrate on finding a way of helping Isla and Alice.

Juggling the white house telephone in her left hand Bethany remembered, 'bloody hell, Isla promised to phone so I would have her new mobile number, I know she hasn't done it,'

'Sod it what do I do now?'

'How the bloody hell am I going to help them now?'

Feeling so helpless, Bethany screamed silently at the empty room and coughed, nearly choking on the rich taste of the whisky.

'How on earth am I going to do anything,' she thought extremely frustrated at her lack of choices to help the girls in the present unfolding situation.

In desperation and having no one else to call, Bethany decided to telephone Ryan, she had only met him a couple of times and didn't quite know how the conversation would go.

'There's no one else,' she consoled herself, 'at least he should understand and must have some idea of what we can do.'

-***-

Ryan had just at that moment lain down, as best as he could, on a blue lounger chair with white legs on the beach at Yanchep lagoon, his mates had kindly raised the back and made sure he could watch their escapades in the surf of the Indian Ocean.

They were headed out into the breaking seas and although he was in pain and not feeling much like doing anything, it felt better lying there getting the rays from the morning sunshine over his left shoulder, than sitting uncomfortably round his mate's apartment watching daytime soap operas.

He was surprised when he heard the Surf's up, by the Beach Boys coming from his tote bag lying on the sand alongside the lounger.

Reaching down with his good right arm, Ryan hooked the white, cord drawstring of the tote bag with the forefinger of his good right hand and deposited it onto his lap, he eased open the bag so he could reach inside and fetch out and answer his tuneful mobile.

Twice with the impatience of someone wanting to know who was on the other end of the cell, he tried to insert his hand into the opening of the bag with it still being too tight.

Getting exasperated by the incessant musical noise of the mobile and his inability to retrieve it from the tote bag, Ryan cursed aloud and screamed at the seagulls wheeling above him in the blue un-clouded sky.

Turning the bag upside down, he shook it hard in anger, at which point the cell flew out of the tight opening and landed with a plop in the sand about five metres from where he was ensconced on the blue lounger.

Momentarily forgetting about his plastered left arm with its finger splint protruding from his white protective sling, Ryan tried to leap from the lounger to salvage the mobile before the caller gave up.

'Damn, that bloody hurts,' he swore loudly at the pain caused by moving too rapidly and without allowing for his injuries.

Typically as he carefully bent down to retrieve the mobile, from the warm, sandy beach the phone stopped its singing.

Brushing grains of sand from the instrument, by rubbing it on his khaki shorts, Ryan checked for the name of the caller.

'Bethany,' said the read out.

Ryan had to think hard for a moment about who Bethany was, having only met her briefly a couple of times and rarely hearing her referred to by her Christian name, he was at first confused.

'I must know her,' he concluded, 'after all my cell recognises the number.'

Then it struck him, 'bloody hell that's Isla's mum,' he remembered, 'she's Bethany.'

'Wonder what she wants?'

'Isla was never her greatest fan,' he recollected.

'Maybe she can give us a line on where they are though, better ring her back,' Ryan thought hopefully.

Having made a decision, Ryan returned to his lounger, glanced up and out at his mates, treading water while they waited for the big one from the blue Indian Ocean, before thumbing his cell and returning the call from Bethany.

Bethany answered the call quickly, almost before it had time to ring a second time, she recognised the number she had just been calling and launched into an outburst at Ryan over the phone.

'Is that Ryan?'

'Yes,' and before he could continue further, Bethany interrupted his train of thought.

'I don't know what happened between you two but Isla's in the crap, big style,' she emphasised.

'She's trying to get away from Luca and there's two horrible east European thugs after her.'

'They really hurt me,' she sobbed as she burst into tears remembering what the twins had done and threatened her with.

Ryan, with his own injuries due to his previous meeting with Andriy and Aleksander was able to emphasise with Bethany's plight but he was embarrassed because he didn't know how to address her.

For a moment there was a long pause, with Bethany sobbing at the end of the phone in Bunbury and Ryan tongue tied on a beach in Yanchep.

Finally, Ryan determined he had to take control of the situation, grasped the nettle and replied, 'Look love I've been there myself, have a broken arm and finger thanks to those thugs.'

'Please tell me what's happened to Isla and Alice, where are they?' he added, concern in his voice.

Bethany now having someone else who had suffered at the hands of the twins to commiserate with, stopped crying and said to Ryan, 'It was awful, they threatened and really hurt me, it must have been awful for you though, having your bones broken like that.'

'They were bloody horrible,' she continued.

'I know, I know but what's happened to Isla and Alice,' repeated Ryan, concern in his voice.

Bethany blurted out, 'they've gone to Victoria, to my brother Brian, I'm really worried, and I don't know how she'll do it on her own with my granddaughter in the back of the car all that way as well.'

'Christ that was quick when did they fly out?'

'No, no you've got it wrong they didn't fly, she's driving that bloody car of hers, she won't give up the Falcon, she says it's the only major asset they've got,' retorted Bethany, regaining some of her spirit and attitude.

'More importantly, what did you tell those gruesome thugs of Luca's?' Asked Ryan, wondering how he could help.

I don't know, all those horrible bloody men know is that she's going to a vineyard in the Yarra Valley, not how she's getting there.'

'Why's that?'

'Isla's decided they will be safer there with my brother, he works near Healesville, at somewhere called Mulroney's vineyard.'

'The only thing is, they've made me tell them where they're going,' sobbed Isla through the speaker on Ryan's mobile.

'Alright, alright,' commiserated Ryan, embarrassed by the sound of a grown woman crying.

'I'll find some way to warn them,' he consoled her.

'Will you, oh that would be fantastic Ryan,' answered Bethany, who in her home in Bunbury, dabbed her swollen eyes with a tissue and stopped crying.

'Of course, of course, I've really messed up, love those girls and I'm not prepared to let that Wop and his thugs mess with my life anymore,' replied Ryan with more bravado than he actually felt.

'I'll have to go now and work out how I'm going to do this, thanks for letting me know.'

Bethany enthused her appreciation, before ending the call.

Eventually Ryan was able to slump back onto his lounger, a look of desperation on his face and a feeling of frustration as he considered all the impossible problems of getting to Victoria and then finding, never mind protecting the girls, even assuming he managed to get there.

'I'm busted up quite badly, I've got no cash and the cops want to know where I am,'

'Oh crap' he swore out aloud at the swooping cawing gulls above him, as he remembered he hadn't telephoned the investigating policeman as he was supposed to.

Now totally depressed, he responded by extracting the card he had been given, from his ever present duffle bag and dialled the number of his tormentor.

'Ah Ryan, glad you called, hope your injuries aren't causing you too many problems?'

'I trust you've called to tell me what really happened and where you are staying?'

Ryan realising how little he could tell the law officer because of the threat from Luca's two Ukrainian thugs replied.

'I've nothing to add to what I told you at the hospital, I'm only calling to tell you where I'm living and to ask if you are going to do anything more about my weed.'

Ryan explained about dossing down on his pal's sofa in Yanchep.

'Okay son,' that's good enough for now.'

'I have to see you about the cannabis though, so I want to see you when I'm next on shift.'

'Let's see,'

There was a pause and Ryan could hear, the Officer he assumed typing heavily on a keyboard at the other end of the phone.

'Right in two days then, present yourself at the front desk at Scarborough nick, CID will also want a chat about those two European thugs as well, hopefully we'll have picked them up by then.'

Ryan replied, 'yes, alright then,' frustrated, disconsolate and feeling trapped by the circumstances, he lay back on the lounger and screamed loudly at the heavens and the wheeling screaming gulls.

19th FEBRUARY LUNCH - ORDERS FROM CASUARINA PRISON

Lunch over, Luca and Spike were locked in their cell awaiting the call to return to their afternoon labours in the prison industries.

Luca, impatient to know what was happening outside and unsuspecting about Isla's disappearance told Spike, 'hand it over and listen out for the screws unlocking, I suspect I don't have much time today.'

'Okay boss,' said Spike retrieving the cell from under his mattress, on the top bunk and handing it down to Luca, sitting perched in green prison dungarees on the edge of the lower bunk.

'Ah Fabio, how's things, trust Isla and my lovely daughter are staying with our aged parents at the moment.'

'Have you found them somewhere to live yet?' He continued.

Fabio, expecting an adverse reaction from his incarcerated, elder brother answered tentatively, 'Luca, I'm afraid there has been a bit of a problem.'

Luca angrily interrupted his brother's response, 'what the bloody hell do you mean by a bit of a problem?'

'It's always the same with you, you can never get anything right, I give you a couple of simple tasks to do and you totally mess up as usual.'

Fabio, who was scared to death of his brother when angry like this, plucked up the courage to interrupt his sibling's diatribe.

'Luca listen, it's nothing to do with me, its Isla, she's cleared off with the kid,' he shouted fearfully down the phone.

'What do you mean she's cleared off, they were only here less than two days ago, she was telling me how much she loved me, there must be some sort of mistake,' replied Luca questioning Fabio fiercely.

'Anyway what happened to Andriy and Aleksander, I told you to get them to keep an eye on her?'

'I did, they had to deal with her boyfriend first.'

There was an explosion at the other end of the phone as Fabio suddenly realised what he had just said.

'BOYFRIEND!' screamed Luca, 'what the bloody hell are you talking about.'

'Shush mate, the bloody screws will hear you and then we'll be buggered,' said Spike forcefully but quietly.

'Yeah, alright, alright,' agreed Luca his face puce with anger at Fabio's announcement.

Fabio could hear Luca's cellmate calling for calm and took the opportunity to try and explain Ryan.

'She's been living with him for months up in Glendalough, I didn't want you to know until you needed to.'

Luca interrupted Fabio's attempt to justify the situation, 'have you no bloody pride, you tell me she's been screwing someone else while your niece has been there.'

'Have you no pride, what about the family, she's been screwing all sorts and you've let it happen.'

'You've let that bitch insult the family name by letting her carry on this bloody affair, you are a bloody miserable excuse for a brother.'

'Okay, okay,' replied an infuriated but compliant younger brother, knowing better from previous demeaning experience, that he could only get himself into serious grief if he disagreed with his elder sibling.

Luca, who had now taken control of his emotions said, 'you better explain what's gone on in the last two days since the last visit, it appears everything totally buggered up.'

Fabio given the chance explained about the crippling of Ryan, the traffic jam preventing the twins from following the girls from the prison, their disappearance, his successful idea about finding Bethany, the twins messing up again in Bunbury and missing the girls again.

'Finally,' said Fabio,' they forced the mother to tell them where Isla was taking Alice next.'

'Where?' interrupted an irritated Luca.

'Victoria.'

'What the bloody hell is she taking my daughter there for?'

'Apparently there's an Uncle there, something to do with wine, and she thinks she'll be safe there from you,' answered Fabio.

At that moment Spike reached down and gripped Luca's shoulder, 'unlock mate, better be quick, you've only a couple of minutes left.'

Thinking quickly, Luca acknowledged by looking at and nodding to Spike.

'I've only got moments Fabio, this is what's going to happen this time and no fuck-ups, you understand.'

'Alright,' agreed his sibling.

'Those two idiots have messed up, it's alright coming heavy in a private situation but it seems to me they've messed up in public, twice.' He emphasised.

'Tell them to get after the bitch, I don't care what happens to her but I want Alice recovered and taken to our parents, where she'll be properly looked after.'

'Tell them to get the plates changed on that bloody tank of theirs because I suspect someone has reported them by now.'

'Oh, and tell them to use out of state plates, it changes the whole perspective of the bloody vehicle.'

'Right one more thing, the three of you had better get this right this time otherwise I won't be answerable for the consequences.'

At that moment, Spike leapt off his bunk grabbed the mobile from Luca's hand and slammed it under the mattress.

Just as he was about to remonstrate with Spike, Luca suddenly realised he could hear voices outside of their cell and a grating as the turned in the lock on the outside of their cell door.

A uniformed Officer with clipboard in left hand and keys in the other stuck his head in the door, 'both at work this afternoon aren't you?'

Luca nodded his head at Spike as if to say thanks for the intervention, 'yes we both are,' he nodded agreeing with the Officer.

19th FEBRUARY PM – FABIO CALLS A MEETING

Fabio was fuming to himself as he drove to a meeting he had called with the twins at the behest of his elder brother.

'The bollocking from Luca was totally uncalled for, I didn't tell him about the boyfriend to protect his feelings,' Fabio excused himself rather than admit to his previous ideas of cuckolding his sibling.

'Anyway he's the stupid sod doing the time, shouldn't have got caught should he?' he thought, conveniently forgetting it was his own grassing that had put Luca in Casuarina in the first place.

Fabio smiled to himself as he realised, 'thanks to Luca's anger, I'm in a great position to pass the bollocking down the line to those Ukrainian idiots.'

'Brilliant.'

Previously, shortly after breaking the news to Luca, Fabio had called the twins and told them about Luca not being pleased and the urgent need for the forthcoming meeting.

Fabio had instructed the twins to meet him at their regular haunt, the Villa Napoli in Fremantle where thanks to the Mancuso connections they were guaranteed a private table no matter the time of day or night.

Parking his vehicle close by the restaurant in the old town of Fremantle, Fabio exited his car, checked his appearance in nearside wing mirror and stroked back his dark full head of hair with the fingers of his left hand and made his way to the restaurant.

He was recognised as he walked through the door and after confirming he needed a quiet table for a business meeting was ushered to a recently closed section at the rear of the pizzeria, which had just been cleared after the late lunch crowd.

'I've two guests arriving shortly,' he explained confirming the identity of the twin's to the maître d.

'I'll need a couple of bottles of Peroni for them and a glass of red for me, the usual please,' he suggested.

'Fine sir, will you be eating this afternoon?'

"I don't think so, if we change our minds I'll let you know.'

What we really need is the privacy and no interference, is that alright with you?' Asked Fabio slipping the maître d a twenty dollar bill.

The maître d acknowledged the tip by saluting unobtrusively and left to arrange the party's drinks. He arranged with the chef for some complimentary antipasto and told the barman to be prompt with the drinks as soon as Fabio's guests arrived.

A few minutes later the Ukrainian brothers entered the Villa Napoli, having just returned from Bunbury and eager to find out what Luca's reaction had been to the events of the last two days.

The maître d recognising Fabio's guests, interceded into the attempt by one of the waiters to seat the arriving party and re-directed them to where Fabio was sitting.

He also indicated to the barman, by using whispering discreetly that the drinks should be served.

By the time the twins were sitting down, a waiter was serving the beers to the brothers and red wine to Fabio.

Another waiter produced the antipasto as if by sleight of hand so the maître d was able to say to Fabio.

'Compliments of the house signor, if there is anything else we can do, please ask.'

'Enjoy your meeting,' he added as he left them to their task.

Fabio who saw no reason to get himself into any further trouble with the Ukrainian siblings had made up his mind to treat this meeting delicately while getting them to retrieve the child and put it into the guardianship of his parents.

'Luca contacted me in the last hour, and to say he is not pleased, is to understate the case,' said Fabio.

'Also he now knows the girl had a boyfriend, since and while Luca has been in prison.'

Andriy went to say something, in between taking a swig of beer from the bottle of Peroni the waiter had placed in front of him.

Fabio held up his right hand, palm towards Andriy to stay the Ukrainian's interruption.

'I need to finish, then you'll get your bloody chance to answer.'

'Luca says you had better find the girls, he doesn't care what happens to the woman now but he wants his daughter taken unharmed to our parents in Rockingham.'

'He also thinks you need to change the plates on your car, or get rid of it, if you've been anything, it's too visible the last couple of days.'

'Okay, now what are you going to do about the situation,' he stated picking up his glass of red wine and sipping it as if in appreciation of its qualities.

Aleksander and Andriy twisted sideways to look at each other, the former nodded, as if to say you tell him, at which point Andriy turned and faced Fabio.

'Sure we'll go after her, it will take a while though, we may have to drive to Victoria and I believe it's a very long way.'

'Why's that?' Interrupted Fabio suspecting he had already guessed right about there being illegals.

'We don't have papers so we can't fly.'

'Anyway it would look suspicious trying to bring the child back on a plane without the correct documentation wouldn't it?'

'You're right,' agreed Fabio nodding his head.

'We like the Ute, so we aren't giving it up especially with the sort of trip you're proposing.'

'Luca's idea about changing plates is a good one, we'll pick out a Victoria registration that's already here in WA and we know someone who'll fix us up with new ones before we leave.'

'Do you know how she and the child are getting to Victoria,' asked Fabio.

'Blast we never asked the mother that,' said Aleksander intervening.

'I agree but we didn't know about needing that information at the time,' agreed Andriy.

'Yes it was a big error wasn't it,' alleged Fabio sarcastically.

'You had better drink up and get to it, let me know what's happening before noon daily, so I can keep Luca informed, otherwise there will be hell to pay.'

Andriy nodded at his brother, both of them realised Luca could cause them a lot of problems even from his cell in Casuarina, especially their being illegal, arrest and return to Kiev was not something to be risked.

'Alright we'll get on it immediately, got plates to change and stuff to pack and we need some kip but should be under way in the early hours, if we both drive we should make good progress.'

'Fine then let's get out of here,' said Fabio knocking back the remainder of his glass of wine.'

'Speak to you in the morning,' he said, 'don't forget to let me know how you're doing before lunch every day so I can keep Luca happy, Okay.'

'Alright,' consented Andriy and Aleksander nodded his head in agreement.

The two parties split up at the entrance to the restaurant and as the Twins made their way down Queen Street, Andriy said to his brother.

'Better sort the vehicle first, I think they're right about changing plates, we're going to Victoria so we need a set of those, let's get hold of Alf at his chop shop, he can make us a set that'll pass muster.'

'Good idea,' agreed Aleksander and if we get on the road really early, we'll be well clear of the CBD before anyone can get suspicious.'

'Right, let's get sorted, fix the car, load it up, get some kip, and light out of here in the early hours.'

'Done,' concurred his brother.

19th FEBRUARY EVENING – ISLA STRUGGLES TO SOUTHERN CROSS

Isla decided they would stop at Northam well east of the Perth CBD, after about three hours driving from Bunbury.

She felt safer, 'they were away from Luca's influence and there would be no chance of meeting Ryan accidentally out there,' she had decided.

'Christ how did I think we could do seven hundred plus kilometres in one day, after the battering Ryan gave me only three days ago,' she said to herself.

They'd had to stop at Northam, the warning light on the petrol tank had been glowing redder and redder for the previous sixty kilometres and a wailing Alice had been announcing her dissatisfaction for the previous hour.

Like most drivers whose fuel warning light has been burning for a while, Isla had been near to panic, scared of running out of petrol, and counting down the kilometres to the approaching town and the chance of refuelling.

Suddenly after what had seemed like hours of arid brown fields interspersed with straggly eucalyptus they had swept round a corner of I-94 into Western Australian suburbia, a local engineering works followed by a school with swimming pool on their right and typical single story Australian houses on their left.

Alice stopped her complaint at the sight of something interesting and before she could start grizzling again Isla had swept the Falcon to the left into Northam's BP garage, which had appeared like a shining beacon, out of the dust of the preceding traffic.

Parking the vehicle alongside a free pump, in the relative shade of the green canopy and close to the garages small shop. Isla gasped at the burning heat which hit her as she opened her car door and eased her aching body out of the driver's seat.

She stood up stretched her arms and bent her back to try and draw out the kinks from her body before easing a tear stained Alice from her seat in the rear of the Falcon.

Isla placed Alice alongside her and opened the fuel cap, the opening gasped because of the vacuum as if in disapproval at the lack of petrol.

After filling the tank, Isla took the little girl into the shop, paid for the fuel and used the opportunity of the available rest room to freshen them both up.

'Where can we get something to eat please?' Isla asked the mature lady in her green and yellow uniform as she paid for the fuel.

'Follow the main highway right across the bridge,' the attendant replied 'then straight left onto the High Street, there's a number of places there love.'

She looked over and smiled at the two girls, 'lovely little girl you've got there,' she said agreeably as Isla turned to leave the shop.

'Thanks very much and have a nice day yourself,' replied Isla.

Shortly after, having crossed the narrow bridge over the nearly dry Avon River, Isla parked in front of a bakery on the High Street.

Lifting Alice out, they made their way past an elderly couple sitting, eating and drinking, at a table on the sidewalk outside the shop. Isla and Alice made their way into the cool interior where they were pleasantly assaulted by the smell of freshly baked bread and pastries.

Isla ordered a carton of strawberry flavoured milk and a gingerbread man at the little girl's insistence, Isla quickly scoffed a pie, and drunk half a litre of refreshingly cold water before returning with Alice to the warming interior of the Falcon, she secured Alice with her food and drink in the rear of the Falcon.

Looking through her road atlas, Isla made note of the individual towns and the distances between them, she almost despaired at the thought of being cooped up in the car with Alice for another five hundred kilometres.

'That's the plan, I made the decision, we'll just to have to grin and bear it,' she said over her shoulder to a placated Alice. Isla didn't bother with the sat-nav she was sure there was only the one road and it would be well sign posted.

She reversed the Falcon back onto the High Street then pointed its nose east.

'Besides we've a motel booked, it's only five hours,' she said to the little girl who was taking in the sights of Northam and slurping her milk through a pink straw as they eased through the town.

Within the hour, Isla was aching again, even though the Falcon was making good progress on cruise control, she couldn't decide, and moaned to herself 'which is the most comfortable position, to put my legs and feet?'

Isla tried different positions for her legs and feet, none of them were really comfortable so she tried to put the discomfort out of her mind.

To help her focus on the journey rather than the planned final days end at Kalgoorlie, Isla decided to concentrate on getting to the next town, which was why she had made the list, which was perched on the dashboard in front of her.

After Northam her next objective was Cunderdin, a distance of 60 kilometres, the road was single track well maintained with occasional passing places to overtake the slower trucks.

Alice had obviously decided she couldn't win by crying and after her brief lunch had to Isla's grateful relief dozed off.

The scenery wasn't the most inspiring with the edge of the tarmac turning to yellow sun bleached sand, flanked by thin, white bleached trunks of leafy eucalyptus.

Occasionally she could see mighty fields, of ready to harvest, golden wheat stretching as far as the eye could see.

They passed frequent turnings onto sandy tracks, marked by colourfully painted metal boxes on rusty steel stakes, awaiting Australia Posts daily delivery.

The turning for Grass Valley and its tarmacked junction flashed by on their left, whilst she automatically slowed for Meckering with its garish yellow Shell Station brightening the otherwise mainly white buildings on either side of the road.

At times the road was so straight in its easterly direction it disappeared into the distance.

Occasional cars flashed by west bound, they overtook little, except occasional lumbering road trains and a few slower delivery trucks.

Thirty minutes later they were approaching Cunderdin as they rounded a left handed bend in the highway Isla could see a large white building ahead, on her left a large white pipeline had for a while been obstructing their view to the north of the road.

'Must be the water pipeline to the goldfields,' she remembered debates about its usefulness in periods of drought.

Isla moved her stiffening right leg to ease the car out of cruise control and down to the new speed limit of 70 as they approached the small town, someone had started harvesting the acres of wheat on their right,

Then they were passing the first of the few buildings, the water pipeline disappeared under the road and a yard full of huge green harvesters loomed to their right as they rushed past.

Isla drove carefully through two crossroads, a sign pointed out Main Street to their left and another brown sign directed visitors to pumping station three, on the other side of the road.

Suddenly they were through and the water pipeline came back under the road paralleling the highway again on the left side of the Falcon.

Isla glanced at her note, Kellerberrin was the next town it indicated, she started to increase speed as the speed limit signs allowed, then there it was to her left a green highway sign Kellerberrin 46, she tried not to notice or think about the bottom town and distance on the sign, Kalgoorlie 439.

Shortly after the distance sign she was able to put the car back up to hundred and ten and reset the cruise control.

Kellerberrin, that's about another thirty minutes, she thought, taking the opportunity to swig from the warming bottle of water mounted in the dashboard cup holder.

Within a few kilometres Isla realised there was a single line railway track the other side and to the north of the pipeline, gradually the trees thinned out and the road was fringed by scrubland with large fields occasionally visible in the distance to the south. There were still the occasional dusty dirt tracks mainly to her left to occasionally visible homesteads.

At somewhere called Tammin the pipeline disappeared under the road and the railway line tracks crossed from one side to the other, the Falcon's suspension hardly transferred the bump of the crossing to Isla and it didn't interfere with Alice's sleep.

The railway track was now alongside only separated from the road by a yellow sandy median with the pipeline to the outer side of the railway track.

The road now started to rise and shortly after they swept past a blue road sign advertising Tammin's facilities.

The first sign of the approaching conurbation was a white sun bleached graveyard on their left side.

Then surprisingly where the railway line double tracked on their left was The Indian Pacific in all its glory, stopped in the siding. The wedge tailed eagle marked each of its silver carriages before at its eastern end they passed the bright blue diesel engine, which was hauling the famous train.

Suddenly they were sweeping round a bend and through Tammin, Isla spotted the huge row of tall white grain silos, alongside the road. These appeared to overwhelm the small town and then they were through, if anything the road ahead seemed even more barren with only the wheat fields either side disappearing into the distance.

Isla saw the green distances sign and despaired at the Kalgoorlie 414 as its bottom reading.

Then as they moved round a left hand bend in the road, the railway returned with the pipeline again on its outside.

In the next fifteen minutes, the scenery of scrub, small dried out trees, and wheat fields didn't change much but the railway disappeared to the south, the pipeline crossed under the road and reappeared on their north side. Shortly before Kellerberrin, they crossed, with a slight bump over the returning single track of the railway.

Kellerberrin passed very quickly, all the commercial properties, butcher, police, bank, pharmacy were concentrated on the south side of the highway with the pipeline and he railway appearing to restrict growth on the north side of the road.

At eastern end of town were the inevitable tall, white grain silos, just before the next green distance sign, Merredin Isla's next target a paltry 55 as against 392 for the inevitable Kalgoorlie.

Isla's aching shoulders and bottom were now numb with sitting in the driver's seat, so as she increased speed back up to 110 she tried to stretch herself while steering the car.

'I reckon we can do this,' she thought, 'Let Alice sleep and keep thinking of it in thirty minute chunks.'

At Hines Hill a tiny hamlet with a fuelling station Isla used the overtaking lane, to pass a huge road train tanker with its three, shiny, stainless steel tanks glinting in the sunlight.

At Merredin Isla was shocked out of her almost automaton steering of the car by a yell from an awakening Alice.

The railway had returned on their left and as they steadily passed through the town on the highway, 'it looks nice and peaceful,' thought Isla, 'everything is so neat.' They soon cleared the small conurbation and then it was back onto the soporific continuation of the journey.

'Hope Alice stays settled for a while,' she wished glancing back in the rear view mirror and seeing the little girl rubbing at her sleepy eyes.

Great Eastern Highway said the sign, Southern Cross 109 was their next target.

'If the plan comes together and you stay with it we'll stop at Southern Cross in an hour,'

'Would you like that?'

Alice yawned widely in answer.

An hour later after spending most of it telling stories to keep Alice happy they arrived in Southern Cross. There was little signage to help to help them find somewhere to eat.

Isla seeing a blue sign indicating a motel to the left turned down the appropriately named Altair Street, just a little way up the red dust covered tarmac was another sign for the Motel advertising food, children welcome and rooms. Isla pulled gratefully in to the Motel car park.

19th FEBRUARY PM – RYAN MAKES A PLAN

Ryan who had dozed off on his sun lounger was woken by shouts from his returning surfing colleagues.

'Ryan you're in enough of a mess, don't want to get burnt to a crisp.'

'Hope you've got plenty of sun cream on.'

'Surf was brilliant, you don't know what you're missing.'

'Hope you haven't let anybody nick our gear.'

'Poor guard dog aren't you?'

Were some of the shouted comments that woke him from his pleasant dreams?

As they all crowded round him collecting their gear together, Ryan interrupted their industry.

'I need to get out of here, got to get to Melbourne as quick as I can.'

'Why's that?' someone in the crowd of friends asked.

'Got to go after Isla, the ex.'

'The two thugs who did this,' he said pointing to his broken arm, 'know where she's going, and I don't think she knows, they know her destination.'

'Just take the plane, there's loads of flights and they're cheap as chips nowadays.'

'Can't the cops want to question me again and they say I can't leave the CBD.'

'There's no way I'll get away with it if I'm on some plane manifest.'

That silenced everyone for a moment, then one of the girls spoke up.

'There used to be a daily coach service, the cheap planes have killed that, the Indian Pacific only goes weekly, even in the sit up and beg, it costs an arm and a leg.' She said referring to the seat only class on the train.

'I don't care if it is expensive when does it go' I need to get there as soon as possible,' answered Ryan in despair.

'No good then she only goes on a Sunday and its Wednesday today.'

'Damn, there must be some other bloody way to get over there, I'd risk taking the Ute but I can't drive because of the bloody mess my arms in.

'It's quite easy to get you a lift, we'll either go on Gumtree or Coseats, maybe both, when we get back, that'll get you a lift in the next 48 hours easy,' declared his mate who was giving him a sofa to sleep on.

'You sure?'

'Pretty certain mate, you'll probably have to sling in some cash for fuel but otherwise there's people advertising daily for companions on the trip.

'Brilliant, let's get out of here,' said Ryan enthusiastically jumping up off the lounger.

Everyone laughed, picked up their wet clothing, surf boards and other gear before heading for the car park and their transport.

-***-

Thirty minutes later back at his friend's house, Ryan was perched on his sleeping sofa, red laptop on the coffee table in front of him.

'Where did you say, which do you reckon has got most chance?' He asked his mate.

'Well with Coseat you advertise what you want first and see if you get any replies, Gumtree may be better, you can see if anyone's offering lifts and answer them straight away.'

'Thanks, I'll try Gum tree first then,' replied Ryan tapping into the computer with his right index finger.

He soon found Gumtree and modelled his request for anything going across the Nullarbor, then glanced through the adverts.

At first it was mainly others looking for a lift, two Italian girls, a French easy going boy called Bertrand, a bunch of people with a pair of trucks going sightseeing on the way with spare seats.

Ryan would have taken that if he could, it might have taken a while but he would have got there.

Almost at the bottom of the page was his ideal, 'Free Ride Perth to Melbourne,' was the headline.

Ryan clicked into the advert for further details, it gave an address for a suburb of Perth and then said,

'Hi I'm driving a small truck from Perth to Melbourne leaving 12pm Friday 21/02/2014, any Backpackers needing a lift.'

'The address it gave was in Mindarie,' Ryan called out to his mate who was in the kitchen.

'Hey look at this Mindarie, that's just down the road from here isn't it?'

'Sure is,' was the reply, 'what's up?'

'There's a guy advertising a lift from Mindarie to Melbourne, Friday,' he said turning the computer so his mate could see the advert.

'Looks kosher to me better get on the blower quick and see what the guy says.'

At that Ryan reached for his mobile and went to dial in the number, then he realised there wasn't a full number, you had to be a member of Gumtree to get that.

'Damn,' he swore out loud.

'I've got to join Gumtree to find out the guys phone number.'

'So'

'I need an address.'

'Use your old one, even if your landlord realises you've done a runner it's too soon for you to be blacklisted yet.'

'You sure,' replied Ryan tentatively.

'Of course you daft bugger, get joined up and get on the blower before someone else nicks the lift.'

Having been given the push, Ryan was soon registered, given a password by return e mail, logged in and was able to access the required telephone number of the person offering the lift.

Ryan picked up his mobile tentatively and looked at it, what if wants someone to share the driving, maybe it's not kosher, could be there's something weird going on,' he expostulated trying to pluck up the courage to ring the number.

His mate strode across the room and grabbed Ryan's mobile from his hand, 'What's the bloody number?'

'You'll never get the ruddy lift thinking about it.'

Looking over Ryan's shoulder at the computer he dialled in the telephone number showing and set the mobile to call.

'Here it's ringing,' he said handing back the cell to the seated Ryan.

Three rings later and a guy answered the call.

'Bruce here.'

'Hi, believe you're offering a lift to Melbourne tomorrow, could use it if you've got no one else.'

'Depends, me and the family are moving over there, they're on the plane but I've got to take the truck across.'

'I'm not sightseeing, am going straight through and we'll be kipping on a couple of mattresses in the back if that's alright?'

'Yeah and if you can fill the tank every other time, that'll be a big help too.'

'Sounds good to me,' replied Ryan.

'I can't help with the driving though I've a busted left arm.'

'That's all right, just have plenty to chat about to keep me awake, will that be okay?'

'That's fine with me, what are we doing about grub?'

'Bring as much as you need, don't intend paying those roadhouse prices and on the other side we'll do some fast food, you reckon.'

'Sounds ace to me,' replied Ryan, 'when and where do you want me to meet you?

'Get your backside with your gear over here about ten the morning after next and we'll get underway.'

'See you then, and oh by the way my name's Ryan.'

'Fine Ryan, Bruce here see you Friday ten sharp.'

Call ended, Ryan repeated the call for his mate.

'Sounds like you've done well there, hope he's got bars on his truck otherwise you might be having a losing scrap with a kangaroo or something else across the Nullarbor if he drives at the wrong time.'

19th FEBRUARY PM – SOUTHERN CROSS TO KALGOORLIE

Isla now partially refreshed, well fed and rested after an hour at the Motel in Southern Cross, drove the Falcon back onto the Great Eastern Highway and pointed its bonnet eastwards towards Kalgoorlie, Alice safely returned to her seat in the rear.

'That was pure luck, the gods must have been smiling us, that place had everything we needed, food, children's play area and changing facilities, the lot didn't it darling.' Isla said aloud to Alice

Alice who had found chasing round after lots of noisy toys, in a large play area great fun; was now happily eying the moving, dusty, scenery of Southern Cross from her perch in the rear of the Falcon, gripping tightly onto a partially full bottle of warm milk.

They were soon edging out of Southern Cross passing between the two dusty forecourts of the petrol stations on the eastern perimeter of the town.

'Everywhere here is covered in red dust, even the tarmac of the roadway,' noticed Isla.

'It's even in my hair,' she realised as she stroked the fingers of her left hand through her blond locks.

'This is real Australia Alice, the outback and the red soil, it's all totally different to back home on the coast.'

Clearing the town they could see Kalgoorlie's lifeline the white, water pipeline about five hundred metres to the South as they approached the 110kph sign.

Isla took the opportunity to ease the Falcon back up to the speed limit as they swept pass the green distance sign. Coolgardie 187 and Kalgoorlie 226, were the two distances designated in white.

'That's good Alice only two hours more, we should arrive before dark, it's just before four now,' declared Isla to her daughter.

At that moment as they were sweeping past a yellow and white striped Tanker with single trailer in the parking area to their left, a small single engine prop plane flew low overhead from the north side towards the dirt runway on their right.

'All happening at once Alice and even the pipeline has gone to the other side of the road,' said Isla to her daughter, noticing its change of position.

At first there were wheat filled fields to the south and on their left dusty scrubland with the never ending pipeline limiting further views.

At Ghooli a crossroads, where the intersecting roads were ones of dusty track they passed Pumping Station No.6.

They were now driving between low lying trees and bushes and except for the very occasional car or truck speeding past in the other direction there was little company except for the grey telegraph poles marking the highway ahead of them.

An occasional dirt passing place would appear after a brief warning, a site where the trees and bushes had been ripped out to leave an indentation in the flora for traveller's emergencies.

These parking places marked only with a yellow waste bin, fixed between two wooden poles, sometimes at a large indentation in the flora there might be two of these bins.

About thirty kilometres from Southern Cross, they rushed through Yellowdine, a yellow Shell garage on the left side appropriately marking its passing.

The distance marker reared up shortly after, Kalgoorlie 194 was its message.

Isla who was settling into the monotony of the journey, was ignoring her aches and pains by concentrating on telling Alice about every last possible thing they saw on the journey.

'Another marker darling, less than two hundred K now, buzzing,' she exclaimed to the little girl.

At somewhere called Karalee Rocks the water pipeline returned to accompany the highway on the north side of the road.

Shortly after, rounding a left hand curve the road appeared to stretch away without deviation straight to the horizon, the wheat fields disappeared and from there on it was bush on either side, telegraph poles and the occasional rest area.

Isla tried singing to Alice and telling those nursery rhymes she could remember from her own childhood.

The little girl seemed happy enough and would occasionally point at what appeared to be her favourite distraction, the large trucks with trailer going in the opposite direction. These would often make the Falcon rock with the wind of their passing, this made Alice giggle every time and she was constantly on the lookout for more of them, peering into the distance ahead of the speeding car.

Just over an hour later they passed a white building on their right, Rock Tavern, 'Last chance Ice Cold Beer and Petrol For long long Time,' said the sign which ran the length of the building.

'Ice cold beer would be nice but the long, long time must be the other way, where we've come from,' surmised Isla as they cruised past the next green distance sign, Kalgoorlie 68 was the indication.

'That's brilliant Alice,' she yelled 'just over half an hour, nearly there.'

The road returned to scrub and sand either side, Isla didn't mind, the end of the days travel was in sight and the longest planned run was nearly over.

Within twenty minutes Isla was easing the Flacon down to the ninety kph speed limit for Coolgardie, a large caravan site on the left announced the first major civilisation for over two hours.

Within moments it seemed Isla was having to reduce their speed down to 60, the warning signs just before the twin welcoming signs for Coolgardie.

The road widened to a broad boulevard, Isla noticed the two story Denver Hotel on their right but little else as she concentrated on their passage down the Main Street, within moments the road returned to normal and they were leaving the western edge of Coolgardie with the Eagle Roadhouse on their right.

Just ahead of them, a large slowing white truck and trailer without markings, indicated and swung right towards Esperance. They carried straight on along highway 94 towards Kalgoorlie, within seconds they had cleared the city limit and there was the usual welcoming green sign 38 kilometres to Kalgoorlie indicated its white number this time.

'Twenty minutes Alice, we've nearly done it,' said Isla enthusiastically.

The sand appeared even redder now dust swept across the road in small whorls as it became obvious there was now a breeze outside, the scrubby bushes and stunted trees marked their passage along the highway.

The occasional turning off the road were now mainly tarmacked, well-marked and more conspicuous as if for use by heavy equipment.

'Probably for those huge open-cast mines they are always boasting about,' said Isla over her shoulder to the little girl.

Once clear of the outskirts of Coolgardie the road straightened and never deviated all the way north-east to Kalgoorlie.

Isla was concerned because she could see the sun getting lower in the sky to the rear of the car, the rear horizon was becoming streaked with purples and reds as the sun made its descent in the west.

There was little warning of their approach to the mining city, after the monotony of the arrow straight road, with no accompanying pipeline or even telegraph poles.

Isla kept glancing at the clock on the dashboard, to see how close they must be to their destination, with the boring sameness of the passing bush and the straightness of the road the last twenty minutes was taking forever.

Alice was getting fractious in the rear of the car and Isla felt like they had both done more than enough for the day.

In what appeared the middle of nowhere and without warning a pair of ninety kph signs sprang up on either side of the road and Isla slowed the Falcon to the new speed limit. An entry on their left with an indistinguishable red and white sign at the entrance was left in their dust trail.

Even though she knew it was coming, it was still a shock to suddenly come upon a rectangular yellow sign with traffic lights indicated and Prepare to Stop, in white letters on a red background.

Isla braked quite sharply and felt the bite from the tightening strap of the seatbelt. She quickly checked the rear view mirror to make sure Alice was secure, before pulling to a stop at the forewarned red traffic light at a major crossroads.

'Wow we must be here little one.'

'This is it Kalgoorlie, now to find our hotel.'

'Look out for it Alice it's called the Kalgoorlie Overland, should be on our left,' cried Isla joyfully.

At first the road had passed through motor courts, garages and industry well set back from the highway now it had become a dual carriageway with residential housing close to and either side of the road.

Just before the sixty kph at the city limit, there it was, their home for the night, Isla swung the car left into the entrance and pulled up alongside a sign advertising the Motel's Reception.

19th FEBRUARY EVENING – END OF THE DAY

Having got their heads down for the afternoon and in the fading light of early evening in a less salubrious part of Fremantle's dockland. The Twins were surreptitiously entering a small metal door set into a larger corrugated ingress at the front of a worn looking brick built warehouse.

A tired looking, square metal red sign adorned the left side of the entry. With its white lettering, streaked by rust, a passer-by would be able to just make out the words, ALF'S Engineering, Anything serviced, followed by a local telephone number.

The location and dingy advertising was meant to make the garage appear legal but put off the unsuspecting public. Inside though was a highly organised workshop where stolen cars were changed enough to sell onto gullible punters.

The brothers passed a number of expensive looking cars, looking freshly painted but were unable to see their Ute in the cavernous dimly lit depository. Taking the metal, grime covered stairs to the top of the building, where the only decent light, shone from the Office they made their way to Alf, the proprietors working abode.

Alf, a short, wiry man, with receding, dark, slick-backed hair, clothed in a once white, grubby, grease covered boiler suit was sitting behind a large wooden desk covered in even grubbier looking paperwork.

Except for the wide open glass fronted door the Office's four sided glass windows gave the owner a complete view of his less than legitimate empire.

Alf not rising from his desk greeted the Ukrainian brothers.

'Hi boys, afraid I've got some bad news for you.'

'Your Ute, she aint going nowhere for a while, you've some major problems with some wheel bearings on your rear axle.'

'Can get it fixed, by just after lunch tomorrow if you want, can't get the parts until the morning,' he said quickly seeing the thunderous look on the approaching Aleksander's face.

'You better not be pissing us about,' exclaimed Andriy furiously while grabbing his brother's left arm with his own right hand to prevent any over-reaction to the disappointing news.

'Look guys would I dare, Luca owns half this business,' Alf stated, waving his left arm to acknowledge the mass of vehicles below them.

'Anyway I've done you a favour, I believe you are going some distance and if you had gone over anything, pot-hole, road kill or something like that you would almost certainly have lost the axle and then you would be buggered.'

'Alright, alright, but you'll let us know as soon as it's ready?'

'Yeah and I've some cracking plates for you, come off a wreck last week, the Ute had an argument with a big red.'

'What's that, big red,' enquired Aleksander.

'A bloody big bastard of a Kangaroo mate, you don't want to hit one of them, they come up to two metres and the big males weigh around ninety kilogrammes and like all the other animals in Australia have no road sense.'

'What about the plates,' said an impatient Andriy, 'why are they so good?'

'They're off a the same make as yours, it was black rather than your blue but their Victorian which changes the whole aspect of your machine.'

'The best thing though the plates will still be on the cops computer as live, the previous machine hasn't been declared as scrap yet.'

Andriy thinking aloud replied, 'good, if we're going to have to wait, put us a couple of cans of extra fuel and water in the rear to save us having to do it when we get the machine back.'

'Alright, we'll get straight on the job as soon as the parts arrive, the boys have stripped it down ready, I'll give you a buzz just before we finish so you can pick it up straightaway.'

'Meanwhile there's a yellow Porsche Carrera down there you can borrow until then,' added Alf handing over the car's keys.

The twins acknowledged their thanks and left a much relieved proprietor at his desk, reaching into the drawer on the right of his desk, he pulled out a bottle of Bundaberg dark rum, uncapped it and with a sigh of relief took a large swig to calm his fractious nerves.

-***-

Over six hundred kilometres to the east, Isla had settled Alice down into the motel supplied cot and was herself easing her aching body, stretched out on the comfortable king-sized bed.

They had eaten in the Motel restaurant shortly after their arrival, Alice had a chance to wander around and meet some friendly other residents before they returned to this, their room for the night.

Safely secure, with the Motel room's entry door double locked with safety chain in place, Isla thought, 'I had better ring Moira and Arthur, then mother to let them all know we are safe.'

After reassuring her Rockingham friends of their safety, plans and progress Isla telephoned her mother.

-***-

After her telephone call to Ryan and encouraged by her actions in communicating with him. Bethany had aroused herself from the lethargy caused by her earlier trauma and went round the property locking doors and windows so she had felt more secure.

After that she had returned to the sofa and present security of the malt whisky bottle.

Sometime later when Bethany had dozed off, Ray had rung to tell her he would be late, having to show prospective buyers round a property. She had managed to acknowledge the news before dozing off again, her previously half empty whisky bottle now fully drained, gripped like a comforter when Bethany was re-woken by Isla's call to her mobile.

It took Bethany a while to come round and she was unable recover the phone before the call ended and it reverted to voicemail.

Bethany scrabbled around, trying to recover the now silent cell as she sat up on the sofa.

"God that hurts,' she realised rubbing her brow, 'must be the beginnings of a hangover,' she realised, glancing down at the now empty bottle gripped tightly in her other hand.

Dumping the bottle on the coffee table, Bethany stretched and tried to remember what she had done with the temporarily lost mobile telephone.

In hope, rather than expectation she thought, 'must find the bloody thing it might be Isla and Alice.'

'Finally she realised it was right in front of her, resting on the coffee table right next to the discarded spirit bottle.

'Bloody drink, doesn't help, my head is banging, my mouth tastes like crap and I hurt from where those bastard thugs groped me,' she realised

Retrieving the cell phone, she flicked open the cover and checked the last call, 'unknown,' said the display.

Hardly daring to hope, Bethany re-dialled and slumped down onto the sofa, tears in her eyes with relief when Isla answered.

'Hallo mother, this is Isla and Alice calling from Kalgoorlie all safe and sound.'

'You were right it was a bloody long drive, I'm absolutely shattered, we've eaten and after this call I'm going to get my head down.'

Bethany blurted out down the telephone, 'Thank god for that, you didn't leave your mobile number, and those two Ukrainian brutes of Luca's were here this morning.'

'Are you alright mother?'

'What happened?'

'Do they know where we are?'

'No I'm not, they seriously assaulted me and they've a rough idea of where you're going but not how,' replied Bethany answering all Isla's questions immediately.

'Have you called the Police?'

'If not, you must, don't worry about us, better they're banged up with Luca than chasing me.'

'You sure?'

'Of course, get Ray to help you, and for Christ sake tell him everything he sounds a brilliant fella,' enthused Isla sitting on the edge of the bed and praying mother would put the cops onto Luca's two heavies.

'Alright darling, I'll do what you say immediately, if you're sure.'

'Yes mother lots of love.'

Give Alice a hug and kiss from me,' said Bethany.

'We'll speak tomorrow, bye,' she finished, ending the call.

Bethany pleased she had told Ray everything the night before called him on his own mobile.

'Ray,' she said when he answered, 'I'm sorry to interrupt, but I need to go to the police I've been sexually assaulted.'

-***-

Ryan was comfortably ensconced in a hammock at the end of his temporary landlord's veranda, a can of half empty Swan in one free hand.

'Last one of these, for a while,' he said to the other surfing buddies, 'got to get my head down and can't miss that lift in the morning.'

'Keep in touch, your lift sounds a bit hairy too me,' declared a voice from the shadows.

'I know but it's free and it'll get me there.'

'The things we'll do for love,' sung the previous commentator, making a passable attempt at the old 10CC hit.

At that everyone joined in on the chorus and a number of ribald remarks followed Ryan as he climbed gingerly from the hammock and made his way towards the sofa bed.

Ryan could hear the good natured laughter from his friends on the patio outside and with their good wishes ringing in his ears and the help of a couple of paracetamol, he was soon drifting off to sleep.

-***-

Ray on receiving Bethany's telephone call about the assault had, with profuse apologies about an emergency at home, handed over his potential purchasers to his able assistant and rushed home to the frightened Bethany.

Once Bethany had told him the story of the assault by the Twins earlier that day he had been in full agreement with Isla and confirmed the necessity of reporting the physical attack to the local constabulary immediately.

Bethany who not having had a drink for a few hours now, could see the sense of this but was still extremely frightened by the thought that the two thugs might return.

'Darling,' said Ray persuasively, 'if they're locked up they can't bother you can they.'

'I'm sure the local boys in blue will do everything they can to help.'

'Shall we go then?'

'Alright, but you'll be with me all the time won't you Ray.'

'Of course I will,' he replied hugging her to him as they made their way to his car.

Within minutes they were arriving at the Bunbury Police Station on Wittenoom Street, somewhere unbeknown to them, Isla had passed and nearly entered about thirty hours before.

Being late evening by now, the police station was busy but within moments of the Reception desk being informed of the nature of the assault a female senior constable had taken over and invited both of them to an interview room.

Just after midnight having given a statement including a description and registration of the Twins Ute, Bethany and Ray were able to return home.

The mention of Luca Mancuso had attracted the Officer's attention very quickly and within moments of them leaving, Police Headquarters in East Perth were being alerted as to the possible implications of the alleged assault and the connections that had been made.

This would alert the State's Crime and Intelligence services who should be able to make all the connections. Unfortunately although an alert was put out throughout Western Australia for the twin's Ute, the connections would only be attended to two days later.

20th FEBRUARY – THE FALCON LEAPS FORWARD

Alice bouncing about in the motel supplied old fashioned wooden cot with counting beads, woke Alice in their motel room in Kalgoorlie.

The three year old little girl had realised, if she jumped up and down and pushed on the upper rail she could make the cot move across the wooden floor of the motel room. Alice was giggling with enjoyment at the new game she was playing and the noise of this, rather than the movement of the wooden cot was what had awoken her mother.

Isla could see it was nearly daylight from the light around the blinds of the single window, she felt stiff and her legs felt sore but even though woken by her daughter, Isla felt refreshed, stretching and yawning in the comfort of the king size bed, Isla rubbed her eyes before glancing at the clock on the table alongside the bed.

'Christ it's only five past six,' she noticed.

'Mind you I was asleep before nine last night,' Isla remembered.

'Come on you little minx, let's get sorted out and get some breakfast,' laughed Isla as she rose from the bed grabbed hold of the little girl and spun her round in an aeroplane spin.

'More, more,' yelled Alice when Isla stopped and put her daughter down on the bed.

'Need the bathroom darling, got to go, see you in a moment,' said Isla disappearing into the toilet.

By seven both females were dressed, ready to go and on their way to the motel bistro which had been open for buffet breakfast since four thirty.

After a substantial breakfast for both of them, bill paid, car re-packed and Alice safely secured, Isla resumed their journey in the Ford Falcon.

The friendly Receptionist who had taken Isla's payment for their food and accommodation had asked their destination, when Isla had replied Caiguna, she had been reminded to change her watch to Caiguna time that is put it on forty five minutes. Isla had expressed her thanks as they left the motel reception.

'On the way now Alice,' said Isla over her shoulder to the little girl as she turned the Falcon towards the centre of Kalgoorlie, they went straight through a couple of roundabouts passing a number of Victorian two story establishments in sometimes garish colours.

Turning right back onto National Route 94, its other name was prominent at this point, Goldfields Highway, they got hit by a sudden heavy shower of rain, within moments the road was awash with red streaked rainwater sluicing across the front of the Falcon and hideous spray from the large trucks and trailers going in the other direction. For moments it was quite horrific, Isla could feel the Falcon wanting to slide on the wet diesel slicked highway, she had the wipers going full blast and Alice was crying in shock at the sudden change in conditions.

Fortunately having only just turned the corner they weren't making great speed and Isla was able to keep control of the vehicle, although a huge overwhelming truck looming large in her rear view mirror wasn't helping her confidence.

Within minutes, but what seemed like longer the rain halted almost as suddenly as it had started and suddenly the greasy wet highway was bathed in sunlight, as they cleared the city limits the road had been unaffected by the previous heavy rainfall and they had returned to the normal dry black tarmac covered in whorls of red dust blown about by the passing traffic.

186 said the distance sign to Norseman as they roared south out past the open casts of the Gold Mining City.

'That's alright Alice less than two hours and we'll stop for elevenses and fuel.'

Isla could see Alice through the rear view mirror thinking about her mother's last statement, her daughters left thumb prominently stuck in the little girl's mouth as she sucked studiously on it.

After a while Alice came back with her answer.

'Are we there yet Mummy?'

Isla laughed and said to Alice, 'shall we have some music?'

'Please,' came the reply.

'Let's have some old funky rock then,' said Isla in a deep voice as she inserted the Rolling Stones, 'Sticky Fingers' album into the car's CD player.

Brown Sugar started its refrain with both girls trying to sing along, Alice's effort was pretty tuneless and not very understandable but to Isla's relief the little girl was having fun and not bored for the moment.

-***-

Ryan's mate pulled the battered old white Ute up outside the address they had been given in Mindarie, it was a modern yellow brick single story building, with an Auction sign, with a sold sticker diagonally across the red billboard.

A battered looking rust red Isuzu pick-up with stainless bull bars prominently displayed in front of the radiator, was the only sign of life, its rear was loaded above the gunwales and a faded green tarpaulin was tied down over the load beneath.

'Should be alright with that Ryan it looks like the 3.5 litre model, they go forever and you'll need to hit something really big, before it messes up your day.'

'Yeah could be right,' the traveller confirmed, 'let's go and find the driver.'

As they exited Ryan's Ute, a short, bald, stocky guy in his late thirties, clad in grubby white singlet, mottled, sky blue and white Bermuda's and red flip flops exited the front door of the property carefully locking it behind him.

Looking up he saw the two approaching lads, Ryan tentatively mumbled.

'Bruce is it?'

'Sure thing, you going to be okay with that arm?' he said pointing to Ryan's crocked, sling held, limb.

'Hopefully, it will have to be, I need the lift.'

'That's great, let's get to it then, you got a bag, hope it's small enough to go in the cab I don't want to unfasten the cover on the back, I've got it good and tight.'

Bruce showed Ryan and his mate by tugging on one of the taut ropes stretched across the tarpaulin.'

'Only this,' answered Ryan pulling his rucksack, with his good hand from the rear of his Ute.

'That'll go fine in the cab, just got to drop these house keys off at the Real Estate Office and we're good for Melbourne, said Bruce waving the keys in front of them.

Within what seemed minutes, Ryan had said goodbye to his mate, with promises to keep in touch, the Agent had received the keys and Bruce had the truck south bound on the Mitchell Freeway.

'Waddya reckon Ryan,' when we get out in the boondocks, I'll get my head down and you can drive this beast with one arm, cause I've only got three days to reach Melbourne.'

'Why's that,' questioned Ryan trying hard not to commit himself to answering the question in the affirmative.

'The bloody house was sold last week at Auction, the removal company was supposed to be out of here two days ago but only picked up the final bits first thing and I'm supposed to be starting work in three days' time on the twenty third.

'Don't want to throw a sickie on the first day of a new job, do I?'

Ryan realising he wanted to get to Victoria as fast as possible himself, thought about how he could manage with one arm, realised he could manage the long boring bits as everything was automatic, came to a decision.

'You do the day, I'll try and do the dark bits then no one's going to see the sling.'

'You did say you were hardly going to stop didn't you?'

Bruce looked across at Ryan and agreed with the answer.

Let's see how we go, it's 550 to Coolgardie before we turn south for Norseman, we should make the latter in daylight.'

'Then top up with fuel have a bite to eat, let it get fully dark and we'll see how you go, alright? Enthused Bruce.

'Fine,' agreed Ryan his spirits raised by Bruce's zeal, 'let's go for it.'

-***-

While Bruce and Ryan were making their way south on the Mitchell Highway with the intention to join the Reid Highway west, Isla, Alice and the Falcon were progressing at speed south on 94 six hundred kilometres to the East.

They had been pushed to the West at Kambalda, by the salt water, Lake Lefroy and joined the Coolgardie Esperance Highway before the road turned south again.

The scenery was much the same lots of red soil and stunted Eucalyptus lining the road on either side.

It wasn't until just before Norseman that the scenery changed much as Lake Cowan, a huge salt flats appeared on the left side of the car, shortly before they reached The town the road traversed the salt flats , the penetrating glare from the sun's rays on the white surround was only partly obviated by Isla's sunglasses and the tinted window. She winced at the penetrating glare and fortunately they were soon past and back into the normal red sand and surrounding bush.

Alice had been happy with the various CD's belting out music from the stereo and the many trucks, their passing buffeting the Falcon as they rattled the other way in a northerly direction.

Shortly before the outskirts of the approaching town a huge lengthy yellow goods train appeared, northbound on the rail tracks to their left.

Moments after and before reaching the rear end of the train, it disappeared into the thickening trees on their side of the highway.

The 80k speed limit signs were passed just before the badge of Norseman perched on yellow stanchions either side of the road greeted their arrival into the last major town before the Nullarbor.

Isla slowed the car in response to the speed limit markers and the sign indicating the left turn onto Highway 1 for Adelaide and Balladonia.

Within moments the poles of the street lights at the junction were visible, and seconds later they were cautiously turning left onto the eastbound highway and then immediately right across the dual carriageway in to the BP service station on the south side of the junction and under the awning to top up the fuel tank of the Ford.

Isla sighed loudly and said to her daughter, 'another stage done Alice, let me fill her up then we'll get some lunch.'

It was only while she was re-fuelling the car that she remembered about the chasing Ukrainian thugs, even though the temperature was around forty, Isla shivered at the thought of them catching up with her and her daughter.

Isla had no qualms about what would happen as she knew she had burnt her bridges with Luca and didn't fancy her chances if it came to a meeting with Luca's enforcers.

'Got to keep going and stay ahead of those bastards,' she thought determinedly as the fuel gurgled through the green nozzle into the cavernous tank of the Falcon.

Completing the refuelling task, Isla moved the car before walking with Alice into the service station, they could see a clock above the counter indicating just a few minutes before eleven.

After paying for the fuel, Isla bought them something for lunch which they ate a table by the window so Isla could keep an eye on the Falcon and watch the highway for any sign of their pursuers.

'Alice,' said Isla, 'we need to go on a lot further than we planned with your Nana.'

'Do you think you can be patient and let Mummy keep driving until it gets dark?'

The little girl anxious to help the person who had just given them a bar of white chocolate, replied, 'okay mummy.'

At that Isla reached for her mobile and quickly cancelled Caiguna and rang the Eucla Motel, with numbers she had already programmed into her cell.

The news wasn't that good, 'You'll have to share with another pair of girls, and I can give you a cot for the bairn,' said the voice at the other end of the phone.

'That's alright, we'll be too tired to notice,' she replied, 'we'll take it.'

Having visited the rest room in the service station the two girls returned to the Falcon and with a sigh while settling her, stiff and sore body into the driver's seat. Isla looked at her bruised cheek the discolouring was now a fine shade of yellow, she rubbed it gingerly, before turning the key in the ignition.

Isla tried to wriggle her sore, tender and bruised body into the most comfortable position in the torture chamber that was the driver's seat and eased the Falcon across the other carriage way and eastwards onto the Eyre Highway.

'Here we go Alice,' she shouted, 'next stop Eucla.'

'Sod the speed limits Alice we're going for the burn,' exclaimed Isla as the passed the green sign with Eucla 710 displayed on it just outside Norseman.

'Let's burn rubber.'

The Falcon seemed to leap forward as Isla kept pushing the accelerator hard before setting the cruise control at 135.

It was 1215 Eucla time.

20th FEBRUARY AM - RYAN AND THE TWINS JOIN THE PURSUIT FROM PERTH AND FREMANTLE

It was nearing midday, and Bruce hadn't been kidding about making good time, once they had cleared the suburbs of Melbourne, he had urged the truck up to 120 and slammed it onto cruise control.

They had swept past anything slower, usually large trucks and trailers bound eastwards to provision Kalgoorlie and its surrounds with necessary supplies.

This enabled the mining of the ore in its mighty open casts and the production of the yellow shiny gold, the reason for the town's existence.

The only time they had slowed was in obedience of the speed limits in the few town's en-route.

'Don't want our country cousins, cash machines having their coffers filled too easily,' explained Bruce when he started slowing as they first approached Northam

'Cash machines?' Queried Ryan.

'Yeah, the country cops like to hide on the edge of their towns and catch us city dwellers ignoring their local speed limits, so because of the fines we call them cash machines.

Ryan who had hardly ever driven inland into the countryside of his home state had never heard of this previously, rubbed his lightly stubbled chin with his free hand and said, 'sneaky bastards.'

'Too right mate, now hand us another sweet will you?'

Ryan found Bruce had few needs, he was more than competent as a driver, the only thing he required from Ryan was the unwrapping and passing over of a fresh boiled sweet about every thirty minutes.

'Keeps the mouth from getting dry and helps the concentration,' had been the explanation when Ryan asked about the need.

Consequently by midday they, even after negotiating the Western Perth City traffic, were already nearly halfway to Coolgardie and their first planned break.

-***-

The Ukrainian twins were having a less than easy ride back in Fremantle, after waiting impatiently all morning for a telephone call from the body shop. They had taken the bit between their teeth and returned to Alf's to see if their presence could hurry along the repair.

Much to their annoyance they could see the Z series Ute up on a hoist with its new Victorian number plates but with the rear axle removed and no mechanic in sight.

'What the bloody hell is going on? Roared Aleksander, 'we need to be on the sodding highway not mucking about here.'

Furious they burst into Alf's office, interrupting a discussion between and elderly lady and the proprietor.

Andriy grabbed Aleksander's left shoulder with his right hand and with his left held his finger to his lips and went, 'shush,' to his brother, who appeared to be about to explode with rage.

Fearfully, Alf ushered his client from the office.

'Mrs Soames, I can only apologise about your car not being ready but it takes more than a couple of days to put it back together.'

'After all you did rather make a mess of the vehicle when you drove it into that articulated truck in the City.'

'Alright, alright but you will let me know when you have repaired her won't you?' Requested the lady as she made her way down the stairs.

Alf returned to his office and the grubby, leather, swivel, desk-chair behind his untidy desk.

'Before you explode, there's nothing I can do, getting hold of a new rear for that,' he said waving towards the broken Ute down below in the workshop, 'is not easy,'

'It's a special edition after all,' he added lamely as Aleksander leaned across the desk, knocking piles of paperwork onto the floor and grabbed hold of the front of Alf's grubby white singlet with his left fist.

'There are no excuses,' thundered Aleksander pulling Alf halfway across the desk so their faces were now inches apart.

Alf's normally well-tanned face had turned white with fright and he tried desperately to think of something to say.

'You can have anything else in the shop I'll even store it up for you, anything you want,' Alf stammered.

Behind them there was a knock at the door, Aleksander released Alf who crashed back onto his chair.

'Hey boss that rear axle and leaf suspension's here for that rush job on that black Ute.' Said a mechanic clad in a greasy blue boiler suit as he opened the office door.

'Here what's going on,' he added seeing Alf's demeanour and the state of the office.

Alf quickest to react answered, his voice shaking, 'nothing Phil, a slight disagreement, get you and your mate on that Ute pronto.'

'Just about to go to lunch boss.'

Looking at the two thugs crowding the office, Alf shuddered and rapidly interrupted Andriy and Aleksander's menacing movement towards the mechanic.

'Double time till you both complete the job and that includes no lunch right,'

Phil, slow on the uptake but finally realising the hostility in the air, shouted 'that's great,' as he departed rapidly banging the office door shut behind him

'Fine Alf, you've finally got the part, we'll give you four hours to have it all ready and we need some bull bars in case we meet any of your crazy indigenous creatures on the road at night.'

'Okay, okay,' agreed Alf, unsure if the job would be done by four but only too willing to agree anything that would speed the departure of these two frightening creatures who were crowding out his office.

'We'll be expecting you to wave us off, so don't think of disappearing this afternoon will you?'

'We wouldn't want to come and pay you, more than a friendly visit, at a later date,'

'Would we?' continued Andriy grinning at his erstwhile sibling, as they departed Alf's office leaving the owner fearfully prostrate in his desk chair.

Reaching inside the bottom drawer of his desk, Alf pulled out a half bottle of Japanese whiskey, unscrewed the top and took a good swig of the raw spirit.

'That'll help calm the nerves,' he said to the empty office returning the now capped bottle to its hiding place.

'Those bastards are real scary.'

'Better make sure those bloody mechanics of mine are earning their corn.'

'I want that bloody Ute pristine and ready to go to hell and back long before four,' he said to himself as he departed his office above the workshop.

20th FEBRUARY PM – PURSUED AND PURSUERS PROGRESS

Half an hour after the Twins left the garage in Fremantle, Isla, Alice and the Ford Falcon were making good progress. Ninety minutes out from Norseman and they were already past the northerly turning for the Balladonia Roadhouse.

Twenty minutes later there was a turning to the north for Balladonia itself and shortly after a brown sign with white lettering.

Isla caught the words 90 mile straight, Australia's longest straightest road and something in kilometres.

The road had been surrounded by red sand with the scrub and stunted eucalyptus trees on each side of the highway.

Alice had seemed to understand the necessity of being strapped into the rear of the car, she had been the epitome of good behaviour with just enough trucks to rattle their passing for her enjoyment. They had sung their way through two CD's already and now Isla switched to some Enya, which Alice had always appeared to enjoy.

Travelling over the speed limit meant they were frequently overtaking other vehicles and Isla had to be careful overtaking the massive trucks and trailers because of their sheer length.

'At least with ninety miles of straight road it will be easier to see something coming the other way,' she realised.

'Let's stop at the end of this straight bit Alice, shall we?'

Alice didn't answer she was too busy looking at the large white truck and trailer they were passing, ten wheels per side, driver and spare ensconced in the cab which had Nullarbor Express inscribed in Australian Green and Gold on the door of the high cab.

The land was barer now red sand and low lying scrub, the landscape didn't change as the Falcon swept along the long straight road.

They passed a lonely metal post box perched on a white painted tractor tyre, a marker for a lonely homestead somewhere to the north of the highway.

Three quarters of an hour later and only three hours after leaving Norseman, Isla seeing the Caiguna sign at the end of the 'straight bit,' steered the Falcon off to the right into Caiguna and came to a halt alongside the front of the Roadhouse.

As she eased her stiff and sore body out into the heat of the afternoon, Isla nearly choked on the small dust storm which was raised by their passage into Caiguna.

Coughing with the choking dust she unstrapped Alice from her seat in the rear, slammed the doors of the car shut and raced into the nearby door marked with a restaurant sign.

It was 1445 Caiguna time.

-***-

About this time Bruce, Ryan and their laden truck were cautiously making their way eastwards down the wide main drag of Coolgardie, Bayley Street looking for refreshment.

Ahead, Ryan spotted the two pair of two storey buildings which could only be a Victorian age building and the sign for a pub.

'Always got to be grub in the pub,' he said pointing across the cab so Bruce wouldn't miss it.

Not that the Denver City Hotel with its Swan Bitter sign prominently displayed on its upper deck could easily be missed.

Bruce indicated and swung their truck across the empty road and drew to a halt alongside the yellow and blue painted two storey building with its red painted upper veranda.

'Right Ryan, 30 minutes as agreed, decent meal, something to drink and back on the road.'

'It's near three now, let's get going by say half past, Norseman by sunset, fill up there and let the sun go down before hitting the Eyre Highway.'

'Fine by me,' agreed Ryan, 'let's get in the pub, I'm starving.'

-***-

By half three at Alf's Body Shop in Fremantle, the Twins Ute was ready to go, the mechanic had just returned from the nearest Caltex, the fuel tank was brimming and Alf had loaded the vehicle with supplies and bottles of drinking water.

'Right get out of here, that's it for the day, I'll get those thugs to get rid of this,' he said indicating the Ute.

'But boss what about the rest of the jobs,' chorused the two mechanics.'

'They can wait for the morning,' replied Alf, 'I want us all safe and clear.'

'See you tomorrow morning, right.'

'Brilliant boss,' they responded as they left the building.

Alf manoeuvred the Ute out onto the deserted street before parking it alongside the wall of the building.

Locking the vehicle he placed the keys on top of the front nearside tyre, hidden by the wall and the wheel arch.

Setting the alarm in his garage, he locked up and proceeded to drive away in his own car.

Once clear Alf pulled to the side of the road and called up the Twins on his mobile.

Aleksander recognising the call answered, 'hope you are ringing to say the vehicle is ready and haven't got another excuse.'

'No its fine, ready parked outside, keys on the front nearside tyre and loaded with fuel and stores.'

'My compliments,' he added grimly.

'What about the Porsche?' Queried Aleksander.

'Put the keys through the letterbox, and leave the car outside, okay.'

'Yeah, it better be right.'

'It is.'

'We're on our way.'

Aleksander explained the situation to Andriy and the latter commented.

'He's obviously crapped himself over our visits, it won't matter he's not there, the Ute will be bang on because he's scared to death.'

'Let's get out of here,' he said grabbing their two hold-all's from the floor of their apartment and heading for the door.

Ten minutes later they had dumped the Porsche outside Alf's, and were on their way joining the busy dual carriage way which is Fremantle High Street with the Royal Fremantle Golf Club to their right.

Gradually the traffic began to thin as the road continued onto the Leach Highway and the Twins continued their eastwards progress south of Perth CBD and the Swan River.

'What do you reckon Aleksander,' Asked Andriy who was looking at the road atlas?

'What's up?'

'By the time we clear the city it's going to be sunset and you know what they said about the animals, those red kangaroos.'

'So, that's why we've got that bloody great lump of metal on the front.'

'What did he call them, Bull Bars?'

'Yeah but he said those 'big red' kangaroos are big enough, so those bars won't do any good, if we hit one.'

'Let's get on 94 then, get some grub and assess the situation,' concluded Andriy to his brother.

-***-

Back on the Eyre Highway it was 1630, Australia Western Standard Time and Isla was starting to get concerned, she was very tired, stiff, sore, aching, uncomfortable and yet parts of her felt numb and welded into the driver's seat of the Falcon.

The brief toilet break at Caiguna had only served to emphasise how tiring the journey was.

In the rear view mirror the partial cloud cover was starting to go red as the sun began to dip towards the Western Horizon.

The only good thing happening was Alice, she was asleep, although after their fifteen minute stop in Caiguna, the little girl had fought her mother, when Isla had attempted, albeit successfully, to return her to the child seat in the rear of the vehicle.

Half an hour before they had flashed past the red roofed roadhouse and petrol pumps at Cocklebiddy leaving it on their southern side.

The kilometre posts sped by in less than half a minute at a time, as Isla desperate to reach Eucla for their own welfare and before the dangers of nightfall pushed the car up to 120kph.

Soon they were approaching Madura, the road switched from the featureless sand and shrub desert of the Nuytsland Nature reserve, and began to rise towards Madura, instead of the boring continuous straightness which could put the unwary drive to sleep, and there were now bends.

Just after a pair of yellow signs indicating, steep hill drop ahead, there was another in white, the lowering rays of the sun behind giving it an orange tinge, MADURA PASS was the wording giving the second indication of the change in terrain.

Isla, eased her back forward, tightened the muscles and slightly adjusted her bottom in the Falcon's seat.

'Hill, a bloody hill,' celebrated Isla in her mind, then she realised the indication had been for a downhill section ahead and the white sign had indicated the top of the hill.

'I never noticed us going uphill,' she realised.

'Oh well this is better and different,' she thought as the swept down the southern side of the escarpment.

Rapidly they swept past the two turnings on their left side indicating the Madura Township, the escarpment rising above them on the Falcon's left.

Soon they were passing the distance sign, Mundrabilla 114, Eucla 182 it indicated.

'Bloody hell, less than two hours if I can keep this up,' realised Isla.

'It's going to be pitch black then,' she thought glancing at her watch, '1650,' it said.

The road levelled and straightened the escarpment still accompanied them at a distance to the north while to the south was the sandy scrub and small tree which she assumed went all the way to the Southern Bight.

Looking again in her rear view mirror the occasional cloud was still tinged with red but still the sun wasn't low enough to be visible so she pushed on hoping against hope they would make Eucla in daylight.

'If its Sunset at seven in Perth, it has got to be a lot earlier out here,' thought Isla forgetting she had adjusted her watch for local time.

The road straightened and Isla could see no deviation in the distance, so when she came up to the rear of a blue truck and trailer with MAIN FREIGHT on its mainly blue tarpaulin sides they were able to pass it easily without pause.

The escarpment continued to accompany them on the north side of the highway, at times it would close in with a rush as if to traverse the road, at other times it was a distant, dark, looming presence as they sped along.

About 20 minutes east of Madura, Isla was surprised she could see a fence stretching north and south to both horizons, then they were on it and the Falcon rattled across what felt and looked like a cattle grid.

Isla guessed, 'maybe it's the rabbit proof fence she thought,' remembering the lessons of her near distant high school days.

The rattling noise made by crossing the grid woke an unhappy Alice, her blubbering caused Isla to address the issue with a Compact Disc in the car's stereo system, Honkey Tonk Woman, burst through the cars sound system, and Isla started to give the little girl a commentary about the rabbit proof fence, which seemed to soothe her wounded feelings.

Ten minutes later Isla was surprised by a yellow sign, in black was an airplane symbol with RFDS EMERGENCY AIRSTRIP, also in black writing.

Keen to distract Alice, Isla shouted, 'look at that darling, this is an Emergency Airstrip for the Royal Flying Doctor Service.'

Then the road was crossed by white hatching at either end of what Isla assumed was the landing area.

Forty five minutes after passing through the Madura Pass, they passed a sign for Madura in five kilometres and less than five minutes later they were speeding past the mainly blue outbuildings of Mundrabilla, its forecourt was covered in white dust and a white truck was kicking up dust as it bore off to the left, ahead of them into the rest stop.

Shortly thereafter they passed the sign indicating that Eucla was only 68 miles away.

Dusk was drawing in now and there were huge shadows from the escarpment caused by the low lying sun which was now a red ball in the rear view mirror.

'Thirty minutes darling,' enthused Isla.

Alice hearing the excitement in her mother's voice, nodded her head in agreement and approval.

'Momma, momma,' she said and then collapsed into a fit of giggles.

The Stones, 'Brown Sugar,' accompanied their conversation and they both attempted to sing along with Mick Jagger.

It was now a fraction after 1800 and they pressed on.

The escarpment was still there to the north but mainly distant, the landscape was the barest it had been with only a rare stunted tree amongst the low lying foliage. The falling red ball in the north western sky was still hanging above the horizon, a long dark shadow now leapt ahead of the front offside corner of the car as they sought their refuge in Eucla.

At 1835 they came upon another section of road dedicated as an emergency airstrip, with growing excitement Isla was able to forget about her aches, pains and tiredness, sure enough at the end of the airstrip was a five kilometre warning for Eucla.

Although the sun was still just hanging above the horizon it was now noticeably darker ahead and Isla had the full headlight beams of the Falcon to presage any risk of collision.

The Ford and its occupants swept into a left turn, Isla caught sight of the Southern Ocean the setting sun's rays glinting off the whitecaps thrown up by the wind blowing all the way from Antarctica.

'Look Alice, the sea,' she pointed to her left and then had to concentrate on the rising hill towards where the escarpment cut across the road.

They entered a cutting with gradually rising rocky slopes on either side of the car.

Suddenly on their side a dusty blue sign pointed its way into Eucla, Isla slowed and gently eased the Falcon across the opposing carriageway. A smart brown concrete sign between two brick pillars pointed the way into their stop for the oncoming night.

Isla slowly drove the vehicle down the dusty slip road, its headlights illuminating the track.

With a sigh of relief Isla pulled into the Hotel Motel, stopped and for a moment rested her weary head on the steering wheel.

'We're here,' was all she said.

It was 1910, and would have been pitch black hadn't it been for the lights from the close by hostelry.

-***-

Back in Norseman, Ryan and Bruce were partaking of a couple of steaks at the BP refuelling station waiting for the setting sun to finish its descent into the western horizon.

The trip down from Coolgardie had been uneventful and now they were discussing the next stage of the journey.

'Look if we ease down a bit say, hit between 90 and 100, we've more chance of avoiding some stray marsupial or road kill, haven't we?' Queried Ryan.

'Also let's do two hours a stint, we'll easily make Eucla or Border village in three stints,' he continued

We'll have to stop around there for fuel anyway, it looks like your truck does about 750k to the tankful,' he added.

'Alright that's okay it will give us more chance of avoiding them, if there's any creatures wanting to play with us,' agreed Bruce.

'If it works out, we'll grab a coffee there and carry on in two hour stints alright?'

'Fine let's do it, it looks dark enough now, you get the truck onto the Highway and I'll take over, and then let's see how I do as a one-armed racer,' said Ryan laughing nervously as his sense of adventure and adrenaline kicked in.

Bruce drove them out across the highway onto the eastward bound dual carriageway, across the railroad tracks and parked the truck under a now lit lamp post.

He then got out and moved round to the passenger side, while Ryan relieving himself of his sling uncomfortably shimmied across to the driver's seat.

Slamming the open door shut and positioning himself Bruce said to Ryan.

'Right let's get going, I'm going to get some kip, give me a shout in about two hours, right.'

By the time Ryan had manoeuvred the truck back onto the Eyre Highway and got it cruising at 100kph he could hear Bruce snoring, the latter's open mouthed head leant against the passenger door.

'I don't care, this is fun, and we must be catching Isla and the little girl,' he thought.

-***-

Just before the sun set the Twin's arrived in Merredin, Alexander asked Andriy for the time.

'It's on the dash in front of you,' responded Andriy, 'its five to seven, what are you thinking?'

'Like we said earlier, let's stop now, get something to eat and drink, top up this gas guzzler and work out a plan.'

'It's alright Luca and that piece of work Fabio telling us to drive across Australia, even when we get hold of the little girl we have to bring her all the way back as well.'

'You're right, Fabio needs to do something about that, perhaps him or the grandparents can pick her up from us once we've fixed the woman and have captured the child.'

'Whoever it is they'll at least need to be in Melbourne waiting our call.'

'You're right,' agreed Aleksander

'Changing the subject, what's this place called again?'

'Merredin, why?'

'Well the highway maybe well lit by the lamp posts either side of the road, it might be a wide road there's nothing but houses,' complained Aleksander.

'Its fine,' said Andriy laughing, 'there's a BP over there on the right, got to be patient, everything comes to he who waits.'

Aleksander pulled in and refuelled while Andriy went and paid the tariff.

'You're alright for food pull in over there,' said Andriy indicating a well-lit brick building with a large red sign on the front on the other side of the highway,' shortly after they left the garage.

'What's chicken treat?' said Aleksander reading the red and yellow lettered sign

'It's the West Australian equivalent of MacD's but with chicken instead of steak.'

'There's one in Fremantle, anyway go through the drive through, we'll eat in the cab and wait until it gets dark, before moving off.'

A short time later the Twins were parked up facing the western red streaked horizon, scoffing their chicken meals while awaiting the onset of full darkness.

21st FEBRUARY EVENING – RUSHING THROUGH THE DARKNESS

Ryan soon settled into the rhythm of the drive his slingless, broken left arm and finger resting awkwardly on his lap, ready for any emergency, whilst his good right hand, mainly gripping the bottom of the steering wheel eased the small truck round the infrequent corners and otherwise kept it on the straight and narrow.

There was little traffic and what was coming towards him were mainly huge freight trains with their powerful lights politely dipped at the sight of the oncoming lesser vehicle.

The full on headlights of the small truck created the effect of never ending cavern between the Eucalyptus trees shadowing the highway.

The cruise control set at 95 pushed the vehicle on seemingly endlessly and there was little to help Ryan concentrate, except for the raucous snores of his partner in this adventure.

About an hour into the trip, Ryan was yawning with boredom trying to desperately trying to keep awake, even though it was only about nine in the evening.

Suddenly he found the nearside tyres of the vehicle, started to rumble as they slid onto the hard sand alongside the highway, he couldn't understand it as he over corrected and nearly pushed the truck of the other side of the fortunately empty road.

'Christ it's a bend,' he realised as he slowed the truck and gripped the steering wheel painfully with both hands, guiding the machine onto the right side of the Eyre Highway as it turned from a north east to south easterly direction.

Gradually he pushed the truck back up to cruising speed, as he tried to settle his now throbbing broken digit back into his lap, the broken arm was complaining as well.

'Bastard, that's going to keep me awake,' he uttered vehemently but quietly to the cab of the truck.

An hour later just as he was due to wake Ryan, he could see lights ahead on his near side, the idea had been to pull into one of the rest stations an swap over but the sight of the well-lit Roadhouse was a place of rest rooms and a lot more hygienic and safer than some desolate camping area.

Ryan pulled in alongside the well-lit building, nudged Bruce awake and said, 'Balladonia Hotel, your turn I'm off to the rest rooms.'

-***-

After a substantial meal eaten at first under the outside lights of the fast food establishment, but their repast quickly interrupted by a horde of large black flies, the twins had retired quickly to the safety of their Commodore Ute to complete their meal.

On completion Andriy dashed across to the rubbish bin and dumped their waste before returning to the vehicle.

'Let's decide what we're going to do from here, before we ring Fabio.'

He'll be doing his nut by now, probably crapping himself, too scared to ring and ask about our progress and needing to know what's happening so he can pacify Luca,' replied Aleksander.

'We'll try driving at night, and see what happens, we're well rested and you can drive if and when I get tired.'

'Where's next?'

'Still Coolgardie about three hundred kilometres,' answered Andriy.

'Get under way,' he said fastening his seat belt, 'and I'll ring Fabio.'

'You'll get cut off when we clear the town and can't get any signal.'

'That's the idea, it'll give him less time to whinge,' laughed Andriy.

Aleksander manoeuvred the Ute back onto the eastbound side of the Highway as Andriy contacted Fabio.

'Where the bloody hell have you been,' retorted a much relieved Fabio when he answered his mobile, on seeing that Andriy was calling.

'Calm down, we're under way, we'll be at some place called Coolgardie about midnight.'

'We didn't get the Ute returned until late this afternoon, so we couldn't start until then.'

'Have you any news about the girl and her kid?'

'It's hard to believe but I think she is driving to Victoria, our contacts at Perth Airport reckon Isla and the kid haven't flown out of Perth, the car isn't in the airport car parks and not in her usual haunts either.'

'You reckon she's got to be ahead of us somewhere.'

'Yeah, I know she's had nearly two days start on you, but she's got the kid to look after and can't drive as long as you two.'

The Ute was now clear of Merredin and its twin beams were cutting a swathe in the darkness ahead.

Abruptly just as they passed the outer sign indicating the distance to four towns further along the Great Eastern Highway.

Andriy recognised the third name, 'Coolgardie, 293,' he stated to his brother.

'Yeah I know, saw it myself, bloody dark out here isn't it?'

Andriy half turned in his seat and could only see the disappearing illumination of Merredin, and the many stars in the night sky, before agreeing with his brother.

'You're right, and we haven't seen anything coming the other way since we left the town, do you think they're right about animals at night.'

'Could be we'll just have to keep an eye out ahead won't we? Replied Aleksander attempting to peer into the gloom far ahead of the headlight beams as he accelerated up to 110 kph.

Ten minutes later they were passing through Burracoppin its streets marked by a single lighted lamp post on a corner on either side of the road.

Aleksander hardly slowed, after all as he had explained earlier, 'what did it matter if they got pinged by a speed camera, they were hardly going to get caught with their Victorian number plates registered to someone else.'

About an hour after their stop they swept through Southern Cross, Aleksander did slow for the town not wishing to attract attention to the flying Ute.

Andriy was dozing, his head resting on the near side door window.

Aleksander was trying hard to concentrate on the road ahead looking into the lighted cavern created by the Ute's full beam headlights.

The monotony was broken after a long straight by some long sweeping bends and then they were powering through a tiny hamlet called Moorine Rock.

Fortunately for the brothers as the Ute completed its passage round a long right hander, Aleksander could see the shining reflection of the water pipeline close to the nearside of the speeding vehicle.

The road ahead was lit by the enormous beams of a large oncoming truck.

Aleksander as a courtesy dipped his headlights, this change concentrated his mind just enough to realise they were quickly approaching a large looming upright shadow on their side of the road.

Having little room to manoeuvre, his heart racing Aleksander wrenched the steering wheel to the right across the path of the onrushing truck.

There was an almighty bang on the front on side of the Ute and the vehicle shuddered up onto its two offside wheels nearly flipping over.

It was the collision that saved them, shoving the Ute further to the right and across the road into the bush on the other side of the road. The diverted machine dropped back onto its four wheels, brushing aside the thin trees close to the road and finally just before Aleksander, braking hard, managed to bring the vehicle under control, it shuddered to an abrupt halt by burying its nose into a larger Eucalyptus.

Behind them the unsighted truck driver roared past eastbound towards Perth and a large injured Kangaroo limped off into the bush.

Fortunately for them the seatbelt and the bull bars had saved the twins from serious injury.

The unforeseen manoeuvre had rudely woken Andriy from his doze, the crashing down of the Ute sent a sharp pain lancing through his lower spine as he tried to understand what was happening, the now tensioned seat belt snapped fast, holding him tightly in place.

Aleksander killed the engine of the Ute, snapped off his seat belt and leaned across towards his injured brother who was complaining vociferously.

'What the bloody hell happened?'

'Where the sod are we?'

'Christ my back's killing me,' he said reaching round with his right hand to grip the base of his spine and try to knead away the pain, pulsating from the injured back.

'Hit one of them crazy bloody creatures they have in this god forsaken land and lucky we didn't get taken out by one of those road trains as well,' explained Aleksander.

'At least the engines still working, if you're alright with it we'll get back on the road, go back to that last town and see what damage there is.'

'Okay let's go for it, think I've bust some ribs where the seat belt grabbed me,' answered Andriy rubbing his chest.

Aleksander started the engine and put the car into reverse, the reversing lights showed the wheel ruts made by their sharp exit from the highway, ahead the beams of the headlights, picked out the white trunk of the eucalyptus reflecting back the lights onto the loose leaves discarded onto the windscreen by the collision of the Ute with the trees trunk.

Looking back over his left shoulder he put his foot onto the accelerator and tried to ease the vehicle back towards the Highway, the car didn't move he could feel the lack of grip and hear at least one of the wheels spinning in a crescendo of noise and digging itself further into the red soil, the truck lurching and sinking into the soil so the driver's side was lower than the other.

Aleksander took his foot of the pedal and put the Ute into sports mode hoping this would give him better grip, it only ended in the same result.

Aleksander cut the engine and extinguished the lights.

'No good Andriy, we'll have to look at it and see how we can get it out of this bloody sand.'

Looking round them at the pitch blackness, with only the rare light of a passing vehicle flashing by on the Highway in their rear, Andriy realised their predicament.

Unless we've got a torch in here and I know we haven't, it's either try and stop a vehicle on the highway out there, and I don't fancy that the speeds they're doing or stay here until daylight.'

'Besides which, who knows what bloody creatures are out there in the dark, killer spiders, vicious snakes this bloody country has the lot.'

'I vote for staying here,' he added in the darkness of the Utes cab.

'Can't say I disagree with you, let's see if we can get some sleep and wait for daylight.'

The pair, Andriy with his painful back and sore ribs made themselves as comfortable as possible before attempting to get some sleep.

_-***-_

Ryan and Bruce's travels across the Nullarbor Plain had gone without incident, the latter had taken over the driving when Ryan had returned from the facilities at the Balladonia Hotel and somewhere around midnight had pulled over to the side of the road at the Madura turning and returned the driving to Ryan.

'Plenty of fuel left, should make Eucla easily, going to get my head down, give me a shout when we get there,' uttered Bruce on returning to the passenger seat of the truck's cab, resting his head against the door window.

Before Ryan had time to take a swig of water from the bottle in the door sill and restart the engine of the truck, his co-driver's gentle snores were already reverberating around the cab.

Just over an hour later a bored but watchful Ryan could see the faint glow of lights ahead, there had only been two road trains going westwards and they had overtaken nothing themselves.

The sign just before the dimly lit fuel station on his left said Mundrabilla, Ryan glanced at the fuel gauge which now indicated a quarter full.

'Stop or not,' he thought.

'No, Bruce said Eucla, so that's where it will be,' he decided as he continued past the inviting lights of the Roadhouse.

Forty five minutes later Ryan gratefully spotted the sign for Eucla pass as the road started to rise into the darkness, shortly after there was the blue sign on the right of the road indicating fuel, bed and other facilities to their left.

Cheerfully and slowly he manoeuvred the truck down the side road towards the dim glow of the filling station and roadhouse.

'Crap,' he expostulated loudly, waking Bruce from his slumbers.

'What's wrong,' he uttered rubbing the sleep from his eyes with his fists.

'The filling station's closed until seven in the morning and we're near out of fuel.'

'If I had known, would have stopped at Mundrabilla less than hour ago.'

'Sod it, nothing for it, find a spot out of the way to park and we'll get our heads down.'

'It's nearly two now, we can get some fresh grub when they open at seven and be on our way shortly after that.'

'Fair enough,' answered Ryan, 'it'll probably do us good to get some kip anyway.

He eased the truck close to the side of the filling station's building and switched off.

22nd FEBRUARY AM – ALL THREE VEHICLES PROGRESS

The Twins were first to make any movement in the morning. Andriy hadn't slept he couldn't get comfortable with his painful back and sore ribs. Besides which it would have been difficult to sleep through the noise of his brother's rasping snoring.

He was pleased to see the red streaks of the sunrise in the clear lightening sky through the side window of the Ute his forward view being partially obscured by the offending eucalyptus and its discarded leaves.

Besides his aches and pains, he was stiff and uncomfortable, dying for a piss and needed to move around and try and stretch the kinks out of his body.

Reaching across he poked his noisy brother, and rasped, 'daylight Aleksander,' through his dry throat, before opening the passenger door and after checking carefully around stepped out onto the sandy red ground.

Andriy looked around him, the other side of the tree they had struck was a mighty field of wheat, he couldn't see any fences and it seemed to stretch towards the horizon. Behind them was the Highway and their tracks at right angles to its trajectory.

There was a crash as Aleksander slammed shut the driver's door and checked round his side of the Ute.

'Dug in here,' he said indicating the front offside wheel, 'get some of this tree bark and wood under the wheel and she'll soon come out.'

At that he bent down and with his large bare hands began to dig a space under the offending wheel.

Andriy, with some difficulty because of his injuries collected plenty of eucalyptus bark and small broken branches which Aleksander used to fill his excavations below the rear of the wheel.

Happy with his work Aleksander decisively declared, 'you drive it off in reverse and I'll push on this corner,' indicating the front offside of the vehicle with his bare outstretched right arm.

'Just reverse it out a bit and we'll see what the damage is.'

Andriy gingerly made his way into the driver's seat of the Ute, started the engine engaged reverse and waited for his brother.

Aleksander dug his feet into the soil, settled himself like a sumo wrestler, in a squat position so he could exert all his strength on the trapped Ute.

'You count, on three,' he shouted.

'One, two, three,' shouted Andriy slowly as Aleksander took a deep breath.

Almost simultaneously Andriy pressed the accelerator hard and Aleksander all sinews straining, exhaling hard, came of his haunches attempting to lift the front wheel out of the hole.

For a moment it appeared as if the Ute would stay trapped, when suddenly it leapt backward leaving Aleksander sprawling on all fours and Andriy stepping hard on the brakes to prevent the vehicle careering backwards onto the highway.

Andriy cursed loudly the sharp movements sending a spurt of pain down his spine and gasped for breath when his sore ribs, agonisingly reminded him of their damage.

Brushing himself off, the fallen twin picked himself up, laughed at his brother and exclaimed, 'easy wasn't it, let's see what damage that night creature caused to the Ute.

Andriy exited the cab of the vehicle and joined Aleksander at the front of the vehicle.

There was blood and gore clinging to the bull bars on the near side the bars were badly bent out of shape on that corner and the headlight glass was cracked and broken where the impact of the collision had driven part of the bull bar inwards.

'Not too bad,' commented Aleksander, 'I would hate to see the kangaroo.

'Mind you it must have been a big bastard to knock us across the road like it did.'

Ever the practical one, Andriy returned to the cab and answered, 'just check those front lights will you,' he switched them on and also put them on full beam whilst flicking the left indicator.

'All working, let's get out of here we've wasted enough time,' stated his brother returning to the cab and replacing his twin in the driver's seat.

Andriy, muttering about his sore lower back and possible busted ribs, made his way to the passenger side of the cab and gingerly returned to his seat

At that, Aleksander started up the engine turned the Ute slowly through the undergrowth and back onto the far side of the highway before increasing speed as they headed towards the newly risen sun.

_***_

Isla and Alice were the next to wake, just before seven the little girl decide she had enough of watching Isla sleep and started loudly, rattling the bars of the motel's cot.

Isla who had slept solidly for around ten hours was happy enough to be woken, they needed some breakfast, plan the day ahead, cancel the previously booked accommodation and make a new plan, and they're being so far ahead of their previous arrangements.

'Right little one, we'll get you out of there, have a shower and get some breakfast.'

'You can help mummy decide how far we're going today.'

By eight o'clock they were both dressed showered and sitting in the motels restaurant consuming breakfast, blissfully unaware Ryan was just round the corner of the motel in the cab of a truck snoring his head off.

Alice was freshly clad in a short sleeved white frock with pink rabbit decorating the dresses front, her brown tanned feet bare of socks and shoes.

Isla in a garish yellow T shirt, khaki green shorts and matching khaki converse boots was ready to go.

Isla cancelled her previous bookings with her mobile and decided, 'I'm stiff but not hurting from where Ryan belted me anymore, and I reckon we can go for a long one again today.'

'Alice darling,' she said to her daughter who was cramming her mouth full of cereal.

'You'll have to be patient again, we are going to try and go a long way today again, and you will have to bear with me.'

'The further we go each day the less times we've got to do it, alright?'

Alice with her mouth full and probably not properly realising what her mother had asked, nodded her head vigorously in agreement.

'That's agreed then.'

'Let's have a look at where we are going today and where we're going to stop,' proposed Isla opening up her yellow Road Atlas.'

Alice reached across to touch the book, but Isla snatched it away laughing, 'can't have you messing it up and putting your breakfast all over the atlas, we still need it.'

Alice giggled.

'Now listen carefully here's where we are going and where I hope we'll stop tonight right.'

Alice answered, 'right,' mimicking her mother and waving both arms in the air in agreement.

'First is somewhere called Border Village, then there is a long stretch to a road house called Nullarbor named after this desert we're travelling through I presume,' pausing Isla made a note of the distances on a beer mat left on the dining table.

Alice her head held in her hands listened intently.

She continued 'then Yalata, Nundroo, Bookabie, Penong and Ceduna.'

'That should be enough, nearly 500kilometres,' proposed Isla to her daughter.

'What do you think?'

'Alright Mummy,' agreed the little girl.

Isla didn't rush, she packed up their stuff back into the car and returned the key to the mature women in a green sleeveless frock in reception.

Isla asked about booking a room for her and the child in Ceduna, the woman replied.

"Depends what you're after, there's five places from really smart to okay.'

'Just something clean with en suite and a cot again for Alice,' Isla responded.

'Oh well the Motor Inn should be fine then, it's on McKenzie Street.'

'Do you want me to book it if they've got any vacancies?'

'Yes please, just one night thanks.'

In moments, or so it seemed to Isla, the telephone call was made and they had a confirmed booking in Ceduna.

Thanking the lady the two of them returned to the Falcon where ignoring Alice's half-hearted protests, Isla re-installed the little girl in the rear of the car before moving it to the petrol pumps and topping off the tank.

By nine in the morning they were back on the highway ten minutes from Border village, Within what to Isla seemed moments the Eyre Highway had become a dual carriageway, shortly after they passed the Western Australian Quarantine station, where a short queue of cars and trucks were awaiting their checks before being given permission to continue west into the wildflower state.

A large pictorial sign welcomed them to South Australia and another smaller notice reminded Isla she needed to put her watch and the car's clock forward another three quarters an hour.

'This is all new Alice,' joked Isla with her daughter.

'A new state for both of us, we're nearly international travellers.'

Alice who didn't properly understand still concurred with her mother by nodding her head vigorously in agreement.

'Mind you the scenery doesn't change, does it?'

'Sand and bushes followed by lot's more sand and bushes.'

Alice had lost interest in her mother's conversation, on her left side were dozens of parked trucks and trailers getting ready for their further journey into South Australia.

Shortly after leaving Border Village and the BP filling station on their south side the dual carriageway petered out and Isla pushed the Falcon up to one ten before re-setting the cruise control.

The inevitable distance sign flashed by, Nullarbor 184 was the next point of civilisation, Isla wasn't really bothered, she knew that this was less than two hours and after the last two days she had settled into a rhythm.

Alice would chatter away about the colour and if a passing or a passed truck had a trailer, while Isla would sing songs to her little girl which Alice would try and join in.

Most of Isla's pain from her beating by Ryan had disappeared and it was only the expected stiffness from long distance driving which made her uncomfortable.

She had quickly realised driving long distances was about concentrating on the road, if you did that, the niggles from sitting in one position for a long time would quickly be forgotten.

Within ten minutes of leaving Border Village, Isla had to pull the car to the side of the road to put on her sun glasses the road having turned to the Southeast and the glare from the rising sun on her left, with the dust from the now frequent passing trucks making it difficult to see.

Ten minutes later the roadside undergrowth had receded and they were running alongside the Australian Bight.

Alice yelped with delight, 'sea mummy, sea.'

'I know darling, I know.'

_***_

Ryan woke groggily and suddenly when Bruce poked him in the ribs and shouted in his right ear.

'Bloody hell we've slept in, it has gone nine.'

'Crap,' agreed Ryan then trying to make the best of the situation said, 'at least we can drive right through after this, now we've had a kip.'

'Mind you this truck seat isn't the most comfortable place to sleep,' he said stretching.

'What do you want to do?'

'Have a hot breakfast fill us up, then the truck and go for a non-stop rest of trip, except for re-fuelling us and the truck.'

'What do you think?'

'Sounds right to me,' agreed Ryan

They both leapt from the truck and headed indoors for an enormous breakfast before continuing their journey.

While at the dining table, Bruce calculated the remaining distance to Melbourne on his I phone.

'We've been playing at it up to now, we need to get a shift on.'

'Why's that countered Ryan?' through a mouthful of sausage.

'We've still nigh on 2000 kilometres to do, allow for stops, that's just about 24 hours.'

'This time in 48hours I need to be at work starting my new job.'

'Okay,' agreed Ryan.

'Two hour stints?' He queried.

'Fair enough let's do it, I'm up first once we get topped up,' agreed Bruce.

By ten they were back on the road and following the Falcon containing the girls.

-***-

Shortly after ten in the morning the twins, in their Commodore Ute, its Perfect Blue body coated in dust and the bull bar looking somewhat the worse for wear pulled into the BP Norseman Roadhouse.

Aleksander had driven all the 373 kilometres from the crash site near Moorine Rock, his brother constantly complaining about his ribs and the stabbing pain in his lower back.

Neither of them had spoken much in the last five hours, Andriy had been making every effort not to complain but groaning with pain when the Ute went over any sort of bump or hole in the road.

Aleksander drove the vehicle into the parking space alongside the children's play area at the end of the Road house, unclipped his seat belt, turned and spoke to his ailing brother.

'You can't carry on like this, you're going to need to see a Doctor.'

'A Doctor won't do any good, there's nothing they can do, and we'll get a stack of ibuprofen and dose me up.'

'I'll be alright to drive then, in fact it will help me forget about the bloody pain having to concentrate on something else.'

'Remember we used to chew on the bloody things like sweets when we were route marching during National Service.'

'You're right let's get your pain killers, something to eat and get back on the road,' agreed his brother. After filling themselves and the Ute with food, fuel and Ibuprofen, a tentative Andriy returned the Ute to the Highway and launched it eastwards about 900 kilometres astern of the girls.

22nd FEBRUARY PM – THE CHASE CONTINUES

For about half an hour Alice's attention was drawn by the regular glimpses of the white capped Southern Ocean on the right hand side of the car. Isla could feel the fresh inshore ocean breeze pushing on that side of the car.

The escarpment to the north vanished and the further east they travelled the flatter the landscape became, shortly after leaving the coast and bearing inland the shrub lessened and deteriorated into a sun browned grassland.

The white dust began to become a problem, westbound trucks and the strong southerly wind covered the Falcon in a layer of this all enveloping white powder.

Isla kept using her windscreen wash and wipers to keep the windscreen clear every time they went through the brief maelstrom caused by the passing road trains.

After nearly two hours when the landscape had reached its bleakest and the suns glare was being reflected back off the dusty tarmac and the white roadside, they passed the Nullarbor Roadhouse.

Isla' impressions were of the Mobil sign, a brown tourist sign announcing Dingo's Den and a huge white dirt car park.

Alice who as much as her mother was bored with the increasingly sparse surroundings shouted, 'Mummy stop,' at this rare sight of civilisation.

Isla though had little sympathy, she was determined to split their drive into two sections and wanted to make Yalata before they stopped for refreshment.

Shortly after the Nullarbor road house the landscape began to change and low dirty green shrubbery began to replace the grassland, a dusty, wide gated roadway to their right was marked by a brown sign announcing Head of the Bight.

Shortly after that the stunted eucalyptus trees began to re-appear on either side of the now undulating highway and they lost the pressure of the ocean wind on the south side of the car and consequently the previously all-enveloping dust.

At about quarter to eleven Isla was relieved to see the white sign with red lettering saying IN and announcing the entrance to the Yalata road house.

Signalling for the left turn, Isla was surprised to see a blue boarded up building and when they got closer a sign announcing the long term temporary closure for renovations of Yalata.

Cursing to herself Isla apologised to her daughter in the rear, 'sorry darling it's closed, it's only half an hour to the next one.'

Alice wasn't best pleased when the without stopping Isla returned the Falcon to the Eyre Highway and set the bonnet towards Nundroo only 50 kilometres to the east.

By the time they reached Nundroo another dusty road house, fuelling station and place to refresh themselves the landscape had changed again, now there was fencing on either side of the highway, occasional farm houses announced their return to a more civilised world and there were even more frequent turnings with metal post boxes, indicating civilisation on either side of the road.

'Here darling,' announced a satisfied Isla to Alice.

Let's get you out of that seat and get something to eat and drink shall we?

Isla found as soon as she entered the air conditioned Hotel that there was a tiny shop and kiosk, there was at least somewhere to sit and Alice could run around safely.

After some lunch and consuming plenty of water bought from the kiosk, and giving Alice a chance to let off some steam, Isla was ready to depart.

Alice didn't want to leave she had made friends with a Golden Labrador called Max who with the couple, who were his owners were headed westbound in their camper.

Fortunately they decided they were ready to leave shortly after Isla. The little girl and her new pal were parted less than an hour after their meeting.

Max looked back at the little girl as he was led on his lead back out into the sunshine his tail wagging non-stop.

Isla and Alice followed and both sets of travellers said goodbye in the spacious dusty car park, Alice hardly noticed her return to the rear of the Falcon she was too busy looking round trying to wave goodbye to her new friend.

-***-

An hour behind Bruce and Ryan were rattling along in the truck, they too eased into Yalata but only to have a piss and swap over positions, Bruce taking over the driving.

They swept into the Nundroo Hotel/Motel, Ryan failed to notice the dusty, blue Falcon departing from the front of the buff coloured, single story block of buildings.

'We aren't going to run short of fuel again,' commented Bruce to explain why they were stopping so early, 'besides I need some more sweets.'

'You get the fuel, I'll top up for my sweet tooth and pay, alright.'

'Fair enough,' agreed Ryan accepting the proffered keys from his driving companion.

'Get some more bottled water, will you,' he added, as he eased himself out of the truck to the departing Bruce.

In reality Bruce should have swapped tasks, Ryan with one immobile arm and hand, found it difficult to firstly unlock the filler cap and then insert the nozzle of the petrol pump into the truck's tank opening.

Finally he managed the task while Bruce watched impatiently from the air-conditioned kiosk.

In the end, fuel tank topped off and cap back in place, Ryan was able to signal his partner that the task was complete.

They left Nundroo about ten minutes behind Isla and Alice in the Falcon at 1310 South Australian time.

Now there were plenty of enormous cultivated fields, the occasional section of trees either side of the road but it was very flat. There was a lot more traffic in comparison with the earlier part of the journey. Most of the time there was traffic in sight coming from the East.

They didn't know it but they were inching closer to the Falcon and its cargo Isla with only 150 kilometres to their next stop was cruising at just over the 100kph whereas the truck's cruise control was set at 110.

The nearer they got to Penong the more of the massive wheat fields lined either side of the road.

There were lots more signposted roads on either side of the road, mainly marked with post boxes for the many farmhouses and some to places Ryan had never heard of, Coorabbin, Fowlers Bay and the like.

By 1400 Bruce was slowing for Penong, and the dual carriageway through the town. As they passed the blue sky sign welcoming them to Penong a light above the road ahead of them started to flash red and Bruce had to brake reasonably sharply to stop before the children's crossing.

A gaggle of young chattering schoolchildren in the dark blue, short sleeved uniform tops matching hats accompanied by three adults were waiting at the crossing to return to the primary school on the south side of the road.

A large over-sized load had shuddered to a halt on the other side of the crossing its escorting yellow truck, its twin yellow roof lights flashing, waiting alongside them for the crossing to clear.

Up ahead they had nearly caught the Falcon, Isla was just increasing speed on clearing the town, she pushed the Falcon up to 115 before setting the cruise control, Alice was starting to complain and she was now impatient for Ceduna it only being 45 minutes away.

Ryan took the opportunity of a phone signal to telephone Bethany.

'Hi its Ryan, am nearly clearing the Nullarbor, do you know where Isla and Alice are?'

'Oh hallo Ryan, she's not rung for 48 hours but should be somewhere around you.'

'I'm a little concerned, although Isla said she would only ring again when they reached Adelaide so I can't really tell you anything.'

'Fair enough, I'll be in Melbourne tomorrow if all goes right and I'll telephone again then.'

His phone cut out as they left Penong no signal being available.

Bruce set the cruise control and the truck roared along between the fenced in golden wheat fields all about ready to harvest.

The tarmac ahead appeared cleaner and had a red tint there was more traffic, a yellow school bus flashed past in the other direction.

'Feels like we're back in civilisation doesn't it?' he suggested to Bruce passing him another unwrapped boiled sweet.

'Good job too, I've had enough of this bloody place, give me the city anytime,' grumbled the driver.

Coming over the brow of a hill they could see the lume of the sea ahead and to their right, they rushed over a level crossing and flashed past a sign advertising Ceduna Keys.

Bruce slowed as they passed a sign pointing to Denial Bay and the warning to stop for Fruit fly inspection. When they reached the upturned red and white boom, a uniformed woman asked if they were carrying any fruit, when Bruce smilingly explained they were carrying none and she waved them on into the town.

Shortly after they were slowly passing along what looked the main street with either side of the road divided from the other by central median lined with tall conifers.

At the second white roundabout, by the Clock Tower a large white signpost directed them to the left for the A1 and Adelaide.

They briefly pulled into a Caltex on the edge of town refuelled and continued their journey after swapping again, Ryan again driving with his one good arm

_***_

Isla had taken the opportunity of the fruit fly stop to ask directions to the Motor Inn, it had been easy to find although on the way out of town.

The Falcon was parked outside the Motor Inn entrance, Isla and Alice checking into their room, when Ryan, Bruce and the truck swept past.

A nice lady called Karen, was so helpful and gave them a room at the rear of the complex, she said it was quieter and away from the traffic.

Isla was pleased to find that even though the Motel was classed as a budget hotel it still had a lot of amenities in the large, cool comfortable room.

'Well Alice do you feel like going into town?'

'It looks very nice.'

'Yes please Mummy,' answered the little girl.

After cleaning up Isla drove the car back to the main street and they went off, in the afternoon sunshine to explore Ceduna it's shopping and sea shore.

-***-

Back in Western Australia, the Twins were making good progress, it might be 1500 in Ceduna but it was now 1630 where they were currently refuelling at Madura.

Alexander who had been driving for the last hour, when the pain of his injuries had caused Andriy to hand over the wheel, was doing the refuelling.

Andriy was in the single storey, red tile roofed, with yellow eaves, kiosk stocking up on snacks and drinks in case they needed them and paying for the petrol. Next to the kiosk was a small two car garage an engineer working under the open bonnet of a white Holden Commodore.

On his return he pulled their road atlas from the glove compartment of the Ute and started to calculate the distances they could continue to travel before nightfall.

'It's nearly 200 kilometres to Border Village, this place Eucla just before it though, looks a better bet to get bed and board.'

'What do you think?'

'Anything will be better than last night, I'm knackered anyway,' replied his brother.

'Let's get this show back on the road, and find somewhere to get our heads down for the night.'

'Also better ring that tosser Fabio, he will be crapping himself not knowing what's happening.'

'You're right,' answered Andriy powering up his mobile before they left the forecourt.

'I've got four missed calls from him over the last two days.'

At that he lost his signal, 'bugger him he'll just have to wait until we're good and ready.'

Aleksander, yawning loudly, tiredly eased the Ute over the cracked dusty tarmac past the truck refuelling pumps of the Shell filling station and out of the eastern exit of Madura back onto the Eyre Highway.

Just over two hours later they had managed to find a double room at the Hotel Motel in Eucla and had both collapsed into the single beds provided. Andriy having taken the precaution of stuffing down four ibuprofen to enable him, he hoped, to sleep through the pain of his injuries.

22nd FEBRUARY OVERNIGHT – RYAN ARRIVES FIRST

The sun was setting behind them as Bruce on his second stint since Ceduna negotiated the truck around the streets of Port Augusta, the four and a half hour trip had been largely uneventful, except when Ryan had nearly missed the sharp left turn at Kyancutta, which could have taken them on a long diversion via Port Lincoln.

The scenery had been unchanging, huge fenced in wheat fields ready to harvest had bounded the highway on both sides. This only broken up by small towns with their massive grain silos and the accompanying grey metal water pipeline.

It had only been as they closed on Port Augusta that the scenery had changed, the famous red earth became apparent again and they could see the Flinders Ranges in the far off distance ahead of them. These disappeared in the oncoming darkness and both of them were glad to enter the lighted streets of Port Augusta without mishap.

They topped up the truck's nearly empty fuel tank, went to the toilet and continued south into the dark night towards the bright lights of Adelaide.

Bruce drove this section, there was some traffic mainly heavily laden trucks hurtling northwards through the night, especially when they left Port Pirie on their western side.

There were few problems overtaking slower southbound trucks with frequent numbers of passing lanes and plenty of warning of their presence.

After about ninety minutes and just south of Port Wakefield the road turned into the easier and faster dual carriageway, they quickly entered the northern suburbs of Adelaide.

'I'll get us clear of the city, we'll find a 24 hour stop and top her up.'

'You can take over once we get close to the Princes Highway,' Bruce concluded.

Shortly after they were in the city, Ryan was quick to spot the sign City Ring Road, Princes Highway East and Bruce followed the A2 round the north eastern outskirts of the City of Adelaide.

Their progress was slow even though it was nearly one in the morning.

'Reckon we're hitting every red light,' complained the driver as he braked again at a large junction.

Never mind that we need fuel before we clear the city, there will be bugger all on the freeway at this time of night.

Coincidentally, Bruce spotted a sign pointing to the left for Coles 24 hour petrol and service, read the white sign with red lettering.

'Hang on,' he shouted to Ryan as he pushed the truck in front of a blaring taxi and round a roundabout, back on themselves before turning left into Wakefield Street and west back towards the city centre.

They were fortunate with the early morning traffic being light in the City and were able to locate their refuelling stop quite quickly.

Bruce having paid returned to the cab of the truck, and said to Ryan his injured arm relaxed in its sling.

'You can't drive in the city with that bloody thing, I'll get us to the first rest stop on the freeway and we'll change there.'

Ryan grunted his agreement with this assessment and looking at the road atlas replied.

'Once we're clear, it will be around two and it's about eight hours to Melbourne.'

'If I do until six or later, you get your head down and then you can finish off in the daylight.'

We've been lucky so far, no cops have caught me trying to drive with this bloody thing,' he said indicating his busted arm in its sling.

'That's fine,' agreed Bruce manoeuvring the truck back onto the Princes Highway before pointing its head in a south easterly direction towards Melbourne.

Fifteen minutes later Ryan was driving himself and they were passing through the brightly lit Mount Barker tunnel, Bruce his head back and snoring loudly was taking Ryan's previous advice.

Two hours later the south eastern freeway/ Princes Highway became the Dukes Highway at Tailem Bend, in the darkness and the radiated glow of the streetlights Ryan little realised they were close alongside the Murray River.

An hour later they were crossing over into Victoria, Bruce noted the sign and yawned loudly, a country station's music was helping to keep him awake.

He realised he should adjust the dashboard clock to the new time but couldn't work out how much he needed to change it by.

'Gawd, I'm knackered,' he thought yawning loudly again.

'The sign back there showed Horsham, 135 kilometres I'll count down to that before handing over,' he decided.

Ryan didn't make Horsham, the sun came up over his left shoulder and a warning sign about, a micro sleep can kill, put paid to his efforts to stay awake.

A single rail track and silver grey silo's too his left and freshly harvested wheat fields on either side of the road were what greeted Bruce as he awakened by Ryan easing the truck onto the grass alongside the highway.

'Where the bloody hell are we.'

'Christ its daylight,' he gasped looking around.

'We're in Victoria, nearly reached some place called Horsham.'

'Brilliant, thanks we're well on our way.'

'Let's swap over and I'll finish it off.'

'We'll be in Greensborough in no time.'

'By the way what is the time,' he said looking at his watch.

'Six thirty, that's South Australian time, so it will be seven Victorian time.'

'Is that what it is, I couldn't work it out earlier,' answered Ryan shuffling across onto the passenger side of the cab.

By the time Bruce had taken a good swig of lukewarm water from an already partially used plastic bottle, undone and started sucking a boiled fruit sweet and ushered the vehicle back onto the highway.

Ryan head resting against the passenger side window of the truck was fast asleep.

The scenery didn't change much for the next couple of hours, the road was mainly lined by Eucalyptus and behind this were mostly recently harvested fields.

They passed by the towns of Stawell, Aarat and Beaufort before being held up by roadwork's at Burrumbeet, the road skimmed the northern edge of the lake.

Shortly after they reached the Western Freeway, now all dual carriageway and were quickly skirting the northern edge of Ballarat, they were still passing between the mainly freshly harvested fields and on occasion Bruce could see a dust cloud where huge green and yellow combine harvesters were stripping the fields of their fertile crop.

They flashed through Bacchus River and began to run into morning, outer city traffic as they merged onto the Western Ring road, Bruce kept pushing, a Qantas jumbo swept overhead inbound to Tullamarine to their north.

Finally about eleven o'clock, Bruce slowed for the traffic lights at the end of the ring road and cautiously steered the truck right of the highway, south on Diamond Creek Road and into the town of Greensborough.

After going round the town's ring road twice he found what he was looking for and pulled up alongside Greensborough railway station.

The eucalyptus shaded car park looked extremely full, there was further evidence of this with all the parked cars on the approach road, so kept the engine running and turned towards Ryan.

'Ryan,' he said loudly to the recumbent figure in the passenger seat.

'We're here.'

'Where are we?'

'Greensborough, we're at the station.'

'Where's Greensborough? Replied Ryan rubbing the sleep out of his gritty eyes and trying to stretch out his stiff limbs.

'We're close by my new place, you'll be able to get a train here into the city.'

'You want to get off at Flinders Street station, apparently there's plenty of backpackers hostels around the station.'

'Also thanks for helping us across, couldn't have done it without you.'

'Thanks, I'll just get my pack,' answered Ryan opening the door and jumping out, reaching back inside for his bag.

Having retrieved it he slammed the passenger door shut, Bruce drove the truck away shouting,

'Thanks again, see ya.'

23rd FEBRUARY – ANOTHER DAY OF PROGRESS

After about three hours of fitful sleep on the motel's single bed, Andriy went back to the bathroom took another two ibuprofen, pulled his quilt onto the floor and tried to ease his painful spine by sleeping on the hard ground.

The anti-inflammatory drugs appeared to help the situation and he didn't wake until about six when sun's rays lightened the room sufficiently, he could make out the horizontal form of his brother in the other bed.

Knowing that his twin would need to do most of the driving, and not wanting to wake him Andriy quietly eased himself painfully off the hard floor, draped the quilt over his shoulders and slumped into one of the straight backed pine chairs alongside the dining table.

Having cogitated on the crash and their present chase for about two hours, Andriy was finally pleased to see his brother stretching himself awake and grunting.

'Morning Andriy, how did you sleep?

'Bloody awful, got a few hours on the bed, then had to kip on the floor, he replied unwinding himself from the chair.

'Thought I might ring Fabio and tell him our progress, what do you think?'

'Yeah alright but let's work out first when we're likely to reach this bloody place.'

'Where is it again?'

'Healesville,' replied Andriy pulling over their road atlas so he could work out the distance to go.

'Eucla to Adelaide is 1261 kilometres, according to this route map and then Melbourne is another 733.'

'Healesville is somewhat north of that so we'll be able to divert before we get to the city.'

'So, we've about 2000 kilometres left, tell him three days,' decided Aleksander who was now sat on the edge of his bed, naked and scratching an itch in his nether regions.

'I'm going for a shower, work out where we're going to stop tonight and then ring the wop bastard.'

Looking at the road atlas Andriy worked out that Ceduna was about 500 kilometres where they would sure to be able to get their heads down for the night, any further and they would be at risk of not finding anywhere to sleep, although Wuddina might be feasible.

Andriy made a note to himself to ask at the Reception desk here in Eucla

Undecided about which destination he should recommend to Aleksander, he rang Fabio.

'Where the bloody hell have you two been hiding, Luca is beside himself,' roared Fabio before Andriy had time to speak.

'Watch you're sodding mouth you tosser, remember what we warned you about previously,' replied Andriy angry at Fabio's attitude.

We're making progress, you can only drive this bloody road in the daytime as we found out, thanks to your dim-witted Australian animals.'

'What happened, where are you?' Answered Fabio cautiously.

'We hit a kangaroo, fortunately our bull bars saved us, and we're just about to cross the border into South Australia.'

'When do you reckon you'll reach the uncle's place?'

'More importantly, have you any news of the girl and the kid?'

'Yeah, Luca reckons she must be driving the Ford Falcon, he says she wouldn't leave that behind it's worth too much.'

'It's why I've been trying to contact you the last two days to tell you to keep an eye out for it.'

'We have,' replied Andriy, 'we haven't seen or passed anything like it.'

'We'll be in Healesville the evening of the 26th we reckon, that's three days from now.'

'If it's like you say with the lead she had and the kid in tow we'll either pass her or arrive at the same time, we reckon,' added Andriy.

'Right, I'll let Luca know,' responded Fabio, accepting the situation but knowing Luca wasn't going to be happy.

'We'll let you know when we arrive or if we catch the Falcon,' said Andriy angrily cutting the connection.

At that moment Aleksander returned from the shower and Andriy passed on the gist of the conversation to his twin brother.

'We shouldn't be bothered by Fabio again for a while then, you get yourself sorted out, we'll get some breakfast and get on our way then,' decided Aleksander.

After a leisurely breakfast, having settled their bill and refuelled the Ute, by 0830 the twins had returned to the eastward bound side of the highway. Aleksander was driving and his aching brother was attempting to make himself comfortable in the passenger seat while chewing on a number of ibuprofen tablets.

'You're not much use with your injuries and don't think I'm going to let you drive if your dosed up on them things,' sneered his twin while steering the Commodore past another huge truck and trailer.

_***_

Five hundred kilometres by road to the east, Isla was putting Alice onto her seat in the rear of the Falcon, this time the little girl went willingly there was a DVD player attached to the rear of the seat in front of her.

Isla had spotted it in a Charity Op shop when they had been strolling the streets of Ceduna the previous afternoon. With the help of a mature lady volunteer, they had made sure it was working, bought up the half a dozen DVD's that would suit Isla and returned to the Motel in a fit of excited anticipation.

There Isla had set it up on a table in their room and while it was being charged, Alice had watched a story about fairies, dressed in a yellow pinafore dress with matching buckled shoes, sitting cross legged on a multi-coloured rattan rug, in front of the little screen, her left fist in her mouth in deep concentration.

Isla had been concerned about the charge not lasting long enough to keep Alice distracted but a helpful receptionist at the Motel had pulled out a bunch of wire from a box under the reception desk and found one that fitted the cigarette lighter in the car.

With the chatter from the DVD player in the rear as an accompaniment, Isla turned onto the Eyre Highway and headed eastwards, they were soon bumping over the railway line on the outskirts of Ceduna and as they passed the low slung white buildings of the local airport, on their right a mainly white commuter aircraft with a multi-coloured REX on its fuselage lifted off towards the east.

The pale landscape helped the glare and as she drove, Isla adjusted the car's sun shield to give her the best protection from that and the rising yellow orb at her left front.

Alice was avidly watching cartoons on her newly bought machine and Isla dressed in cut-off blue denim shorts, matching t shirt and red sandals soon settled into her driving routine.

They stopped twice briefly to changeover Alice's DVD's, before reaching Port Augusta about one in the afternoon, Isla felt quite refreshed, the drive had been relatively simple and Alice had hardly uttered a sound.

'Let's find some lunch darling,' she shouted to the little girl.

At first there wasn't much evidence of the city the road became a divided dual carriageway, the ready to harvest yellow fields disappeared and the green fairways of a golf course were visible through the trees on their left.

It wasn't until they turned south at a large junction, that they started to meet the first real evidence of the many inhabitants with a petrol station on their left.

After that it was all houses, local traffic, fast food and hotels, seeing a Road House, with food and refuelling station, Isla pulled in intent on lunch, refuelling and a decision about how much further they should go that day.

Putting the un-protesting Alice into a high chair, Isla bought the drinks and a light lunch from the counter to their table, before looking again at her road atlas.

'We can go on from here and stop at tea time, that will take us down to Adelaide, unless we go the country route,' she explained to Alice, who was listening, while happily chomping on a large white choc chip cookie.

'Or we can stop here, there's really not much by the looks of the map between here and the City,' she thought out aloud.

'Let's ask the garage about what's best,' she decided.

'What do you think Alice?'

'Yes mummy, was her answer.

To which Isla laughed and tickled Alice under her chin.

Isla decided as they had crossed the Nullarbor and were back in civilisation again she could safely call her mother.

Pulling her mobile from the voluminous white handbag she always used, Isla powered the fully charged phone into life and speed dialled her mother.

While she waited for it to ring she spoke to Alice, 'just going to talk to grandma and then we'll be on our way.'

As soon as it rung it was answered by Bethany who exploded with relief over the air waves.

'Darling, thank god you've rung.'

'Are you both alright?'

'Where are you?'

'That lousy Fabio rang last night and threatened us.'

'What happened mother?'

'He telephoned last night, Ray answered and he threatened all sorts of things if we wouldn't tell him where you and Alice were.'

'Ray didn't properly understand, and it was only when Fabio said I would get something worse happen to me next time,' that he slammed the phone down.

'I had tell Ray what's going on, what happened to me and about them horrible criminals chasing you both, so we've been to the police.'

'It's so awful,' wailed Bethany.

At which point Isla could here Ray reassuring and calming her mother.

'Isla, its Ray.'

'Yes.'

'Firstly, your mother Bethany.'

'I took her to the police and they've treated her right, now we've been threatened by the brother we can report him as well.'

'Now about you and Alice, I don't think we need to know where you are, just that you're safe.'

'I'm also aware that you are, from what your mother tells me clear of the Nullarbor and somewhere in South Australia by now.'

'Yes that's right.'

'Piece of advice,' recommended Ray.

'When you get to Port Augusta, that's the end of the route everyone has to take, most people going to Melbourne go via Adelaide.'

'Don't do that, it's almost certain those two dangerous heavies will go that way.'

'You must keep to the north and go down the Goyder Highway to Mildura, have you got that?'

'Yes,' replied Isla uncertainly, 'is it much further that way?'

'No, about an hour if that,' re-assured Ray.

'Have you a piece of paper and pen available?'

'I'll give you my mobile number, you can ring me, daily or if you need help at any time.'

'Thanks.'

'Hang on a sec,' exclaimed Isla rummaging in her bag for a pen.

'Got it, go ahead,' exclaimed Isla with paper napkin and Red Cross pen poised to write.

Ray gave her the mobile number and the code to dial from South Australia and then Victoria.

'Don't forget, ring any time day or night.'

'Oh something else I nearly forgot.'

'Your ex is in a Backpackers Hostel in Melbourne, he wants to help and intends being at the Post Office in Healesville from midday on the 26th.'

'He says to ring when you can, he's really desperate to help you both and has had his own run in with those two creeps, so use him if you need, he really cares you know.'

'Alright and thanks very much, I'll have to think about Ryan, we had better get back on the road,' replied Isla uncertainly.

'Look after mother and we'll ring tonight to see how it all went.'

'Thanks again,' she added shutting down the mobile to save the battery.

Isla looked at Ray's suggested route and realised they would come into Healesville from the north and avoid the cities and their traffic altogether.

She liked the idea.

Having noted that they needed to turn east off the Adelaide road just before Crystal Brook 115 kilometres to the south of their present position, Isla felt anxious after the conversation with Ray and eager to get onto the new route before the Twin's Ute could appear over the horizon.

Isla retrieved Alice from her chair, cleaned and tidied her up, before they both walked out to the Falcon.

23rd FEBRUARY PM – CEDUNA TO BURRA

Isla refuelled the car after re-installing Alice in the Falcon's rear and making sure the little girl had a new DVD in place.

Soon they were southbound and crossing the bridge before leaving the city centre on their left.

It was now just gone 2pm and Isla had no idea where they would stop that evening all she cared about was clearing the Princess Highway at Crystal Brook.

The telephone call with Ray had frightened her, in her mind she knew it was unlikely the Twins would spot them.

'Still it's unnerving to think those two bastards could be anywhere by now,' she shivered at the thought.

Clearing Port Augusta the road crossed a viaduct between two masses of blue water before they cleared the city and the dual carriageway petered out.

For most of the way down to Crystal Brook Isla broke the speed limit wanting to reach the relative safety of the town and clear the main highway as soon as possible.

At first the road was similar to the Nullarbor mainly scrubland, only the mountains to the left breaking the horizon and the occasional glimpses of the Spencer Gulf to the West.

After a while a single track railway hugged the road on their nearside and the monotony was only broken by the light traffic they were overtaking.

As the kilometres rapidly clicked past, the land began to change with distant farmhouses and sun-browned wheat fields.

They raced past the two Port Pirie junctions and through Warnertown, Isla was, after just over an hours fast driving pleased to see the green sign indicating the B64, Goyder Highway, Burra and Crystal Brook to their left.

Glancing in her rear view mirror with no indication of a blue Commodore Ute, she indicated and swept the Falcon off the highway and into the approach to the town of Crystal Brook.

Shortly after a sign indicated it was four kilometres to the town and somewhere called Burra was another ninety five,

Isla liked the name and she was certain they could manage another hour, she decided to risk it, she was sure there must be food and accommodation.

Isla slowed down to the requisite sixty kilometres per hour as the car dropped into a dip on the now tree lined road.

It was easy to follow the signage for Burra, and the Goyder Highway through Crystal Brook, a ninety degree right turn followed by a similar left turn shortly after they rumbled across a rail track put them back on course.

It was now three pm.

-***-

At the same time, the Commodore Ute with Aleksander still driving, was halfway between Ceduna and Port Augusta.

They had cleared the Nullarbor at Ceduna in less than five hours and were now racing along the Eyre Highway towards Port Augusta.

They had stopped briefly for fuel and to top up with snacks in Ceduna. Andriy had taken no part in the driving he was stoically trying to survive the ride, the discomfort from his painful injuries partially helped by liberal doses of the shop bought analgesics.

Aleksander was not sympathetic and made occasional comments about carrying passengers.

'This Port Augusta seems to be the only place we can reasonably stop, is there anywhere else further on?' Asked Aleksander.

His brother wearily and gingerly reached onto the dash and pulled the already open road atlas onto his lap.

Looking at the map he concluded and informed his brother, 'there's nothing really, anyway you'll already have done nearly a thousand kilometres today, I think we should stop there, at this place Port Augusta.'

'Surely we must be catching them?'

'Yeah almost certainly, and on this road we're goanna spot them if we catch them up.'

'Those Falcons are distinctive and there's only been this one road they can be driving on since we left Norseman,' concluded Aleksander.

By six in the evening they had found and checked into a roadside motel on the north side of Port Augusta, with the intention of starting early the next morning.

-***-

Shortly before, Isla, Alice and the Falcon had entered the town of Burra, looking for a bed for the night.

The trip down the Goyder Highway had mainly been uneventful except when they reached the T junction with the Northern Highway, with Burra not indicated on the green signposts, Isla had guessed and turned to the right guessing that going south was the best idea.

Within the next kilometre there had been another sign confirming her deduction, indicating Burra at sixty-six kilometres.

A few kilometres later they had turned east again back onto the Goyder Highway and briefly thereafter passed through the northern edge of Gulnare.

Throughout the road had been surrounded by harvested brown fields on either side, the terrain had become more hilly and bendy with occasional switchbacks.

About thirty kilometres out of Burra, they passed round the southern edge of Spalding before continuing their journey.

Isla was pleased they had made it this far and felt safer now they had diverted to the slightly longer country route.

Now all she wanted was a bed and a meal for both of them, as she steered the car off the Highway and into Burra.

Two tall white silos marked the town to their right and unsure where to go Isla stayed with the Highway until a road sign indicated the town centre and Adelaide on the B32, Barrier Highway to their right.

Meandering down the road they eventually came across the Burra Motor Inn, on the left side of the road and just before the main street of the town.

Pulling in, between the gap in the yellow stone wall and with crossed fingers, Isla drew to a halt outside the Reception of this National chain's motel.

She was much relieved to find an available room, happily they were able to settle in for another night of strange beds and bedrooms.

-***-

In Melbourne, Ryan was hanging around the Back Packers Hostel he had found on Flinders Street

The room was shared, clean, comfortable and most importantly cheap, with his busted arm and finger he couldn't even grab a couple of day's casual work because of the injuries and cash was fast becoming a problem.

He had worked out he would need to be up in Healesville in a couple of days and already made his plans. A train to Lilydale and then a bus from there.

'All I need to know is when,' he thought as he made his way back from wandering around Melbourne's CBD.

He felt grubby and in need of a shower but happy he was doing the right thing following Isla and the little girl east to Victoria.

'I'll telephone Bethany in the morning,' he decided.

24th FEBRUARY PM – OUYEN FRIGHT

The Twins were awake early, Andriy was feeling better having dosed himself up again on more ibuprofen, his supreme fitness assisting his restorative powers.

Both were dressed in black singlet and similarly coloured jeans looking at the road atlas and discussing their plan for the day.

'I reckon I can help with the driving today, commented Andriy to his brother.

'Had my first good night's sleep for three days last night,' he added.

'About bloody time,' yawned Aleksander, maliciously, 'save me killing myself.'

'We've got to decide which way we're going to go later on this morning,' pointed out Andriy.

'It's either through Adelaide or cross country along something called the Goyder Highway.'

'Alright,' asked Aleksander, 'which is best do you reckon?'

'Going through Adelaide is only slightly shorter, than the other route which is more northerly but we've got false number plates and we don't know if the West Australian cops are onto us.,

'I think we had best avoid the city then and take the country route, less chance of police and we'll avoid the city roads of Melbourne.'

'That's it then, country route, we'll try you out first, see if you can cope and I'll navigate for a change.'

'Mind you first thing is food and fuel.'

'Think they'll have a MacDonald's round here I fancy some breakfast.'

At that they checked out, paid their bill refuelled and went in search of their breakfast.

'MacDonald's, there must be a bloody MacDonald's somewhere in this town,' exclaimed Aleksander, rubbing his ample belly as they headed out across the Spencer Gulf Bridge, towards the main part of Port Augusta south of the crossing.

Andriy who was adjusting to driving with his injuries, didn't reply for a moment or two, and who didn't really want to leave the main highway was saved when he spotted a sign pointing out the Port Augusta Trotting Track to the left.

'There, see that sign, Hungry Jacks 2 kilometres on the left.'

'I there's one of them there's surely got to be a place with enough McMuffins for you close by.'

'If not, we'll just have to use one of the others.'

'Alright,' agreed Aleksander tetchily.

At that moment Aleksander's favourite food outlet hove in site and Andriy pulled the Ute into the car park.

'I'm not moving out of this seat, now I've got myself comfortable, you go and get us breakfast and we'll eat here in the cab.'

His brother departed rapidly for the fast-food restaurant and within twenty minutes, Andriy having broken his fast and with his twin still chomping away on the remains of their repast, they had returned to the Highway and were making rapid progress southwards, it was only eight o'clock in the morning.

-***-

In their motel in Burra, Isla was feeling safe and luxuriating in the thought of not having to rush out of bed that morning.

'There's no way those bastards of Luca's are going to follow me now,' she thought happily.

Alice for whom there had been no cot available, after sleeping in a single bed in the corner of the room, had risen earlier and was now contentedly sitting on a green and yellow rug in her pink pyjamas, happily playing with her rag doll.

'What do you reckon Alice?'

'Think we had better get up?'

Alice swivelled round on her bottom so she could face her mother, who was now sitting up in bed starching her arms clear of the red kaftan she used as her nightdress.

'Yes mummy, breakfast please.'

'Okay darling, I'll have a shower and we'll both get dressed.'

An hour later, Isla dressed in her denim shorts and fresh white T shirt was with Alice, in her own yellow T and green shorts sitting in a café in the centre of Burra eating breakfast.

Finishing breakfast, and completing their toilet, Isla settled Alice into their fully refuelled car, set a DVD going and steered the Falcon north out of the Burra town centre and back to the Goyder Highway, where she turned them east towards Morgan, the next town on the Highway eighty five kilometres to the east. It was coming on for nine thirty in the morning and the Twins were closer than Isla realised.

-***-

At the same time, Aleksander was sitting in the passenger seat of the Ute trying to work out from the road atlas where they were meant to turn off the Princes Highway to avoid going through Adelaide.

'It's no good,' he said to his driving brother.

'You know I've never been able to follow these bloody things,' he declared angrily.

'You're always the Navigator and I'm the driver, we should stick to what we're best at.'

Andriy, trying to concentrate on his driving and not think about the pain from his lower back, sighed exasperatedly and angrily replied.

'Bloody hell you never know what you want.'

'We'll change again as soon as I can stop and I'll try and work out where we are.'

'What did that last signpost say at that junction?'

'Someplace called Crystal Brook,' answered Aleksander sulkily.

'Oh Christ, I'm sure we were meant to turn off there, I couldn't see the sign because we were passing that tractor and trailer.'

'Bloody hell we'll have to stop and work out how to get back on track, he cried, slowing the Ute whilst looking for somewhere convenient to stop.

He was glad he had slowed because as they came round a bend in the highway he could suddenly see two police vehicles parked astern of a massive, high sided grey truck and trailer on their side of the road.

Aleksander drove the Ute sedately past the parked vehicles.

'Well that's it we can't go back just in case these plates are hot, we need to get off this road soonest as well.'

Fortunately they found an unsigned right turn within half a kilometre and Aleksander swung the Ute into the turning heading towards the massive white silo on the horizon.

'If we're lucky that's our town,' he said pulling the Ute over to the side of the road.

'Here you take over the bloody driving and I'll tell you where to go.

'It's a bloody long way to nowhere, if we get lost in this country,' Andriy added, gingerly easing himself out of the now open driver's door.

'Christ I'm stiff,' he winced from the pain of his crash injuries.

Once they had swapped positions, Andriy instructed his brother to drive towards the silo, the road they were on wasn't marked on the map but as he thought, Crystal Brook the start of their cross country trip was.

Fairly quickly Aleksander was having to slow at the 80kph sign as they drove between the brown, freshly harvested fields.

Shortly after they slowed for the 50kph sign they went straight across a dusty cross roads, a small blue sign indicated they were on Frith Road, this didn't help Andriy who was trying to navigate from a small scale map which only showed the major routes.

They passed a number of single story white with red tiled roof's residential buildings, many had silver corrugated fencing surrounding their properties.

Aleksander pulled up at a give-way sign, the town's huge white grain silo was directly ahead of them, and fortunately nothing was astern of the vehicle.

'Where now Andriy?'

'I'm not sure.'

'Take a left, there must be a sign somewhere around here,' he surmised loudly.

The road was tree lined on their near side, through the trees Andriy could see massive grain hoppers lined up behind two huge yellow diesel engines.

Aleksander pulled up at a red stop sign at another cross roads.

Frustratingly the only road sign was on their left but it was the back of the metal sign.

'Pull forward a bit, so we can read that sign,' he told his brother.

His sibling obliged and Andriy was with some difficulty able to read the two green metal boards with their yellow writing.

'Left,' he shouted to his brother.

'It says B64, that's what we want.'

'Hope it's the right way this time,' grunted his brother in turn as he steered the Ute towards the Town Centre and across the train lines.

Andriy looked back at another sign on the opposite side of the road.

'Damn,' he swore, we should have gone straight across, back there.

'That sign we passed shows Burra to the left, we're going the wrong way.'

'Quick, quick, turn around,' he added urgently as they bumped across the rail tracks.

'Hang on a bloody minute, let's just find somewhere to do a U turn.'

'It isn't that ruddy easy,' he continued exasperatedly at his sibling as they went straight across the crossroads.

Fortunately there was an almost empty parking area in front of the tractor supply depot on the left and he was able to swing the Ute round and back onto the road behind a mature lady in a small red Echo.

Just as they cleared the crossroads the red warning lights on the level crossing started to flash and a cacophony of noise from the warning bells reverberated around the cab of the Ute.

Expecting the little red car ahead of them to go across the crossing, Aleksander tail gated her hoping to make it himself and nearly ran into the rear of the car when the driver decided to stop.

He was now too close to whip around the offending vehicle and couldn't reverse due to a heavy tractor and trailer, which had just pulled up behind them, realising they were going to have to wait, he swore.

'Damn and blast, stupid bloody woman we're going to have to wait bloody ages.'

'Calm down, calm down, we both got it wrong.'

'How long can it take for a train to come across, its only single track after all.'

It appeared an age before the two, massive, dirty, gold and green, diesel engines in tandem, hauling a seemingly never ending line of grey 100 tonne grain hoppers, started to slowly pass across their front.

The Twins, impatiently watched the cause of their delay in silence while seething at this unfortunate delay, which only happened because Aleksander had failed to note the correct turning earlier.

About forty trucks had passed them when with much clanking the train shuffled to a halt in front of them.

'For Christ's sake,' swore Andriy, 'what now?'

'Can we get round this if I can turn round,' asked his brother.

Andriy picked up the road atlas and glanced at the small scale map of Crystal Brook and its surrounds.

 'Nothing, we're stuck here until this bloody thing moves on,' he concluded waving his right arm at the stationary train in front of them.

They didn't know that the train was still being made up and it was a good twenty minutes later after some backing and forwarding that the lengthy train cleared the level crossing.

Finally they resumed their journey, after the delay and their missed turnings, they were now over ninety minutes behind the Falcon and its occupants.

-***-

Meanwhile back in Melbourne Ryan telephoned Bethany's mobile, to check on the progress of Isla and Alice.

Ray answered, 'Hi Ryan, how are you getting on?'

'Struggling a bit, cash is a bit short and with this buggered arm I can't even earn anything either.'

'How's Bethany, and what's the news of the girls?'

'Bethany's doing okay, we've been to the cops and they really looked after her.'

'They've put a National all-points bulletin out for those two Ukrainian thugs, we've told the cops what we think they're doing and they're going to pass it onto the Victorians.'

'Isla reckons they'll reach Healesville tomorrow evening, so you'll need to be at the post office in the afternoon.'

'Oh and we can't get hold of Bethany's brother, his mobile isn't answering and there's something wrong with the landline to the Vineyard.'

'Right, I've worked how to get up there, its train and bus and doesn't cost a lot, so I'll be there from noon ready and waiting,' said Ryan enthusiastically.

'Fine, I'll get off the phone and save you some call time.'

'Good luck and keep in touch.'

'Thanks,' replied Ryan as Ray cut the connection.

-***-

At first after leaving Burra, the road continued as the previous day with rolling hills, long sweeping bends and recently harvested fields on either side of the highway. About twenty minutes into their journey, the road straightened, the fields disappeared and the surrounding land reverted to bare scrub, with the occasional small trees breaking up the scenery.

Shortly before arriving at Morgan there were the occasional harvested fields on their north side, a warning to eat their fruit and a large blue sign welcoming them to Riverland?

They drove straight through Morgan, turning left at the dust lined T junction and continued on the B64 towards Monash and Renmark.

Another hour later around ten thirty they were bearing left onto the Sturt Highway and finally leaving the Goyder. Isla pulled over onto the sandy hard shoulder for a quick drink of water and to change Alice's DVD.

The little girl appeared to have got used to the long days in the car and no longer complained.

Isla took the opportunity to refill Alice's mug with juice before setting off again, east towards the town of Monash.

The green Sturt Highway mileage sign indicated Mildura to be 166 kilometres and with it only being eleven thirty Isla wondered whether they should have a late lunch there instead of stopping earlier.

They rolled through Monash passing between some vineyards, before accelerating away as the speed limit allowed.

Shortly after Isla, Alice and the Falcon, drove into the busy town of Renmark, firstly passing between vineyards and then onto a dual carriageway lined with trees.

There was plenty of industry and commercial premises with fast food outlets, the dual carriageway was wide and every business on each side of the road, had plenty of frontage space.

They passed under the Town Centre sign, a white half ships wheel with yellow nineteenth century steamboat at its centre, showing the history and the town's connection with the River Murray.

At the point when the central median widened into well-tended lawn surrounded by flowering plants, a sign indicated a left turn across the oncoming carriageways towards Mildura.

Isla indicated, pulled into the outside lane and was able to steer the Falcon serenely across the other carriageway and onto a single carriageway road, they were soon clear of the town and passing a bend in the Murray River which made the Sturt Highway veer sharply to their left.

Caravan sites on the left side of the road reminded Isla how close they were to Australia's premier river, shortly thereafter they were crossing the river itself the muddy brown water of the gently flowing wide watercourse below them as they rumbled across the north side of the red, steel, structured passageway.

As they left a yellow bricked red roofed Lutheran Church on their left the highway sign indicate that Mildura was 139 kilometres ahead.

Isla looked at the dashboard clock, 'twelve thirty, Alice with a bit of luck we'll be at Mildura for two and have lunch there.'

'Alright?'

Alice was engrossed in something on her own personal video screen and ignored her mother.

At first the Murray followed the road but then disappeared as they passed between numbers of vineyards, at Yamba a large sign shaped as a half a black tyre stretched over the road its writing thanking them for visiting Riverlands.

For the next forty kilometres until the state border their passage was accompanied by rows of vines and freshly harvested fields.

At the border a large purple sign thanked them for visiting South Australia while a smaller blue one welcomed them to Victoria.

At this point for the next ten kilometres or so the highway passed between low lying scrub and bushes with countryside returning to its natural state.

After about ten kilometres the landscape flattened and harvested wheat fields bounded both sides of the highway.

After Cullulleraine there was a massive stretch of vines to the north, Isla had visions of cool glasses of Chardonnay and licked her lips at the thought.

Soon the scenery reverted to the mainly harvested fields and as they approached Mildura itself there were cattle grazing behind fenced brown shrubbery.

There wasn't much warning on reaching the town, a large roundabout with Bendigo and Melbourne signed to the right encouraged her to follow the traffic round the busy junction.

Isla was now in urgent need of the toilet and seeing the sign for Hungry Jacks rapidly turned off the highway, parked quickly outside the fast food restaurant before rushing into the restaurant.

-***-

At the same time 1400 in Renmark having spotted the big M sign, the twins parked up and were making their way towards a late lunch themselves.

Aleksander looked at his brother who was limping and holding the base of his spine with his right hand.

'You don't look too good, how's it going?' He asked his twin.

'I'll be alright, just stiff from sitting still for so long,' he answered with a grimace as he stretched out his arms and tried to ease the tightened muscles in his back.

Aleksander led the way into the restaurant and made their orders.

Whilst sitting at a table consuming their food, Andriy opened up the road atlas.

'You still alright with the driving?' he enquired.

'Yeah fine, what are you thinking?'

'We can do about three more hours and stop before it gets dark.'

'There's a town called Ouyen which looks big enough to have a couple of motels, we can stop there and do Healesville by the following afternoon.'

'Sounds good to me,' grunted his sibling through a mouthful of burger.

'All agreed then,' commented his brother, 'by tomorrow night we should know where the bitch and the kid are and be able to do something about it.'

By 1420, they were back on the Sturt Highway eastbound towards Mildura.

_***_

Up ahead on the outskirts of Mildura Isla and Alice were taking their time and didn't actually leave the fast food restaurant until around 1500.

They little realised that Andriy, navigating astern of them had calculated that if the twins went through Meringur, they could cut out Mildura and shorten their journey by another fifteen minutes.

Relatively, the threat to the girls was closing fast, not only were both vehicles and their passengers aiming to stay in the same town that night, the threat of the Ukrainian thugs was now only forty minutes astern.

Isla eased the Falcon left and out into the light traffic southbound, on what was now the Calder Highway.

'Just an hour left today darling,' Isla said over her shoulder to the little girl in the rear of the car as they increased speed on clearing the outskirts of Mildura.

At first they passed between miles of vineyards and harvested fields, accompanied by the inevitable rail line close by on the west side of the highway.

At Carwarp a massive grey, grain silo towered over the surrounding land close to the highway and briefly divided them from the rail line.

Soon they were running between the inevitable bush of stunted Eucalyptus, bushes and yellow dusty sand.

It was only as they approached Ouyen, that the road was bordered by harvested fields, the inevitable agricultural support businesses and the inescapable rail line.

Soon they were bumping slowly across the railway while Isla was looking on both sides of the road for a possible motel.

Finally she spotted a motel sign on their side of the highway, Ouyen Motel said the sign at the entrance to the Budget Motel its red and white bricked buildings at variance with the surrounding scenery.

Isla steered the Falcon into the Motel grounds past the red lettered vacancy sign and alongside the Motel Office astern of a green station wagon with at least three children running wild in the rear of the car.

Isla stepped out into the afternoon heat, released Alice from her car seat in the rear, before entering Motel's reception.

A harassed looking woman, in mainly white, short sleeved dress and yellow apron, stood behind a bar height reception desk. She was trying to persuade the middle aged couple, presumably from the station wagon outside that the only room that was still vacant wouldn't be large enough for the couple and their brood.

'Sir, I am really sorry because of this weekend's fair we only have that room and it's our smallest.'

The guy answered, 'that's alright darling we'll take it and make do.'

'Sir, I'm afraid you can't because of the fire regulations.'

'The room is limited to two persons and just isn't big enough to hold anymore.'

'Come on darling,' said his partner pulling at his right sleeve with her right hand, 'we have plenty of time, Mildura is only an hour up the road, it's bigger and will have ample spare accommodation there.'

'Alright it's a bugger though.'

'Thanks anyway love,' he said to the receptionist as the pair made their way out of the doorway.

'It was worth a try,' he could be heard saying to his wife as the screen door crashed back into its frame as they left the building.

Isla having overheard the conversation spoke to the lady behind the counter,

'Can we have the room please?'

'Sure love if there's only the two of you, it has twin beds, is small and I'm afraid I haven't a cot left for your little girl, we're so busy.'

'That's alright,' assured Isla gratefully, 'Alice will be fine.'

'Won't you darling,' she said to her daughter who was busily fingering some old magazines, lying on a brown wooden coffee table.

By the time Isla had completed the paperwork, paid for the room, received instructions from the Receptionist and learnt about local eateries; the Twins and their Ute were minutes from the Ouyen welcome sign to the north of the town.

Isla sat Alice in the front passenger seat of the car and drove the car into the first clear parking spot, next to a battered, dirty yellow, working Ute, which was itself facing the building in the first space adjacent to Reception.

Grabbing Alice and setting her onto the pathway, Isla opened the screen door and unlocked the door to their Motel room. Pushing Alice inside, she laughingly joked with the little girl, 'You explore darling and choose your bed, I'll get some stuff from the car.'

Leaving the door open, Isla went between the Ute and the Falcon, opened the rear inside door and bending reached inside for their overnight bag.

Behind her she could hear the noise of a large vehicle pulling up outside Reception.

'They'll be unlucky,' she thought as she tried to select clean clothes, from the rear of the car, to stuff inside the bag.

The doors of the vehicle behind her, slammed in unison as its passengers exited the vehicle.

Having, she thought, put everything they needed inside the bag Isla stood up and looked behind her over the rear of the dirty yellow Ute.

In front of her was the large deep blue Commodore Ute and disappearing through the outside door of the Reception, were Luca's Ukrainian enforcers.

24th FEBRUARY EVENING - SAFE, TONIGHT AT LEAST

For a moment despair overwhelmed her, 'how the hell did they find us here?'

The despondency and feeling of hopelessness lasted for what seemed eternity but was in fact only moments.

The determination which had got her through the past few days, quickly kicked in.

Throwing the overnight bag back into the car, Isla pushed the open car door shut as quietly as she could and retreated rapidly across the concrete pathway, into the open door of the Motel room.

Quietly pulling the screen door too she eased the door eased itself closed until the lock engaged.

Behind her, Alice bouncing on the nearer of the two single beds screamed loudly, 'look mummy, my bed.'

Isla grabbed the little girl and snapped fearfully at her daughter, 'quiet!'

At this show of temper from her mother, Alice burst into tears.

Isla hugged her daughter to her breast and tried to console the little girl, while desperately attempting to peer through the grey net curtains covering the rooms' only window.

-***-

Inside the Reception Office the lady proprietor still in her apron, had again left her kitchen to respond to the Reception desk bell, was trying to explain to the unsympathetic twins, why the vacancy sign was still lit and the fact, there were no rooms that night.

'I'm sorry lads, I just recently rented that room to a woman and a little girl, there's nothing available here because of the fair this coming weekend.'

Andriy angrily retorted, 'why's the vacancy sign lit then.'

'It's my fault, I forgot to switch on the No sign,' she replied, reaching to and flicking a switch, on the wall behind her to the on position.

'There it's done now, I'm awfully sorry fellas,' she apologised.

'If you turn right at the next junction and go into town the pub will probably still have vacancies for tonight, they don't normally fill up until the fair at the weekend.'

'I bloody well hope so,' grumbled Andriy as they departed the office.

Aleksander angrily slammed the screen door to as they returned to their vehicle.

He made sure he left deep ruts in the Motel's gravel driveway as he turned the Ute, before showering the yellow Ute and motel walls with loose gravel.

Following the woman's advice they made their way into Ouyen, the flashing no vacancy sign mocking them as they turned left out of the motel's environs.

They easily found the two storey Victorian pub and were able to book a room for the night.

Thirty minutes later they were both nursing a beer while standing at the bar of the local hostelry.

Both were still a bit annoyed about the Motel and the vacancy sign.

'Bloody woman shouldn't have the place if she can't do her job properly,' grumbled Aleksander wiping froth from his upper lip after his first gulp of the cool refreshing beer.

At this point Andriy realised the woman might have said something important but couldn't remember what it was exactly.

'Aleksander, never mind complaining about the sign what else was it she said.'

'Bloody hell, she said a woman and young girl had just booked in.'

'It couldn't be could it?'

'Don't know but we need to check now,' urged Andriy slamming his half-drunk beer onto the bar counter and making for the outer doorway.

Aleksander reaching into his trouser pocket for the Ute's keys, urgently followed his rapidly departing brother.

-***-

As soon as the Ute disappeared out onto the highway, Isla ran from their room in time to see it turning right at the next junction.

Returning to the room she snatched Alice from the bed and made their way into the Office.

Hearing the bell again, the proprietor angrily left her cooking once again and stormed through to the Reception desk, cursing people who couldn't see the no vacancy sign.

Her anger evaporated when she saw Isla holding Alice in her arms.

'Is there anything wrong with the room darling?' She asked.

'No, I'm sorry something has come up and we can't stop I'm afraid, do you think you can let the room again, I can't really afford to pay twice.'

Being a sucker for little ones and girls in distress, certain she would fill the vacancy, she switched the no vacancy sign off and re-assured Isla.

'Look darling there's nothing goes on the Credit Card until the morning, if we don't fill the room I'll charge you fifty percent, otherwise there'll be no charge.'

'How's that?'

'That's fantastic, we'll get out of your hair and thanks again,' she said as Alice and her departed.

Determined the Twins, if they even guessed about Alice and her even being in Ouyen, wouldn't know where they had gone, Isla steered the Falcon left out of the motel.

Instead of doing the obvious and going south, not caring about the direction, she steered the Falcon left and east onto the Mallee Highway, they soon exited Ouyen and Isla had the car flying along, in a sort of controlled panic.

Alice in the rear of the vehicle, wasn't best pleased at being suddenly bundled into the car again and started to whine.

'You said we were staying there and to pick my bed,' she whined.

This was the last thing Isla needed, she needed to control the car and think, think, think.

'Shush Alice please, we need to get away from some really bad men.'

Alice, her senses attuned to her mother's moods, stopped whimpering and rubbed her eyes dry with the backs of her hands.

Almost before they knew it he Falcon was rushing through a tiny place called Kulwin, there was no visible habitation only the sandy track off either side of the highway.

Twenty minutes later Isla had to slow their rush between the freshly harvested fields as they approached the town of Manangatang, a rickety wooden sign with yellow painted lettering announced its entry, the highway split, at this point into a dual carriageway.

Although the town looked large enough, Isla didn't consider it far enough away from Ouyen to be safe from their pursuers. They continued their journey through the town and out the other side.

There was no sign of Melbourne on the signpost only places Isla had never heard of, worryingly she did recognise the place at the bottom of the sign, Sydney.

Just over an hour out of Ouyen, it now being quarter past five and only an hour from sunset they reached Piangil, Isla gratefully pulled into the Caltex station and refuelled the Ford.

Only taking the time to pay, and still very scared, she leapt back into the car and pointed its bonnet eastwards out the other side of the small town.

Even at sixty kilometres an hour they quickly passed the bowling lawns of the RSL, CFA Fire Station and the single storied houses, with their freshly cut lawns. They were soon through the small town and back on the highway with a vineyard on their left side.

Very quickly Isla was braking hard for a give way sign at a T junction, the road ahead crossed from north to south. Isla guessed and turned right, southbound behind a crossing, high-sided, grey truck and trailer.

'Should all be right now Alice,' re-assured Isla.

'Must be headed in the right direction again, we're going to someplace called Swan Hill, should be somewhere to stop there.'

Alice interrupted her mother's chatter and shouted excitedly while pointing to the left side of the road, 'ship mummy,'

Isla looked to the indicated point of the excitement and sure enough there was an old fashioned paddle steamer making its way down the Murray River which was now close alongside.

They were soon clear of that bend in the river and passed a sign indicating they were on the B400, the Murray Valley Highway and only forty two kilometres north of Swan Hill.

-***-

Only twenty minutes before the Falcon and its occupants made their southward turn onto the Murray Valley Highway the Twins stormed into the Reception of the Ouyen Motel.

There was no one to dance attendance on them and the Vacancy sign was still lit outside.

'Where the bloody hell's that woman, growled Aleksander viciously banging the desk bell to call for attention.

They waited impatiently for what seemed ages for someone to answer the bell.

Andriy marched up and down the reception while Aleksander gripped the counter, his knuckles white, as if he was about to rip the whole place apart.

A small man in green, greasy overalls put his head round the entry door, half in and half out of reception, holding open the screen door with the index fingertip of an oily right hand.

'Help you, lads?'

Andriy stepped forward and spoke quickly before his angry brother could say anything, 'we're looking for our niece and her daughter,' he lied.

'She told us she would be stopping here tonight.'

'I don't really know,'

Andriy interrupted, 'the Receptionist would know wouldn't she?'

'She sure would, that's my wife, we run the place,' he explained, 'but she's gone into town for stores and I'm working on an old banger out back.

'Drove in recently,' explained Andriy.

'Yeah saw that one, girl and a kid, in the first room, doesn't look like they're here at the moment though, car isn't here,' he said glancing outside.

'God it was filthy though looked like it has been across the Nullarbor,' he said without realising the truth of his comment

'Can you check the name for us, save us wasting our time?' queried Andriy pleasantly.

'Sorry lads, she will have locked the book away and she's a stickler for the guest's privacy.

'It's more than my life's worth to tell you even if I could.'

Aleksander's face began to redden and his brother who wasn't best pleased himself, realised he was going to have to do something before his erstwhile twin over reacted, grabbing his brother's arm with his own he interrupted.

'If you know about cars, you'll know what she was driving then,' he declared with a certain amount of sarcasm not expecting a comprehensive answer.

'Of course one of those new Falcon's, V6 engine, its own special blue paint job, were the bees knees when they were brought out a couple of years ago.'

'That what you looking for, would know it anywhere, even covered in all that crap.'

Andriy still holding his brother's thick, muscular right arm with his left could feel his twin relax as the nodded their heads at each other in agreement, replied.

'Thanks, sounds like it could be them, we'll be back later to catch up.'

The brothers brusquely brushed past the mechanic and returned to the Ute.

'What'll we do?' Grunted Aleksander once they were securely ensconced in the cab of the vehicle.

'Get some dinner and walk back a lot later.'

'Once the girl is back with the kid, she'll think they're secure for the night.'

'Fine with me,' he agreed turning the Ute round in the parking area and setting about returning to the Pub.

After a couple of more beers the Twins ordered their evening meal from the bar, sat down to fill their bellies and await sunset.

_-***-_

At the point at which her pursuers were sitting down to their meal at the Pub/Hotel in Ouyen, Isla and Alice had just completed their unexpected journey into Swan Hill, they had followed the Murray Valley Highway south between lots of vineyards and occasionally closing with the river itself, New South Wales visible on its far bank.

Swan Hill had greeted them with a large roundabout its concrete white centre increasing the glare factor from the setting sun.

Having previously passed a couple of motels on the Highway, Isla had determined after the experience at Ouyen to get off the main Highway and find somewhere more hidden to stay.

Consequently after bumping across the railway, she had taken the second turning off the roundabout, which directed them towards the city centre.

They passed through the city centre and nearly returned to the Murray Valley Highway, before Isla was able to find what she wanted, the Lady Augusta Comfort Inn Motel, just off the main drag.

Its welcoming Vacancy sign was just what they needed, Alice had been becoming irritated with the extra diversion and Isla was very scared, the closeness of their pursuers, and their escape, left her exhausted.

Now they were booked into a comfortable room and Isla was lying on one of the twin beds trying to calm her nerves.

Alice was excitedly rushing round the room exploring.

Isla couldn't believe how close they had come to meeting up with Luca's, Ukrainian enforcers.

'How the ruddy hell, have they got so close,' she cursed to herself while for Alice's sake trying not to show her agitation and burst into tears.

Trying to be decisive and react to the situation, which was going to occur sooner or later anyway she made some decisions.

Reaching into their overnight bag she gave Alice something to drink, turned on the Television, sat the little girl in front of the screen and pulled her mobile out of her handbag.

First she tried Uncle Brian's work at the vineyard, a computer generated voice repeated the previous message about there still being a problem with telephone connections to Healesville and the surrounding Yarra Valley due to local fires.

Next she telephoned her mother.

This time Bethany answered herself.

Isla explained about her near miss with the twins and told Bethany, they expected to reach Healesville the following day.

Isla asked about her mother's health, after all the recent trauma, she was re-assured by her parents reply and the support she was receiving from her partner.

Finally Isla, at her mother's insistence called Ryan.

Ryan who was lying on his bunk in the Back packers Hostel on Flinders Street, didn't recognise the number but answered anyway.

'Ryan,' asked Isla tentatively, 'is that you?'

'Sure is babe.'

'Where are you both?'

'How are you?'

'When do you get to Healesville?'

'I'm so very sorry for.........'

'Bloody hell Ryan will you let me get a word in,' interrupted Isla.

'We'll be in Healesville tomorrow afternoon.'

'We nearly ran into those awful thugs of Luca's this afternoon, so they're going to be around when we get there.'

'There has to be a visitor centre, we'll meet you there at say four, if we're going to be later than that, I'll stop somewhere and phone.'

'If you see them bastards, don't let them realise you're around, they're bloody dangerous.'

'I know to my cost,' replied Ryan to a dead phone as Isla terminated the call.

-***-

It was gone eight, by the time the sun disappeared in the north west, after a substantial dinner and a number of beers the Twins reeled out of the front of the Victoria Hotel and across the railway line at the Station in front of them. They were only a short jog across the Calder Highway to the front of the Ouyen Motel.

'Shush,' cried Andriy to his brother who had belched loudly.

They walked onto the well-lit car park and began to look at each of the cars, parked in the marked spaces' outside each of the individual rooms.

Reaching the end of the row, they looked at each other and shook their heads.

At that point someone exited one of the rooms in front of them.

Guiltily and with the effects of the booze, both of them ran off towards the exit from the motel, onto the Highway.

'Hey,' shouted a male voice behind them, what the bloody hell are you doing?'

Neither of the brothers bothered to reply as they stumbled across the highway, and the railway before arriving panting in front of the pub.

They leant against each other trying to catch their breaths, 'she definitely isn't there, she might have been but the place is full and there's no sign of the Falcon,' panted Andriy.

'What the hell, we'll find them in Healesville, sometime after we arrive tomorrow, let's not worry about it, time for another beer, suggested Aleksander making for the bar as he said it.

25th FEBRUARY AM - ON TO HEALESVILLE

Isla had difficulty sleeping because of the near miss with the Twins. It made her despair, even though they had driven across Australia, she hadn't been able to escape Luca's influence.

Isla woke up early, tired but determined to complete their journey, across the continent and hope that Uncle Brian would be able to protect them.

Even before she woke Alice, Isla had calculated their route and the nearly four hundred kilometres to their final destination Healesville. She had surmised that if they went via North Melbourne, it was only possible, although highly unlikely, they could meet up with the Twins and their Ute.

So Isla had determined to go via Bendigo and the lesser roads, through small towns like Broadford and Glenburn, where they would join the Melba Highway, south into Yarra Glen, before completing their journey into Healesville.

Having made a note of distances and junctions, Isla woke Alice.

By eight they were dressed, breakfasted and on the road to the south east, the glare of the rising sun, on her left side attempting to distract Isla.

They continued to follow the Murray Valley Highway, the harvested fields and scrubland bounding the road was broken up by frequent lakes. After three quarters of an hour they crossed a stream and entered the outskirts of Kerrang.

Isla pulled into the side of the road at the entrance to a Budget Motel and checked her notes.

'Right onto the B400 and the Loddon Valley Highway towards Bendigo,' she said aloud to Alice.

Alice waved at Isla from the rear of the car and concentrated again on her television screen.

Isla resumed their journey, steering the Falcon back onto the Highway, leaving the bright green lawns of the local tennis club on their left.

Within moments she spotted the sign indicating the right turn towards Echuca and Bendigo, she found the highway, departed leaving the town on their left, they soon cleared the outskirts and were quickly passing the green signpost, its yellow lettering confirming that Bendigo was 125 kilometres to the south.

It wasn't quite nine o'clock as they continued their journey past cattle, vineyards, scrubland and freshly harvested fields.

-***-

Isla would have been pleased, if she had been aware of what was occurring in the Pub in Ouyen.

Andriy was awake, his throbbing head stuck to his pillow, Aleksander himself was fast asleep, his unshaven face, surrounding his wide open mouth from which their emitted, a full and deep throated sonorous snore.

'Why oh, why did we have all that beer,' thought Andriy groaning to himself.

'It must be full of chemicals, my stomach feels awful and I could do without the pounding in my head.'

Finally the pressure on his bladder, forced him to stagger from his bed and into the toilet, his noisy closure of the bathroom door, waking his somnolent brother.

Almost before he had completed his ablutions, his sibling banged open the same door.

'Some night that was,' he declared to his ailing brother.

'After you, then let's get a nice big fry up and get out of here.'

'Should make Healesville easy today then we'll have some fun.'

'Bloody hell, don't know how you do it, I've got a crappy hangover and you're talking about breakfast, I would vomit if I tried to eat anything.

Aleksander as the driver had his way, and while he consumed a massive fry up, Andriy gobbled paracetamol and drunk litres of black coffee, to try and still his thumping head and queasy stomach.

Between mouthfuls, Aleksander queried, 'What's the plan?'

Andriy after glancing at the Road Atlas he had brought from the Ute replied.

'About 500 kilometres to Healesville, the nearer we get to Melbourne the faster the roads, there's a bit of country road at the end but that's it.'

'Right,' said Aleksander glancing at his watch, 'on the road by half ten, let's say six hours, Healesville by tea time.'

'What about digs?'

'We'll have to see when we get there, there doesn't seem to be a lot but there's a visitor centre marked on the map, they'll point us in the right direction.

'Besides which we might not be staying around.'

'Why not.'

'If we find the bitch and her sprog, we'll need to get out of there.'

As forecast they were back on the highway by ten thirty, the Ute's nose pointed towards Melbourne.

_***_

The Falcon was just approaching Bendigo, after days and days of little traffic, Isla had forgotten all about this and city driving. The closer she got to the city centre the worse the movement of cars and public transport became.

She knew she had to keep going into the city until she reached the A300, at times as she pushed the Falcon through the busy city, it appeared like she would never find the turning and she kept thinking she must have missed it.

Near to panic and there being nowhere convenient to stop and ask, Isla was relieved because suddenly there was the green sign, just before an exceptionally busy junction, indicating her left turn.

Isla gratefully eased the Falcon into the flow of traffic and slowly they made their way through the centre of Bendigo alongside the vintage tram tracks, until she found what they wanted, the right turn onto the B280.

Immediately the traffic eased and within minutes they were back out into the countryside.

After the flatness of the Murray and Loddon valley highways, now there were hills and fenced off fields with sheep, horses and cattle. There were plenty of trees, both sides of the road being lined with tall thin eucalyptus.

As they approached Axedale, the world went dark about them and Isla had to put the Falcons lights on full beam as a very heavy rain squall swept over them, the automatic wipers, struggling to keep the glass clear, swept rapidly across the windscreen in front of her. Isla reduced her speed and drove slowly through the small town, the rain bouncing off the black tarmac ahead of them.

Almost as soon as it arrived it was gone, the only evidence the greasy slippery wet road and the lightning flashes from the dark clouds to the north of them.

Isla accelerated as she cleared the township, just for a moment the front wheels spun and the car twitched and slid briefly towards the near side ditch on the wet road surface.

Isla corrected, vowed not to get too close to any other traffic and allow longer distances for braking. The rain, mixing with oil and muck on the roads surface, making it extremely dangerous and slippery.

An hour after Bendigo, just before eleven, Isla realised they had been diving for three hours and determined to stop for a break, they had passed through Heathcote shortly before and Isla was beginning to wonder whether they should have stopped there.

Speed reduction signs gave evidence of civilisation ahead, and sure enough as Isla eased the speed of the Falcon they swept out of the tree lined highway round a right hand bend and into Tooborac. There were still green fields on their right, a welcome, freshly, renovated, two-storey bluestone and ironstone, Tooborac Hotel appeared ahead on their right. Isla pulled across into its hospitable, near empty, car park.

It was now just gone eleven in the morning, before releasing a complaining Alice from her seat in the rear, Isla checked her road atlas.

'Don't worry Alice, we'll take our time, an early lunch here and then a relaxed couple of hours to Healesville.'

'Nearly there,' she added triumphantly as she eased herself out of the car and stretched her stiffening muscles, before letting Alice out of the back of the car.

-***-

 Further north about fifty kilometres south of Ouyen the Ute was making good progress on the Calder Highway and following Ryan's earlier passage towards Melbourne.

Andriy was sitting scrunched up in the near side seat, eyes closed and regretting his alcohol intake of the night before. It had done little to ease his painful lower back and he felt excruciatingly miserable.

His sibling was humming happily as he steered the Ute past the freshly cut sun drenched fields, although only single carriageway, there was little traffic to pass and he watched the railway line accompanying their passage, in hope of seeing a train as a break from the norm.

His anticipation was rewarded by another grain train stretched out alongside the grain silos in the small town of Berriwillock.

Happy to be driving and in anticipation of completing the first stage of their task, Aleksander reached across the cab and punched his dozing brother on his arm.

'Berriwillock,' how long have we got to go?'

Andriy grunted and reached for the road atlas, after a few moments to check where Berriwillock was, he forced out a reply.

'Four and a half hours.'

'Eleven now then,' replied Aleksander glancing at his watch.

'Let's say 30 minutes extra for traffic and a piss break, reckon we should be there around four, all things being equal.'

At that he resumed his humming, much to his twin's annoyance as they continued their journey towards the south east.

_***_

After a long leisurely lunch and a walk around, Isla and Alice returned to the Falcon and resumed their journey towards Healesville in good spirits.

Alice was re-assured by her mother's bonhomie, the days of sitting in the back of the Falcon were nearly over and she chattered happily away in the rear of the vehicle.

Isla, although very happy to have nearly completed the journey, was really worried about Luca's acolytes and being determined to stay as far away from the normal route to their destination, had taken advice of the kindly land lady back in Tooborac.

She had suggested they follow the Northern Highway south until just before the town of Kilmore, when they could turn east towards Broadford, before taking the more easterly route towards their destination.

Opinion in the bar when it became common knowledge about their destination, that it was probably quicker that way, so Isla had determined to take the advice she had been given.

After about twenty minutes of travel, through the greener countryside of fields of cattle, orchards and vineyards on the rolling hills, she easily spotted the hairpin turn left to Broadford.

After a short passage along the tree lined road past the green fields she steered the car carefully into the town and found the well-marked turning for Flowerdale. It was easy enough to spot also being the turning for the Hume Highway.

Shortly after the turn they crossed a bridge over a three track railway, then they were above the Hume, its dual carriageway gleaming after the recent rainfall, the foremost highway between Sydney and Melbourne.

The road narrowed as it rose into the hills, at times there were precipitous drops and hairpins, where Isla had to reduce their speed to a minimum, to negotiate the corners safely.

By the time they reached Strath Creek, they were surrounded by fresh green fenced pastures and undulating hills and valleys.

'Wow,' said Isla to her daughter, 'look darling horses,' as they passed a field with half a dozen thoroughbreds cropping the green grass in a sunlit meadow.

Farm entrances proclaimed horse studs, rare breed sheep and prize winning cattle.

Isla who had never seen scenery like this her whole life, almost forgot their troubles as she enjoyed the vistas set before her.

Shortly after Strath Creek they came to the promised T Junction and Isla turned towards Yea as she had been told. There was little traffic on the road, and usually it was a tractor or a dirty mud streaked farm truck.

At Flowerdale they had to stop at the T Junction and Isla giggled at the sign indicating a Fish farm circus, she just couldn't imagine such a thing.

Then because Alice wanted to know why her mother was giggling, Isla had nearly to stop the car because she was laughing so much, trying to explain the concept to the little girl.

With all the merriment, they nearly missed the turning for Glenburn and Isla had to brake hard, the Falcon juddered to a stop, before she was able to steer it across the carriageway onto Break o Day road.

The name of the road caused another fit of giggles as she guided the car onto a narrow steeply rising side road.

At the top of the hill they could see a other green hills in the distance, ahead of them.

They now began to make their way between burnt out Eucalyptus trees, the lower vestiges starting to recover from recent fires, the blackened trunks a stark reminder of the horrendous fires, that had befallen the region the year before.

At Glenburn they joined the Melba Highway and descended between recovering but mostly fire blackened Eucalyptus trees, finally they came back into the open and were immediately greeted by a multitude of vineyards on either side of the road, the fields in between were straw brown and parched from lack of water, unlike the hills from which they had just descended.

They reached a new four way roundabout and turned left onto the Old Healesville Road, Little knowing that their pursuers had just turned east off the Calder Highway, onto the Western Ring road north west of Melbourne and were only an hour astern.

Within ten minutes they were entering Healesville itself, Isla followed the town centre sign as they passed the RACV Country Club and gently drove towards the town centre.

They rumbled across the single rail track, past a bottle shop and there in front of her on the other side of a roundabout, was a pale yellow single storey wooden panelled building, with the blue and yellow sign marking it as the Visitor Centre.

Isla steered the car into the side road to the right of the building, parked the Falcon's bonnet facing the Visitor Centre and slumped back in her seat.

She should have felt elated but just experienced a feeling of exhaustion.

Suddenly there was a commotion and Alice shouted, 'Ryan,' pointing out of the car window towards the building, sure enough there he was exiting the centre, ripped blue jeans, black vest, white cast, left arm in a sling lugging a large khaki rucksack.

26th FEBRUARY PM - ARRIVAL AT HEALESVILLE

Isla leapt from the car ran up to Ryan, who was just exiting the wicker gate at the entrance to the visitor centre and with her strong right hand slapped his left cheek.

'You bastard,' she screamed then burst into tears and hugged him busted arm, knapsack and all.

Ryan didn't know what to make of these conflicting emotions, his face red and stinging from the assault, dropped his rucksack on the floor and with his good right arm hugged Isla to him.

Alice interrupted this greeting by yelling at the top of her voice, 'Ryan.'

Isla stepped back and laughed with tears still streaming down her cheeks, 'children who'd have them eh!'

Ryan now having a chance to interject, broke into the emotional reunion.

'We need to get you both away from here and out of site in case those two bastards turn up.'

'I've booked you a room until we can find your Uncle Brian, the Mulloneys vineyard is about three miles to the west and their telephones and broadband will be back on tomorrow.'

'They've been down while Telstra have been repairing the damage from last year's fires and updating the fibre optics or something,' Ryan explained.

'Fine Ryan,'

'Where's the Hotel?'

'You'll need to put your rucksack on your lap, while we go there, the car's full of our stuff,' said Isla over her shoulder, while returning to the Falcon.

Ryan squashed himself and his rucksack into the front of the Falcon and directed Isla the short distance to the Bed and Breakfast.

'It's no good,' declared Isla dejectedly, when they pulled up outside the Tuck Inn on Church Street, 'there's nowhere to hide the car.'

'I've thought of that,' answered Ryan positively as he unwound himself and his rucksack from his awkward position in the car.

'We'll get you both checked in, empty the car of both your belongings, then I'll take it somewhere else in Healesville and hide it.'

'Okay, okay sounds like a good idea to me, I'll get checked in, you can look after Alice.'

'Don't suppose you have any cash yourself,' she laughed cynically at the thought as she entered the reception and checked in.

About forty minutes later a one armed Ryan and Isla with the helpful, joyful, hindrance of an enthusiastic Alice, had managed to empty the Falcon and transport it to their room.

'Right I'll get the car hidden and will be back shortly.'

'Fair enough,' agreed Isla,

'Refuel the car first and bring us back enough food so we don't have to leave the room tonight,' she told him pressing a fistful of dollars into his good right hand, while looking around their large well equipped room complete with kitchen.

Don't forget we can always cook, so find a supermarket.

'Back soon,' shouted Ryan as he closed the door behind him.

It was just a few minutes before four.

Whistling happily, unaware of the nearness of the blue Ute and its fearsome threat, Ryan made his way to the Falcon.

He released his painful left arm from the black sling and settled himself into the driver's seat.

Because it was facing downhill he drove down to the first junction and realised the Maroondah Highway was the main road crossing ahead of him.

On a whim he turned right into the centre of Healesville. The place was alive with people sitting at tables, set outside the numerous cafes and restaurants and shaded by the tree lined sidewalk.

There was a passageway left for shoppers, visitors and the like at the many varied small shops either side of the street. The highway was itself busy and he could only drive the Falcon slowly past the many parked cars on either side.

Outside the Grand Hotel were about a dozen, very shiny, well, maintained motor bikes and their tattooed riders in black leather trousers, and garish T shirts, he noted the Coles supermarket on his near side before spotting a Caltex on the right.

Pulling alongside a spare pump, Ryan proceeded to top-up the Falcon, before going inside the shop to pay for the fuel.

Getting back into the Falcon the pump ahead of him having just been cleared by a red Commodore, Ryan started the engine as he prepared to move off a large, filthy, blue, Commodore Ute, cut in front of him and halted, its front squarely across the bows of the Falcon.

Ryan enraged by the stupidity of the driver ahead, started to get out of the vehicle, only to realise as the offending driver exited his own vehicle that he was in serious trouble.

_-***-_

It was Andriy half asleep most of the day's trip, who had been wide awake, body now clear of the hangover and looking eagerly out of the Ute as they entered Healesville from the west, who had spotted the Falcon ahead of them.

They had been held up at the crossroads by the Grand Hotel and lost the car ahead.

It was only after they were well past the Caltex garage that Andriy looking searchingly around the surrounding area, spotted the parked Falcon and Ryan refuelling the car.

'Behind us, behind us in the petrol station,' shouted Andriy.

His brother braked sharply and was greeted by the honking of a horn astern of the Ute, from the offended driver behind them.

Aleksander continued round the right hand corner, before finding a plant shop to turn into on their left. He turned the car round eased out across the highway onto the other side. They returned to the garage just in time to see Ryan returning to the Falcon.

'Hang on,' shouted Aleksander, 'we've got the bastard.'

He swept past the petrol station and in the far entrance, flicking round another stationary car and placed the Ute diagonally across the front of the Falcon in the recently vacated space.

-***-

Ryan didn't panic, sat himself back in the car put it into reverse and glanced in the rear view mirror, unfortunately there was a little old lady close up behind in a small silver grey car.

Ryan pressed the horn hard and could see the woman behind frantically trying to reverse away from him. Suddenly she shot straight back into a dirty, battered, lime green Ute, which was just entering the garage. Steam started pouring from its bonnet and the two red brown dogs in the back of the Ute, started barking furiously, adding to the mayhem.

Ryan glanced ahead and saw the looming body of Aleksander jogging towards him.

Taking the opportunity presented by the crash behind, he reversed into the space, managed to turn the Falcon across the forecourt and out of the exit which had previously been behind him. He pushed his way into the oncoming westbound stream of traffic and back onto the Maroondah Highway.

'I daren't go back to the Hotel,' he thought while concentrating on manoeuvring the Falcon through the busy town. Behind him, in his rear view mirror he could see the Twins blue Ute, exiting the petrol station, there were about a dozen vehicles between them.

At the Grand Hotel cross roads, Ryan gained a march as the traffic lights turned red just after he passed them.

Internally scared to death, his mind racing at the thought of the near miss with the two Ukrainians, Ryan didn't know what to do, he just drove westwards a picture of indecisiveness.

Clearing the town he swept past a Toyota Garage and the road cleared ahead of him, he stomped on the accelerator, raced around a left hand bend and up a tree lined hill, backed by a row of one storied houses on either side.

He could feel the knife he had kept in his pocket since his previous run in with the Ukrainian thugs, if it came to it he was determined not to go down without a fight, he knew if they caught up with him there would be no mercy this time.

The road continued up the relatively steep hill and Ryan riskily overtook a white panel truck which was slowing him down. He could on the straight sections no longer see the Blue Ute and this made him finally start to think of a way out of his desperate situation.

'I need to get off this highway as soon as possible.'

'I need to get back to the girls and leave the car somewhere safe.'

At the top of the hill the houses ended and he was back out into the country, frantically Ryan looked for a suitable turn off.

'I want something quiet and with no obvious destination,' he concluded anxiously.

At the cross roads for no other reason, than it looked most promising, the road disappeared over a hill, Ryan turned right onto Heritage Lane.

He was fortunate, seconds later the Ute went speedily by, straight though the cross roads.

-***-

Back at the Hotel, Isla was in near panic, she didn't know what to do or where to turn, in the end she fed Alice and herself from bits of food they had collected during the journey, double locked the outer door and also wedged a chair under the door handle.

After an hour she tried Ryan's mobile, only to hear it ringing on a bedside table where he had left it on charge.

Finally she put Alice to bed and lay on the bed herself cuddling the little girl for comfort, eventually exhaustion overtook her and she fell asleep.

26th FEBRUARY EVENING - DESPERATE STRUGGLE

The Twins quickly realised that the Falcon and its driver must have turned off the Maroondah highway when the road ahead straightened out and Andriy could see nothing down the only turn-off, the Woorl Yallock road.

'Definitely not ahead or gone left must have turned off before this,' he exclaimed to his brother.

'Quick turn round otherwise we'll lose the bugger again,'

For a moment Aleksander could do nothing except continue their trip down the Maroondah Highway, there being nowhere to turn.

They crested a hill the long, nearly empty, straight, road, ahead helping confirm Andriy's suspicions of Ryan having diverted from the highway.

Halfway down the hill, well beyond the crest, Aleksander was able to swing the Ute across the oncoming traffic and onto a loose grey gravel turn out and set their vehicle to returning the way they had just come.

'You tell me which way then when we get to the other side of this hill.'

Andriy replied thinking aloud, 'Don't think it can be that last turn, it has got to be closer to the town, after all we could nearly see the car until just before we cleared the houses.

They cleared the Woorl Yallock turning at the bottom of the slope before the road rose again, ahead of them, quickly approaching at the crest of that slope was a cross roads.

'Which way?'

Andriy couldn't make up his mind so his brother made the decision for them, with oncoming traffic, making it difficult to turn right, it being easier, he turned left into Heritage Lane.

-***-

Shortly before Ryan had sighed with relief, once he thought he had disappeared behind the hillcrest and out of sight of the highway.

He steered the Falcon gently down the slope and quickly had to make a decision whether to continue straight on, either onto the continuation of the lane which turned into a single lane gravel track, or to follow the tarmacked road to the right.

Being easier and taking him further out of sight of the Highway, Ryan's decision was simple, he turned right, firstly passing two men closing a gate at a VicRoads depot, then the entrance to a SES depot on his right.

He didn't really notice the closed yard with tree trunks and sawed timber in the closed compound on his left because the road suddenly ended. It bent left, at a low grey, timber panelled gate.

Although both the gates were open, it was obvious this was the end of this particular road, a sign on the dirt bank to his left, indicated this was the entrance to the Yarra Valley Water Purification Plant.

Frustrated he did a three point turn and rushed back to the junction, still not wanting to risk the highway, Ryan turned onto the grey, gravel track and rushed along the lane, leaving a plume of dirty, grey, dust behind the Falcon.

He passed the entrance to a farm on his right and a couple of brightly painted corrugated huts above him in a field on his left, before suddenly at a closed pair of metal grey gates mounted on orange brick posts the road ended.

Ryan could see a red brick bungalow beyond the gates but it was obvious there was nowhere else to go, resigned to having to return to the Highway, he began to retrace his tracks through the cloud of dust created by his previous passage.

Passing the huts he was struggling to see far ahead of him because of this own made fug.

The further he made his way down the road the clearer became his visibility.

Suddenly rushing towards him was a blue Ute.

'Christ it can't be,' he screamed aloud at the windscreen.

He realised it was.

The road being too narrow to pass and there being no time to turn or escape he hurriedly pulled to a halt on the left verge.

Almost before he had time to react the blue Commodore Ute was upon him, it slammed to a halt in a cloud of dust, almost but not quite ramming the driver's door of the Falcon.

Its nose prevented Ryan exiting the car on the driver's side. He struggled, with his useless left arm impeding his progress, across to the passenger side of the car, whilst trying to grab the knife from the side pocket of his shorts.

Just as he reached the passenger seat and was reaching uncomfortably across his body with his good right hand, to unlatch the door it burst open and Aleksander loomed in front of him.

Ryan couldn't believe his luck but determined not to suffer at the hands of the Ukrainians without some effort to defend himself, gripping the kitchen knife with his good right hand he swung it wildly at the Ukrainian thug who by now had gripped Ryan's throat with his left hand.

Ryan's undisciplined swing with the kitchen knife went straight into the offending lower arm of the Ukrainian colliding with bone.

Aleksander grunted in pain, and stood up letting go of Ryan's neck. Unfortunately as he took his arm away it ripped the knife out of Ryan's hand, leaving it poking out of the stabbed arm, its black handle vibrating.

Alexander's tempestuous side took over, his face red with anger, with hardly a thought for the pain, or the necessity of questioning Ryan for the girl's whereabouts, with his good right hand he ripped the knife out of his arm and slashed the blade in a horizontal arc.

It tore open Ryan's throat cutting his jugular and he died almost immediately.

Aleksander casually ripped Ryan's T Shirt off his body and bound it round the bleeding knife gash in his left arm, and turned to find Andriy behind him.

'What the bloody hell have you done?'

'Is he dead?' He asked trying to peer round his brother, who was blocking his view of the unfortunate Ryan.

'The bastard stuck me,' complained Aleksander waving the offending weapon at his brother.

'Nobody does that,' he whined

What about the woman and the kid we'll never find them now.

'Stuff them, let's get out of here,'

'You'll have to drive for now, till I get this arm fixed up.'

'He cut me.'

At that they left the scene, Andriy turned the car south down the Maroondah, towards Melbourne wanting to put distance between them and the unfortunate scene outside Healesville.

At first Andriy just hammered along the road not caring what happened, he was angry with his sibling and worried about the repercussions

Andriy's idea was to put as much geography between them and the murder, as possible.

His sibling was compressing the remains of Ryan's black T Shirt onto his wound and complaining.

'The bastard stabbed me.'

'Andriy he stabbed me.'

'Never mind that you've dropped us right in it, with the woman's help, they'll soon work out it must have been us.'

'You stupid bugger, why did you have to kill him?'

Aleksander who was still in shock could only wave his arm forlornly at his brother and say, 'but he stuck a knife in me.'

Andriy slowed their precipitous rush from the scene of the crime and returned the Ute to the local speed level as they rushed past the surrounding vineyards. It was only six in the evening and it was going to be a good couple of hours before the sun began to wane.

The adrenalin filled rush created by the crisis, meant that at first, Andriy hadn't felt his back pain or other injuries.

He had also taken a few risks overtaking in tight places, this had earned them, honking of horns and flashing lights, from other irate drivers he had endangered.

Now he could feel his back again, he decided he would have to ignore it and continue their flight.

'Christ he's lost it,' he thought looking at his brother in the passenger seat who was still compressing his wound with the now ragged, bloody, black T Shirt and whispering continually with a surprised look.

There was no improvement from his brother who had very quickly descended into a catatonic state, he had now reverted to his mother tongue and was now repeating, 'he stabbed me,' in Ukrainian.

As he drove down the Maroondah Highway, Andriy could think of only one way out of their situation and that was to get back to the haunts they knew in Western Australia.

He drove and drove, joined the new Melbourne East Link road, at Ringwood and kept going west.

Aleksander was still repeating the same phrase only now in an incomprehensible mumble, while tightly gripping the dirty cloth around his arm.

At sunset, just after eight in the evening they were closing on Ballarat, the setting sun ahead of the Ute had been giving him a headache and it was only when he rubbed his forehead Andriy realised he wasn't wearing his sunglasses.

Realising he wasn't thinking rationally, made Andriy wake up from his only inclination of just fleeing the scene, he realised he had to do something other than just drive westwards.

They left the lights of the Ballarat junction behind them and continued for a while on the dual carriageway of the Western Freeway.

Finally at Beaufort where the Freeway had become a single carriageway through the town, Andriy realised what they needed, was a petrol station, with a decent shop. Coming up on one in the town he drove the Ute in topped up with fuel and parked up in the car park.

His brother had now fallen asleep and was snoring loudly, Andriy was able to leave him securely in the Ute when he went to pay for the fuel and shop in the Handy Mart alongside the garage.

Andriy filled a basket with ready edible foodstuff, crisps, pies and the like; he also bought a first aid kit, antiseptic cream, paracetamol and bottles of water, plus high caffeine drinks for himself.

Taking a moment in a parking area of the garage, he rang Fabio briefly, 'It has all gone wrong, the boyfriend is dead, Aleksander isn't well and we're coming back to Fremantle as fast as possible.' He then switched off the mobile before Fabio had time to reply, consumed a pie, a high caffeine drink before setting out, for Adelaide and beyond.

27th FEBRUARY DAWN - DAWN ON HERITAGE LANE

The rising sun crept slowly into the red sky above the Yarra ranges, Brian Steele, a fit looking, fifty year old ruddy faced man; wearing a short sleeved, red checked, collared shirt, beige shorts and light brown sandals, a Bush hat perched across his short cropped fair hair, cycled briskly, in an easterly direction towards the newly appearing red orb. He was fully refreshed from a good night's sleep and looking forward to a new day at his work as the Winemaker for Mulloney's Vineyard on the Maroondah Highway south of Healesville.

Brian, a third generation Australian of Anglo/German stock, had only recently moved to the Yarra Valley, after having been pursued and head hunted by Mulloney's, who due to the unexpected demise of the previous incumbent had found themselves short of an experienced leader.

Until recently any thoughts of a move away from the Margaret River area of Western Australia, his family's home for at least three generations would have been beyond Brian's comprehension.

A change in Brian's personal circumstances of seismic proportions, had made him susceptible to a move from a similar post, back in his previous haunts of the Margaret River.

Brian's adored childhood sweetheart and wife Melissa, died due to Breast Cancer two years previously, ever since he had since been using alcohol as a substitute, to help erase these memories.

The horrific memories of her struggle for life and initial relief at her release from the torment, had surrounded and threatened to overpower him.

Brian thought back to the aftermath of Melissa's demise.

'He couldn't walk out onto the veranda of the house back in WA, without remembering balmy evenings sat together, her in the swing chair, him on the old carved eucalyptus bench, sipping red wine from the vineyard.'

Except for a few really decent friends, and caring colleagues at the vineyard, Brian's descent into alcoholism through depression and despair would have continued un-abated.

Finally with the help of those caring souls and a severe warning from the family doctor, had finally woken Brian up and shaken him out of his guilt-stricken fall, into an alcoholic abyss.

'You're drinking too much, you're one step away from a breakdown, you need to change your life, get away from here and the memories.'

'I won't be held responsible for your wellbeing otherwise,' the concerned Doctor had threatened him.

'There's obviously now nothing for you here, the kids are long gone, they may return but I wouldn't count on it, especially looking at the mess you're in,' the Doctor had said cruelly, hoping to break the self-destructive trend of his friend and patient.

Brian and Melissa's children were abroad and far away, their son Bruce, a 27 year old, oil rig engineer in the North Sea was settled, enjoying the excitement and challenges of his chosen profession.

Charmaine a 25 year old fine arts graduate, from Perth University, completing a post-doctorate course at Oxford's Magdalene College was busy getting on with her life. She was looking for opportunities in London and had worked summers at a big London Auctioneers.

Both had been badly affected by their mothers' death nearly two years ago but they were both busy people, with other outlets and been able to get on with their lives.

Charmaine on her last visit, especially had made it quite clear to her Dad, 'Mum would be disappointed in you, she told all of us in those last horrific hours to get on with our lives, think of her fine.'

'For Christ's sake Dad what do you think she would say if she could see you now?'

'You stink of booze, you're unshaven, unwashed and a right bloody mess.'

'We love you but only you can get yourself out of this.

'Bloody wake up, it's bad enough losing Mum we don't want to lose you as well,' she had finally broken down and sobbed.

It had been the final straw which had made him look at himself and attend the Doctor's surgery.

Brian's passage along Heritage Lane, a drought effected, dusty red track was accompanied by the rising dawn chorus of the Cockatoos, perched high in the eucalyptus trees lining the road, the noise of crickets in the verges, which in the dry Summer had taken on the colour of ripened hay. He could smell the dryness of the air, his nose wrinkled and he felt an itch in his nose, which he rubbed gently with the outside of his right wrist, it was probably the dust irritating his nasal membranes.

Brian's progress was marked by the small cloud of trailing dust and the fresh indentations on the roadway, from the two rubber tyres of the bicycle.

'It might be lovely weather for the grape harvest, but it's too dry, ideal for bush fires,' Brian grumbled to himself, if that happens we'll lose half the pickers to the CFS (Country Fire Service,) and the others to the SES, (Victoria State Emergency Service,)' he grumbled.

'Still mustn't complain, we'll muddle through somehow, after all they're all volunteers and do a fantastic job, we'd be buggered without them.'

A flash of colour made Brian lift his head, the progress of the bicycle slowed as he watched a flock of bright, red and green, lorikeets flash across his eye line. The glare of the large red plate which was the now fully risen sun made him look away and pull the front brim of his battered hat to shade his eyes from the glare.

This distraction brought his attention to a previously unnoticed dark blue Ford Falcon, with WA plates. It was facing away from him towards the Maroondah Highway, its passenger door wide open to the elements, as he got closer he could see the vibration and fumes, bubbling out from the twin exhausts, and realised the engine was still running, closer inspection showed a hairy, obviously male leg protruding from the open door, a discarded blue flip flop littered the verge outside the open car door.

'What on earth is that doing there?' Brian thought.

Subdued by the sight of the apparently un-moving hairy limb, the unexpected vehicle and the interruption too his personal space, Brian approached the car with caution and some trepidation.

A pair of large black ravens which had been inspecting the scene, jumped up and flapped away a few yards at Brian's approach.

Reaching the vibrating Falcon, Brian could hear the big V6 grumbling away, he dropped the bike to the near verge and ran the last few yards to the passenger door. The thick smell of oil and diesel, impinged upon his senses.

Even though moving rapidly - time seemed to stand still as the scene opened to his gaze.

The first impression was blood - it was everywhere, car seat, dashboard, door but especially all over the young man's half naked body. The left leg was the one protruding from the door; the right was bent up into the foot well, while the rest of the body lay partially, on its back across the passenger seat.

It was a young man, unknown to Brian; in his mid-twenties with, blond straggly, tangled hair, long unshaven face, dressed only in crumpled, dirty looking, knee-length, khaki shorts.

The source of the blood was immediately obvious, a gaping wound about 5cm long, horizontally across the young man's throat. The blood must have gushed from the wound, it had dried into the poor man's chest hair and matted there, the shorts had absorbed some of the blood which had further congealed into a now dried pool in the passenger well of the car.

Brian's ruddy face paled, he felt nauseous and retched loudly, it wasn't as if he hadn't seen a dead body before he had suffered through the death of his beloved Melissa as he watched her pass from this world. The violence of the wound, was horrific and totally unexpected on this quiet country lane.

It was like a scene from a horrific movie, but this scene wouldn't go away and move on, like in a Film, it was real and all the more shocking because it was right in front of Brian.

You read about the smell of death,' thought Brian, 'it's real, you can't quantify it it's not quite tangible but it's there,' he grimaced at the suggestion.

For some reason the noise of the V6 engine, began to intrude upon his panicky thoughts.

'I've got to turn that off,' he decided as he raced around to the driver's side of the machine to reach the ignition.

'Damn, it's still locked,' he realised stumbling back round to the horrendous passenger side of the Falcon

Bracing himself and returning to the open door, Brian although not normally squeamish, felt his insides curdle as he steeled himself to delicately reach across the young man.

As careful as Brian was he couldn't help but brush against the naked corpse, his body flinched at the unexpected touch and he recoiled from car.

'Ugh,' he winced, then steeling himself, he forced himself to reach across the corpse and turned off the engine. Leaving the keys in the ignition, Brian leapt back quickly, quailing as he accidentally brushed against the lifeless body again.

Brian inhaled loudly and sucked in a huge breath of fresh air, the tension of the operation had made hold his breath throughout.

'That was bloody awful,' he thought, his insides churned at the thought of having touched the dead body, 'must get help,' he decided, his initial panic now well and truly resolved.

Heritage Lane being a dead end there was at this time of day, unlikely to be any traffic. Brian reached into his shirt pocket for his mobile telephone, 'damn,' he swore under his breath, he visualised it lying on his bedside table connected to its charger, 'I've bloody forgotten it again,' he cursed to himself, 'every time I put it on charge I do that,' he cursed to himself.

'Anyway the transmitters down,' he remembered.

Brian looked north towards the Yarra Valley Water Purification Plant, on Argon Road, and made a decision!

It being just after six in the morning, he felt it would be best to continue towards the Highway. There was no point in returning to the rented house, his temporary home at the far end of the lane.

'I hope those lazy buggers at the Vic Roads depot, on the Maroondah are going to start at a decent hour for a change?' He hoped earnestly.

'Otherwise there will be someone I can flag down and they will be able to communicate news of this mess to the Vic Police.'

Brian grabbed and re- mounted his bike, a mainly blue 'Trek Superfly Hardtail 29er,' a present to himself when he moved from WA.

The idea had been to get himself fit, to explore his new home area and sweat out some of the alcoholic abuse of the previous two years. Instead Brian had just used it to travel leisurely the 2K, to and from the vineyard.

He pushed off and immediately knew something was wrong, 'bloody hell that poxy chain's come off again,' he swore as he gashed the inside of his right leg on the pedal when his foot slipped off due to lack of pressure.

Dismounting, Brian quickly turned the bike upside down, knowing what was wrong; he was able to quickly re-align the bike chain.

Rapidly turning the 'Trek,' the right way up, he remounted and started pedalling, within seconds the chain came off again.

Brian lifted his head and screamed obscenities to the heavens, the noisy Cockatoos, frightened by Brian's yells, scattered from the nearby trees in a cacophony of sound. Disgusted he threw the useless Trek onto the dusty track and started to run. The distance to the Vic Roads Depot and Maroondah Highway was about half a kilometre.

To Brian, running was different from cycling, only slightly fitter because of the cycling, it hadn't helped with his running. Within seconds he was puffing and within 50 metres he had a bad stitch in his left side.

'The gash in his right ankle must have been worse than I realised,' thought Brian, he could feel the blood running into his shoes and dampening his foot

'Christ that hurts,' he gasped to himself imperceptibly slowing, kneading the source of a sudden stitch pain, on his left side, with his left fist.

Remember the sports masters' shouted advice from his schooldays many years before, 'Should be able to run it off,' he hopefully agonised through the pain.

'It might be late summer but it must be nearly 30 degrees already,' thought Brian as he stumbled along the road, 'alright for ripening the grapes but not much good for my temperature,' he concluded as he gasped for air under the inexorable tormenting red ball, of the sun on the Eastern skyline.

Dust rose from the track with Brian's passing, and furrows of sweat ran down his quickly dust covered face. He tried to wipe this away, ineffectually brushing the brow of his face, with the too short sleeves of his shirt. The sweat began to sting his eyes and cloud his vision.

Under the dust and sweat his face, unbeknown to him, had now changed from its previously pale countenance, to a grey unhealthy sheen.

The squawking of the returned roosting Cockatoos appeared to mock his passing. Brian felt he was now beyond pain and just concentrated on putting one foot in front of the other. He didn't realise how much his gait quickly changed, the initial rush had become a pain filled jog, and he was now weaving and staggering from side to side, along the highway.

Just before he reached the junction with Argon Road, Brian slowed almost to a walk and glanced hopefully to his left, he didn't notice the flies buzzing above the black sleeping cattle in the small field on his left side, or the smell of dried dung, just the padlocked and closed entrance gate of the Vic Roads Depot, the other side of the field.

Brian muttered something indecipherable under his breath.

Panting hard he tried to speed up, his mouth wide open gasping for every scrap of oxygen, Brian left the Argon Road entrance to his left, he continued straight on towards the nearing but still distant Maroondah Highway.

If he had any breath left Brian would have wasted it cursing, the road now began to incline, he felt pain everywhere, he had stitch both sides now, both fists were kneading at the source of the pain his knees hurt badly and his feet were already sore from the pounding. The sweat in his eyes was making him wince with irritation.

Suddenly he got hit by the most excruciating pain in his upper chest; it felt like a tight band was compressing his upper body. His vision faded, he stumbled, stopped and collapsed onto the Heritage Lane roadway.......

27th FEBRUARY – PANDEMONIUM

At about the same time Uncle Brian was having his heart attack, Isla was woken from her sleep of exhaustion by Alice kicking her in the face as the little girl reacted to something she was dreaming about.

Isla realised she had fallen asleep fully clothed, next to Alice and even though stressed out at the missing Falcon and Ryan himself, she realised she had been too exhausted to stay awake.

Looking around her, she realised Ryan hadn't returned, she could see that the sun had risen as it was light outside. Isla rose from the shared bed and made her way to the bathroom, glancing at her wrist watch as she went, it showed her it was ten to seven.

Isla felt desperate and full of despair, 'we've got here after all, now Ryan's disappeared.'

'What the bloody hell am I going to do?' she cried to herself in the bathroom, her head in her hands.

Hearing a thump from Alice moving around in the bedroom, Isla washed her face and prepared to face their uncertain future.

Plastering a smile on her face she went back into their hotel room, to find Alice jumping up and down on the bed and giggling loudly.

'Good morning darling, sleep well,' asked Isla who just caught her daughter before she crashed towards the floor having bounced off the springy bed.

Alice laughed in reply and rushed off to the bathroom.

'No matter about me, I've got to protect Alice, we'll have to go to the police,' Isla concluded, remembering the Police Station, next to the visitor centre

Isla quickly dressed in cut-off red denim shorts, white T Shirt and red flip flops, sorted out Alice by plonking her into the slightly grubby white pinafore dress from the previous day.

She drank some water, gave Alice some cold milk left over in the fridge, before carefully taking them both out of the hotel. Checking carefully, Isla gripping Alice's left hand walked out carefully onto Church Street, a side road uphill and south of the main road through Healesville.

As they turned uphill and crossed over the road, they could hear the siren of an Ambulance coming along the Highway below them, Alice who was looking back, pulled at her mother's hand and shouted dah, dah, in tune with the siren, they both saw its mainly white body, flash across the junction below them.

'Hope they're all right,' empathised Isla to her daughter as they continued their short walk towards the local forces of law and order.

Just after eight, they had crossed the Maroondah Highway and were approaching the small Healesville Police Station, with its blue and white police sign, tall grey radio aerial and orange brick single storey entrance.

Isla approached the counter and the Victoria policeman in his blue shirt, with a single white chevron on his epaulette, indicating he was a First Constable, said to Isla.

'I'm sorry, I have to ask, is this really important, can it wait?

'Yes, it is rather,' replied Isla, tightly gripping Alice's left wrist with her own right hand.

'We've a big crisis outside town and everyone is up there at the moment,' interrupted the policeman.

'Oh no,' thought Isla, 'it's not Ryan is it?'

Almost on the edge of hysteria but determined to have her say, Isla whispered, 'your problem it doesn't involve a Perfect Blue V6 Ford Falcon with West Australian plates does it?'

The First Constable's face changed perceptibly and the muscles tightened when she said that, he suddenly took an overwhelming interest, in her statement.

Seeing Isla's distress, not wishing to upset her unduly but needing to find out as quickly as possible what Isla knew he said, 'please sit down,' while ushering her round the counter, to the far side of a large teak computer desk.

Isla in a daze led Alice to the chair indicated and slumped down onto its wooden seat.

Alice ever sensitive to her mother's mood burst into tears and tightly grabbed hold of her mother's knees.

'Would you and your little girl like a drink?'

'Just water, for both of us please,' replied Isla haltingly.

At that moment the telephone on the counter started ringing and at the same moment the policeman's radio crackled into life.

'VKC to Healesville 210,' heard Isla

'Code 11,' he replied into his personal radio.

'Means I'm busy,' he shouted to Isla in explanation as he leapt across to the ringing telephone.

'Please can we get back to you about that, there's no one available at the moment,' said the Officer to the person on the other end of the phone before replacing the receiver and reaching for his radio.

'VKC this is Healesville 210, please tell Healesville 105 at the Heritage lane IBR, that I may have part of the answer at the home station.

'Roger that VKC out.'

'I'm First Constable Terry Costello,' explained the Officer handing both the girls a polystyrene cup of water each, from which they both drank greedily.

By way of explanation and to help Isla get started, he asked her their names.

'I'm Isla and this is Alice,' she answered indicating the little girl who was now sat on her mother's lap sucking her thumb and looking at the police officer with curiosity.

'We've found a car like you described not far outside the town.'

'Who do you think was driving the vehicle?'

'Ryan,'

'Please madam what did Ryan look like and do you know what he was wearing.'

Isla described her ex-boyfriend, the blue flip flops, khaki shorts and black T Shirt he was wearing, when she had last seen him the previous evening.

-***-

Shortly after Brian collapsed halfway up the final slope of Heritage Lane just before the Junction with the Maroondah Highway, a silver grey Commodore saloon rushed onto the Lane from the Highway.

Inside were two employees of VicRoads late and about to start their day at work. They were arguing about last night's AFL game at the G.

The driver spotted the bundle, which was Brian, just over the brow of the hill lying in the middle of the Lane and reacted quickly by braking hard and slewing his vehicle onto the free grass verge on the left side of the road.

'Get on the blower,' he shouted to his mate as he rapidly exited the car.

'Cops and Ambulance.'

He bent down to Brian and sighed heavily in relief as he could see the faint rise and fall of Brian's chest, which meant he was still breathing at least.

He easily turned the pale-faced Brian onto his side and checked the open mouth for foreign objects and then ran back to his vehicle for the blanket he knew was lying in the trunk of his car.

Meanwhile his workmate had dialled 000 and asked for assistance, fortunately the problems with the local signal didn't apply to emergencies.

'On their way,' he said.

'What's wrong, do you know?'

'He's breathing, just got to keep him warm,' the driver answered covering Brian with a blanket from the trunk of the car.

Better go up to the Highway and stop any traffic, coming down here, besides which you can show the paramedics and cops where we are.

As his mate jogged up the slope, he looked the other way down the lane, he could see the Falcon half on the verge a few hundred metres away, its door open and the rays of the rising sun glinting off its blue roof.

Brian kept breathing and within what was only minutes but seemed like hours to the waiting Good Samaritan, he could hear the distinctive notes of a multitude of sirens.

First a local ambulance screeched to a halt alongside and a following White police Holden placed itself across the road to prevent anyone else accessing the lane.

A single first constable exited the car and approached the scene, by this time Brian was being attended to by the paramedics and his rescuer stood up to greet the oncoming copper.

'What happened mate,' enquired the Officer?

'Just on the way in to open the VicRoads depot, found him lying in the middle of the road, maybe heart attack,' guessed the driver.

'There's a blue car down the road with its door open may be his,' he continued pointing west further down Heritage Lane.

'Alright I'll go have a look see, thanks mate,' said the copper realising he would have to walk there with the road being blocked, he set out strolling casually towards the Falcon.

A few minutes later, on arriving at the vehicle he became a lot more agitated, after finding the body, and was rapidly on his radio to control, calling for immediate assistance.

He ran urgently back to his Holden, his blue cap gripped tightly in his free left hand.

Stay here, you and your mate don't go anywhere there's a body in that car, wait until I get some assistance.

Reaching the paramedics, who were just putting Brian strapped tightly on a stretcher into the rear of the white ambulance.

The Officer explained the situation, to the two women paramedics.

'You sure it's a body,' asked one because we can't leave this one he's almost certainly had a heart attack.

'Yeah definitely deceased, been a while he's going stiff.'

'Where you taking this one we'll need to talk to him,' he asked the paramedics.

Just into Healesville I'll shout you another ambulance to get the other one sorted, can you move your car said the driver of the paramedic as she closed the rear doors of her machine on her partner and their patient?

Making his way to his cruiser, he told the two Vic Roads men to wait for back-up, before taking the car to within, about ten metres of the crime scene.

By the time he had reached the Falcon and was taping off the area the duty sergeant arrived with another First Constable and parked their Cruiser next to the first one.

After a brief consultation and checking the situation in the Falcon, the Sergeant sent the new Officer off to take statements from the VicRoads men. He then contacted Division for assistance.

It was only after, that he received the message about Isla and Alice, from his only remaining Officer on duty back in Healesville.

Making a decision he headed back to the station, leaving the other two in charge of the crime scene.

-***-

By lunch time Isla had told the story of her trials and tribulations and their epic journey from Perth to Healesville.

She had been told about Ryan, who she had helped identify by explaining about his broken arm.

Alice had been with Isla's agreement taken to a local kindergarten, the little girl had complained at first but soon settled in to play with the other children once the first tears had been dried from her eyes.

In the afternoon they had been taken in a police car to visit Uncle Brian who was sedated and connected to all sorts of tubes, the nurse in charge confirmed his diagnosis of a heart attack.

Bethany would be on her way with her partner Ray as soon as they could get a flight.

On being told Bethany had telephoned Charmaine in the UK, who promised to get herself and Bruce on the first available flights out of the UK

A search was on for the Perfect Blue Commodore Ute and its occupants.

_***_

The runaway Ute, now in Adelaide, made a brief stop for coffee, food and an attempt by Andriy to bring his brother out of the catatonic torpor.

Andriy filled himself with food and availed himself of his brother's, as well as his own caffeine filled black coffee.

Andriy didn't feel too bad, just a bit hyper with all the caffeine, so after topping up with fuel he continued north out of the South Australian capital.

At the time Isla was being released from her interview and re-united with Alice, the Ute was negotiating its way slowly, through a busy Port Augusta.

_***_

In Perth at the airport, it was three pm, Fabio had decided to run and was booked on Singapore Airlines SQ214 to Singapore at 1710, with a suitcase full of all the cash he could grab.

Similarly Bethany and Ray were arriving at the airport, after one of the office girls had managed to get them the 1730 flight to Melbourne.

Fabio just dumped his car in the long stay car park never expecting to see it again, while on the same level Ray was parking their vehicle.

They passed each other without realising, Bethany and Ray bound for Terminal 3 and Fabio for Terminal 1.

'I'm sure I know that bloke,' commented Bethany shortly after passing Fabio.

Victoria Police had got their act together, with the help of the Federal Police, had agreed Fabio should be picked up and charged with conspiracy to kidnap a child.

West Australian Police had been rather pleased, to be asked to arrest a known drug dealer of Fabio's reputation and after finding him not in residence, had put out an all points request.

A police car stopped at a red light on the Guildford Road had fortunately seen Fabio running a red light, when he turned off the road and onto the Tonkin Freeway towards the airport. He had been in no position to pursue but recognised the plate from the recent message over the police net.

Consequently from his arrival at Perth International Fabio was followed on the security cameras, while an Inspector and Sergeant rushed to the airport, where they would meet up with two constables who were already on patrol there.

The Inspector in charge made the decision to pick up Fabio as he cleared security, thus ensuring he couldn't be in possession of a weapon.

Fabio feeling full of himself and quite safe now he was checked in and cleared through security, was quite shocked and disillusioned to be confronted by an Inspector, Sergeant and two constables belonging to Western Australian Police and gave up easily.

Once handcuffed and on his way to gaol the Inspector and Sergeant made their way south west to Casuarina Prison.

The day's head of the prison, who had been alerted to the visit smoothed their passage through to an empty visits room.

Luca who was within six months of discharge, didn't take kindly to being re-arrested and had to be forcibly removed from the visits room by three uniformed prison officers after the Police Inspector had charged him.

From Isla's information the Inspector was also able to inform the prison staff about the presence of the mobile telephone in Luca's cell.

-***-

While all this was going on Andriy had reached the Nullarbor proper, having arrived in Ceduna. He was still coping though by now he hadn't slept for nearly forty hours. He felt beyond pain, all he could do was keep driving and ignore the discomfort.

Aleksander wasn't eating or drinking and somewhere in his own little world of shock, neither asleep nor awake.

Topping up with fuel and caffeine drinks, Andriy set the Ute back onto the road and turned it towards the setting sun. He wasn't worrying about distances or possible collisions with Kangaroos or the like, he just knew they had to get back into Fremantle and felt then everything would be alright.

Just after midnight he was really struggling to keep awake, only the jarring of the offside wheels every time he drifted off the Highway had kept him awake, realising he could go no further he determined they would stop at the next place and kip in the Ute.

Fortunately the lights of Border Village loomed into sight, he passed the BP station and had to stop to avoiding shunting the rear of a large trailer ahead of him.

He wanted to turn off but a line of cones and an inside lane of trucks prevented this, gradually they moved forward towards a well-lit hangar like building, open at both ends.

Andriy remembered dozily, 'no problem it's the Quarantine Station.'

A blue uniformed quarantine officer directed him to follow the truck into the right hand lane, next to the Quarantine Station Offices, another truck was directed into the same lane astern of the Ute.

He could see from the lights of the truck and trailer ahead of him, a blue sign indicating a rest area on the left side of the road.

'That'll do,' he decided

The female Quarantine Officer walked towards him from the offside of the trailer ahead of him. He wound down the driver's window.

Suddenly she turned round and rapidly departed back the way she had come.

Andriy twisted his head round looking to his left.

A steely voice said into his left ear, 'Armed police, you're under arrest.'

'Leave your hands on the steering wheel where we can see them and don't move,' ……………………

Printed in Great Britain
by Amazon